Mandy lives in leafy Wiltshire and has Sting as a neighbour. She lives with her husband, two daughters and two cats (Kravitz and Springsteen). When she isn't writing she loves to sing and do Lady Gaga impressions (check out You Tube). She will soon be working on her fifth novel – if she can stay off Twitter for long enough.

Praise for Mandy Baggot

I've just read your book and thought it was excellent! It had a real 'feel good' factor about it. (Excess All Areas)

I was entertained by the book from beginning to end and when I finished reading it, I felt the same satisfied feeling I have after watching a good film. (Breaking the Ice)

The book takes a thorough look at relationships, love, commitment and honesty and all the complicated baggage that comes with the territory. It is chick-lit to its fingertips! (Knowing Me Knowing You)

Strings Attached

To,
Rachel

Best wishes!

Mandy Baggot

Published in 2011 by FeedARead Publishing

Copyright © Mandy Baggot

First Edition

This one's for you Granddad. You always believed in me and I miss you every day.

Set the mood for Strings Attached with this suggested playlist!

Crazy in Love – Beyoncé
The Time (Dirty Bit) – The Black Eyed Peas
Wherever You Will Go – The Calling
Beat Again – JLS
The Thong Song - Sisqo
Sweet Child O' Mine – Guns 'n' Roses
Have You Ever Really Loved A Woman – Bryan Adams
Use Somebody – Pixie Lott
Thunderstruck – AC/DC
Is This Love? – Whitesnake
(I Just) Died In Your Arms – Cutting Crew
Let Love In – The Goo Goo Dolls
Back in Black – AC/DC
Someone Like You – Adele
Secret Smile - Semisonic
Back to Black – Amy Winehouse
Running Scared – Ell & Nikki
Bailamos – Enrique Iglesias
Smooth – Santana
Stay With You – The Goo Goo Dolls
White Wedding – Billy Idol
Grenade – Bruno Mars
November Rain – Guns 'n' Roses
Like I Love You – Justin Timberlake
Are You Gonna Go My Way – Lenny Kravitz
Rebel Yell – Billy Idol
Let's Make A Night To Remember – Bryan Adams
Cosmic Girl – Jamiroquai
Bamboleo – The Gipsy Kings
Amazing – George Michael
Light On – David Cook
Just Another Day – Jon Secada
Marry Me – Train

One

'Damn it!' George yelled, racing over to the tap with her bloodied finger.

Cuts were an occupational hazard, but this time she'd been slicing up chillies. Sliced pepper, sliced finger, and now the spicy contents of the Mexican plant felt like they were burrowing to her core. This was typical. She was under pressure, she was rushing to get things finished and her mind was on another job. Sometimes multitasking was just plain dangerous.

'Bugger!' George roared angrily as she continued to hold her finger under the tap.

What she really wanted to say was 'f**k', really, really loud. She wanted to stand in the middle of the kitchen and release the word from her mouth with the ferocity and venom of a wronged banshee or, maybe, Pink. She took a deep breath and tried to swallow down the feeling. Nope, it was still there.

'You alright? Or are we having flesh sandwiches again?' Marisa asked, raising her low-lighted head to look at her boss.

'Have you finished buttering yet?' George questioned in reply.

She wasn't in the mood for sarcasm, particularly sarcasm with a thick Welsh accent and plenty of attitude. Marisa had already pissed her off singing badly to

7

Beyoncé all morning; she didn't need her questioning her ability right now.

'No, like there's loads.'

'Well, stop worrying about what I'm doing and get on with it. Or it's only thirty minutes for lunch,' George told her.

'That's like totally not fair, in fact I think it's against the law,' Marisa remarked, jabbing her knife into the margarine tub.

Nothing had gone right today. George was short of supplies, the radio couldn't find a decent station and they were behind schedule. She could also feel a headache coming on. It always started in her ears, a build up of pressure like she was at thirty thousand feet, then the pain would slowly move to the back of her head and spread until it had enveloped her entire skull. Then she couldn't think, let alone function. She needed Ibuprofen washed down with a nice cold beer. There was a six pack of bottles in the fridge. They were Mexican too. How ironic was that?

It was only 3.00pm though and having beer would be wrong when she was so busy. She needed to stay focussed, she needed to regain some momentum on the order they were finalising. And drinking beer in the afternoon was highly unacceptable in front of someone as impressionable as seventeen year old Marisa. She already knew Marisa dabbled in alcopops and needed little encouragement. She caught her once, snogging the lad from the butchers outside the Co-op, a half empty bottle of WKD in her hand. At 10.30am. George had laid out Butcher Boy when he'd suggested she 'f**k off and mind her own business'. Marisa was frogmarched back to George's and a gallon of strong Costa Rican poured down her neck before she was taken home contrite and hickey ridden. She hadn't mentioned the alcohol to Helen and Geraint. She knew the evidence of intimacy would be enough to warrant a severe ear bashing for the girl. In truth, George sympathised. She'd been there, done that, worn the rock band motif t-shirts, but she wasn't that person anymore. She'd turned a corner a long time ago; she was responsible now and awfully grown-up. Thirty four in fact.

She let out a sigh and ran her uninjured hand through her short crop of blonde hair. There was still so much to bloody do and Marisa was back to singing. Adele this time. The myth that all the Welsh had voices to die for wasn't true. In Marisa's case, she had a voice to die by and that was verging on being kind. The passion was there but the execution wasn't even debatable. George looked at her watch; thankfully Helen was due back any minute.

The phone rang and Marisa bounded over to it like an overeager puppy, catering hat askew on her head, hair flapping wildly, chewing gum close to spilling out of her mouth.

'Hiya, Finger Food.'

George cursed under her breath and shook her head in irritation. Every day she had the same conversation with Marisa. Greet the potential customers in a friendly yet professional manner, state the company name, try not to sound like you're chewing gum even if you are. And do not say 'hiya' unless you're referring to a fee agreement or something on a very tall shelf. Marisa changed grip with the phone and succeeded in wiping egg mayonnaise all over the handset.

'Tonight? A hundred people? You have got to be joking,' Marisa exclaimed, her Welsh accent becoming broader and thicker by the second. She almost sounded like she could round up sheep. Without a dog.

George turned off the tap, rushed over to the telephone and relieved Marisa of the call. She shook her cut and burning hand around, hoping the air would cool it.

'Hello, this is George Fraser, the owner, sorry about that, foreign staff. Can I help? Tonight? Yes, we can do tonight. A hundred people at the Hexagon. OK, hot or cold? OK. Yes, that's not a problem. As it's short notice I would usually charge an additional fee, say - oh - could you clarify that amount, my phone line's been playing up and - yes that figure is absolutely fine. We'll see you tonight, bye.'

A smile crossed her face as she replaced the handset. The headache was easing a little; the painful hand was temporarily forgotten. Perhaps today was going to pick up after all.

'Are you like totally insane? We have Archie Reeves' sixty fifth birthday party to cater for tomorrow and I don't know about you but I'm kind of struggling with Katie Murray's princess shaped sandwiches for the party in like two hours,' Marisa said, wiping her hands on her apron and planting them on her hips.

'Marisa, I thought we talked about telephone answering again this morning. I thought we decided you were going to say 'Good morning Finger Food' or 'Good afternoon Finger Food' depending on the time of day. I thought we said that 'hiya' was categorically banned,' George said, looking at her young employee.

'We did, but like I was trying to be efficient and 'hiya' just comes out quicker.'

'OK, well, telling a potential customer that they have got to be joking isn't efficient, it's bloody rude. Rude might be the trend right now if you're Puff Daddy, or P Diddy or whatever he's calling himself, but it won't wash here,' George told her.

Shit. She was starting to sound like her mother. 'It won't wash here'. What was she thinking? This was what the stress was doing to her. It was starting to make her talk like someone from the 1950s, or Nigella, pouting over her pert meringues.

'I was just thinking time management, you know, getting to the point,' Marisa answered defiantly.

'You're lucky we didn't miss out on two grand.'

10

Despite the words she'd chosen she had to hammer the point home.

'Two grand! Jesus! Just for a hundred people! Is it for Elton John?' Marisa exclaimed her eyes bulging.

'It's an after-show party at the Hexagon, obviously I'll pay overtime. Could you call Callie, Alison and Bianca, see if they can help serving?'

'Callie's got glandular fever,' Marisa replied.

'OK, well someone else who's helped us out before, but not Gina. I know it isn't her fault she's got a brace but she spat over everyone's food at Mr and Mrs Wong's wedding anniversary.'

'She does do that a lot,' Marisa admitted.

'Right, so do you want me to help you with the sandwiches?' George offered.

She could never be angry with Marisa for long and the news she was going to get a large fee had considerably improved her mood.

'Why couldn't the spoilt little madam have butterfly sandwiches instead of princesses? I can do butterflies and she had butterflies last year. She totally enjoyed picking all the wings off, knowing they took me bloody ages to stick on,' Marisa moaned, scowling like an irritated child.

The back door swung open and crashed against the worktop as Marisa's mother Helen Thomas entered, two carrier bags swinging from each arm. She huffed and puffed and groaned loudly and George hurried to relieve her of some of the load.

'Thank God I'm back. It's murder out there. It's market day isn't it and you know what that means,' Helen began unfastening her coat.

'OAPs and job dodgers,' Marisa remarked not looking up from her sandwiches.

'Yes, exactly and both move as slow as each other 'cause they've got nothing better to do. Anyway, I've got

11

more prawns, more chillies and Simon's bringing extra bread later on,' she said with another sigh.

'Great, let's stick the kettle on and then we can wrap this job up,' George suggested.

She carefully carved the white bread to show Marisa how a princess was constructed out of Hovis' finest.

Helen had worked with George since the beginning, some ten years ago. They had met at the local pub where Helen had worked in the kitchen providing the town with a combination of hearty pub grub (steak and mushroom pie) and fine dining (breast of ostrich, fine green beans and potato shavings in an oyster vinaigrette). George had treated The Bell as a second home back then. She had always gone in after college, always managed to find someone to buy her beer and had always won enough from hustling on the pool table to afford a meal. She knew Helen felt sorry for her back then and she had played on that. She could think what she liked as far as George was concerned, there were always others who thought worse, like her own mother. She was worse than The Boston Strangler in her mother's eyes.

She'd qualified from college with a distinction and after helping Helen improve her own pastry making, Finger Food was born.

The business was George's pride and joy. It hadn't been easy building a company from scratch when you had no idea where to start. George had struggled at school much to the horror of her parents, because apparently Frasers don't struggle at anything. But, despite their insistence that she retook her GCSEs, she enrolled on the catering course at college. Two years and a lot of hard work later she achieved a hospitality and catering qualification. Cooking was something she had always enjoyed and, before things got complicated, she and her mother had cooked together all the time. It seemed like a lifetime ago.

Baking for buffets wasn't the usual job of choice for a jeans wearing, rock music listening, pool playing chick. But, for whatever reason, it worked. When she was creating something new she immersed herself in the recipe, focussed on making the ingredients gel together in new and unseen ways. She was concentrating on that moment with the food and nothing else. She could only manage to do that stood next to a hot oven with her hands in a mixing bowl.

But apart from the therapeutic reasons as to why she cooked, it was fun, she was good at it and she could see the money making potential. She had a heart full of woe but a head full of ambition.

At first she started making sandwiches and selling them at offices, on building sites and business parks, anywhere she could. She researched areas that already had a regular service and she undercut them where she was able. Then when she had the money to take on staff she started catering parties. Gradually the functions became more frequent and her customer base grew. It was then things really started to take off. She got a loan from the bank and used it to build a state of the art kitchen as an annexe to her two bedroom terrace. It had meant losing most of the garden but she didn't really do gardens anyway and it was also an excuse to lose the hideous love seat her parents had bought her one Christmas. She didn't know what was behind their thinking on that one; most of her boyfriends never made it to a second date, let alone got invited to sit in the garden.

In fact she had only introduced one boyfriend to her parents and that was nineteen years ago. Her mother had hated him, but George had expected that. She hated everyone. George could have brought home Jesus himself and she would've commented on the state of his sandals. She forbade a fifteen year old George to see him and when that didn't work she tried to get his parents to forbid him from seeing George. Any male acquaintances she had

had since didn't last. She found meeting someone new was just full of empty expectation. You knew immediately if there was a connection or not and if there wasn't, the best you could hope for was that he paid for dinner and he didn't have a tongue like sandpaper.

But right now she was happy on her own. She was in a good place. She loved her work, she adored Helen and Marisa and she quite enjoyed flirting with Simon who worked at the bakery.

Simon was tall, dark haired and smelt of Hugo Boss aftershave. He had been trying to ask her out for as long as she could remember. The trouble was he was just too obvious. It reeked of desperation, even over the rather fresh cologne. He was nice enough, he was fun to banter with but that was it, there wasn't *anything*. There was no spark, no charge in the air. And rightly or wrongly she got bored rapidly, their conversations never ended with her desperate for more. Accepting a date would only raise his hopes. More importantly, as far as the business was concerned, she didn't want to lose the twenty percent discount she had worked so hard to get out of him. She could imagine things might turn nasty if she went out with him and then decided one date was enough. Which she would.

'You'll never guess what happened while you were out,' Marisa spoke.

'Don't tell me Archie Reeves cancelled the birthday party! Please don't tell me that, I'm liable to go round there and make sure he doesn't make sixty six! Five hours it took me to ice the cake. He hasn't has he?' Helen asked, taking off her coat and shaking out her bubble-permed hair.

'No, but you might want to sit down. George has taken on a catering job for tonight, an after-show party at the Hexagon. But there is an upside, wait for it Mum – it's two thousand quid!' Marisa exclaimed.

'Tonight! But we're so busy,' Helen remarked as she washed her hands and prepared to get back to bread buttering.

'I know, but catering a party there could be really big. We do this well and we could get recommended for more of the same. And Marisa just said, it's two grand,' George reminded.

'We've only got an hour or so to finish the food for Katie Murray's party and then it's...' Helen began.

'I know Helen! I know what we have on. Look if you don't want the overtime I'll do it all myself. I want this job,' George said with steely determination.

'I don't think Mum was saying that, were you Mum?' Marisa spoke hurriedly, worrying her extra cash was evaporating.

'No of course not, I just...' Helen started.

'Good, right, well Marisa I'll get these sandwiches done and you get on the phone to your friends, rustle up some waitresses,' George ordered, taking a deep breath.

'I could ask my friend Shirley if you like, she enjoyed it last time and she was ever so good,' Helen offered.

'Oh God, not Curly Shirley! You two look like a couple of prize poodles entering Crufts when you're together you do. She's the only person I've met with curlier hair than you!' Marisa remarked.

'I was complimented about my hair at the shop just now,' Helen told her.

'What shop was it? RNIB?'

'Marisa!' George exclaimed.

'Don't worry George, the next time she wants to borrow money, I know what to say.'

'Oh Mum, I didn't like really mean it, I mean your hair's individual isn't it? Unique,' Marisa said realising she had gone too far.

'If you could ask Curly Shirley that would be great,' George replied.

A loud knock on the back door interrupted them.

'That's early if it's Simon, he could have given me a lift back from town in the van. Half a mile I struggled with those bags. My hands are red raw. They look like overcooked saveloys they do,' Helen moaned.

'You need to pass your driving test Helen; at this rate Marisa will be driving our van before you,' George remarked as she went to the door.

'Overtime will pay for more lessons Mum,' Marisa remarked carefully cutting around the princess template with a sharp knife.

George opened the door and revealed a tall, slim, dark haired man, wearing a beanie hat and a big smile.

'Hello Sis. Need some help wrapping and stacking?' he greeted.

'Adam!' George exclaimed excitedly and she threw her arms around the eighteen year old, enveloping him in a tight hug.

'God, can't breathe, let go, you're squashing the street cred right out of me.'

George let him go and smiled up at him.

'What are you doing here? Why aren't you at uni?' she enquired.

'God, you're sounding more like Mum every day, that's exactly what she said. Don't know whether it was because she thought I was skiving, or whether it was because she didn't like the big black bag of washing I gave her,' Adam spoke as he stepped into the kitchen.

'So, why aren't you at uni?' George repeated.

'Hello Helen, hi Marisa. I love what you've done to your hair,' Adam said, giving both the women the benefit of his charming smile.

'It's supposed to be magpie,' Marisa replied, looking at her blue/green streaks, her cheeks flushing.

'Well it really suits you. So, what jobs have we got on today?' Adam asked, looking around at the organised chaos.

16

'All sorts. A princess party, a sixty fifth birthday tomorrow and an after-show party at the Hexagon tonight. It's like totally full on,' Marisa answered.

'After-show party at the Hexagon? Wow, you know who's playing there tonight don't you?' Adam said, his eyes lighting up.

'No idea. Someone from Rock It Music just called me,' George replied.

'George likes Radio Two these days; I think it's like an age thing,' Marisa spoke cheekily.

'Hey that's unfair, you know the radio's broken at the moment,' George responded.

'Well it's Quinn Blake. That's why I'm home. Me and Tom are going tonight. Quinn Blake's awesome on the guitar and the piano; you got me the DVD remember?' Adam said excitedly.

'Er, yeah,' George answered not remembering.

She knew who Quinn Blake was, everyone did. He was always on television and in glossy magazines about celebrity lives, but she didn't really pay attention to any of it. Perhaps it was time she paid more attention to the things Adam was interested in.

'Marisa, please tell me you've heard of Quinn Blake,' Adam continued, picking up a sausage from a tray and eating it.

'Of course, he's like totally cool and really hot,' Marisa answered.

'You can be cool and hot at the same time can you?' Helen enquired.

'He can,' Marisa answered.

'Has he had a number one record?' Helen asked.

'Mother! You are like *sooo* embarrassing. He's had about a million number ones. And I keep telling you they aren't called records anymore!' Marisa exclaimed, raising her eyes to Heaven.

'Are you missing any lectures?' George asked Adam, moving the tray of food out of his reach.

'No,' Adam answered.

'And now the truth please?'

'It's just one, it isn't important. I mean, I *am* studying music. I think watching a Quinn Blake concert will be more beneficial than listening to Professor Moreton bang on about scores for two hours,' Adam said.

'You like *sooo* rehearsed that excuse,' Marisa remarked.

'But you love all that stuff,' George reminded him.

'It's only one lecture George. I'm sure you'll catch up won't you Adam? He'll catch up. Won't you?' Helen said, encouraging the teenager to agree with her.

'Of course and I've brought all my books with me,' Adam added.

'Hello Alison. Listen, can you waitress tonight? At the Hexagon. Oh, you're going to the concert. You lucky cow! I couldn't get tickets. Well it's after the concert if you're interested. We won't need you until eleven...' Marisa spoke on the phone.

'You better not be lying to me,' George warned him.

'I'm not, I swear.'

'...and don't forget it's double time after midnight,' Marisa added, as George pulled a horrified face and began shaking her head.

'I can be a waiter for you,' Adam said, trying to distract his sister and find some more food.

'You don't have to do that. It'll be late and you've driven three hours to get here.'

'Who else have you got?' Adam asked.

'Well there's me and Helen and Marisa and probably Alison now Marisa's offered her double time and Curly Shirley...'

'Who else reliable?'

'Are you calling Marisa and Helen unreliable? Shame on you,' George remarked.

18

'Come on, you know what I mean. You need me! Admit it! Besides, Quinn Blake might be there. It would be so cool to meet him,' Adam said.

'But you couldn't ask for his autograph or anything Adam, you would have to be professional. You'd be representing Finger Food and...' George reminded him.

'Yeah I know. You still got the penguin suit I wore for that wedding reception?' Adam enquired.

'It's in the spare room,' George responded.

'Great, then count me in. And shall I ask Tom? We're both poor students who could do with the extra cash and I can teach him the ropes. I'm sure Dad must have an old tux knocking about he can wear,' Adam offered.

'It doesn't sound like I have much say in the matter does it?' George answered with a smile.

Two

Everything was set in the upstairs suite at the Hexagon. It was almost 11.00pm, the hot platters were warming, the cold platters were ready to go out and George had six staff, all dressed smartly in white shirts and black bottoms. She couldn't help thinking Marisa had been right about Helen and Curly Shirley though; there were enough ringlets between them to rival Mel B in her Spice Girls days.

'I wonder if he's actually going to be here, like you know, really in the room,' Marisa remarked for at least the tenth time.

'Marisa, remember we have a code of conduct. We only speak when spoken to, unless we're introducing the food,' Helen said, brushing down her daughter's skirt as she tried to escape her scrutiny.

'I know! I'm not a novice. Don't drop food or drink down anyone's clothes and talk in my posh voice,' Marisa replied.

'Do you have a posh voice Marisa?' Adam teased, smiling at her.

'Actually Sir, I do. Would you care for an asparagus spear?' Marisa asked, batting her eyelashes and quelling her Welsh accent as best she could.

'We don't have to talk posh do we Hel'? I never talked posh the last time. One bloke asked if the snacks

20

had capers on 'em and I had no idea what he was talking about; I thought he was asking me on a date,' Curly Shirley announced with a loud laugh and an unexpected belch.

'I just offer the tray and keep chat to a minimum. I'll run through the ingredients for you,' Helen offered kindly, passing Shirley a packet of Rennie from her handbag.

George looked at her reflection in the window and swept a hand through her hair. She got closer to the pane and checked her minimal make-up. She looked so tired. Her skin was pale and her eyes were puffy and sore. She needed to invest in some sleep, either that or some significantly better concealer. Tonight would be another late night, but this function could be the most important event she had ever catered for, if the fee was anything to go by. She needed to be at her best.

She straightened the waistband of her skirt and tucked in her crisp white shirt. She was nervous, more nervous than usual. She wanted everything to go well. If people liked her food they would recommend her and recommendation was the best way to get new business. That, plus a thick wad of business cards sat by the crudités.

She did hate dressing up though and wearing a skirt was against her whole ethos. She always felt so uncomfortable and she knew skirts didn't suit her. She was strictly a jeans and t-shirt kind of girl, always had been. Her mother hated that about her too. She had tried to get her to wear Monsoon's finest to anything and everything when she was a child, but she wasn't having that after about the age of six. Heather Fraser had finally got the message when, aged eight, George had taken a pair of scissors to a particularly floral pink dress and slashed the skirt up to her thigh. There had been a lot of shouting and bitter, angry words, a smacked leg and no television for a week. That had just been the start. Her relationship with her mother had gone downhill from then. Her dad said they were too similar. George frequently slammed her bedroom door and turned up Aerosmith.

But business was different. Her company was everything to her. She couldn't let the fact she was a tomboy at heart get in the way of her success. In this business people had certain expectations and she needed to exceed them all. She wanted to be the best and she would. She was nothing if not determined.

She looked out into the function room and saw guests had started arriving and were being served drinks by the Hexagon staff.

'OK everyone. Listen, thanks for helping me out tonight at such late notice. People are arriving now so let's get this food out there. Helen, keep an eye on the hot platters and bring them out in twenty,' George instructed.

'Gimme those pâté parcels. If anyone's getting the first look at Quinn Blake, it's me,' Marisa exclaimed, darting towards a plate of food.

'Oh no you don't sweet cheeks, that hunk is mine,' Curly Shirley announced, pushing open the swing doors with a cackle.

'Don't look so nervous George. I told you, the concert was awesome, no one's going to notice if the food's crap,' Adam told her with a grin.

'Thanks Adam.'

'Just kidding, the food's great isn't it Tom? Especially the chilli pork - I've had four of those,' Adam replied.

'You better be joking! Now, take a platter and go and serve,' George told him.

'Yes Boss,' Adam answered cheekily.

George watched the two young men leave the kitchen and then she turned to the hob to finish off preparing a sauce.

'Growing up so fast isn't he? A proper young man now,' Helen remarked, turning things over in the oven.

'He certainly is, but still bloody cheeky.'

'He's just the same as Marisa really, full of youthful innocence and excitement. When she really grates on me I try and remember what I was like at her age. I mean I used to hang around outside the chippy and drink Diamond White, Marisa's nothing like that. I should be grateful shouldn't I?' Helen told her.

George shook the memory of Butcher Boy and the Blue WKD incident out of her mind. Now wasn't the time to contradict her opinion.

'Oh. My. God! He's only bloody here! He's here! Looking *sooo* absolutely bloody gorgeous it's scary. He's wearing like really nice jeans, you know, like figure hugging and this really plain white t-shirt, but oh my God it *sooo* suits him. Curly Shirley's edging her way into his group, it's *sooo* gross,' Marisa babbled as she and Alison burst back into the kitchen to collect another tray.

'Two glasses of water please Helen and lots of deep breathing before you let them go out again,' George said.

She picked up a tray and prepared to leave the kitchen.

'He's over by the big palm plant, chatting to some totally skinny blonde-haired trollops who look like *sooo* desperate,' Marisa called as George swung through the doors.

She entered the function room which was filling up rapidly with party guests. It was an eclectic mix with every 'something' between twenty and sixty. Some were dressed casually in jeans and t-shirts; others had dyed hair and were wearing leather. There were a group, of what looked like, transvestites in one corner. They were all six feet tall, wearing over the top outfits, big wigs and too much make-up. And there were several men in dinner jackets, accompanied by ladies in cocktail dresses, in various cliques around the room. It was alive, buzzing with excitement and showbiz.

23

'Canapés gentlemen?' George offered, holding her platter out to a group of six who were sharing a bottle of champagne.

'Well hello! Doesn't this all look ravishing,' one of the men in the group greeted excitedly.

The owner of the voice was in his forties and was dressed in a navy blue suit, teamed with a lilac shirt. He had a perfectly round face with a wide, permanently upturned mouth. His loud booming voice ensured he got attention, because it sounded like he was making a heart stopping announcement every time he spoke. He had well conditioned glossy, hair for a man of his age and it flopped over his eyes when he talked. He looked like a rotund, cheeky version of Hugh Grant.

'I'm famished, what are they darling?' he asked camply, turning to look at George.

'Asparagus and brie on the left and feta and red onion on the right,' George directed.

'God man! I hate cheese. Have you got anything less dairy?' a leather clad man questioned with a groan.

Compared to the perfectly presented owner of the floppy hair, this man was positively the missing link. He had unkempt, shoulder length hair that bushed out like a Leylandii and a row of six hooped earrings in each ear.

'Yes, of course. There are some meat dishes being taken round. Would you like me to get you an alternative?' George offered to the sullen expression.

'No lovey, you will not. You will stay here with me until I've cleared the plate. These are divine! And you, Belch, you can go and find the Neanderthal section of the buffet by yourself. Honestly! He becomes a rock star and forgets all his manners.'

George couldn't help but smile as the leather clad man let out a discontented grunt and headed in the direction of the bar.

'Sorry about his rudeness, I can't bear rudeness. I don't care who you are or what you do, it doesn't take a lot of effort to be polite does it? Gosh, these are really truly delicious. Who made them? What is the name of your catering firm?' the man demanded.

'We're called Finger Food,' George announced proudly.

'Finger Food, I like it! Very good! And who is your MD? I may have business to pass his way.'

'Actually I'm the MD. George Fraser,' George spoke and she balanced the tray of food on her arm and held out her hand to him.

'Gosh really? And you're serving as well, admirable, admirable indeed. Well George Fraser from Finger Food, I will take one of your little business cards and recommend you to anyone and everyone. I am loving the feta and onion. Oh, dear, excuse me, overindulging again,' the man spoke as he let out a loud hiccup.

George smiled.

'I'm Michael by the way, Michael Lambert, Quinn Blake's PA.'

'Pleased to meet you.'

'Oh lovey, the pleasure is all mine after those gorgeous nibbles. Right, must mingle! Toodle pip!'

It was going well. People were being really complimentary about the food. George turned round to head back into the kitchen and replenish her tray. It was then that her attention was drawn to the large palm plant Marisa had mentioned and the people stood by it.

There were at least half a dozen perfectly preened women in figure hugging designer dresses, straight off the pages of *Grazia* magazine, forming a circle around someone. They shuffled themselves further forward with every breath, tightening the ring and George looked at them, enthralled by their behaviour. It was like watching a nature documentary where a large pack surrounded the prey before attacking in team formation.

And then almost divinely the circle parted, like the Red Sea, and the person from the middle made a break for freedom. Suddenly George was stood right in front of the most gorgeous man she had ever seen.

He was of medium height, slim and perfectly proportioned. He had dark brown hair, cropped close to his head and dazzlingly turquoise blue eyes. He was wearing a tight white t-shirt and jeans which clung in all the right places. George could definitely see why Marisa was making such a fuss over him.

She knew she was staring, but she couldn't help herself. He moved towards her and she stood paralysed to the spot like she was stuck in position by Solvite.

'Hi,' Quinn Blake greeted with a smile.

'Canapé?' George responded hurriedly, offering the tray forward as quickly as she could. It was good to have a prop when the way he looked had almost disabled her vocal chords.

'I would, but you're all out,' he answered, indicating the empty platter.

Shit prop.

'Oh, yes, sorry, I was just going to get some more,' George replied.

This was great, now she felt like a complete idiot.

'They're very good. Especially the chilli pork, I've had five of those already, but who's counting?' Quinn informed her.

'Thank you,' George responded, blushing.

Why was she blushing? He was paying her wages; she shouldn't even be talking to him. She had a code of conduct. She should have just carried on to the kitchen. She didn't know what to say, she didn't want to say anything, but he was looking right at her waiting for some sort of conversation and suddenly she couldn't seem to string a sentence together.

'I'm Quinn,' he introduced, holding his hand out to her.

Like she didn't know! He was the one person everyone in the room wanted to be near. She could almost feel the various sets of female eyes on her, burning a hole in the back of her neck.

'George,' she replied, balancing the tray on her forearm and taking his hand.

This just wasn't normal. Usually the guests at parties looked straight through her or completely ignored her presence until she waved the platter under their nose. Introductions and hand shaking were an oddity and this was twice in one night. This was no ordinary party.

'Ah, so you're George Fraser. My PA, Michael, just told me and everyone else in the group all about the merits of Finger Food,' Quinn said still smiling.

'Oh, well, that's very nice. I'm amazed he's been able to spread the word so quickly, especially with the hiccups,' George spoke.

'If there's one thing Michael knows how to do well, it's work a room,' Quinn answered.

George didn't know what to say next and she just couldn't stop looking at him. She felt like she was fifteen again. No, she felt like Marisa and she was starting to get concerned that at any minute she was going to say something completely inappropriate like 'D'you know I think you're like completely hot and cool all at the same time'. Probably in a Welsh accent for authenticity.

'Sorry, you'll have to excuse me, I need to speak to someone before they sneak out and I can see them heading for the door. Good to meet you,' Quinn said, moving past George and giving her the benefit of another sexy smile.

'Nice to meet you too,' George answered, watching him go.

She carried on staring after him as he approached a couple by the door and began shaking hands with them.

'George! Mother is like doing her nut. She says the hot platters need to come out now or they're going to

27

be overdone! What are you looking at?' Marisa asked, bursting out of the swinging doors and bounding up to George.

'Nothing, I was just coming back in for the next batch,' George spoke hurriedly averting her eyes from Quinn.

'Oh God he's over there now. He is like so gorgeous, like even more gorgeous than David Beckham. Nicer arse and less tattoos,' Marisa said as she drooled.

'In the kitchen with you. Professionalism,' George ordered.

She glanced back before she opened the door, taking one last look at Quinn.

Three

He'd seen her the second he'd entered the room. He couldn't put his finger on what it was but his attention had been drawn away from the high fashion, intense make-up, of the usual set of women at his after-show parties and been drawn to her. This blonde-haired woman wearing a plain black skirt she looked uncomfortable in.

And now he had spoken to her his guts were churning. He was exhausted and hungry. He could happily eat a whole tray full of canapés himself and now he had to make small talk. He didn't want to make small talk and work the room; he wanted to speak to her. George Fraser from Finger Food.

This was insane. Tonight he was supposed to be enjoying the company of pole dancer Amber Range, but right now he couldn't face it. No, the only woman he wanted to spend more time with was serving his guests.

'Canapé Sir?' Adam offered.

'Thanks,' Quinn accepted.

Eating was good. Eating would keep his hands occupied if nothing else.

'...and so I said to her, I said "Darling, everyone knows they're fake boobies, you all have the same

29

surgeon"!' Michael spoke loudly to a group he was entertaining.

He burst into high-pitched laughter and reached behind him to take a mini prawn wrap from the platter George was holding.

She held the tray closer to him and looked across the room at Adam.

He looked even more grown-up tonight than usual. Now he was so much more manly than gangly and not at all the little boy she remembered running around the house dressed as Batman. She swallowed a lump in her throat as he caught her eye and smiled, holding aloft an almost empty tray so proudly.

'Have you tried one of these prawn things? Have you? What are they called George? This is George everybody, she is the MD of Finger Food and she will be catering every party I organise from now on, if I have my way,' Michael spoke, turning to her and demanding her attention just by the volume of his voice.

'They're prawn and Tabasco,' George informed with a smile.

'Who would have thought it? I mean prawn and Tabasco; I would never have thought it, would you?' Michael said, shaking his head in admiration.

George watched as Adam handed out canapés to the guests and then she saw him offer one forward to Quinn Blake himself. The musician took another chilli pork parcel and Adam said something to him that made him laugh and smile. Quinn offered Adam his hand and the two men became engaged in conversation, both surrounded by the group of beautiful women that seemed to swarm around Quinn like wasps around an open can of Coke.

'So are you going to cater for me? I absolutely need you to cater for me,' Michael carried on, bringing George back to his conversation.

'I'd be delighted to, but I am pretty booked up, I mean...' George started.

'Cancel them! Cancel them all! We will pay you twice what they are paying you. No! Make that three times, in fact, name your price! We have another four nights of concerts here, could you cater the after-shows? Vary the menu? Whip up some new creations every night? Could you George? It would make me so happy. Look at all these happy, smiley people and your very empty silver dishes. They all have expressions of deep delight because of your marvellous culinary expertise,' Michael rambled on.

'Well, I guess...' George began.

'Marvellous! That's settled! Now, tomorrow night, I would quite like to see what you can do with lamb. I like a bit of lamb, but not with anything minty, too tart. Surprise me,' Michael ordered and he let out a hearty laugh that was heard at the other side of the room.

'No problem,' George answered tentatively, wracking her brain for a long forgotten about recipe.

'Oh goody!' Michael said, clapping his hands together in delight.

George looked over at Adam again. He and Quinn were engaged in what seemed like a deep conversation, completely oblivious to the presence of the beautiful women encircling them. Adam was leading the talk. George watched as he passed his platter to one of the women in the group and then suddenly he and Quinn were studying each other's hands.

'So you're a student,' Quinn spoke to Adam.

'Yeah, I'm at uni, in Wales, got another year to go, but I gig with my band. I mean, we're nothing like you guys but...' Adam started, blushing.

'Hey, we all started gigging in bars,' Quinn answered, taking another canapé.

Is that where he had started? Had he gigged in bars? He had no idea, but it seemed the right thing to say. George was smiling and laughing with Michael. She was drop-dead gorgeous when she smiled, her hair dropped slightly over her face and her eyes lit up.

'So, how come you're here?' Quinn asked Adam.

'Here's home. My sister runs the catering company, Finger Food. Over there,' Adam indicated, pointing her out.

This was great, he had engaged in conversation to take his mind off the caterer and now he was being made to look at her again.

She glanced over and Quinn felt something inside him lurch. It wasn't unpleasant, but it was unexpected. God, he definitely didn't want the pole dancer tonight. No, it had to be her, Miss Finger Food. But he needed to play it right.

It was 3.00am before all the guests had left. The Hexagon staff had finished tidying the bar area and George, Helen and Curly Shirley were almost at the end of clearing up the kitchen.

'Van's loaded up, ready to go; waitresses have gone off in taxis and Tom's gone on to another party. Some ex-girlfriend of his wants to rekindle things I think. Marisa's waiting in the van,' Adam informed as he re-entered the kitchen.

'OK, well Helen and Cur - I mean Shirley - why don't you go with Adam and Marisa in the van. I can finish tidying up here,' George suggested.

'Oh George are you sure? I mean I can stay and finish that washing up if you like,' Helen began, preparing to grab the dishcloth.

'Boss says go Helen, you don't quibble about it,' Shirley remarked, putting a vice like grip on her friend's arm.

'Helen you look done in. It's been a really busy day and you're heading up the sixty fifth birthday party tomorrow afternoon. Go home, get some sleep and I don't want to see you until at least ten tomorrow. And Shirley, thanks for all your help, you've been brilliant,' George said.

'Did you hear that Helen? I've been brilliant. How brilliant exactly? Triple time brilliant?' Shirley asked, cracking a crooked smile.

'Don't push it.'

'I could just finish these before we go,' Helen started, her hand dangerously close to making contact with a soiled platter.

'Put the cloth down darlin',' Shirley said forcefully.

'Adam, take the women home will you?'

'I'll drop them off and come back for you,' Adam told her.

'No, you go home and get some sleep too; you've had a busy enough day as it is. Don't worry about the van, I'll come round for it later,' George told him.

'OK, we're out of here. See you later,' Adam said, linking arms with Helen and Curly Shirley.

'See you and thanks again. It was a really successful night,' George said.

'Come on girls, which nightclub we going to hit? Have you tried Strikers Shirley? They play some great retro Eighties stuff,' Adam joked, making the women laugh and weakly protest.

George waited for them to leave and then she hurried over to the fridge and swung open the door. She grabbed at an ice cold bottle of lager she had been coveting all night. She took the lid off it with a bottle opener, put it to her lips and took a long swig. She closed her eyes and let the cool, refreshing taste fill her throat. She so deserved this, she was totally wiped out, exhausted beyond belief.

Quinn looked through the door at her. She was necking a bottle of beer like if she didn't drink it there would be an apocalypse. Christ, he was nervous. His palms were sweating and he didn't dare take a breath. He didn't want her to hear him; he needed to be in control of this. But he wasn't. The tightening of every muscle in his chest told him that. What was going on here? He could get sex anywhere he wanted, with anyone he wanted, why did he want her? He swallowed and then taking a deep breath he quietly opened the door.

When she opened her eyes she almost leapt out of her skin as someone was standing in the kitchen right opposite her. It was all she could do to hold onto the bottle. It was Quinn Blake. How hadn't she noticed someone enter?

'Oh shit. I mean, sorry, excuse me. I didn't think anyone was left up here. I was just finishing the clearing up,' George spoke hurriedly, putting the bottle down on the side and picking up a dishcloth.

'Do you mind?' Quinn asked, reaching for the lager.

George shook her head and waited to see what he was going to do.

He circled the bottle in his hands and then put it to his mouth, taking a mouthful of liquid and swallowing it down. George watched him. The most simplistic movement, just drinking, and she couldn't take her eyes off him. She felt a flush run up her whole body as he took a second swig.

'I thought everyone had gone,' George repeated as Quinn put the bottle down and looked over to her.

He was so hot, so perfect looking, so ruggedly beautiful, just the way a man should be. The kitchen was

34

silent apart from the drip of the tap into the washing up bowl.

'Everyone *has* gone,' he replied, moving closer to her.

'Then, what are you still doing here?' George enquired her breathing quickening as he took up a position just inches away from her.

She could smell him. His light fruit and musk aftershave, the heat off him, the scent of Fast Fret wax and guitar strings. It reminded her of her youth.

'I'm looking for you,' Quinn answered his eyes not leaving hers.

Before George could react to what he'd said, he stepped forward and took her face in his strong hands. She could feel the intensity, his lips were on hers and she was backed up against the worktop, the pressure of his firm body on hers.

She kissed him back, tasting the lager on his tongue, enjoying the way he was holding her so hard against the kitchen unit. She suddenly felt so completely out of control.

And then she could hear voices heading their way. He pulled away, as quickly as he had grabbed her, returning to his position across the kitchen. It was seconds before Michael burst in, waving his hands excitedly.

'Ah here you are Quinn! Roger's phoned, *again*! Was concerned you weren't back at the hotel. I am your personal escort and the car is waiting. Let's not dilly-dally,' Michael spoke, opening the door to the function room.

'I was just talking to Miss Fraser about the catering. I wanted her to tell me what her secret is,' Quinn said his eyes locking with hers.

'That is completely unethical! I hope he wasn't trying too hard with the charm offensive. He's such a naughty boy! Anyhow, we will find out the extent of George's talents over the next few nights. She's catering all the after-shows here. If you approve of course,' Michael spoke.

'Oh I approve, wholeheartedly. In fact I can't wait,' Quinn answered, smiling at her.

George had been struck dumb by his kiss. She was unable to speak or move or even breathe. She just kept looking at him, unable to believe what had just happened between them. Perhaps she was out of touch, maybe this was what happened to all caterers when they provided food for a rock star's after-show party. Maybe it was after-show party etiquette.

'Right, so, tally forth Quinn! It's another big day tomorrow. See you tomorrow night George, don't forget a foray of lamb,' Michael spoke, smacking his lips together.

'See you tomorrow,' Quinn said the satisfied smile still lingering on his mouth.

'Goodnight,' George managed to reply stiffly.

And with Michael leading the way they were gone.

As soon as the door swung closed and she could hear them making their way up the corridor, she let out a long, slow breath. What the Hell had just happened? She turned and caught sight of her reflection in the window. Her cheeks were flushed, her eyes were sparkling; for a second she didn't look exhausted.

Subconsciously she put her hand to the ring on the chain around her neck and held it in her fingers. She felt giddy and excited. She almost felt like a teenager again.

He was still shaking when he got to the car. He sat down on the white leather seats of the limousine and stared at his trembling fingers.

'A marvellous party tonight, marvellous! The catering was a delight don't you think?' Michael said, joining him on the back seat.

'Yeah,' he answered, coupling his hands together and having no idea what to do with them.

'I never thought I'd be saying that in Basingstoke. Life is full of little surprises,' Michael said with a titter.

'Yeah, it is,' Quinn agreed.

Four

It was almost 9.00am when George got to her parents' house the next morning. She'd got in from the Hexagon at just before 4.00am but hadn't been able to sleep. She'd been on a high, completely wired. She had still been able to feel Quinn's lips on hers and it bothered her. It bothered her because it had been reckless behaviour, behaviour that was no longer in her make up. It also bothered her because she'd enjoyed it so much. He had kissed her and she had been powerless to stop him. She hadn't wanted to stop him. She'd been out of control for the first time in a long time and that worried her too. That was the person she used to be, not the George she was now. That George had been boxed up and put away long ago.

She stood outside her parents' house, looking at the twee net curtains in the window, the perfect borders edging the beds filled with rose bushes and winter pansies. She approached the door, acknowledging the welcome doormat and the bell that chimed 'Greensleeves' and the 'William Tell Overture' on alternate days. She paused, her hand hovering over the button. She didn't want to go in. She wanted to just get in the van and get back to work. She was busy, they had Archie's party and then she had to produce something amazing with lamb for Quinn Blake's after-show. She had received a voicemail from Michael earlier agreeing two thousand pounds for each show. She would be able to afford a new van by the end of the week.

She had the spare van keys with her in her bag; she didn't need to go in. But then she thought about Adam. He was probably in there being smothered. Her mother feeding him up with fatty meats drenched in gravy, her father trying to get him to take an interest in golf. The cat, Lesley, farting all the time and her mother trying to cover it up with lavender room fragrance spray. That was her strongest memory from childhood, the scent of cat farts mixed with stew and lavender. It wasn't the greatest of recollections.

She breathed in deeply and then pressed the bell as hard as she could. It was 'Greensleeves' today and the song had almost played out before her mother opened the door. She was smiling initially, probably thinking it was a neighbour or someone from the town magazine committee, but when she saw who it was the smile was replaced with a look of indifference.

Her hair looked like it had been shampooed and set that very morning and she was wearing an apron tied around her middle, which covered the majority of a nylon A-line skirt. She had always looked like a cover model for *Woman's Weekly* and nothing ever changed, not in this house.

'Brian, it's Georgina,' Heather called to her husband.

That was it. That was the greeting she received after not seeing either of them for at least two months. She had been busy, she hadn't returned a few of her mother's phone calls, they had stopped calling round, she had stopped calling round. And here they were.

Heather opened the door a little wider to allow George to enter and she stepped in just as Lesley appeared in the hallway, lifted her tail and filled the narrow space with the pungent stench of cat arse.

Automatically, George reached for the lavender spray, which was positioned in various locations around the house and gave it a good few pumps.

'Hello Georgina. Got time to watch a bit of golf? It's the Masters,' Brian called from the living room.

'Sorry Dad, really busy today. I just came for the van keys,' George called back.

She put her head around the living room door and there was her dad, his head shining like a snooker ball, his favourite maroon sweatshirt on. He was sat on the floral sofa they'd bought in Courts circa 1984, remote control in one hand, his 'I love Nick Faldo' mug in the other, watching the golf on Sky Sports. Sky was the only newfangled appliance they had in the house, that and the forty two inch LCD television he had bought with a big premium bond win. He didn't even look over to her.

Heather led the way through to the kitchen, pulled the van keys from the hook on the wall and put them down onto the worktop in front of George.

'Is Adam in?' George asked hopefully.

'He's in bed. I don't know what you were thinking of, keeping him out until the early hours working,' Heather said as she turned her back on George and stirred a vat of something on the hob.

'He offered to help and I will pay him, more than the going rate,' George replied.

'You take advantage of that boy's good nature,' Heather continued.

'He was happy to work. Ask him if you don't believe me.'

'He's too polite to say no to people, you know that,' Heather said sternly.

'I want to see him,' George said, heading towards the kitchen door and the stairs.

'I've told you, he's asleep. Now take the keys and get that heap of a van off the front drive. Mrs Weeks can't abide cluttered drives. She phoned the council last week

40

because number nine's plastics and cardboard bin was overflowing. I don't want to give her any cause to call about this house,' Heather spoke.

'Is he staying all weekend? I'd like him to work again tonight,' George said and with a sigh she picked up the van keys, moving them from hand to hand.

'He should rest. He has exams coming up and he needs to practice his piano. I have Mrs Rowland coming round this afternoon,' Heather said.

Mrs Rowland was half French and half psycho. She was a piano obsessive with half moon glasses and her hair tied tight in a bun. She had attempted to teach George how to play too, until George realised hanging out with her friends after school was preferable to Mozart and practising scales. She took the month's grounding for not wanting to continue with lessons, knowing that after that month she was free. She felt for Adam having to endure an afternoon of 'you are not hitting the phrasing with enough passion - FROM THE TOP.'.

'George! Hey,' Adam greeted, entering the kitchen and smiling at her.

'Hey Adam. Thanks for helping last night, I was just coming to collect the van,' George said.

'I'm not sure it's running right you know. I'm pretty sure it has an oil leak. I could take a look if you like. GCSE mechanics might not be able to solve all the issues, but I could give it a go,' he offered kindly.

'I said it didn't look roadworthy,' Heather commented.

'That's OK, don't worry. I'm hoping to buy a new one next week. I've been asked to cater the rest of the after-show parties for Quinn Blake's concerts at the Hexagon. It's big money,' George told him.

'Wow! That's amazing isn't it Mum? I'm staying till Monday; do you want me to help out?' Adam asked.

'Well, I...' George began not daring to look at her mother.

She could imagine the expression. The disdainful look, the thin, tight-lipped mouth, as if she had just suggested Adam become a rent boy.

'Adam, you need to revise and Mrs Rowland is coming round this afternoon remember? We were lucky to get her at short notice,' Heather reminded.

'Yeah I know but George won't need me until ten-ish; Mrs Rowland will be here at two and gone by four. She likes to get to Waitrose just when they start reducing the stuff from the deli counter,' Adam responded with a grin.

'Listen, your uni stuff has to come first though. Are you behind?' George enquired.

'No! I'm straight A's George; you know that. Tell her Mum,' Adam urged.

'But straight A's have to be worked at,' Heather responded, glaring at George again.

'Look, I'll be fine. I'm sure Marisa can rustle up an extra friend or two,' George said, heading for the door.

'No, I want the gig. I could do with the cash, guitar strings and sheet music don't come cheap and, I want to see Quinn again. He's a cool guy; he gave me some good advice last night and I showed him some hand exercises to help with his shredding,' Adam told her.

At the mention of his name George was transported back to the kitchen of the Hexagon, the weight of his body against hers, the urgency of his kiss.

'I'll meet you there, ten-ish,' Adam promised, walking her to the door.

'OK, but listen, don't rub Mum up the wrong way. Clean out Lesley's litter tray for her or something,' George suggested.

'Will do. See you later Sis,' Adam spoke as George opened the front door.

'Bye. Bye Dad,' George called.

'Oh bye love. Try and catch some of the tournament if you can, Tiger Woods is blowing everyone away,' Brian called back.

'So I've heard,' George remarked.

Five

When George got home she dumped the van outside and raced indoors. She hated her mother. She always made her feel inadequate, always tried to shut her out of family life. So many years had passed since she had taken on the black sheep role. She had hoped one day she could shrug the stigmatic fleece off, or at least have been allowed to have it highlighted. But no, it seemed she was still paying for her actions all those years ago.

Up in her bedroom she rifled through the back of the wardrobe for a faded green wallet file. It was all she had to remind her of the family they used to be.

But if she was honest there weren't many photos of happy times before Adam was born. There was a photo of George at her fifth birthday party, almost setting light to her fringe as she blew out the candles on her cake. In that photo her mother was actually smiling in the background and clapping her hands with glee. There were a couple of others pre-Adam, George and her dad eating ice creams on a day out at the farm, her mother pushing her on a swing and a photo of the three of them standing to attention next to a Busby at Buckingham Palace.

She smiled as she moved on to the pictures of Adam. There he was, paper crown on his head, at one particularly awkward family Christmas. That day, her mother had blown up over forgotten bread sauce and charred stuffing balls. Dinner had been eaten in virtual silence after that, apart from Adam telling cracker jokes and making sure he got everybody's novelty prize.

Then she pulled out another photo and felt her chest tighten as she looked at it. All this time and she still felt so strongly about someone she hadn't seen in so long.

She had been sixteen, sixteen and madly in love. Yes, George Fraser had been madly in love. It seemed hard to believe now, because she hadn't felt anything remotely like love since. Nowadays she flirted and she had sex, but it was just fulfilling a physical need. It was lust, nothing like love. What she had with Paul back then, despite their age, had definitely been love. She had no doubt about that.

Paul Robbins was the same age, bright, funny, cool, good looking. Everything a fifth former's dreams were made of. Everything George's dreams were made of. He rode a motorbike and had shoulder length hair. He introduced her to lager and he played guitar in a band.

She let herself smile now as she remembered him. He had made her laugh every single day. Whenever she was with him she'd been happy. He didn't care what people thought about him, he just did his own thing, ran from the mainstream, embraced originality, laughed in the face of rules.

She loved him, he loved her, they were going to be together forever. Back then she had never even contemplated life without him. Their feelings ran deep, they were for keeps. Her mother hated him; he was everything she despised about 'feckless teenagers'. She called Paul an 'irresponsible, long-haired hooligan' and it only made George love him more.

Then, one day, Paul announced he was leaving. But not just leaving the town, leaving the country. His mum had been ill for as long as George could remember and she was getting no better. She needed pioneering treatment that was unavailable in the UK. His dad had got a new job in Canada and the family were leaving for a new life on the other side of the world.

When he broke the news he had sobbed. Her tough, strong, guitar playing boyfriend had wept inconsolably, worried for his mother and unable to imagine what his new life would be like minus George.

She remembered the day he left like it was yesterday. Standing in her school uniform - skirt trimmed three inches above regulation - clutching a photo Paul had given her of them. They were both smiling and laughing, happy together after one of his gigs. In the picture her hair was long and streaked with pink and she was wearing his leather jacket. Her eyes were heavy with eyeliner and her mouth was decorated with pillar-box red lipstick she knew her mother hated. But it was her expression that said so much. She was smiling, not just with her lips, but on the inside. And their hands were clasped together tightly like an unbreakable link.

The moment the car engine started up she had burst into tears. She ran alongside it as far as the end of the street, her hand touching the glass where his hand was pressed up against it. She wanted to smash the glass, she wanted to feel him kiss her again, and more than anything she wanted him to stay.

She had taken one last look at him, his handsome face, his sad eyes and then finally she had let go.

Two weeks after he left she found out she was pregnant. She'd been too busy pining for him and trying to ring him on an apparently unobtainable number to think about things like periods. It hadn't arrived, she had started to feel sick and her friend Tracey suggested she ought to do a test. Tracey knew everything about everything; she read *Just Seventeen* and *More!* and she smoked Marlboro Lights without coughing like an asthmatic and puking up.

So with Tracey giving careful instructions from behind the school toilet door she had done the test, in between science and drama. And it was positive. Sixteen and pregnant. She had never felt so ashamed.

They were usually so careful. But sometimes things between them were so intense; practicalities took a backseat to desire. When they were together the real world just didn't exist.

George knew when it had happened. They had stayed at a hotel, saved up for months to jump up and down on the bed wearing nothing but complimentary robes. They had been Mr and Mrs Robbins for only one night and they had drunk smuggled in Asti and made love to Whitesnake.

She had continued to call him - no answer - she wrote - no reply. She didn't know what she expected him to do or say but she just wanted him to know. Deep down she would have loved for him to come back and take her away from her spirit-crushing mother. But she knew his parents would never let that happen. They wanted the best for their son and having him tied to a pregnant sixteen year old was never going to be it. Besides, they had bigger things to think about, like his mother's deteriorating health. Compared with that, her issues seemed almost insignificant.

She touched the ring on the chain around her neck now and closed her eyes.

Her mother had been despising her ever since. She had brought shame on the family by getting pregnant. Apparently she was no better than Debbie O'Connor from number twenty three who had given birth long before her sixteenth birthday and was now on a Methadone programme.

That black fleece had weighed heavily on her shoulders since then.

'Cooee! George! Are you here?' Helen's voice called from the annexe.

'Yep, I'm up here, just coming,' George replied hurriedly, piling the photos back into the folder and stowing it back in the wardrobe.

No one knew about the pregnancy, apart from her parents. Heather said if people knew, her life would be over. They would label her a tramp and a failure. 'It might be the en vogue thing to do in the eyes of this current society, Georgina, but I am telling you, if people find out then you're tarnished for life,' Heather had said. She hadn't really believed her, but pregnancy had seemed to quash the rebel in her and it was easier to just agree.

'You're early. I said not before ten and it's five to,' George remarked as she joined Helen in the kitchen.

'I couldn't lie in. Geraint had to get up for work. I tried to lounge around reading magazines, but I couldn't relax knowing there was so much to do today. Shall I start buttering? Marisa will be here soon, but she was slightly better at lying-in than I was,' Helen informed as she put gloves on her hands.

'Yeah that would be great. I need to look through my recipes and find something new and exciting to do with lamb. What d'you think?' George asked as she got some files out of a drawer.

'Well, mint always complements it.'

'No, not mint. Too tart apparently. I need something that hasn't been done before, something you wouldn't think of. Something a bit out there.'

'How about jam?' Marisa suggested as she crept up behind the pair, chewing gum and clutching *Star Life* magazine to her chest.

'I need something edible not revolutionarily gross.'

'You want edible, let me show you edible. I almost hyperventilated in the newsagents. I give you Quinn Blake, almost naked in this week's *Star Life* magazine,' Marisa exclaimed.

She laid the magazine out on the worktop and opened up the centre pages. With nothing to cover his dignity but a strategically placed violin, there was Quinn Blake, oozing sexuality and staring out from the photo like he was personally undressing every voyeur.

George swallowed as she looked at him. There probably wasn't a woman alive that didn't feel something stir inside her when looking at a photo of him. And she had experienced the man at close quarters last night. Very close quarters.

'I hear they airbrush a lot of things in magazines these days. I mean, he has to be airbrushed there doesn't he? I mean, that isn't how a man looks is it?' Helen remarked, staring at the magazine all too enthusiastically.

'Mother! He isn't airbrushed! He isn't like Dad is he? He doesn't sit on his arse all day eating cheese straws and reading *Nuts*. Quinn Blake is perfect in the photograph because he's perfect in the flesh!' Marisa announced swooning.

'Hmm, well I'm not so sure. I mean his skin is flawless, you just don't get skin that flawless do you? He must use some wonderfully expensive moisturising cream,' Helen continued.

'I wonder who rubs it in for him?' Marisa asked excitedly, letting out a shriek of delight.

'OK, on that note let's get rubbing some ingredients together. Let's check what needs to be done for the sixty fifth this afternoon and what we need to get ready for the Hexagon tonight,' George spoke, shutting the magazine up and clapping her hands together.

She couldn't look at him a second longer. She was already conjuring up a recollection of the texture of his tongue.

'What? The Hexagon again tonight? With him?!' Marisa exclaimed excitedly.

'Didn't you tell her Helen?' George enquired.

'Not yet. I thought she might spend all morning heavy breathing into the fillings.'

'Oh. My. God! Another party? Another Quinn Blake party! Do we need staff? No one is going to believe this! Once was like mega but twice...' Marisa carried on.

'Yes we need staff, for the next four nights. Ring around,' George said, smiling at her enthusiasm.

'You realise we have Lady Harrison-Bowater's ball to cater for at the end of the week and you know how much planning that involves. We're talking crusts off and complicated arrangements. She inspects everything personally before it even makes it through to the banqueting hall,' Helen reminded.

'I know,' George answered.

'And the Army party. Crusts on, but mountains of everything,' Helen continued.

'I know Helen, it's under control,' George insisted, flicking through her recipes.

'Oh. My. God Callie! Can you speak? Is your throat OK yet? If it is, then you are going to like love me forever!' Marisa gabbled down the telephone.

Six

She had made lamb, spinach and sesame canapés.
It was a recipe she found on the internet. It had been
insanely difficult to get them wrapped up and looking
pretty and Marisa was all but useless at it and kept saying
'f**k it' like a member of a punk band every time one fell
apart. In the end, George had sent her to join Helen at
Archie Reeves' party, to assist in overseeing the tea
dance. They would be tucking into corned beef and Spam
sandwiches followed by scones. He had insisted on a
wartime theme. He was going to be dancing to Glenn
Miller and had put blackout curtains at all the windows of
the hall. George only hoped he wouldn't throw the hall
into complete darkness or sound an air raid siren, or there
could be injuries. Some of his guests were in their
seventies.

She looked around proudly at the spread of food
she had prepared for the after-show that night. The lamb
canapés, the gammon and honey, the brie and grape
tortilla wraps, the seafood medley parcels. It was her best
work yet. It had challenged her but she had risen to that
challenge. She smiled at the cellophane covered platters
and let out a sigh of satisfaction.

She was just considering indulging in a lager
while no one else was around when there was a tap at the
back door.

She knew the tap; he always knocked the same way, with confidence, perhaps a little cockily.

She opened the door and there he was. Thick dark hair, easy smile, dressed in jeans and a checked shirt.

'Hello sexy,' he greeted, looking George up and down the way he always did.

She looked anything but sexy in a hair net, gloves and an apron, but she smiled anyway, knowing the compliment was well meant.

'Your bread M'lady,' Simon spoke, putting a container of white and rye down on the worktop as he entered.

'Thanks Simon,' George said appreciatively.

'No problem. Wow, you've been busy today. Hope you're not working yourself too hard,' Simon remarked, looking around at the platters of food.

'You know me,' George replied with a shrug.

'Actually I don't. Well, not well enough by half in my opinion. I mean I've tried to charm you with my thick sliced wholemeal, but I think it's high time you and me had a drink sometime,' Simon suggested, smiling at her.

'How about a coffee? I was just going to make one,' George offered, picking up the kettle in an attempt to distract him from his offer.

'That wasn't what I meant and you know it. Come on George, we could just go to the pub or for dinner if you'd rather. I'm easy,' Simon continued.

'Yeah? Well I'm not,' George snapped rather more viciously than she'd intended.

'Whoa! Hold on a minute...' Simon started.

'Look, I've got a big job on tonight and I need to get organised,' George spoke, lowering her eyes so as not to meet his gaze.

'I was just asking you for a drink George, no strings. Just a chance for us to get to know each other better that's all,' Simon insisted.

'I know. I'm sorry. I'm just totally manic at the moment. We will have a drink sometime. Hey, I might even let you win at pool,' George answered, trying to diffuse the awkward atmosphere that had descended.

He was sweet and he was handsome in a boyish sort of way, but he just wasn't for her. She didn't know how she knew that but she knew it. There was no spark, not one.

'Sure, I understand. Listen, I'd better get on. Got to deliver to Mrs Devonish at the tea rooms next and you know how much she talks. I'll catch you later,' Simon said, replacing his smile.

'Yeah, sure and thanks for the bread,' George replied lamely.

'See you.'

He closed the door behind him and George let out a sigh. She hadn't meant to be quite so hard on him. She had basically insinuated he was desperate to get her into bed. Which he probably was, but he wasn't brazen in his attempts to woo her and she had been flirting with him for months, albeit in front of Helen and Marisa. She probably owed him a date.

But she didn't want to owe anyone anything. She didn't want to feel obliged to do anything she didn't want to do. There was no future in her and Simon. He would most probably take her on a great date, she might even sleep with him, but as much as he was good looking she couldn't imagine eating food off him or letting him cut her hair. And that was the sort of relationship she craved. It had to be intense and powerful and it had to be wild and passionate to be enduring. She wanted a soul mate. She wanted someone who 'got' her.

The phone began to ring.

'Good afternoon Finger Food,' George greeted.

'George, you have got to like come now, right now. It's all kicking off here,' Marisa's voice shouted down the phone.

'What? What's happening? What's that noise I can hear?' George questioned as she battled to hear what her employee was telling her.

'That's the band playing Guns 'n' Roses. They've all gone hyper from the Spam or something in the Spam, there's like *loads* of really old people dancing really badly and head banging. Oh and Archie Reeves is being tended to by the paramedics. Seems he has a nut allergy he neglected to tell us about. Mum said she needs you here 'cause everyone is like looking to her for an explanation,' Marisa tried to explain.

'I'll be two minutes,' George replied.

'Can you like make it one minute, if you drive really fast? Mum's getting a migraine,' Marisa responded.

'Heading for the van right now, bye.'

When George arrived at the hall the ambulance was just leaving, blue lights flashing. She parked up and entered the foyer. Hearing the strains of Bon Jovi coming from behind the double doors she pushed them open and was greeted by, what could only be described as, utter carnage.

Thirty or so OAPs were on the dance floor thrashing themselves about to the band's rock music. The blackout curtains had been torn down from the windows and were mostly being worn as capes or headdresses by the pensioners. There was food all over the floor and Helen and Marisa were trying desperately to contain the guests in the hall as a few giggling invitees were threatening to turn the occasion into an impromptu street party.

'Who's in charge?' George asked, grabbing Marisa by the arm.

'Er, well I don't know really. Archie's wife was kind of trying to keep things under control, but when he like keeled over she obviously like couldn't carry on and now she's gone in the ambulance with him,' Marisa said.

'Doesn't he have any other family here?' George enquired, surveying the room for someone who looked remotely sensible.

'That's his dad over there, the one using the broom as a microphone. He's ninety four,' Marisa replied.

'Well, great! That's just great. No children? A nice sensible daughter maybe?'

'He does have a daughter, Sandra. She was here earlier, but he called her a money-grabbing bitch after he cut the cake and she made a comment about savouring every special occasion. She left, like just after that.'

'OK, well the first thing I'm going to do is stop the band. You go and make strong black coffee in the biggest pot you can find,' George ordered.

She hurried across the room, mounted the steps to the stage and grabbed hold of the lead singer. He was dressed up in 1940s military attire, as the theme of the party had demanded, but was now swinging the microphone around like he was a 1980s rock god.

'Wind this performance up now and get off the stage,' George hissed in his ear.

He immediately stopped his impression of the lead singer from KISS and signalled to his band mates to end the frenetic playing.

'You were supposed to be playing Glenn Miller and Vera Lynn, not Bon Jovi and Def Leppard,' George told him sternly when the music had finally ceased.

'They asked for something more up tempo. We didn't want to disappoint them and they really got into it,' the lead singer replied.

'Yeah, I know. Have you seen the destruction?' George asked him, indicating the flailing arms of the partygoers and the upturned chairs and tables.

'Sorry,' he replied.

George jumped down off the stage and looked for the worst case of hyperactivity amongst the guests.

A woman with a pink rinse looked like her first point of call. She was still thrashing her head about, holding hands with an elderly man who seemed to have become as stiff as a board and was likely to be done an injury if she carried on shaking him with such ferocity.

'Hello there, my name's George. I've got some great coffee over here, just like the stuff you had back in the Forties, you know, before it was rationed. Shall we go and have a sit down?' George suggested to the woman as she tried to capture her attention.

'Coffee? Like mother used to make?' the woman enquired her eyes turning to George and a look of excitement spreading across her face.

'The very same. Let's go over here and have a sit down,' George encouraged.

She shepherded the woman over to a chair and managed to sit the stiff gentleman down next to her. It was then she noticed a huge tureen of something bright orange in the middle of the table of food. It looked like jelly and it certainly wasn't something she had provided.

Marisa came out of the kitchen carrying a tray of coffees and Helen, looking red faced and flustered, was dragging a gyrating pensioner over to a chair at the side of the room.

'Helen, what's this?' George questioned, pointing to the suspicious looking substance.

'That's the jelly Archie's granddaughter made, apparently it's very nice. No Mr Kendal, it's best if you just sit still,' Helen spoke, trying to hold her charge in his chair.

Marisa began passing out cups of coffee to the guests who were slowly coming off the dance floor and looking for somewhere to collapse.

'Please tell me you haven't eaten any of it,' George said, picking up the bowl and sniffing at it.

'No of course not, I just served it up.'

'To everyone?'

'Well, everyone that wanted it. That was most people,' Helen replied as one of the old ladies vomited into her lap.

'Great. Get the paramedics back here. Apart from being loaded with E numbers it smells like it's got rum in it and pretty soon everyone's going to get really sick,' George announced.

'Shittin' Hell!' Marisa remarked as the stiff man keeled over on the floor.

Seven

By the time the after-show party began that night George was exhausted again. It was just after 11.00pm and since the unplanned pensioners' punk party she hadn't had a minute's break.

She, Helen and Marisa had stayed at the birthday party until they were sure all Archie Reeves' guests were being attended to by paramedics or escorted home to bed. The hall had been a mess; there was food everywhere, streamers all over the place and blackout curtains lying forlornly on the dance floor, where they had been discarded during the frenzied dancing.

She knew she looked awful but she hadn't had the time to care. She couldn't wait to get home to bed, even though she knew she would only get four or five hours sleep before getting up to start catering for the party the following night. Sleep was all she could think of and she let out a yawn as she offered the platters around the packed function room, wondering if a seafood medley parcel could possibly prop her eyelids open if inserted correctly.

'My dear George! Miss Finger Food herself! My darling, tell me what you have done to this lamb! It's gorgeous, it's divine, it's delicious, it's delectable, it's every word beginning with 'd' I can think of and more. It's wonderful!' Michael shouted excitedly, slapping her on the back as he bounded up to her and jolted her away from thoughts of sleep.

'Oh Michael, thank you,' George responded, stifling another yawn.

'No, thank *you* darling. People think I am a party planning genius and guests are picking up your business cards, like they were money off vouchers for Harrods,' Michael informed her.

'That's really good,' George answered.

'I'm sensing a slight lack of enthusiasm here. Your company could be huge I tell you. Huge!' Michael exclaimed, waving his arms about theatrically.

George smiled and offered him the tray of canapés she was holding.

'Oh, the seafood medley is tempting me. Should I indulge?' he asked, gazing adoringly at the plate.

And then her attention was diverted to the double doors of the function room as they were fiercely swung open.

Quinn Blake entered, an acoustic guitar slung around his neck and Belch at his side. They began to play as they walked across the room, enthralling all the guests with an instantly recognisable melody. It was one of Quinn's biggest hits 'By Your Side' and even George had heard it played over and over on the radio. It sounded different now though; there were no electronic overtones, no drum and bass keeping a rhythm, just two guitars and Quinn's smooth confident voice.

He moved into the centre of the room singing and playing, bewitching every guest present, stopping all conversations and turning every head. George watched as he mounted a table and began to strum out the crescendo to the song. Then in one swift movement Belch jumped up alongside him and the two men duelled on the guitars, encouraging people to clap along in time.

George fumbled with her tray, trying to hold it and clap at the same time. She glanced over at Adam. His tray was abandoned on the floor in front of him and he was watching Quinn and Belch in awe, mesmerised by their performance.

Marisa was also enjoying the show, hopping about in an excited state, giggling and glowing as she stood in prime position at the foot of the table Quinn and Belch had got up on.

With loud, raucous strumming and harmonised vocals the musicians ended the song and the whole room erupted into rapturous applause.

George watched as Quinn jumped down from the table and passed his guitar over to Belch. Guests hurried to surround him and compliment him, but although sharing a few words and smiling, he began to walk purposefully away from the crowds and straight towards her.

George quickly picked up her tray which contained less than half a dozen seafood medley parcels and prepared to leave for the sanctuary of the kitchen. Her heart was thumping in her chest.

But there was a large group in her way, giggly from champagne and blocking her route. She wasn't quite quick enough. Before she could disappear Quinn stood in front of her, his soulful eyes fixed on her.

'Hello,' she greeted in her weakest voice ever, trying desperately not to fixate on his lips.

'Meet me outside. Fire exit door, ten minutes,' he told her.

She looked directly at him now, her eyes widening with every second that passed, trying to digest his words.

'Ten minutes,' he repeated leaving no doubt.

Then he reached out, took a seafood medley parcel from the tray and turned back to his adoring public, smiling and accepting their appreciation of his music.

George swallowed a knot of fear and excitement and looked at her watch. No, what was she doing? Why was she looking at her watch? She didn't need to know when ten minutes was, because she was not going to have some clandestine meeting with someone she barely knew. OK, so she knew what the inside of his mouth felt like, but she knew nothing about him in the ordinary sense. He was a celebrity, a rock star who adorned magazine covers and she was not in the market for being anyone's plaything.

She squeezed herself past the large group in her way, trying to avoid looking anywhere in Quinn's direction.

'Oh. My. Life! Did you like hear what he just played? That is *sooo* my favourite song in the world ever!' Marisa exclaimed excitedly, buzzing about the kitchen waiting for Helen to serve up some more food.

'How are we doing? Running low on anything?' George enquired trying to remain focussed and forget she had been propositioned by the best looking guy in the room.

'No we're absolutely fine,' Helen replied, passing out trays to Marisa.

'George did you hear Quinn Blake singing? Isn't he just *amazing*?' Marisa said again.

'Make sure you work around the room with the trays; check the crudités aren't running low and that the business cards are still in the best position,' George ordered, taking a deep breath and ignoring her comment about Quinn.

Yes he was an amazing performer, in more ways than one and he had invited her to an exclusive, private, meet and greet in ten minutes. Well, approximately nine minutes now.

'Did you know Adam spoke to him last night? Very unprofessional I thought,' Marisa piped up.

'Marisa, you're just jealous. Now take those trays out please, before things start getting cold. I don't know! One nice looking chap and your head's in the clouds isn't it?' Helen told her daughter.

'Thank you, I'll take those, just run out,' Curly Shirley announced, whipping the tray from Marisa's grasp and hurrying back towards the function room.

'Mother! Will you stop her! She's trying to get Quinn Blake! She's like old enough to be his grandmother. Give me the sausages!' Marisa ordered, snatching up another platter.

George waited for the young girl to disappear and then she bolted to the fridge and got out a bottle of lager. It was petty theft for the second time in two nights she knew, but she really needed a drink.

'Is everything alright?' Helen asked as George rifled through a drawer for a bottle opener.

'Yes fine,' George replied, rattling utensils around looking for what she needed.

If she didn't find one she would use her teeth. It wasn't like she had never done that before.

'Are you looking for this?' Helen enquired as she passed the implement over.

'Thanks,' George answered.

She removed the lid and took a long swig. A wave of calm ran over her as the sharp liquid coated her throat. She felt better already.

'Something's on your mind. I always know when something's on your mind,' Helen reminded her.

'Nothing's on my mind, I'm just tired that's all after the 1940s Bacardi party. You've got to admit that was hard work,' George said, taking another drink.

'You're doing too much in my opinion, taking too much work on. You're seeking solace in lager, you've started listening to Metallica again, you're not eating properly...' Helen started.

'I am eating properly. I ate half a lamb trying to get the canapés just right,' George insisted.

She couldn't deny the other points. She had dusted off Metallica's *The Black Album* the other week and she suspected Helen counted the number of bottles of lager in the catering fridge. She didn't know what was in the other fridge though. Or what wasn't. That was definitely a good thing.

'You need to make time for some fun,' Helen told her.

'I do! Come on, parties like this are fun. I'm having fun. See! This is a smile,' George answered, grinning a little too forcefully.

'Hmm,' Helen replied unconvinced.

'OK, well, say I was thinking about having some fun and it was all a bit impromptu and maybe a bit strange but I quite, you know, liked it - what would you say?' George questioned, looking directly at Helen.

'You know what I think George. You need more time for you. Have you thought about going out with Simon from the bakery? He seems such a nice lad and he's very keen on you. He was only saying the other day he thought you two should have a drink together or something. He'd be nice to have a drink with wouldn't he? Have you thought about having a drink with him?' Helen asked, quickly opening the oven door to check on progress.

'No, not thought about that,' George answered, taking another swig of her drink and a look at her watch.

What was he doing? She wasn't like other women. What if she didn't know the drill? He knew nothing about her. Apart from the way she made him feel and how soft the inside of her mouth was. God she was driving him crazy! He hadn't been able to sleep last night. He'd gone running at least five miles through the town at 4.00am. No one had ever done that to him before. And he needed to know why she was getting to him. No. This was stupid. He was meant to be mingling with record company executives and influential players from the media. He wasn't thinking straight. He took a deep breath and moved closer to the edge of the roof. He could get down and disappear back to the hotel. He looked at his watch. What if she didn't come? That thought unsettled him more than it should.

It was twelve minutes since he'd said 'ten minutes' and she was standing by the door to the fire escape, staring at the white character man simulating running for his life from a deadly inferno. What was she doing? She should be serving canapés and directing her staff and keeping an eye on Adam. Instead she was loitering by an exit door wondering whether she should open it or not.

Why was he having an effect on her? Why did she want to see him? Why had she enjoyed his kiss so much the previous night? This was uncharacteristic. She was usually the one driving situations, but now, here she was, on the inside of the fire door, responding to someone's order. And there was no doubt it had been an order. He couldn't have made it clearer.

There was loud giggling and George heard the doors along the corridor open. People were coming. She needed to make a decision. Open the door? Or go back to the party?

The voices were getting louder, people were approaching. She took a deep breath and pushed open the door.

She stepped out onto the fire escape expecting Quinn to be waiting for her, like some gorgeous, brooding knight, all bolshy and irresistible. But to her dismay there was nothing but the oily black sky and the chilly air to greet her. She was on her own and suddenly she felt very stupid. What an idiot! He must think she was some sort of pathetic fan, who would let him kiss her and order her about just for the thrill of being in his presence! He'd had no intention of meeting her, it was just a game. He probably did this stuff all the time. She should have known better. She did know better.

'Hey! You're late!'

It was him. She heard his voice but she couldn't see him. She looked down to the bottom of the fire escape, but there was no one there, apart from two security guards stood by the doors to the Hexagon's back entrance.

'I said you're late. Ten minutes I said, this is almost fourteen,' Quinn called again.

George looked around her; she still had no idea where the voice was coming from.

'Hey! Up here!' Quinn shouted.

George looked upwards, towards the roof of the theatre and there he was, stood on the very edge, looking down at her, a broad smile on his face.

'What the Hell are you doing? Are you mad? You could fall!' George exclaimed in horror.

'Yeah, dangerous isn't it? So, are you coming up? I have beer,' Quinn enticed.

He picked up two bottles and chinked them together temptingly.

'How did you get up there?' George enquired, wishing he wasn't stood quite so close to the edge.

'Same way you're going to get up here. Give me your hand,' Quinn ordered, leaning over the edge of the roof and holding his hand out to her.

'I'm not coming up there,' George told him, folding her arms across her chest in a show of defiance.

She was a grown-up and in charge of catering an important function. She was not stupid enough to be climbing up on roofs at the age of thirty four.

'Of course you are. You know you want to.'

'I do not.'

'Sure you do. Come on, live a little,' Quinn spoke.

George looked at the hand he was holding out and then looked down at the drop below. This was insane! One slip and it was goodbye life, hello tarmac.

65

'Take my hand, put one foot up onto the bar there and I'll help you. View's great by the way,' he said.

George felt a rush of excitement run through her. It was dangerous, it was reckless; it was like when she was a teenager and had found all sorts of new ways to annoy her mother. She had loved rebellion and a little danger then, perhaps she had forgotten how to live for the moment.

Quickly she took off her shoes, put one down as a wedge to keep open the fire exit door and dropped the other.

She reached up, firmly took hold of Quinn's hand and pulled herself up onto the metal fire escape. With another stretch and a scramble she arrived on top of the roof.

'You've done this before,' Quinn replied as they sat down on the tiles and he handed her a bottle of beer.

'Not for a long time and only on a three storey,' George answered, taking a much needed drink.

'This is the sort of extreme length I have to go to to get away from people,' Quinn said with a laugh.

'And you enjoy every minute of it,' George answered, looking at him.

'Yes, I do,' he replied, looking back at her.

It was those eyes again, like turquoise glass, clear yet dense. Something about the intensity of them reminded her so much of Paul.

They were sat very close together enveloped by a black blanket of night, both staring out at the town's skyline. She didn't really know what she was doing here, sat on a roof with the biggest rock star of the moment when she should be wowing people with her buffet. But her heart was thumping a rhythm it hadn't performed in such a long time and she was finding it hard to care what she should be doing.

'Are you cold?' Quinn enquired suddenly breaking the silence.

66

'A bit,' George admitted aware she was shivering.

Without saying another word Quinn put his arm around her and drew her closer to him in one quick action. She was suddenly wrapped up in warmth.

She was a grown-up, yet she felt like a girl on some sort of awkward first date where no one knows the rules. It didn't feel like she was sat in the arms of a major rock star, it felt like she was in another time and another place where she was young again. Young and alive.

'If I could, I'd ask you out to dinner,' Quinn spoke as he stroked her arm, keeping the cold at bay and sending delicious shivers down her spine.

'If you could?' George queried.

'It's complicated. I'm watched, all the time, which is why...'

'You climb on roofs,' George finished off for him.

'Exactly. But I like you you know and...'

'So what do we do?' George asked him.

'What do you wanna do?' Quinn replied.

'I don't know,' George answered almost in a whisper.

'Yes you do,' Quinn told her his eyes looking deep into hers.

Before she could stop herself she had reached out and touched his face with her hand. She felt the firm line of his jaw and looked into his eyes, waiting, pausing in anticipation. He just matched her gaze, not letting his eyes drop from hers for a second and as her hand fell to his chest she could feel the strength of his heartbeat.

It was then he moved, taking her face in his hands for the second time in as many days and their lips were together, his mouth hot and sensual on hers.

He lowered her down onto the roof tiles and the raw cold slate sent shivers down her back as he sat astride her. He kissed her jaw, her neck; he ran his hands through her hair and then started to unbutton her blouse.

She thought she was going to combust with the desire she felt. She had never experienced anything like the longing she felt for him now. She wanted him to touch her everywhere.

Wantonly she pulled his t-shirt over his head and admired the perfect body underneath.

And then, completely shattering the moment, a mobile began to ring.

'Shit,' Quinn remarked, moving off of George and hurriedly fumbling for the phone in the pocket of his jeans.

She sat up and began to refasten her shirt buttons. Suddenly she felt a bit stupid, sat on the roof of a theatre, half undressed with someone she knew had two platinum albums and liked her canapés, but that was where the knowledge ended.

'Hey Roger! Yeah it was another great show tonight. Where am I? Well I'm at the party, there's a good turn-out. Yeah back to the hotel afterwards, sure I know and no late night poker with the boys. Yeah, OK, tell her the same,' Quinn spoke into the phone.

He ended the call and snapped the phone shut, turning around. George's shirt was tucked primly back in and she got up from the tiles and stood in front of him.

'I'd better go. I should be serving your guests,' she spoke, trying to move away from him without him touching her again.

'Spend the night with me,' Quinn said, grabbing hold of her arm.

George saw the sincerity in his expression and felt the tight grip on her arm. She swallowed, not knowing what to say. A night with a rock star, a hot rock star and someone who made her burn up from the inside out. She liked sex, it would be fantastic sex and she hadn't had sex in almost a month.

'Not on the roof, obviously. I have a hotel room,' Quinn spoke hurriedly.

'And you're watched all the time,' George reminded him.

'Yeah, I know, I am. But we could work something out.'

'I'm not that sort of girl, sorry. I'd better go,' George said.

'I think your brother's really cool by the way. He knows a lot about music,' Quinn said quickly, as George began to balance over the roof edge.

She stopped and looked back at him. He was still shirtless and the sight of his perfection did nothing to strengthen her resolve in turning him down. It wasn't too late. She could change her mind. Her foot was only dangling toward the fire escape, no contact had been made.

'He's very talented, I mean *really* talented. He was grade eight piano at age eleven,' George informed him, a swell of pride coating her voice.

'That's seriously good. I didn't do grades, at least I don't think - well anyway - he could definitely teach me a thing or two,' Quinn answered.

'He thinks you're a great artist. He admires you and your music very much,' George told him.

'Well maybe we could spend an hour or so together doing something on the piano,' Quinn suggested.

'Don't say things like that unless you mean them, not where my brother's concerned,' George ordered almost angrily.

'I don't say things unless I mean them. Tell him to ask for me tomorrow afternoon before the show, say four?'

'Four,' George repeated.

'Yeah and if you wanted to come along that would be good too,' Quinn said his turquoise eyes studying her.

'Sorry, four's no good for me, I'll be busy coordinating an Army party and trying to create something exciting and never seen before, using salmon as my muse,' George answered as she clambered carefully over the side of the roof and her foot made contact with the fire escape. No going back now.

'I want to see you again,' Quinn said, leaning over the edge and watching her descend.

'You will. I'll be one of the waitresses holding a silver tray at your party tomorrow night,' George answered.

She jumped down onto the fire escape, put on her shoes and went back inside, closing the door behind her.

Once inside she leant against the door and tried to get her breath back. If the phone hadn't rung would she have stopped him? Would she have stopped herself? Or would she have had sex on a rooftop without thinking about the consequences? Why did he have this effect on her? Yes he was gorgeous, but there was more to it than that, something about him was different. He got to her.

He was buzzing from head to foot, even more than from the gig. His heart was racing like he'd taken a shot of something. She was hot and sexy and she'd tasted like all his fantasies rolled into one. He stood up on the roof, stretched his arms up to the sky and howled.

Eight

'Oh. My. God. Like, could my life get any better? I've just finished spreading three hundred slices of bread, we've got an Army party this afternoon, with like *loads* of gorgeous blokes, and tonight we've got another after-show party full of more eye candy, including the totally awesomely hot, Quinn Blake,' Marisa announced over strains of The Black Eyed Peas.

The radio was picking up Radio One again although George wasn't entirely sure that was a good thing. Marisa had a limited knowledge of music when it came to the 1970s and 1980s and that meant less singing and more work getting done. Marisa fighting Will.I.Am for lead vocals, meant time management went out the window.

'You can do some egg separation for me next. I need yolks please, put the whites to one side, in a bowl obviously,' George ordered, ignoring her excited comments and studying a recipe book.

'Like what did you think I was going to do? Break them open on the worktop?' Marisa replied huffily.

'Is Adam working tonight?' Helen enquired as she washed her hands.

'Yes, last one though; he's driving back to uni straight after the party,' George replied not raising her head from her work.

71

'Would you like a cup of coffee?' Helen offered.

'No thanks. I want to get this finished and we need to get the Army stuff organised and the van loaded. What time is it? We have to be there at one,' George said, checking her watch.

She didn't want coffee, she wanted beer. She was tired and she was under pressure and she couldn't stop thinking about Quinn. She hadn't wanted someone so badly in such a long time. Conjuring up images of his naked torso in her mind was affecting her concentration.

'It's only eleven; we've got plenty of time,' Helen reassured.

'Right, OK, good,' George replied, burying her head back into her mixing bowl.

Suddenly the back door burst open and Adam flew through it. He ran up to George and grabbed hold of her arm.

'Is it true?' he questioned with wide eyes.

'Well, I...' George began her chest tightening.

'I got your message about Quinn Blake. Is it true? He wants to jam with me this afternoon?' Adam asked, his excitement clear for all to see.

'Oh, yes that, yes it's true. I mean I didn't actually speak to him, of course, because he's ultra important and that wouldn't be professional. But his PA, Michael, said he thought you were very knowledgeable about music after your conversation the other night and he wanted to get together with you this afternoon,' George explained haphazardly.

She could hardly mention the rooftop could she?

'Man, this is the most amazing thing that's ever happened to me, I can't believe it!' Adam exclaimed, taking off his beanie hat and beaming.

'Neither can I! You jammy sod! Private lesson with Quinn Blake! I wouldn't mind a private lesson with him, although I wouldn't want to learn piano. I could think of something better to practice like...' Marisa began.

'Thank you Marisa, your mother is in the room. I am here aren't I? With my hands in a mixing bowl of tuna,' Helen clarified.

'Yeah but you said here, we're like just colleagues,' Marisa replied, screwing her face up.

'What should I take with me? What should I wear?' Adam questioned as nervously as someone about to have a job interview.

'Whipped cream and strawberries I'd take,' Marisa answered hurriedly.

'It isn't an audition for *The X Factor*, just take yourself. He isn't going to judge you. He already thinks you're knowledgeable, well that's what Michael said,' George answered, a flush covering her cheeks.

The lager, the cold tiles, the flawless torso, it was all so easily recollected.

'Yeah, but he's really amazing and this could be a chance to get into the industry. If he likes me he could tell other people about me and...' Adam gushed.

'I've no doubt he's going to be blown away by you. I mean you play that piano like a demon and he hasn't even taken one piano exam,' George said the words tumbling from her lips before she could do anything to stop them.

'What?! Hasn't he? Not even I knew that. Where did you read that?' Marisa exclaimed eyes bulging at the new information.

'I don't know, in one of those magazines of yours I guess. Now, you, go home and stop panicking. Enjoy the afternoon; show Quinn Blake how a piano should be played, you know, hitting the phrasing with lots of passion. Isn't that what Mrs Rowland is always telling you to do?' George said.

'Thanks George. This is down to you you know, getting the catering for these shows. I can't thank you enough,' Adam spoke.

He put his arms around her and gave her a firm squeeze.

'Yeah, go and have a little practice at your scales or something before I nick your hat and coat and pass myself off as you. Can't play the piano though. Do you think he would notice? Especially if I just kind of like stripped off and got on top of it? Or him,' Marisa asked.

'Marisa!' Helen exclaimed.

'I don't think any normal red-blooded man would fail to notice you Marisa,' Adam told her with a smile.

She blushed immediately and tried to avoid catching Adam's eye.

'Go on, go! I'll see you at the Hexagon about ten thirty,' George ordered, shooing him to the door.

'OK, see you later,' Adam said.

'Bye Adam and good luck,' Helen called after him.

'Yeah good luck and if you finish before the hour's up, I'll entertain him for the rest of the time. Just text me,' Marisa added.

'What's got into you Marisa?' Helen asked when the door had closed and Adam had left.

'What?' Marisa asked innocently.

'Since we started doing the catering for Quinn Blake you haven't stopped talking about him for a minute, usually with sexual connotations attached to every other word,' Helen said, facing her daughter.

'Yeah well, he's hot and I've seen him in the flesh like every night and so what?' Marisa snapped.

'Well, it makes you sound cheap,' Helen replied.

'Me! Cheap! That's rich coming from someone who models herself on Tina Turner in her Mad Max phase and uses Value antiperspirant,' Marisa exclaimed, turning to face her mother.

'Hey, guys, could we stop the confrontation about sex and deodorant and concentrate our efforts on the food?' George suggested.

'Well she started it! And anyway, it isn't like I'm going to exactly leap on Quinn Blake is it? I mean he's engaged isn't he!' Marisa shouted, crossing her arms defiantly.

George dropped the book she was holding and it hit the mixing bowl of egg whites. Almost in slow motion the bowl tumbled off the worktop and smashed on the floor.

'Oh shit!' George exclaimed angrily, looking at the mess.

Quinn was engaged. No, he couldn't be. Marisa must have finally read one *Star Life* magazine too many.

'Oh George, let me clean that up for you. I'm sorry, that was our fault for arguing and disturbing your concentration,' Helen said, hurrying to the cupboard.

'No, it's OK, I'll do it,' George said with an aggravated sigh.

'Shall I do some more eggs?' Marisa offered sheepishly.

'No, it's OK, I'll do it later, let's just concentrate on the Army stuff for now,' George said, taking the cloths Helen was offering.

She began to clean up the sticky egg mess but curiosity was getting the better of her. Was Quinn really engaged? She had kissed him, she had almost had sex with him and he was with someone. And not just *with* someone, planning a wedding with someone. She hadn't supposed she was the only woman he had hit on this month or even this week, but being committed to someone else put a totally different slant on things.

'So, Quinn Blake's engaged? I didn't know that,' George remarked as casually as she could manage.

'Are you serious? Don't you like know who he's engaged to?' Marisa questioned in astonishment.

'Well, no, I don't, otherwise I wouldn't be asking,' George almost snapped.

'Taylor Ferraro,' Marisa informed, biting her nails.

'Taylor Ferraro?'

'You know! The actress! She's in that American soap opera with all the beautiful people in it. You know, the one where they're all at college even though they all look like thirty,' Marisa explained.

'I've not seen it,' George said.

'She had a bit part in the latest Brad Pitt film. She was his love interest for about three scenes until she got bumped off by someone from the Mafia.'

'I don't know her.'

'Yeah well he's marrying her in the summer. She's blonde and thin and rich and her father's the head of Rock It Music,' Marisa explained.

'Right,' George answered as she finished wiping up the floor.

Hearing the description of some sort of angelic-looking nymph was not making her feel better.

'Apparently she's having two wedding dresses made because she can't decide which designer she likes best,' Marisa continued.

'OK, that's fine, enough information, thanks. I wasn't really that interested, just you know, remotely curious,' George told her.

'Well all I know is she is one lucky, lucky bitch. I wish I was shaping up for her wedding night,' Marisa replied.

'Actually Marisa, could you do some more eggs for me please?' George decided not wanting to hear another word.

'Sure. Is that coffee ready yet Mother? I'm like dying of thirst over here,' Marisa called.

'Don't you just love the Army?' Marisa remarked as she came back into the kitchen.

She had just taken another tray of sandwiches out to the partying soldiers and needed to restock.

'A lot of those men and women out there have looked death right in the face. I take my hat off to all of them,' Helen spoke as she stirred a creamy mint dip destined for the pork and red onion skewers.

'I was thinking more of the sexy uniforms and the toned physiques really, but bravery is all good,' Marisa answered.

'I'll take the sausages and potato wedges out if they're ready now,' George said with a sigh.

She wasn't supposed to be here. She was supposed to be finishing off platters for the after-show party that night, but since Marisa's bombshell that Quinn was engaged, she hadn't been able to think about anything else. She shouldn't care, he was completely unsuitable anyway. She was just one in a long line of conquests. She'd suspected that, had known it really. After all he had kissed her without knowing the first thing about her, what did that say about him? In fact, what did that say about her?

She'd needed a distraction and surrounding herself with a hundred or so hungry squaddies was better than brooding alone, with only salmon and chive mustard butter for company. She wasn't sure the recipe was going to work anyway and at the moment she didn't care. If it didn't work she would just serve up sausage rolls and cheese and pineapple on sticks and call it retro party food. She was certain Michael wouldn't be opposed to a bit of retro.

She was angry with Quinn. Who did he think he was? Kissing her like she had never been kissed before, taking off her shirt, asking her to spend the night with him. She didn't do 'the other woman', she had never done that, it wasn't her. And how dare he think it was. She could just about cope with being just another conquest but she felt sullied for being made to be a party to real adultery. He was going to exchange wedding vows with someone in a matter of months, stand up and declare his love for someone, pledge to be faithful. She hated herself for letting him fawn over her so readily. She hated him for wanting to.

'Hey love, got any more of those ham and mustard baps?' a tall, burly soldier called to George as she arrived with the sausages and wedges.

'No, I'm sorry we don't, I have kebabs coming out in a second though,' George informed the group.

'Oh, Jonesy would rather have a nice couple of baps, wouldn't you Jonesy?' another soldier piped up, smothering a gurgle of laughter.

'Yeah, I would and yours are lovely. Nothing too over the top, just a nice handful,' Jonesy informed grinning.

With that remark made he grabbed hold of George and attempted to manhandle her chest.

Quick as a flash she dropped the tray of food, pushed the solider away and held her fists up threateningly. Her whole body was shaking with rage. She was so angry about Quinn taking advantage and now this soldier thought he had the right to do the same. She was not someone who could be used. If anyone did the using she did, on her terms.

'Touch me again and I'll put you on the floor,' she hissed her eyes wild, the whole battalion looking at her.

Marisa entered the room with quiche. She stopped and her mouth dropped open as she took in the scene in front of her.

'Whoa! You've picked a manic one Jonesy.'

'I like 'em a bit on the feisty side,' Jonesy replied a smirk appearing on his lips as he faced George and looked her up and down.

George still had her fists up, and she stood her ground as Jonesy moved steadily towards her. He was six feet tall and as wide as a Sherman tank. An arrogant, self-satisfied smile was set on his face and all his mates were watching and waiting to see what he was going to do next.

He took another step towards George, still smiling and she didn't wait for him to move any closer. She stepped forward, punched him hard in the face and followed it up with a swift knee to the balls. Then, without saying another word, she fled from the room, flying past Marisa and the tray of quiche.

'We're leaving. Turn the oven off, turn everything off, throw the food in the bin and get whatever belongs to us,' George ordered Helen as she started to pick up platters and cloths in a frenzy.

'George, what's happened? You're shaking,' Helen remarked as she watched her boss manically collecting everything together.

'She just laid out one of the biggest squaddies out there. Writhing on the floor he is, clutching his bits,' Marisa exclaimed as she put her platter down on the side.

'George?' Helen queried, concerned.

'He touched me, inappropriately. I gave him what he deserved. We're leaving, hurry up and get everything in the van,' George ordered.

'It was a cracking punch, like something out of *Rocky*,' Marisa added.

Nine

After tonight there were only two after-show parties to cater for and George was glad. She hadn't had a proper night's sleep in ages and she was getting sick of the pressure of creating a culinary masterpiece every day. It wasn't something she liked to rush; it was usually something she had time to plan for. Tonight it was salmon canapés with chive mustard butter. They were good, but she was too exhausted to care what anyone thought of them. And she was still so angry about Quinn and his utter arrogance. Jonesey, the soldier, had copped a punch, not because he thought he could get away with touching her, but because she'd been so mad about Quinn. She hadn't been that furious for a long time and she didn't like it. It showed a lack of control and it was a reminder of the old George. The George who started fights in pubs and played pool for money. So tonight, to save herself from karate-kicking Quinn in front of a room full of people, she was hiding in the kitchen.

She had sent Helen out to be the face of Finger Food with Marisa, Adam, Tom, Alison and Curly Shirley assisting her with distribution. She had put herself in charge of preparation, because this way she didn't have to be nice to people when she really didn't feel like it and she didn't have to even set eyes on Quinn Blake.

When they had got back to her house after the Army party Adam had called, gushing about his time with Quinn. Apparently he had played every guitar Quinn had available and the ridiculously expensive grand piano Quinn played in the gigs every night. Quinn had apparently played him a song he was working on and Adam had made a suggestion about incorporating a violin part. Quinn had thought it was a great idea. They had worked together on the section and then Quinn had picked up a violin, played the part and it had brought the whole song together. In fact George had been so entirely sick of hearing the name 'Quinn' by the end of the conversation she thought she might vomit if she ever heard it again in her life.

She was pleased Quinn hadn't let Adam down though and glad Adam had enjoyed himself. She knew he would be glowing from this experience for a long time to come. Unlike her. She would be annoyed with herself for a good long while, wondering why she had momentarily fallen for the charms of a superficial pop star who treated people like pawns on his celebrity chessboard.

'Empty tray,' a voice spoke.

'OK, put it down. I've got another platter of salmon and chicken if you just hang on a second,' George said, putting the finishing touches to the tray she was decorating.

'I can wait,' Quinn replied.

George looked up and saw him standing in the kitchen, hands in the pockets of his jeans, a plain black t-shirt hugging his all too moulded chest.

'What are you doing here?' George questioned angrily.

'Just helping out.'

'Well we don't need any help. Where are my staff?' George enquired.

'Listening to Belch rock out to one of my songs,' Quinn answered.

81

'I don't pay them to join in with the party, I pay them to serve,' George replied.

'Are you angry?' Quinn enquired, looking at her with interest.

'Yes!' she answered.

'Why?'

'Lots of reasons.'

'Such as?'

'It's none of your business.'

'I think it is. This is my party after all,' Quinn reminded her and he moved nearer so she could no longer avoid looking at him.

'You're engaged,' George stated, staring him straight in the eye.

'Yes,' he replied nonchalantly.

The matter of fact tone to his voice, coupled with the devastatingly handsome jaw line was enough to irk her into action. George slapped him hard across the face and then let out a gasp realising what she'd done. Before she could put her hand back down Quinn grabbed hold of it and gripped it tightly in his.

'Spend the night with me,' he said his eyes meeting hers.

'You're getting married! I'm not stupid enough to think you want me for more than a bit of fun, but I won't do that!' George shouted.

She was trying desperately to ignore her racing heart as he gripped her hand. His palm was warm, he was so close to her she could feel his breath on her face, smell the musk on him. It was intoxicating.

'Spend the night with me,' he repeated unfazed.

'No,' George answered through dry lips.

'I'm not going to stop asking,' Quinn told her still looking at her with his intense eyes.

'And I'm not going to stop saying no,' George assured him in as strong a voice as possible.

'Yes you are,' Quinn answered with a smug smile.

George swallowed and looked at him looking at her. Her head was starting to spin. She hated him didn't she? She despised him for being the philanderer he was. Then why was there nothing else she wanted to do more than spend the night with him? She wanted to let him undress her, touch his lips on every single part of her. She wanted sex with him, hard, fast, dirty sex. It was like he was infectious and although she wanted to be immune, she definitely wasn't.

The door flew open and Marisa stomped in carrying two empty platters. George hurriedly moved away from Quinn and picked up the nearest thing to hand, which happened to be a rolling pin.

'Oh. My. God, like you totally missed Belch doing a whole rock guitar version of 'Mine'. He was like totally ace and...Oh. My. God,' Marisa said as she dumped the platters on the work top and suddenly noticed Quinn was standing in the kitchen.

'So, salmon is Michael's thing, not mine. I don't want to see another salmon canapé tomorrow night, d'you understand?' Quinn said to George in a manner appropriate to a telling off.

'Yes, of course, I understand,' George replied, playing along.

'Hello, er Mr Blake, I'm Marisa. I'm like one of your biggest fans and...' Marisa began.

'Hi Marisa. I'm sorry, I've got to go. No more salmon,' Quinn said, wagging a finger at the young girl.

'Salmon sucks,' Marisa replied with a hasty nod, her face glowing with embarrassment.

Quinn left the room and George let out a sigh of relief. He only had to look at her and a part of her melted; it was like a personal global warming crisis.

'Oh. My. God! He hated the salmon! But everyone else loved the salmon, it's almost all gone. I can't believe he came into the kitchen to tell you he hated the salmon. I mean *him*, himself, not like just sending

83

someone to tell you. He actually told you in person,' Marisa gabbled.

'Yeah, fancy that. The personal touch,' George replied with a nervous swallow.

'Why are you holding a rolling pin?' Marisa enquired.

She knew about Taylor. Well, it was inevitable wasn't it? Taylor had them featured in as many magazines as she could get access to. Brand Blake! That was a f**king joke!

He put a hand to his cheek and felt the heat. She'd done a good job of slapping him, his face was stinging, but bizarrely it was really turning him on.

'Ah there you are! I was almost thinking of sending out a search party for you. Timothy Moulineux from *Ultimate Guitarist* magazine, could you give him a few moments?' Michael asked, taking hold of Quinn's arm.

'Sure, lead on,' Quinn said, taking a breath.

For once the party was wrapped up before 3.00am. George sent Helen, Marisa, Alison and Curly Shirley off in a taxi and that left her, Adam and Tom to finish loading the van. With three of them it didn't take too long and then it was time for Adam and Tom to make the long drive back to university.

'Now, are you sure you're not too tired to drive?' George asked as Adam put his beanie hat on and prepared to get in the driving seat of his Fiat Panda.

'I'm sure, plus it will be better driving through the night, less traffic,' Adam assured her.

'OK, well, just take care won't you and Tom, can you sing to him or something? Keep him awake,' George ordered, looking in on the other youth.

'He won't need to sing. I've got the CD me and Quinn made this afternoon. I haven't been able to stop listening to it, it's only one track but he says he's going to credit me on the CD, as a writer,' Adam informed her proudly.

'Well that's great but, you know, don't be upset if that doesn't happen, you know how these things are,' George spoke.

She couldn't believe a word he said no matter how he made her feel in the knicker department.

'You worry too much George. By the way Quinn's dead impressed with Finger Food. He talked quite a lot about you,' Adam remarked.

'Well let's hope he tells all his celebrity friends. I could do with the business,' George answered quickly.

'I'd better go, promised I'd ring Mum when we got back and you know she won't sleep until I do,' Adam said, getting into the car.

'Yeah well don't drive too fast and text me when you get there too,' George told him.

'OK, see you,' Adam said.

'Bye,' George replied, closing the door for him.

She watched him start up the car, reverse out of the parking space and drive off up the road, waving to her. She swallowed as the car went out of sight. She had enjoyed spending time with him, even if they had been working for most of it. It had been nice to just have him around, although it always reminded her just how much she missed him.

'George Fraser,' a deep male voice spoke.

George spun around quickly and was confronted by a rotund black man wearing dark trousers and a black puffa jacket. Ordinarily, he would have looked quite like a mugger not to be messed with, given his size and slightly scary voice, but he knew her name and he was holding out an envelope to her.

She took the envelope and looked back to the man for some sort of explanation. However he had already turned away from her and was making his way back to wherever he came from.

George ripped open the envelope and took out what was inside. There was a plastic credit card shaped item and a sticky yellow note attached to it which read:-

Highgate Hotel Suite One – Q x

It was a hotel key card.

George looked at the card and the note and a shiver of excitement ran through her, like it did whenever she thought about Quinn or whenever he was anywhere near her. He was dangerous, he was spontaneous, he had complete disregard for anyone but himself. He may be engaged but he was everything she looked for in a man and hadn't been able to find since Paul. He was unreliable, he couldn't be trusted but he made her feel unbelievably alive.

She dropped the keys to the van in her haste to get inside it and it was enough to make her stop and think. She disliked him didn't she? The way he was so cocksure of himself, so confident of his ability to woo her, or was disliking him part of the thrill? She may not agree with how he behaved, but she couldn't deny she still wanted him. She got into the van, closed the door and started the engine. She knew where the hotel was.

Ten

She stood in the lift, looking at her reflection in the mirror and listening to the burr of the wheels as it transported her between floors. It had stopped at the right level four times, but she couldn't bring herself to get out. She kept asking the doors to close, hoping that the next time they opened she would have made up her mind whether to step out or whether to descend to reception again.

Giving her a key to his room was presumptuous. She'd told him no and he didn't believe her. Was he right? Even if she didn't go to his room tonight was she just fighting a losing battle with her own desires as well as his? Perhaps it was just something they both needed to get out of their system. Yes, if she had one night with him it would all be over. She would stop wondering what it would be like to sleep with him and he could stop pursuing her. After all, the buzz came from the chase didn't it? Once their sexual needs had been fulfilled he would move on to someone else and she - well she could always make do with Simon.

She wouldn't come tonight, he knew that. She wanted to, but she wouldn't. She wasn't ready yet. She wanted to be ready but it was too soon for her, for whatever reason. Maybe she had someone. Shit, he didn't want to think about that. He didn't want to think of her ever having had someone else. That was unrealistic, but he wasn't big on the whole talking about previous partners thing. That was something Taylor did. He was convinced she had a chart with penis comparisons on somewhere at the bottom of one of her giant handbags. That was the sort of stupid, dumbass shit Taylor did.

George was different. George wasn't twenty-five going on twelve; George was a grown-up, a real woman, someone who made him hard just by looking his way. Shit, he was hard now just thinking about her.

He turned the shower down a couple of notches and put his face right into the water flow.

The lift doors opened again and George took a deep breath. Besides, even if she got out now and went to his room she could always just give him a piece of her mind when she got there. If she really didn't want to spend the night with him.

She stepped out of the lift and walked down the corridor, following the signs for the suite. And then she saw it, at the very end of the corridor, a huge oak panelled door with a gold sign stating that it was the entrance to Suite One.

The slot to put the key card in was flashing ominously. Was that because she ought to go in, or because she shouldn't? She wished it would speak. What was the matter with her? She was a grown woman; she could make decisions herself without looking for hidden meanings in inanimate objects and willing them to share their thoughts with her. This was ridiculous.

She smoothed down her white shirt and pulled at her skirt. She had a sauce stain on the left hand side of it and she knew she was hot and sweaty from spending all evening in a kitchen. Not exactly the best outfit for seducing someone. And then it dawned on her that Quinn had never seen her in any other clothes. Perhaps he had a thing for waitresses. The thought made her shudder.

She put the card into the slot and pulled it out. It flashed green and she cautiously leant down on the handle and opened the door.

She stepped onto soft, thick, cream coloured carpet and walked into the most luxurious room she had ever seen. There was a huge bed to her right, covered in cushions and fur throws. There was a full sized dining table to the left and two large chocolate coloured leather sofas, again adorned with sumptuous cushions. There were full length patio doors at the far end of the room, which seemed to open out onto a balcony. The whole room was decorated to perfection, there wasn't a thing out of place. In fact if it hadn't been for two guitars leant against the wall she wouldn't have thought anyone was staying in the room at all.

She could hear the sound of running water coming from the bathroom and suspected Quinn was in the shower. What to do? Should she announce her arrival? Should she whip off her sweaty clothes and join him? Or should she just sit, read the Gideon's bible and wait for him to come out? The other alternative, of course, was to leave while she still could. He didn't know she was there, she could disappear and he would be none the wiser.

She was just contemplating doing exactly that, when the water was turned off and Quinn strolled out of the bathroom completely naked.

'George,' he stated seeming surprised she was there.

'Hello,' she replied, tearing her eyes away as he hurriedly wrapped a towel around himself.

'I didn't think you'd come,' he told her, running his hand over his cropped hair.

For once he didn't look quite so self-assured. Perhaps it was just being caught without his clothes on, but she suspected it wasn't the first time that had happened.

'You sent some huge, scary guy to give me the key card,' George reminded him.

'Yeah, I know. I just didn't think you'd come. Not yet,' Quinn replied.

'Do you want me to go?' George said suddenly feeling a little bit awkward.

'No! No, of course not. Of course not. Have a seat, would you like a drink?' Quinn offered, securing the towel around his waist.

'A beer would be good,' George answered.

Perhaps she had given in a bit easily if he really hadn't been expecting her. She felt disappointed and internally kicked herself for it.

'Sure,' Quinn said and he opened the mini-bar, which didn't appear to be so mini and stocked every drink known to man and some that probably weren't known to many men.

He took out two bottles of beer, opened them and handed one to her. She accepted it and quickly sat down on one of the leather sofas.

'So, here we are then,' she remarked not knowing what else to say to someone she had only thought about sleeping with and not considered talking to all that much.

'Yeah, here we are,' Quinn replied with a nod.

'Right, well, to be honest, I don't know what I'm doing here. I should know better, I do know better. In fact I think I'm just going to pretend that I didn't drive over here like some sort of aged groupie and just leave,' George said, standing up and starting to move past him.

'No, don't do that,' Quinn said, grabbing her arm to stop her.

'Why not?' George asked, staring him in the face.

'Because I want you to stay,' Quinn told her sincerely.

Her heart was hammering again, threatening to explode as she looked at him, looking at her.

'Why?' George enquired.

'I don't know, but ever since I met you I haven't been able to get you out of my head,' Quinn admitted.

'I offered you a canapé from an empty tray.'

'It wasn't anything you said or did, I don't know what it was. I can't explain it. I just can't stop thinking about you George, I mean that. You're just everywhere, all the time,' Quinn told her.

He traced his finger down the line of her jaw and she felt herself quake beneath his touch.

'I want you to know I don't make a habit of kissing men I know nothing about.'

'I know that. Your brother tells me he can't remember the last time you had a boyfriend.'

'Did he also tell you he's away at university and I don't tell him everything that goes on in my life?'

'So will you tell him about this?' Quinn asked his fingers travelling quickly to her shirt buttons.

'About what?'

'About this,' Quinn said and in one swift move he picked George up and carried her over to the bed.

He threw her down, straddled her body and looked down at her. She couldn't control her breathing, she thought her body was going to combust unless he stripped her right now and made love to her. All thoughts of his fiancée were pushed out of her mind. It was his problem, not hers. It wasn't as if he was going to leave her. It was just an animal attraction, it was just sex. In a few nights he would be gone, doing gigs in Manchester and probably sleeping with someone else. That alone should bother her, but right now it didn't.

'What do you want to do now?' Quinn asked her as he unbuttoned her shirt and slipped his hands inside.

'Everything,' George replied and she pulled at the towel around his waist and discarded it on the floor.

His fingers were plucking the strings on his guitar, but his eyes were fixed on her. There she was, George Fraser, Miss Finger Food, in his bed. Misson accomplished. Or was it? Just watching her now he wanted to go back over to the bed, pull the covers off her and touch her like he'd touched her last night. He'd touched her everywhere and the way she had touched him – well it was a class apart from what he'd experienced in the past and he'd experienced enough to know. But it wasn't just the sex. Afterwards he'd found himself wanting to talk to her. F**k! Wanting to talk! He'd managed to stop himself but the feeling was there all the same. What was it about her that got to him?

When she woke up the first thing she saw was a fur cushion only inches from her nose. Then she breathed in and the musk and lemon fragrance filled her nostrils. It immediately reminded her where she was and who she was with. Last night had been one of the best nights of her life. Her skin actually ached from his touch and there wasn't a centimetre he hadn't made contact with. She closed her eyes again and replayed the sex in her mind. She stroked the sheet around her with the flat of her hands, remembering the way the linen felt between her fingers. She had clung to it, clawed at it and then clung to him, Quinn Blake, pulled him into her like she had been starved of physical contact for a hundred years. He had taken her breath away, he had whispered all sorts of words into her ear and his voice, the sound of his urgent need had left her with no choice but to submit to him completely. He was the whole toe curling, fingernail scratching, head spinning package. She'd had nothing left.

As she let out a breath and opened her eyes again she heard a guitar being played. She hurriedly sat up, drawing the covers closer around her naked body.

'Hey,' Quinn greeted.

He was sat on one of the sofas, wearing a hotel robe, an acoustic guitar around his neck. He looked more gorgeous now than he ever had.

'What time is it?' George asked, looking around the room for a clock.

'Almost nine thirty,' Quinn informed her.

'Nine thirty? Shit, I've got to go. Marisa and Helen will be at my place waiting to get in,' George exclaimed in horror.

She bounded out of bed and began picking up her clothes from the floor, where Quinn had thrown them in the early hours.

'I could order some breakfast. You shouldn't go without breakfast, that would make me the worst host in the world,' Quinn told her.

'I have a kitchen full of food, I'll be fine,' George replied, pulling on her skirt and zipping it up.

'Shall I arrange a car?' Quinn asked, putting his guitar down and standing up.

'No need, I have the van. Look, last night was really great and...' George began.

She was struggling to put her bra back on and he was looking at her. It wasn't going to happen. She hurriedly buttoned up her blouse and stuffed her bra in her bag, her cheeks flaming with shame.

'Can I see you again?' Quinn questioned.

George tucked in her shirt and turned to look at him.

This was supposed to have been an itch that disappeared when it had been scratched. And it had been scratched, several times in fact. In the bed, on the floor, in the shower, up against the patio doors. Her temperature shot up as she remembered everything they'd done.

'I don't think that's a good idea,' George said.

'I do,' Quinn replied.

93

'I've got to go,' George insisted, putting on her shoes and heading for the door.

'Keep the key,' he said as she prepared to leave.

George looked at the plastic card in her hand.

'Keep it,' Quinn repeated an edge of determination to his voice.

George looked at it again and then dropped it inside her bag.

'I'll see you at the after-show,' she spoke, looking back at him.

'Don't I get a kiss goodbye?' Quinn queried before she could open the door.

George let out a sigh and crossed the room towards him. She pecked him on the cheek and was about to make a hasty exit when he grabbed her and pulled her to him. Being so close to him she was completely powerless to stop whatever was coming next. She was behaving like a pathetically weak heroine in a dodgy romance and she couldn't do anything to fight it.

Just having him look at her the way he did, was enough to make her want to take her clothes off again. This was bad. This was almost like Paul.

He kissed her, deeply and passionately and she didn't want him to stop. She clung to him, closing her eyes and remembering how he had made her cry out with delight.

'This isn't what you think it is,' Quinn told her when their mouths had finally parted.

'I don't know what I think,' George replied her hands lingering on his chest.

'You think I'm fickle. You think I have a girl at every venue,' Quinn spoke.

'I need to go now,' George said, letting him go and checking her watch.

'That isn't how it is,' Quinn assured her.

'I've really got to go,' she said again.

He reluctantly relinquished her and she hurried out of the door.

'George...' he called after her.

She almost leapt out of the room, not wanting to hear what he was going to say. She slammed the door closed and leant against it for support. What had she done?

Shit! Why had he lied to her? He did have a girl at every venue. Well, not every venue maybe, but most of them. She knew that, he knew that, why hadn't he just told her the truth? He had a girl most nights, but none of them came anywhere near close to her. He never wanted the girl to be there in the morning. He never offered breakfast and he never, ever, wanted to see them again. He wanted to see George again. Again and again and again.

Eleven

'So then, who were you with?' Marisa questioned as she mashed up eggs later that morning.

'Marisa!' Helen exclaimed.

George couldn't blame her for asking. She had turned up late, in the van, wearing last night's clothes - the skirt of which was torn and her hair was spiked up like Shirley from *EastEnders*. She had managed to avoid earlier questions by running upstairs to shower and change before they started work. But she had known it was only a matter of time.

'No, it's OK. I bumped into a friend from school, we went back to hers. I had too much to drink and I crashed there,' George explained.

It was amazing what you could get to trip off your tongue, without too much thought, when you were backed into a corner.

'A friend from school,' Marisa repeated suspiciously.

'Yeah, Tracey,' George added, hiding her face and trying to concentrate on what she was doing.

She hadn't seen Tracey since school and was still visualising her in ripped jeans and a New Kids on the Block t-shirt. Still, it didn't matter for alibi purposes.

'Tracey,' Marisa said.

'Marisa, will you leave George alone. She doesn't answer to you does she?' Helen told her daughter.

'Well, I don't believe a word of it, I mean 'bumped into a friend from school'! Well where? The car park of the Hexagon at two in the morning? What does this Tracey do? Is she a pole dancer or a taxi driver? Because I can't think of another reason for her to be out at 2.00am,' Marisa continued.

'Well Marisa, where do you think I was?' George enquired, looking at her employee and feeling very certain there was no way in the world she was going to guess.

'With a man. It's like *sooo* obvious,' Marisa answered confidently.

'What man?' George enquired.

'Well I don't know, someone you're like hiding from us obviously,' Marisa said, starting to blush as her confidence unravelled.

'I'm glad you think my life's *sooo* exciting,' George mimicked.

She was trying desperately not to think about Quinn, but even after her shower she could still feel him on her skin. She had finger shaped bruises at the bottom of her back, along with a friction burn and as she filled Marisa's suspicious head with lies, the injuries smarted in retaliation.

'Well you're acting all mysterious and like that's what people do when they're hiding man action from their friends,' Marisa concluded.

'Who told you that? I think you've been watching too much *Desperate Housewives*,' George answered her with a laugh.

There was a knock on the back door and George stiffened. She knew exactly who that was.

Helen opened it and there was Simon with the bread delivery. George turned to greet him, thinking it would be best to get any awkwardness out of the way. She smiled at him but he didn't meet her eye. In fact his head was bowed so low that if he opened his mouth he could probably lick his shoes.

'Oh Simon, perfect timing as usual, thank you. We're getting through it today aren't we George?' Helen said, trying to draw her into conversation.

'Would you like a cup of coffee?' George offered, giving him another hesitant smile.

Simon not speaking to her like he usually did would set off Marisa's questioning again and she didn't want that. She just wanted to try and put the whole date refusal thing behind them and move on, like the professional business people they were.

'No thanks, got a lot on,' Simon said briskly and before anyone could say anything else he left the kitchen, closing the door behind him.

'Now that was suspicious. Not wanting a coffee, not looking you in the eye, not trying to flirt with you. Were you with him last night?' Marisa demanded to know.

George swallowed. She really couldn't bear any more interrogation, she felt guilty enough as it was.

'Marisa! I won't tell you again! Leave George alone,' Helen warned.

The phone rang and, glad of a distraction, George picked it up.

'Good morning Finger Food.'

'Georgina, is that you?' her mother's voice queried.

'Yes it's me.'

'Good, now listen. Your father and I have had to go up to Wales so we won't be at home for a few days,' Heather informed her.

'Wales? Well why? Is it Adam?'

'Adam had an accident this morning, hit a parked car,' Heather said like she was giving the bare bones of a news report.

'Oh my God is he OK? I'll come up. I'll just arrange a few things here and I'll be there in a few hours,' George exclaimed in panic.

'Don't be so overdramatic, there's absolutely no need for you to do anything. He's fine, just cuts and bruises, we're with him now and he's telling you to stop making a fuss,' Heather continued.

She couldn't hear him making a fuss; she couldn't hear anything apart from her mother's businesslike voice holding her at arm's length as usual.

'I want to speak to him,' George said, putting a hand to her racing heart.

She hadn't checked for Adam's text last night. She had asked him to message her and then she'd been too busy having her clothes ripped off to bother even looking at her mobile. This was payback for her involvement with a betrothed man. This was the sort of thing that happened. This was retribution.

'That isn't necessary. I told you he's fine. I just thought you should...' Heather began again in her best secretarial tones.

'Put him on the phone Mother! Don't mess me about, put him on the phone right now,' George ordered knowing her anxiety wasn't going unnoticed by Helen and Marisa.

'For goodness sake Georgina, it was only a small accident, the car took the brunt of it and Adam is fine,' Heather spoke all too calmly.

'Mother I swear to God, if you don't put Adam on the phone right now I am driving up to Wales to see him for myself,' George threatened.

Heather let out a loud frustrated tut of annoyance and then there was background movement as the phone was passed over.

'Hello,' Adam spoke sheepishly.

'Adam what happened? I thought I told you to drive carefully,' George reminded him harshly.

'I did drive carefully; it was foggy when we got back to Wales. Stupid f**king car was parked on a bend! Lucky I was only doing thirty,' Adam told her.

'Adam! You do not use that word!' George heard her mother retort in the background as Adam swore.

'Are you OK?' George asked.

'Yeah, I'm fine; car isn't though, the whole front caved in.'

'It's a write off? God Adam, you were so lucky. Is Tom OK?'

'Yeah he's fine and the best thing is I managed to get the CD out of the car before they towed it away.'

'CD?'

'The one I made with Quinn Blake. I would have been gutted if I'd lost that.'

George let out a sigh of irritation at the sound of his name. This was all his fault. She should have been checking Adam was safe, not acting like a slapper.

'Look, do you want me to come up?' George asked him.

'No, course not. Mum and Dad are already fussing round me and you have the after-shows to do. I'm fine really,' Adam assured her.

'Well, if anything changes I want you to call me or text me and I'll come up,' George told him seriously.

'Cluck cluck Mother Hen. Isn't it about time you had some kids, then you might stop worrying about your little brother so much,' Adam spoke.

'Kids? Me? I wouldn't know what to do with one. I mean do I cover them in breadcrumbs? Or drizzle them with oil?' George answered with a laugh.

'Just kidding Sis, I like all the fussing really.'

'Yes, well you take care and phone me once in a while will you? Even if it's to tell me how drunk you are or how many hours of study you haven't done,' George ordered him.

'Will do. See you,' Adam replied.

'Happy now?' Heather's voice spoke as she came back on the line.

'Not really, he's had a car accident. What's to be happy about?' George answered.

'Yes and the accident may not have happened if he hadn't been driving through the night, too tired after you made him be a waiter at a party,' Heather snapped.

'So it's my fault,' George said with a heavy sigh.

'Fatigue was a factor in the accident, yes.'

'Why do you still hate me so much? I mean how long is this going to go on for Mum? What exactly did I do?' George wanted to know.

'You know what you did, you let us down,' Heather retorted.

'I made one mistake. People do make mistakes you know. It doesn't mean they have to go on paying for them forever.'

'Goodbye Georgina, I'll let you know when we're back home,' Heather spoke and she ended the call.

George hung up the phone and Marisa and Helen hurriedly recommenced their work, pretending not to have heard the conversation.

'Is Adam OK?' Helen asked when George had hurriedly turned back to making pastry.

'Yeah, I think so,' she answered.

Her heart was still palpitating, but now she had spoken to Adam she felt better than she had at the beginning of the conversation. He was in hospital but it could have been so much worse.

'Why don't you go upstairs and have a lie down? Marisa and I can cope here and you can't have had much sleep last night - on Tracey's sofa. It was Tracey wasn't it? Your friend,' Helen said.

'Yes it was,' George replied, sensing the tone of her voice.

'Well go and catch up on some sleep now. I can finish the pastry and do the chicken and garlic parcels and

Marisa can do the sandwiches for the WI. You do look terrible. She looks terrible doesn't she Marisa?' Helen said.

'Dog rough,' Marisa replied without looking up.

'Thanks, both of you,' George answered.

'Go on, shoo! And I don't want to see you back down here until well after lunch,' Helen ordered.

'OK,' George replied.

She didn't have the energy to contest the idea and the thought of a couple of hours with her head on her own pillow was literally pulling her up the stairs. Sometimes you just had to give in. Like last night.

The show that night had been awesome, but more importantly she was in the room now and she looked amazing. A white shirt and black skirt had never been so appealing. Not that he wanted to look at it on her; he'd much rather it was spread across his hotel suite, like she had been.

His palms were itching, he was nervous. He wanted her again but he had rules. You didn't go there twice. Once was testing the water, a little fun on the side, no harm done, twice indicated intent. But this wasn't just about the sex, he wished to God it was. No, this went a whole lot deeper. He walked over to join Michael.

'My dear I missed you last night. What did you think you were doing hiding away in the bowels of the Hexagon? Surely your staff should have been beavering away in the background, while you shone out here with your delicious concoctions,' Michael exclaimed as George brought another platter into the buzzing after-show party that night.

'Ah well, I was preening and perfecting and those details could only be attended to by the creator,' George replied swiftly, offering the plate of food to him.

'What do we have here?' Michael asked, picking up a pastry parcel and scrutinised it.

'Chicken and garlic with honey overtones,' George informed him.

'Honey overtones! My dear, you are starting to speak my language. Oh! Oh! I have officially died and am feasting at Paradise's table. These are special I tell you! Delicious!' Michael exclaimed, chewing the food and enjoying every bite.

'Michael you're my biggest fan. I've never known anyone enjoy my food quite so much,' George told him.

'I definitely want to vie for the title of super fan, these are excellent.'

George had been avoiding even looking in Quinn's direction all night and had made sure she was always standing near a large group when handing out food. Now, here he was, stood next to Michael, eating one of her parcels and looking straight at her, bringing back all the memories she had of the night before. She had kissed every inch of him; he had kissed every inch of her. They'd had sex over and over again. At first, fast and passionate, then much slower and more sensual, and the final time she had cried out his name when she came. She couldn't stop looking at his lips as he ate, remembering how they tasted, recalling what they'd done to her.

'Isn't she wonderful? I can't tell you how glad I am the original caterers pulled out,' Michael said with a big smile.

'I'm with you. So, how are we fixed for Manchester?' Quinn asked.

'In what department my man?' Michael enquired.

'The catering department,' Quinn said, looking at George.

'Well we've got a local catering firm. I can't remember their name off hand, not something nice and punchy like Finger Food. Probably something really dull like Sally's Sandwiches,' Michael said with a guffaw.

'Cancel them,' Quinn ordered 'I want George.'

'Oh what a marvellous idea! I love it! Yes! Perfect!' Michael exclaimed excitedly, clapping his hands together.

'I'm sorry. I've got other commitments and Manchester's a bit of a commute to be honest,' George answered hurriedly.

'Darling! You wouldn't have to commute, would she Quinn? We would put you up in a hotel, get you some staff to boss around, all the ingredients you need, whatever you wanted.'

'Sorry, I've got long-standing bookings and they're people who've put a lot of business my way,' George answered firmly.

'I've put a lot of business your way,' Quinn retorted almost angrily.

'Yes, I know, I realise that and I'm very grateful but...' George started.

'Five thousand pounds a night and you can bring your team,' Quinn stated.

George held onto her breath as much as she could. Five thousand pounds was about three times the amount she would get from the bookings she had and that was just for one night. She knew he was in Manchester for four nights. She was ashamed to admit, she knew his whole UK tour itinerary now, thanks to Marisa and *Star Life* magazine.

He was looking at her, undressing her with his eyes, a slight smile on his lips. It was hard enough to resist him now, she didn't know if she could bear another four nights. And despite him making her feel like no other man had in years, it was going nowhere.

'I'm sorry, I'll have to decline. Excuse me,' she said and she turned her back on Quinn and Michael and made her way back to the kitchen as quickly as she could.

He was so angry he had trashed his dressing room. He'd also had Belch up against the wall by the collar of his leather jacket. Now, he was halfway through his sixth bottle of lager, on top of all he had drunk at the party. How dare she turn him down? What was wrong with her? She'd been keen enough to take her clothes off last night. Once couldn't be enough for her! He was Quinn Blake! People didn't say no to him. He was shaking again. What was wrong with him? He should put a stop to this and go and find another distraction. He could go to the casino with some of the other guys, or a club. He couldn't stop thinking about her. He knew she wanted him, so why had she said no?

'Ready to go?' Michael asked, opening the dressing room door and popping his head around it.

'No, I'm not and since when did you come in here without knocking?' Quinn blasted.

'Oh, well, I apologise my man, a thousand pardons and...' Michael started, taken aback but trying his best to hide it.

'Shut up Michael for Christ's sake!' Quinn ordered, sucking in a breath.

This was her fault. George Fraser, the woman who was taking him over and not giving a damn about it.

By 3.00am the Hexagon conference room was empty and George was collecting up the final plates. It had been a busy night, all the food had gone and guests had been particularly complimentary about the canapés.

As she prepared to go back to the kitchen to pack up the last of the stuff, her phone vibrated as a text message came through.

She looked at it and saw it was from Adam.

Mum n dad drivin me mad - cant sleep - food terrible send canapés x

George smiled and was about to text a reply when the swing doors banged open and Quinn marched into the room, a thunderous expression on his face.

'How dare you!' he greeted, striding up to her.

'How dare I what?' George replied, standing her ground and looking at him.

'How dare you refuse to come to Manchester, in front of Michael!' Quinn yelled.

'How dare I?! How dare you put me in that position!' George exclaimed angrily.

'It was just a catering job,' Quinn said, standing opposite her, so close it was a little unnerving.

'No it wasn't,' George snapped back.

Quinn just kept his gaze focussed on her, staring at her as if he was daring her to look away. George swallowed, knowing what was going to happen next.

His lips crashed against hers a second later and he was holding her so tightly she thought the breath was going to leave her body entirely. She melted into him, like she did every time they were together and only let go when she just had to stop to take in air.

'Quinn...' she began as he moved his lips down to her neck and began lightly kissing her shoulder blade.

He didn't reply. She could feel the tip of his tongue brushing against her collarbone.

'Quinn...' she repeated, trying not to shiver as his hot breath warmed her entire insides.

His fingers were at the buttons of her shirt now and she was perilously close to letting him carry on.

'Quinn,' she said firmly.

Finally he stopped, and brought his head back up to look at her.

'We can't keep on doing this. I won't be that girl,' George told him seriously.

Quinn just gazed at her, his eyes shining with emotion and then he took a step back from her and held onto her hand, his fingers softly caressing hers.

His whole persona had altered and for a moment he looked completely fragile, not the self-assured, confident individual she was getting used to seeing at close quarters.

He opened his mouth as if to speak but then closed it again and swallowed poignantly.

He squeezed George's hand and she saw his eyes well up with tears. All of a sudden he looked like a different person, someone with the weight of the world on his shoulders. The change in him shocked her. He looked lost, like he didn't know what to do next.

'This is stupid, come on,' George spoke, squeezing his hand and leading him towards the door.

Twelve

This was insane behaviour. He felt sick and there were tears in his eyes. Tears for crying out loud! He was losing it big time. He needed to stop this and he needed to stop it now. He should just let go of her hand and head off to the nearest hot spot where he could lose himself in any woman he fancied, or didn't fancy. But he couldn't. He wanted to talk to her; he wanted her to talk to him. He wanted to hear all about mixing fillings for wraps and the intricacies of pastry. He wanted to hear anything that came out of her mouth and then hold it close to his and part those full lips with his tongue. Shit, he was weak! He couldn't let her see that, he couldn't instigate conversation, that wasn't what men like him did. Was it possible though, that Quinn Blake had an Achilles heel? And that it was her? She was creeping under his skin and he had no idea what was going to happen next. Could he tell her how he felt? Should he tell her she had swept into his life and taken the Earth from under him?

She clambered up onto the railing and held out two beers to Quinn. He took them, put them down and grabbed hold of her arms, hoisting her up onto the roof.

'You can almost see my house from here. If you squint and bend your head to the left,' George remarked as she sat down and opened up the bottles.

'Let me guess. That one?' Quinn asked, pointing to the left of the skyline.

'I wish! That's Bowater Manor,' George responded.

'That one then?' Quinn said, pointing at a group of tower blocks.

'Nope, that's Triplet Towers. And that's not because there are three of them, that's because that's the number of children per single mother,' George explained.

Quinn nodded and took a swig of his lager.

'It's over there. Raleigh Crescent,' George informed, pointing in the direction of her home.

Quinn didn't reply and when she turned to look over at him, his eyes were shut. She watched him, wondering what he was thinking. She didn't know anything about him; they hadn't really had a chance to talk in any of their snatched moments together. It had seemed more appropriate to act rather than speak and you couldn't talk when someone was trying to kiss your face off.

He opened his eyes and took another drink.

'I can't come to Manchester you know, I have commitments. I can't just travel to the other end of the country because you click your fingers,' George stated.

'I know,' he replied simply.

'Then what were all the theatrics?'

'I don't know,' Quinn responded with a shrug.

'You don't know.'

'No,' he answered.

'Well, that's not good enough. I mean I'm just a caterer you met a few nights ago, you know nothing about me. Why I am suddenly so important to you, you have a full on hissy fit? I'm really not someone worth having a tantrum about,' George exclaimed.

'I wouldn't say that.'

'Well...'

'Look, I don't know. I can't explain it. I haven't felt like this before.'

'You're engaged to some beautiful actress and yet you've spent the last few nights desperately chasing me. What's that all about? I mean, just maybe I can understand the wanting illicit sex, but we've done that now, isn't it time you moved on? I mean Manchester must be full of good looking women, dripping with anticipation for your arrival. Me, I don't even know if I like your music.'

'What d'you want me to say?' Quinn asked, turning to look at her.

'I want you to tell me what's going on, because to be honest I've never been pursued as much and that's nice and everything, but I don't understand it,' George told him.

'I find it hard to believe you're not pursued on a very regular basis. Weekly at least.'

'Stop the flattery and talk to me. We've spent the night together but we haven't had one proper conversation.'

'Conversation's overrated.'

'Quinn!'

'I like you, you like me, what's there to say?'

'You have got to stop seducing me,' George told him.

'You could always say no.'

'I do! All the time!'

'Yeah, but you don't mean it.'

'I do mean it. And I definitely mean it about Manchester,' George insisted.

'OK,' Quinn answered.

'OK?'

'Yeah, OK, I get it. You can't come to Manchester. It doesn't mean I won't wish you were there,' Quinn told her.

'See! You say things like that and I don't know how to take them. You can't want me! I've seen the women who hang around your parties; they're preened and perfect, with less meat on them than a chicken satay. I barely run a comb through my hair and I stink of shortcrust pastry and I mean you're getting married! Why *are* you getting married?'

'Pass. Next question.'

'You must love her.'

'Must I?'

'Well that's usually what prompts a proposal and a wedding.'

'Is it?'

'You know it is. Look, this is stupid, if you aren't going to talk to me then...'

'Let's just go to bed. Let's go back to the hotel and pick up where we left off,' Quinn suggested, taking hold of George's hand.

'No. I told you before; I don't do that sort of thing. This isn't me; this isn't what I do any more...'

'I think you'll find you did that sort of thing just last night, several times in fact,' Quinn reminded her.

'Yes, but that was last night and last night I was just scratching an itch. You know, facing up to the inevitable, getting off on the adrenalin. I was stupid.'

'You were amazing,' Quinn responded, squeezing her hand and smiling at her.

George felt heat rush to her cheeks as she remembered being in bed with him the previous night. It had been amazing; they had been a fantastic combination. She still got chills when she thought about it.

'Stop it, it's not fair. I don't know anything about you and I can't be doing any of this with someone I don't know,' George exclaimed.

'What d'you want to know?'

'I don't know. Where you come from? How you got into music? How you met Taylor Ferraro? What you like for breakfast? What you feel about global warming? Normal stuff, you know, things ordinary people talk about,' George said, verging on exasperated.

'Global warming's a worldwide problem and we should all really cut down on our fuel emissions and CO_2 production,' Quinn replied with a smirk.

'Don't you take anything seriously?'

'Life's too short.'

George let out a frustrated sigh, picked up her bottle of beer and took a long swig.

'Look, I'm sorry. I've not had a good day and the idea of only having two more nights with you kind of tipped me over the edge earlier. I was acting like a jerk before. You've got more important things in your life than me, I get that,' Quinn told her in sincere tones.

'You don't need me. Look at you! You're a successful musician with the world at your feet. You've got a glamorous fiancée according to *Star Life* magazine and your album's about to go platinum,' George informed him.

'You don't know whether you like my music, but you've been reading up on me. That's sweet.'

'When I work all day with your greatest fan it's very hard not to soak up the information being thrown about across the bread buttering.'

'Bread buttering. I'm flattered.'

'So you should be. Marisa talked about George Clooney for a week once, when she was going through her 'older man' phase, but I didn't end up knowing half as much about him,' George told him.

'You're funny and you're feisty and you don't look like you've spent a month in a tanning booth,' Quinn spoke, touching her hair with his fingers.

'Was that a compliment? Or a not so subtle way of telling me I have the complexion of someone close to death?'

'It was a compliment.'

'Well actually, I snore quite badly, I used to have a big crush on Billy Idol and I've got twenty five pairs of jeans,' George said, drinking more beer.

Quinn took a deep breath and then looked at her. His eyes, the colour of the Med, were so intense, every time they locked with hers it felt as if he could see right inside her soul.

'Things with Taylor are complicated. It isn't at all like you think. She's young and she's pretty, but that's all. There's no connection. The minute I saw you I felt something. I don't know what it was but it blew me away,' Quinn tried to explain.

'You're not expecting me to believe that are you?'

'It's true.'

'Yeah, of course it is. You've never said that before to get someone into bed.'

'Sure, all the time.'

'At last! The truth.'

'But I've never actually meant it. Until now,' Quinn told her.

His eyes told her he meant what he said, but she still didn't understand it. She was just George Fraser, caterer, black sheep, rock music loving jeans wearer; no one had ever wanted her like he seemed to want her. No one except Paul.

'It's just a physical thing. It's just nerves before the wedding. You want one last fling before you settle down,' George spoke quickly.

'No, it isn't like that. It's more than that. When I saw you it was like I had to be with you,' Quinn continued.

'Do you love Taylor?' George asked him bluntly.

'No,' Quinn answered with conviction.

113

'But you're marrying her, you're engaged. What happened? Have you fallen out of love with her? Because, if you have, then you just have to tell her. Then you can go and shag whoever you like, go and live at The Playboy Mansion or something.'

'I was never in love with her,' Quinn replied with a heavy sigh.

George looked at him, not understanding what he was trying to tell her. She hadn't understood a word he'd said since they got up on the roof. He was telling her everything but nothing all at the same time.

'It's difficult. It isn't just about her, it's about me and it's about Roger,' Quinn said, taking another much needed swig of his drink.

'Roger? Who's Roger?'

'Roger's her father. He owns Rock It Music, the record company I'm signed with,' Quinn informed.

'OK. Still not getting why you're going to marry someone you don't love.'

'Look, I can't tell you any more.'

'Please tell me we aren't having some sort of 'unless you marry my daughter I'm going to drop you from the record label' kind of blackmail scenario here, because that is so 1970s cult movie and it really doesn't happen in the real world,' George spoke.

'I've said too much already. Look, I'd better go. If I'm not back at the hotel he'll be calling and I don't want to speak to him,' Quinn said, getting to his feet.

'Well, let me drive you back,' George suggested.

She didn't want to leave things like this. She had assumed he was a player, after all weren't they all? They had money, a luxury lifestyle, people at their beck and call; they took advantage and why shouldn't they? He was a star, he had earned the right. She had completely expected it. But the things he'd said were not the words of an egomaniac with the world at his feet. They were sad words, the words of someone who was drowning in a situation.

'No, it's OK. The paparazzi are still outside, I don't want them to see me, or you for that matter. I'll walk.'

'Look, I didn't mean to pry and I'm not judging you. God, I've been judged so much in my life I know what that's like. It's really none of my business what you do, or who you do it with,' George started.

'Yes it is,' Quinn told her bluntly.

'No, really it isn't and I apologise if I've given the impression that I'm some sort of bunny boiling stalker chick who wants to know the ins and outs of your entire life. The sex was fine, we'll leave it there. I'll go back to whipping up trout mousse and you can go back to whipping teenage girls into a frenzy,' George said.

'You're kidding right?'

'Kidding about what?'

'The sex was *fine*? That's what *fine* feels like to you? God, I thought I was doing OK all this time and really I've only been hitting the *fine* mark? Man that's disappointing,' Quinn replied with a shake of his head.

'You're not listening to me.'

'And you're not listening to me. I want to be your business. I want my life to be your business. I've spent all of a few hours with you and it isn't enough. I want more,' Quinn clarified roughly grabbing her hands.

'I don't know what you want me to say.'

'Change your mind about Manchester,' Quinn suggested.

'I can't,' George answered with a sigh.

'Then come to my gig tomorrow night, see what I do. Bring that mad girl that works with you or whoever you want. I want you to see the show. I want you to know why I do what I do; I want to show you the part of my life I do understand. I want you to see how much the music means to me. The music - not the after-show parties full of people I can't stand,' Quinn said gently caressing her fingers with his.

'I'd like that,' George found herself admitting.

'And then, after the party, spend another night with me. We'll go somewhere else, anywhere you like,' Quinn added.

George shook her head as she looked at him. He probably had a high-class call girl agency on speed dial. If he wanted someone, anyone, he could have them. Yet, he was sitting on a rooftop with her. She saw him swallow, his Adam's apple bobbing nervously and he smiled almost hopefully at her, waiting for a reply. In his beautiful eyes she saw honesty. He didn't need to waste his time on her, he wanted to.

'I promise to do better than *fine*. I'll have the Kama Sutra sent by room service,' he told her.

'If I say no...' George began.

'I won't stop asking until you say yes, you know the drill,' he answered.

'I've never met anyone quite like you.'

'Is that a yes?'

Shit, was this what it was like? The whole heart skipping a beat, chest in a spasm, tingling from head to foot feeling. Was this what people felt? He had told her more than he'd told anyone, almost too much. He had wanted to tell her, the words were at his lips, ready to fall out, but self-preservation had taken over. He felt wonderful and near death all at the same time. Was this what love felt like?

Thirteen

'What the bloody Hell is this? Heavy Metal FM? Has the radio broken again? I mean, I know I moaned about Radio Two but Jesus! I can't be listening to this all day; I won't be able to work, like not one bit, not with that noise going on. It's like totally criminal. Ow! Eardrums actually like splitting now,' Marisa exclaimed the next morning in the kitchen.

'Come on Marisa this is AC/DC, it's classic,' George announced, smiling at her staff as they took their coats off.

'Oh. My. God. Are you getting this Mother? Something's happened. She's either won the lottery or she's in love, or both. No sane person smiles that much first thing in the morning and listens to this music so loud. Get her a coffee, she's been on the lager for sure,' Marisa continued, staring suspiciously at George.

'Can't someone be a little cheerful in the morning without getting accused of drinking?!' George said, holding up her already full coffee mug.

'So, which is it? Lottery win or new romance?' Marisa enquired.

'Neither actually. Sorry to disappoint you. But you are going to love me later,' George told her, still smiling.

'Why? What's happened? Don't tell me you've finally got that gig at the rowing club! I knew it! I knew

117

they would go for the meat and potato parcels!' Marisa exclaimed excitedly.

'It isn't the rowing club and we have to be very nice to your mum today, and I mean extra nice. Making her lunch and supplying her with endless coffee. I might even buy Eccles cakes to really butter her up,' George said, looking over at Helen.

'I'm not sure I like the sound of where this is going. You want me to do some really difficult icing job don't you? Not more than three tiers George, we agreed no higher than three didn't we?' Helen began, getting flustered.

'It isn't a cake, it's tonight. Would you be able to set up for us at the Hexagon?' George asked.

'Why? Oh don't say we've got another function and I'm going to miss out on a night with Quinn Blake! Oh George, please let me go to the after-show party, please, please,' Marisa said, grabbing hold of George's sleeve and tugging it like a child.

'You're not going to miss out on the party, but you and I are going to the Quinn Blake concert. I have VIP tickets,' George announced, waving the laminated passes at her.

Marisa let out an ear-splitting scream and threw her arms around George, almost bowling her into the worktop.

'Oh I'm not sure I can set up all on my own. I mean there's so much to do! All those heavy boxes and arranging the tables. I'm sorry you'll have to forfeit the tickets,' Helen said in as serious a voice as she could manage.

Marisa spun around, an expression of woe on her face. Helen laughed and smiled at her daughter.

'Just kidding! You two go and have fun,' Helen spoke.

'Oh. My. God, they're really VIP passes! The best seats! Access all areas! Wait 'til I tell Callie! She will be like so miffed! Where did you get these from?' Marisa wanted to know as she bounced from one foot to another.

'I, er, got them from Michael Lambert, Quinn Blake's PA, the one that booked us for the catering. It's kind of a thank you for all our work at such short notice,' George hurriedly lied.

That excuse sounded plausible enough. The reality was the huge black man, who had accosted her in the Hexagon car park with the hotel key card, had knocked on the door before 9.00am that morning and handed her an expensive looking parcel.

Inside had been a pair of gorgeous designer jeans in her size and the VIP passes. There was also a note.

Pair number 26 – hope you like them
Q x

The jeans were a perfect fit and she had tried them on immediately, turning around and checking every angle out in her full-length mirror. The denim was the softest she had ever felt and skimmed her thighs in the most flattering of ways. She couldn't wait to show Quinn. It was the most appropriate present anyone had ever given her.

'This is the best day of my life! Officially!' Marisa yelled, hugging the passes to her chest.

'You look brighter today; did you get a bit of sleep? Have you got hold of that pomegranate juice I told you about? The one with ginseng,' Helen asked as George got back to concocting something new for the party that night.

'Not yet, but I slept better,' George informed with a smile.

'Oh. My. God. Mother what am I going to wear?! I have like *nothing* to wear. I mean *nothing*!' Marisa exclaimed in horror.

'Well it's a rock concert isn't it? Don't most people just wear jeans? In my day you wore something you weren't worried about getting sweaty and covered in beer. Have things changed? I'm sure people still sweat,' Helen said.

'Yeah, but not in the VIP section! I can't imagine anyone sweating in there. No, I need to buy something new. I need to go into town,' Marisa announced.

'Marisa, you haven't got time for that. We've got work to do. We've got four loaves of bread to butter yet and then someone needs to shred the chicken,' Helen reminded her.

'It's OK. Let her go, you too if you like. I'm totally on top of the WI stuff and I've already found something 'delectable' to do with beef. Take her shopping, tire her out. She might have come down from Cloud Nine by the time you get back,' George suggested to them.

'I won't,' Marisa answered already putting her coat back on.

'George are you sure? I mean the WI is catering for a hundred and they want quiches...' Helen began.

'Quiches are done; I did them before you came in this morning. Go! Go on, before I change my mind. See you after lunch,' George ordered them.

'George, you are like the best boss in the world ever,' Marisa said her eyes shining with excitement.

'I'll remember that when you're swearing at me, the next time we need complicated sandwich shapes.'

There was a familiar tap on the door and Marisa opened it up.

'Hi Simon! You won't believe it; I'm going to the Quinn Blake concert tonight with a VIP pass! Me! A VIP!' Marisa screeched in a frenzied fashion.

'Well, wow, that's great,' Simon answered in a completely unexcited voice.

'We won't be long. I can only stay so long in Topshop. The music's too loud and the mannequins scare me,' Helen said as she followed Marisa out of the house.

George smiled as they left and offered the same smile to Simon. Hopefully, now more time had passed, he might be ready to slot back into their professional friendship.

'Morning,' she greeted.

'Morning. Brought the bread,' Simon informed, putting the tray on the worktop.

'Thanks. Would you like a coffee?' George offered.

'Well, I've got to get on really and...'

'A quick one?' George suggested hopefully.

'Well, OK, a quick one,' Simon agreed, closing the door.

George put the kettle on to boil and got the mugs ready. The atmosphere still felt awkward. She could sense he was looking at her as she spooned the coffee out. She didn't want this complication, but maybe she only had herself to blame. She had flirted quite a lot with him.

'So, how's business?' Simon asked, breaking the silence.

'Good thanks, really good. And with you?' George returned the question.

God this was so stilted. Usually they were already talking local bands and how many Stellas made a hangover.

'Yeah, not bad, considering how things are in general. You know, with the recession and that,' Simon answered, shifting his feet about.

George looked at him and let out a sigh. This wasn't good. She didn't talk current affairs with anyone, especially not an attractive thirty-something. Had her denying him a date really been the nail in the coffin of their relationship?

'We never talk about the recession and business. Is this how things are going to be from now on?' George blurted out.

'I don't know. I don't know what you want,' Simon admitted harshly.

'I want things back the way they were. You teasing me about my fancy snacks and me telling you you're late again and asking about the pool team,' George said.

'I asked you out,' Simon said.

'I know.'

'And you said no,' Simon reminded.

'I know.'

'And I don't understand why. I mean it was just a drink, where's the harm?' Simon questioned.

Shit. He wanted a logical explanation. That was never going to happen, because there wasn't one. She liked him, she knew he liked her, but she just didn't like him enough. How could you tell someone that? He was a man. He wanted a date. She was single. He was good looking and fun. A refusal with no good grounds was going to put a sizeable hole in his ego.

'Si, I don't want to go over it again. Let's just get things back to how they used to be,' she suggested hopefully.

'What if I can't do that? I mean, I really like you George and I don't know if I can go back to just talking about your fancy snacks,' Simon replied his doe eyes meeting with hers.

She was ripping the heart out of Bambi. That was just what she wanted! She couldn't deal with this. She shouldn't have to deal with this. Why couldn't he just take no for an answer?

She turned her back on him and began to make the coffee she was starting to wish she had never offered.

'Just come out with me, one time. If you think it's so awful after one date then fine, I won't ask again,' Simon carried on.

Was he ever going to stop asking? Suddenly there was a direct comparison with Quinn. The difference was, when he asked, she had to fight with herself to say no, not think of all the reasons why she couldn't say yes.

'One date, come on. You can choose where we go.'

'No.'

'Why?'

'Because I don't want to ruin our friendship and...'

'It wouldn't ruin our friendship, I promise. One date, come on.'

'No, I can't.'

'Why not?'

'Because I'm seeing someone,' George blurted out desperate to stop the conversation.

She saw his face drop and his whole persona slump like she had inflicted a fatal blow. Bambi was floored, bow legs flat out and unresponsive.

OK, so what she'd said wasn't strictly true. She wasn't having a proper relationship. But it was true she was kind of, loosely, seeing someone. Quinn Blake, pop sensation and all-round hottie. Just thinking his name made her simmer under the apron.

'Look, maybe you should get your bread from another supplier,' Simon suggested as he went towards the door.

'Oh Simon don't do that, that's just stupid. I'm a good customer, I always pay on time and we're friends aren't we?' George exclaimed.

'It's not enough,' Simon stated, looking at her with hurt in his eyes.

He opened the door, closed it sharply behind him and left the house.

George took a deep breath. She felt sorry for him. This was usually how every one of her brief relationships ended. The guy would like her a little too much. She wouldn't like him enough and inevitably it would come to this same conclusion. It didn't always finish with her needing to find a new bread supplier though. That was bad news.

She took the AC/DC CD out of the player and slipped in a Billy Idol album. She had new jeans, expensive new jeans, and a night of passion with one of the world's biggest pop stars to come; it wasn't the time for dwelling on a baker who had a crush on her.

Fourteen

On her impromptu shopping spree Marisa had bought six tops and two pairs of trousers. Wet look leggings and hipster jeans. She had changed three times in the Hexagon toilets and had finally opted for the leggings and a long tunic-style top with black and red stripes. She teamed that with the highest pair of platforms George had ever seen and huge silver hooped earrings. Her make-up left a bit to be desired though. George wasn't entirely sure how she was going to avoid looking like a panda by the end of the night with the amount of eye liner she had under her eyes. Still, Marisa was young and hadn't she worn similar when she had snuck out of her bedroom window and shinned down the drainpipe to meet Paul?

She smiled now as they took their seats in the concert hall. She remembered falling off the drainpipe once and landing in a heap at Paul's feet. It had been raining, she was covered in mud and her arm hurt like Hell. But, Paul had helped her up and they had run down the road towards his motorbike before her parents came out of the house to see what the noise was about.

They'd gone to see a band that night, some awful student indie band at the college. They hadn't played a chord in tune the whole evening. In the end, during the interval, Paul and his band mates had invaded the stage and taken over the instruments to play their music. They had been amazing and were so well received, the original band never made it back on. She'd had the hangover to end all hangovers the next day courtesy of Dry Blackthorn and blackcurrant.

George held onto the ring on the chain around her neck and looked at Marisa's radiant face. She was so excited about seeing the concert. She was sat on the very edge of her seat now, looking around at the other people in the VIP section, enjoying every second of the experience.

George smoothed her hands down her jeans. They were so gorgeous she didn't know whether she would ever wear any of the other twenty five pairs again. Quinn obviously had good taste. Either that or his personal shopper did. She didn't want to think about that. She hoped he had chosen them. But she wasn't really that naive.

'Look at the people standing down there? Don't they look squashed and like really uncomfortable. Don't we have like the best view?' Marisa exclaimed, looking at George.

'We certainly do,' George agreed.

'Oh. My. God! It's her! Taylor Ferraro! Look!' Marisa blurted out loudly as she looked to the door into the VIP area of the seating.

George's blood ran cold, but she quickly turned her head in the same direction as Marisa, to catch a look. A tall, very thin, blonde-haired girl in her twenties was being escorted to a seat by Quinn's PA Michael.

'That's Quinn's fiancée?' George found herself asking as she watched the woman move along the row nearer to them.

'Yeah. She's like so pretty isn't she? I wish I looked like her,' Marisa said with an appreciative sigh.

'She doesn't look like she eats much,' George remarked unable to draw her eyes away from the actress.

'Well no, they don't do they? People like that, you know, celebrities. She's probably on the new pea and apple diet,' Marisa answered knowledgeably.

George continued to watch as Michael and Taylor sat down about ten seats away. She let out a grateful breath; the last thing she wanted was to have to sit next to her. Seeing her in the flesh made her real. She was going to marry Quinn. She was here. There would be no night of passion in his hotel room, or anywhere else. Well, not for her anyway. She swallowed and looked back to the stage, as the lights began to dim. She felt huge disappointment, like a shine had been taken off the evening. Had their one night together really been just that? One night.

The drummer began to bang out a beat; the other musicians joined in and then, descending on a platform from the roof of the stage, came Quinn playing an electric violin. The crowd went wild. Marisa started screaming at the top of her voice and George watched him, as he greeted the crowd and began to belt out a classical version of one of his well-known hits. The light show was amazing, with explosions and strobes flickering, as the dancers pulsated to the beat. Marisa stood up and already the eye liner was making a break for freedom.

George glanced across at Taylor Ferraro and watched her as she slipped a nail file out of her designer handbag. She looked intently at her fingers and began to shape and buff them.

Quinn was a born performer. Apart from being something of a musical genius, he was also adept at crowd pleasing. He enchanted them with his musicality, his voice and his moves. George was certain every member of the audience had just experienced the best night of their lives.

Marisa's face was awash with tears and make-up and her voice was now as husky as a forty-a-day smoker, because of all the screaming she had done.

'...and now a song that was only written a couple of days ago, by a very talented musician called Adam Fraser. It's going to be on my new album and it's called 'Sunrise',' Quinn announced through the microphone.

George felt like her heart was going to burst with pride. A thousand people had heard Adam's name, heard he had written a song with Quinn Blake. She looked over at Marisa and the young girl screamed at the top of her voice.

'I know Adam Fraser! He's like my best friend!'

Belch began the song and then Quinn started to sing, his voice soft and soulful. It was a beautiful melody with moving lyrics. George immediately recognised the section Adam had written. He had a certain style when it came to composition that was uniquely him.

She clapped along with the audience, as Quinn encouraged everyone to join in. She could just envisage Adam's excitement when she told him about this. He would be made up.

The song came to an end and the audience applauded, screamed and made noise any way they could to signify their appreciation. George and Marisa rose to their feet and clapped excitedly, as Quinn and his band accepted the adoration.

George looked over at Taylor, expecting immense animation from her, but instead she was checking her Blackberry, looking bored. Michael, on the other hand, was clapping loudly and yelling 'bravo' as loud as he could, hair flopping in front of his face; smile as broad as a wide chasm.

Taylor had just sat through an amazing concert, that had moved everyone in the hall, and she looked like she would rather be somewhere else.

'We'd better go and get changed and get ready with the platters,' George said, looking at her watch and returning to work mode.

'Oh! But we've got backstage passes. Can't we go backstage? I bet they have really cool dressing rooms and like loads of lilies and M&Ms,' Marisa remarked reluctant for her adventure to end.

'I don't want to leave your mum for too long. She's already had to do all the setting up,' George reminded.

'She won't mind and Curly Shirley should be there by now. Please! Pretty please!' Marisa begged, putting her teeth together and grimacing like a desperate toddler.

'Alright. One look backstage but then we're going straight to the function room,' George told her.

'Yay!' Marisa said, jumping up and down.

The silly bitch had arrived and he couldn't have been more pissed off. This was Roger's doing. He had got a sniff of something from one of the hired helps and he had flown in Taylor to keep tabs on him. This was the shape of things to come for him. He knew that and he hated it. But he couldn't do anything about it. Not if he wanted to keep the life he knew. He wanted George more than ever, especially now he knew he couldn't have her tonight. Well, he shouldn't have her, but maybe there was still a chance. He just needed to charm Taylor the way he knew he could.

Backstage wasn't exactly the glamorous setting Marisa had envisaged. The narrow corridors of the Hexagon's behind the scenes area were full of equipment and people rushing from one end of the corridor to the other, shouting instructions and asking where certain people were. George felt very out of place and was beginning to wish she hadn't given in to Marisa's demands.

'Oh. My. God. There's Belch! Can we go and speak to him? I've got a camera; can you take a picture of us?' Marisa squeaked as she noticed the guitarist about to head into a dressing room.

'OK, quick then! Before he goes into his room,' George said, propelling Marisa down the corridor.

'BELCH!' Marisa screamed at the top of her voice, bringing him to an immediate standstill.

'Man, that's an enthusiastic greeting,' he said, turning to greet them before letting out a trademark burp.

'Can I - I mean like - could I - we...' Marisa began, awestruck and lost for words.

'She'd like a photo with you,' George informed, waving the camera.

'Sure babe,' Belch said, slipping his arm around Marisa, much to her very obvious delight.

For once the guitarist was smiling. George wasn't sure she had ever seen him smile before. He still looked completely unkempt, but a smile definitely improved him.

George took the photo and then the door of Belch's dressing room burst open and Quinn came out. He was sweating from the show and was wiping at his neck with a towel.

'Oh. My. God. George, take a picture of me and Quinn, please, please,' Marisa said excitedly as she flashed a much practised smile at the pop star.

George was staring at Quinn and Quinn was looking back at her. It was as if there was no one else there.

'George! Photo!' Marisa repeated in annoyed tones.

'Sorry,' George responded hurriedly.

Quinn joined Belch in putting an arm around Marisa and all three of them smiled for the shot.

'Belch, why don't you show Marisa around. It is Marisa isn't it?'

'Yes,' Marisa said her eyes glazing over with admiration.

'Get her a drink or something and maybe some of that great candy,' Quinn suggested not taking his eyes from George.

'Vodka?' Marisa asked hopefully.

'I don't think so,' George answered sternly.

'I'll look after her,' Belch insisted, slipping his arm around Marisa and hugging her to him.

The guitarist seemed positively ecstatic to be Marisa's escort. George hoped he wasn't high.

'Ten minutes and I'm coming to look for you,' George warned as Marisa bounced up the corridor hanging onto the tassels on Belch's leather jacket.

Quinn waited until they were out of sight and then opened the door of the dressing room.

'In here,' he ordered.

Without saying anything George entered the room. It was certainly not the tranquil, flower and chocolate filled environment Marisa had spoken of. There were half a dozen guitars stood around the room and clothes lying on every available space. She was just deciding whether to find somewhere to sit when Quinn spun her around and kissed her hard on the mouth.

He was hot from the show, his t-shirt was wet but he tasted so good. He backed her up against the wall, his hands in hers, pressing them against the paintwork as he kissed her neck.

She let him kiss her, enjoying every tiny sensation of his mouth on her skin. She released her hands and moved them underneath his t-shirt, touching the taut stomach and the smooth, hairless chest. She pulled the top over his head and looked at him, willing him to know what she wanted to do.

131

Suddenly there was a knock on the door and George froze, her heart flying up to her mouth.

'Yeah?' Quinn called his hand on the belt of George's jeans.

They both watched the door, waiting for something to happen. The door handle moved down but then sprang back up. Thankfully, it had locked.

'Is Belch there? He's needed for an interview,' the voice called through the barrier.

'Try Quinn Blake's dressing room,' Quinn replied, muffling his voice with his hand.

'Thanks,' the voice replied.

George was still holding her breath. Only when she knew they were safe, did she finally let it out and let go of Quinn.

'Hey, it's OK. Door's locked, no drama,' Quinn stated, holding her hand.

'I saw Taylor,' George said, straightening her top and smoothing down her hair.

'I know. I didn't know she was coming here, she just turned up this afternoon.'

'Look, I'd better go and find Marisa before she steals away in a tour bus or something,' George said, heading for the door.

'You're wearing the jeans,' Quinn remarked.

'Yes, they're beautiful. Your personal shopper has great taste,' George replied with a smile.

'My what? Are you kidding me? I had Zara open at 8.00am for me. If I could have made it to D&G and back I would have,' Quinn told her.

'Oh,' George answered feeling bad.

'I ran my hands over at least a dozen pairs before I found these,' Quinn said, pulling her back to him by the waistband.

'I have to go.'

'I won't let you,' he stated firmly.

'I have to, I've got a party to run. Your party.'

'That wasn't what I meant,' Quinn said, looking at her seriously.

'Tonight was fantastic. Your music, your performance, well I'm so glad you showed me that. I can see your passion on that stage, how driven you are. Spending another night with you would have been amazing, but things change and Taylor's here. And, you're going to Manchester tomorrow,' George reminded him.

'I won't let you go,' he repeated and he kissed her again.

George clung to him, feeling his strength, wanting to close her eyes and forget everything else but the moment. It had been a brief liaison, but she knew this was the end. She wouldn't see him again. He was leaving tomorrow; he was going back to America soon. It had been a fantastic few nights and she would never forget him.

'Goodbye Quinn,' George spoke, kissing his cheek and swallowing a knot of emotion in her throat.

He looked at her and then he took hold of her hand and placed it tight to his chest. His skin was warm beneath her fingers and she could feel his heart beating double time. She took hold of his hand and mirrored his actions, placing it on her chest so he could feel the rhythm her heart was beating out.

'This isn't goodbye,' Quinn told her, squeezing her hand in his.

Unable to speak, she hurriedly fumbled with the lock on the door and let herself out into the corridor.

There was no time for contemplation; the scene that greeted her outside the door took her breath away in a not so good way.

Marisa was pressed up against Belch, one hand in his crotch, the other in his abundant hair. It looked like they were performing a tonsillectomy on each other.

'MARISA! We're leaving! Now!' George yelled at the top of her voice.

Marisa broke away from the guitarist, lipstick all over her face and cheeks as red as a cherry.

'Is this your idea of looking after her? She's seventeen!' George exclaimed angrily at Belch.

'Whatever,' Belch responded with a burp.

'Bye,' Marisa said miserable that her passionate encounter had come to an abrupt end.

George grabbed hold of Marisa's arm and marched her up the corridor.

'What the Hell did you think you were doing? He's old enough to be your father,' George said angrily.

'Oh he is not; he's like thirty or something. We weren't doing anything wrong, we just...' Marisa began.

'I saw what you were doing?! You had your tongue stuck so far down his throat you could have licked his stomach lining. Haven't you learned anything from your encounter with Butcher Boy?' George continued, pushing open the door and leading the way upstairs to the conference rooms.

'It isn't like I had anything to drink and I am seventeen, not like ten! I mean I could get married if I wanted!'

'You'd need permission unless you went to Scotland actually! Right then, let's go and tell your mum you've been getting intimate with a bushy-haired bassist shall we?'

'Oh please don't tell Mum she'll freak!' Marisa said suddenly scared about the prospect.

'How many years do you think she will ground you for? Especially if I go on to tell her about the Blue WKD incident!' George enquired, staring at the teenager.

'About a hundred at least. Please don't,' Marisa begged.

'Look, believe it or not Marisa, I remember what it's like to be seventeen and have everyone telling you what to do. But you have to promise me you'll be careful and that you'll never do anything like that again when I'm supposed to be looking after you. I don't care what you do when you're not with me, but you don't go snogging the face off guitarists on my watch. Got it?' George told her seriously.

'Understood,' Marisa responded.

As it was the final night at the Hexagon, the after-show party was buzzing more than ever. George was introduced to several potential clients by Michael, who couldn't seem to sing her praises highly enough. Marisa kept looking lustfully at Belch, who was constantly surrounded by a bevy of women and everyone had been complimentary about the food.

George had managed to avoid being at close quarters with Quinn so far, but she couldn't stop herself from watching him. Taylor was at his side, holding his hand one minute, slipping her arm around his waist the next, laughing at things he said, smiling at his guests, looking comfortable amongst the other celebrities. She was the perfect hostess and George couldn't help but feel a stab of jealousy at how she looked, how she was able to work a room and how she could hold Quinn without worrying who might see.

'Darling, why the long face? I think the beef and cucumber sauce is your best work yet. Everyone's said so,' Michael spoke, standing in front of George.

'Thanks Michael and as it's the last night, I want to thank you for the job here. It's been really - good,' George said, trying to find the right words and failing miserably.

'No my dear, thank you. You've done a marvellous spread every night and you took on the job at such short notice. I would have loved you to continue the work in Manchester but it's not to be. *C'est la vie*,' Michael said.

He'd had to listen to her bleat on and on about some stupid designer handbag she was on the waiting list for and now she was parading him around the party like he was auditioning for *America's Next Top Model*. It would be worth it though, when she let him out for the night to 'play poker'. It would be risky, but another night with George was more than worth the risk. It might be the last time. No, it couldn't be the last time, not yet.

George suddenly stiffened and tightened her grip on her tray as Taylor Ferraro arrived at Michael's side and took hold of his arm.

She was even more stunning up close. She was wearing a beautiful peacock blue dress which emphasised her slight frame. She had clipped her hair up into a chignon, which showed off a large diamond stud in each ear. Everything about her was immaculate, from her pedicured toes to her perfectly threaded eyebrows.

'Hello darling. How are you enjoying the party?' Michael asked, turning to look at the actress.

'I'm so jet lagged Mikey. I don't think I'm going to last much longer,' Taylor spoke in a voice like Minnie Mouse.

George hadn't been expecting that. But it was comforting to know there was a rogue cell amongst all that perfection.

'Oh you poor dear. Here, have a canapé, they're truly delicious,' Michael said, indicating George's tray.

'Oh I couldn't. I ate on the plane and I'm still bloated from that. It was all starch and carbohydrates,' Taylor spoke.

'Only the finest ingredients here, local produce too. Isn't that right George? This is George by the way, MD of Finger Food. George, this is Taylor Ferraro, esteemed actress and Quinn's fiancée,' Michael introduced.

God why had he done that? She'd never known someone introduce her to so many people before. Usually it would have been a good thing, excellent for business, but she didn't want to be introduced to Quinn's fiancée. She wanted to be a faceless name to her, or a nameless face, she didn't mind which.

'Nice to meet you,' George spoke, holding out her hand and hoping it wasn't shaking too much.

'Likewise,' Taylor said her tiny little hand meeting George's and performing a weak, wet fish shake.

'Oh gosh! I've just had the most amazing idea. Have you settled on a caterer for the wedding yet?' Michael enquired.

George's heart leapt into her throat. She knew what he was about to say. This was really a step too far.

'I'm choosing between two at the moment, both very different. It's going to be really hard to decide.'

'Well, do not look any further. I think George could be your woman,' Michael exclaimed excitedly, clapping his hands together like a toy monkey with a pair of cymbals.

He'd said it.

'Do you do weddings?' Taylor wanted to know, focussing all her attention on George.

'I - er - yes, of course, but not usually in America,' George spoke quickly.

Ha! That would put a spanner in the works. It would be impossible for her to cater a wedding that far away. It was impractical and she'd never done it before. Result!

'Oh they aren't getting hitched in America, kitten,' Michael said.

'We're getting married in Spain. We have a villa there,' Taylor informed her.

Still abroad and George had no experience in catering outside of the UK. Taylor needed someone experienced in that department, therefore not her. A lack of experience would surely hit her right between the eyes.

'Oh well, I can't say I've done any weddings in Spain either. In fact, I've done nothing abroad,' George replied awkwardly.

'But there's a first time for everything. You need to tone up your self-promotion techniques darling! George is a genius in the kitchen. We've had so much top-class food here, I don't know how I'm going to cope when we get to Manchester. I'll probably never be able to eat again,' Michael spoke his hair bouncing around.

'Well, I'll bear you in mind,' Taylor said, looking at the tray of canapés and then again at George.

She smiled politely. Thank God she seemed completely disinterested! That was one catering job George would definitely not want to take on. It would be almost incestuous.

She looked over at Quinn. He was chatting to a group of people in the centre of the room. He had changed from his show clothes and was now wearing an olive green t-shirt and combat trousers. He looked up and caught her eye. He smiled at her and she smiled back. She was going to miss him. She was grateful for the time they'd had. He'd taught her how to feel again. Perhaps he was the kick-start she'd needed to leave the past behind and move on.

'I'm like completely knackered,' Marisa remarked as she helped George, Helen and Curly Shirley finish loading up the Finger Food van.

'I'll second that,' George replied, shoving in another box.

'Me too,' Helen agreed with a yawn.

'Oh hark at you! You sound like you're halfway to the old folks' home. I'm wired after that party, ready for dancing,' Shirley announced, throwing her arms in the air and jogging on the spot.

'I have no idea where you get your energy from Shirl'. Are you drinking that new pomegranate juice?' Helen asked as Shirley continued to bust some moves.

'We did well tonight and we got a bonus. An extra grand which I shall be divvying up tomorrow,' George told them.

'Oh wow! I've almost got enough for a car!' Marisa said excitedly.

'Oh God! Have you?' Helen exclaimed concerned.

'And I'm going to have enough for a new van,' George said happily as a taxi pulled up alongside them.

'That must be ours.'

'Thanks for your help Shirley. I'll see you two in the morning, no more late nights for a while, just a funeral tea and a teddy bear's picnic tomorrow,' George spoke as the three women approached the taxi.

'Goodbye glamorous parties and shoulder rubbing with celebs. It was freaking sick while it lasted,' Marisa remarked with a sigh.

'Sick? What do you mean sick?' Helen queried.

'It's a good thing nowadays apparently. But I think you've had enough excitement for quite some time don't you Marisa?' George said, giving Marisa a knowing look.

'Well maybe for this week,' Marisa admitted with a coy grin.

The taxi pulled away and George turned to put the final box inside her van. She went to close the door when suddenly she was forcefully pushed and bundled into the rear of the van. She screamed out loud and turned to put up a fight, but someone had jumped in after her and slammed the doors closed.

139

'You touch me and I'll kill you. I have mace!' George shrieked hysterically, trying to get her eyes to adjust to the sudden blackness.

'Cool, but I have beers and fries,' Quinn replied, switching on the internal light and revealing himself.

'What are you doing here?' she asked, taking a breath of relief and trying to keep the excitement out of her voice.

'I'm doing what I want to do for once, not doing what I think I should be doing,' he told her.

'What about Taylor?' George questioned.

'What about her?' Quinn asked, moving towards her.

Fifteen

George woke up feeling freezing cold. Her head ached, one arm was stuck underneath her and she had pins and needles in her leg. She attempted to turn onto her side, but she couldn't move. She was naked, covered by nothing but a silver tablecloth and she was surrounded by boxes. In fact, her foot was actually inside a box containing paper plates. Not a great look. She pulled it out and deposited a few plates onto the floor of the van as she did.

It was light outside. She could see the Union Jack waving from the roof of the Hexagon, against a cloud ridden sky. She looked at her watch and saw it was almost 8.00am. She gently shook Quinn's arm and he opened his eyes, smiling when he saw her.

'Morning,' he greeted, stifling a yawn.

'It's eight o'clock. I've got to get home,' George told him, searching around in the debris of cardboard for some of her clothes.

'No breakfast first?' Quinn asked, stroking her arm.

'There's a café just down the street, does a great full English,' George told him.

'Who was talking about food?' Quinn replied, pinning her down and rolling over on top of her.

George looked up at him and smiled. They had talked more than they had ever talked last night. She'd told him things about herself she had never told anyone. The twelve pack of lager had gone straight to her head and she'd relaxed enough to tell him all about her controlling mother, her dislike of red wine and her desire to be the best in the catering industry. And when they'd finished talking, he had undressed her so slowly by the time she was naked she was begging him to take her.

'You're insatiable,' George told him as he pressed himself against her.

'Ditto.'

'I wasn't like this until I met you,' George answered.

'I don't believe it,' Quinn said, kissing her.

'You'd better go,' George said, cupping his face with her hands.

'Yeah, I'd better go. Toe the line, do as I'm told,' Quinn answered with a sigh.

'If it's that bad why do you do it?' George asked him.

'Because I don't know how to do anything else,' he responded.

'I don't understand.'

'No, I know you don't,' Quinn replied.

He moved off her and began looking for his clothes.

'But if you're not happy...'

'It isn't that simple OK. I can't just up and leave, I just can't,' Quinn insisted, buttoning up his shirt.

George hugged the tablecloth to her, feeling colder than ever. She didn't want to end their last night together like this. She didn't understand, but she was in no position to question it.

'I want your number,' Quinn said, doing up his trousers.

'My number?'

142

'Yeah, your number. I want to call you, I want to text you, I want to speak to you in the middle of the night and tell you what I wish I was doing with you,' Quinn told her.

'Isn't that dangerous? What if Taylor...' George began.

'Taylor's my concern.'

'I know but...'

Quinn took hold of her hand and placed it on his chest, just like he had in Belch's dressing room.

'That's what's real, the way you make me feel. I'm yours,' Quinn told her.

George swallowed and shook a memory from her head. Paul had always said those very words to her. For a second, the chain around her neck felt slightly heavier. Why did those age-old memories keep forcing themselves into her mind? She couldn't keep holding onto the past like a crutch. She had a life to live and this time with Quinn had been living to the extreme.

She took hold of his hand and put it to her chest, squeezing it tightly in hers.

'I'm only going to say it once OK? So I hope you've got a good memory,' George told him.

'You have no idea.'

'D'you know, I can't make up my mind which is my favourite Quinn Blake song after last night,' Marisa said as she iced fairy cakes for the teddy bear's picnic later that morning.

'Does it matter? Do you really need to know which is the sickest?' Helen enquired.

'Yes Mother. I bet you can tell me your favourite Duran Duran song. Whoever they are,' Marisa commented.

'Well obviously that would be 'Girls on Film' but...' Helen began.

'No way, 'Rio' was much better,' George interrupted.

'God, you are both like *sooo* uncool,' Marisa said with an exaggerated sigh.

George's phone beeped as a text came through. She picked it up and saw it was from Adam.

Quinn B mentiond me in show last nite! Cant believe it!

George smiled. She wondered how he'd found out. She hadn't had a chance to tell him. Perhaps one of his friends had been at the concert. She would ring him later; find out how he was and whether her parents were still there. She hoped they weren't, her mother was smothering at the best of times but a thousand times worse when he was ill.

Her phone beeped again as a second text came through, this time from an unknown number.

Can still taste you Q x

Just reading the words made her blush and she looked around at Helen and Marisa, feeling immediately guilty.

'Someone's popular today. Either that or you've requested a ringtone and are now getting bombarded with texts asking you if you want to win ten grand,' Marisa spoke.

George didn't reply but sent texts back, first to Adam.

i know i was there so proud of you mum n dad still there?

And then to Quinn.

Ditto G x

She felt like she was sixteen again, it was fun, it was exciting and it was bad.

Her phone beeped again.

'For God's sake! Trying to like work here! Can you put it on silent?' Marisa exclaimed.

They r leavin 2day speak soon sis x

'Sorry! I'll turn it off,' George said about to press the off key.

It beeped again, Marisa let out a loud tut of disapproval and George read the message.

C u soon Q x

George smiled. He made her feel how she used to feel with Paul. Maybe she should have taken the job in Manchester. She could have had four more nights with him before he moved on to Glasgow. But then he might have asked her there too and where would it have ended? No, they needed some space. She needed to take a breath. It was all too intense too soon and he was getting married. She couldn't forget that, no matter what he said.

The phone in the kitchen began to ring and Marisa put down her icing bag and went to answer it.

'Don't know why I'm bothering, it will be whoever's texting you. Hiya Finger Food - yes she's here. Who's calling? Taylor Ferraro? Oh. My. God. As in *the* Taylor Ferraro?' Marisa exclaimed her eyes bulging.

George suddenly felt sick. There could only be one reason Taylor Ferraro was on the phone. She knew. She knew about her and Quinn. She was probably going to arrange to meet and then murder her. She had seen the length of her nails; she did not want her eyes scratched at by them. This was a conversation that was going to end things with Quinn and probably earn her a reputation as a slut.

'George! It's Taylor Ferraro!' Marisa said, holding out the phone dramatically.

George wiped her hands on a cloth and took the phone from Marisa. She had to be calm, she didn't want Marisa and Helen knowing what was going on.

'Hello George Fraser,' she greeted.

'Hello Ms Fraser, it's Taylor Ferraro. We met at the party last night.'

Today her voice was more Joe Pasquale than Minnie Mouse.

'Yes, we did. Hello,' George replied with a swallow.

It didn't sound like Taylor had spent all morning sizing up concrete boots. George only hoped she didn't sound like she'd been performing fellatio on her fiancé.

'Michael Lambert hasn't stopped pressing your business card into my hand since last night, suggesting I employ you to cater my wedding,' Taylor told her.

'I see,' George said not knowing what else to say.

'I'm here at the Highgate Hotel until early evening. Would it be possible for you to make up, say, three menus, and bring some samples? I'd like some buffet options and a three-course suggestion,' Taylor spoke.

'Today?' George said stupidly.

'Yes, I'm here until six then I'm getting a flight to Manchester. Could you make that work?' Taylor asked again.

'Um, yes - I guess,' George answered unenthusiastically.

'Good. So shall we meet in the restaurant at four thirty?' Taylor suggested.

'Forty thirty,' George repeated.

'See you then,' Taylor said, ending the call.

146

George replaced the handset and was greeted by curious looks from both her staff.

'Well?! What did she want?' Marisa demanded to know.

'She wants Finger Food to tender for her wedding,' George said almost choking on the words.

'Oh. My. God! Quinn Blake's wedding! Oh. My. God!' Marisa said, looking like she was about to faint.

'Oh George, that's a massive contract. Her wedding is going to be the celebrity event of the year, all the magazines say so,' Helen said.

'I know, but she wants to meet me at four thirty with sample menus and some food to taste. It's a tall order. I don't know if we can do it,' George said.

She didn't want to do it. She didn't want to look into the eyes of the woman. She had slept with her soon-to-be husband over and over again. She didn't know if she could sit across a table from her.

'How about those menus you did for Lord Barrington's wedding?' Helen suggested.

'Yeah, I guess,' George answered.

'What's the matter with you? Don't you want the job? This is the sort of job most caterers would like kill for. Like seriously...' Marisa began.

'Sick,' Helen added with a proud smile.

Yes, Marisa was right; it was the sort of job most caterers would kill for. She should be lapping up this celebrity attention and thinking of the prestige and great fat fee at the end of it.

'Yeah, I know. You're absolutely right,' George said a hundred different thoughts going through her head.

It was Quinn's wedding; she was going to pitch to cater for Quinn's wedding. It was the biggest opportunity of her career so far. She would be a fool to turn it down. This was the sort of break she had been looking for. This event could make Finger Food into an internationally renowned company. This could rocket the firm into the catering orbit she wanted to be part of.

'Well let's get those menus out and get preparing shall we?' Helen said momentarily taking charge.

'Yeah, let's do that,' George agreed, clapping her hands together.

She needed to try and get this contract. She had to do it, for so many reasons.

Sixteen

Only that morning, she had woken up naked in the back of her van, having spent the night sleeping with Quinn Blake. Now, she was entering the hotel she had been in only a few nights before, with the aforementioned Quinn Blake, destined to meet and discuss wedding catering with his fiancée. It was a mixed-up state of affairs and she wasn't relishing sitting with Taylor Ferraro, three sample menus and some food to taste.

George entered the restaurant, carrying the bag full of delights she, Marisa and Helen had made earlier that afternoon, including a brand new main course she had created. It was chicken breast with a cream and garlic sauce and it was gorgeous. If that didn't impress Taylor then nothing would. It was the tastiest thing she had come up with in a long time.

She saw Taylor immediately. The American was sat at a table near the window, overlooking a fishing lake in the hotel grounds. George had seen the view before, from Quinn's room. His suite had overlooked it and they had had sex up against the full-length windows, too desperate to get with each other to worry about any paparazzi that might be camped out in the bushes. She hadn't thought about it at the time, but if there were photographers in the shrubbery, it was likely they would have snapped a perfect picture of her not so perfect arse.

Taylor was wearing a navy blue dress which skimmed her mid thigh. She had huge sunglasses on her face that were far too large for her tiny features but again her hair and make-up were flawless. She was like a perfect little Barbie doll complete with accessories.

George approached the table and put her bag down on the floor. This made Taylor turn away from the view of the lake and greet her.

'Hello Ms Ferraro, sorry if I'm a bit late, the traffic was terrible,' George greeted.

'And it's raining. It rains a lot here doesn't it,' she replied, indicating the weather outside.

'Most of the time actually,' George said, taking a seat opposite her.

'OK. So, do you have what I asked for?' Taylor enquired.

'Yes, I do. Here are three menus, two buffet style and one for a three-course sit-down meal. As the wedding's in Spain, I went for a starter of local citrus fruits made into a sorbet with sweet biscuits, followed by chicken breast in a cream and garlic sauce with lemon infused rice and mixed leaves. For dessert, a chocolate orange flan with chilli cream. I've got a sample of all of those and a selection of the canapés from the other two menus,' George told her as she began to get both insulated and cool boxes out of her bag.

Taylor let George open the boxes and make a display of the various items for her. The American then picked up a fork and ate the tiniest mouthful of the chicken, sipped at her water and followed it up by taking a small half-teaspoonful of the flan and cream.

George couldn't tell what she thought, from her non-existent expression. Taylor hadn't spat anything out, but perhaps she would wait until George had gone to do that.

'Michael's right,' she said after she had eaten a bite from two different canapés 'it's very good.'

'Thank you,' George replied, struggling to know whether to feel pleased or terrified.

'Can you do the date? It's August 28th, in La Manga. I'd need you there a week before. I have a bachelorette party I'll need catering for and you'll need to get accustomed to the cooking facilities. I have staff, they can assist you,' Taylor spoke.

'Actually, I have my own staff. We come as a package,' George told her.

'Fine. So can you do the date?' Taylor queried for the second time.

'Yes,' George answered.

'Good. I'll get my wedding planner, Pixie, to liaise with you about flights and ordering the ingredients etc.,' Taylor said, standing up and picking up a handbag that was almost as big as a suitcase.

'Which menu? You didn't say,' George spoke, watching her fasten the clasp on the bag and put it over her arm.

'The three-course, with a vegetarian option too and vegetarian canapés for the bachelorette party. I have to go, I need to see the beautician before my flight,' she informed.

'Don't you want to know my fee?' George asked.

'I just want the best. How much that costs is irrelevant. It was good to meet you,' Taylor spoke and she moved gracefully out of the restaurant, her handbag looking oversized for her stick-like arm.

George watched her go and then looked at the table of food. She hadn't eaten since the chips she had shared with Quinn in the early hours. She was starving. It seemed a shame to see it go to waste and perhaps having a full stomach would give her the courage to come to terms with the fact she was going to be catering Quinn's wedding. But then again, she wasn't sure anything was going to prepare her for that. No, she was being over the top. It was just a fling. A few days in Manchester,

151

probably another woman or two, he would barely remember her name. She needed to focus on her future, the future of Finger Food, not spend time dwelling on someone who was getting married in a month.

She took a mouthful of chicken and put her mobile phone to her ear.

'Hiya, Finger Food,' Marisa greeted.

'I think your boss said on several occasions that it's supposed to be 'Good afternoon Finger Food',' George told her, spooning more food into her mouth.

'Oh God, the meeting's over already! Didn't it go well? Did she eat anything? If she turned you down without eating anything then she's a sick bitch,' Marisa rambled on.

'Better dig out your sunscreen. We're going to Spain,' George informed her.

She held the phone away from her ear and waited for her reaction.

As predicted Marisa let out a loud ear-splitting scream of excitement and George smiled to herself. If she tried really hard she could think of it as a holiday. A holiday with a job that was going to make her year, and hopefully lead to lots more lucrative opportunities, catering for the rich and famous. Quinn would have forgotten all about her by the time the wedding arrived. Whether she would forget about him was another matter entirely.

Seventeen

At 1.00am George was on her fourth lager and three quarters of the way through chicken curry, chips and egg foo yung from the local Chinese takeaway. You could get a bit sick of fine food when you spent all day working with it and everyone needed to indulge in a bit of comfort eating once in a while. Besides, this was a celebration meal. This was a treat for managing to land the function of all functions, a wedding every caterer in the modern world would have poked their own eyes out for a piece of. And it was hers.

She was just deciding what to watch on TV when her mobile beeped as a text message came through.

Wish I was there Q x

George looked at the words and suddenly the event that was going to turn her business into an international success diminished dramatically in her mind. She wished he was there too. She wished she could put her arms around him, strip him of his clothes and lose herself in him. He seemed to instinctively know what she wanted every time they were together.

She picked up her phone and began to type a message back.

Im catering ur wedding

She put the phone back on the table and ate another mouthful of food. She hadn't told him yet. She wondered how he would feel. Perhaps he would persuade Taylor that her food wasn't that great, say he had tasted it for four nights, it sucked and she should consider another catering company.

The phone beeped again and she picked it up.

I know cant wait to show u the infinity pool x

George looked at the text and took a deep breath. Nothing seemed to faze him. He took everything in his stride, he didn't worry about anything. She was like that once. She missed being like that. But she was responsible now; she had a business and a professional reputation to protect. She had to think twice about what she did. Didn't she?

The phone beeped again.

Want to c u

George let out another sigh and hastily text a reply.

Ur in Manchester

Within seconds it beeped again.

Guess again

George looked at the text and was about to reply when her phone made a loud, determined beeping noise and the battery died.

'Oh shit! Bugger! Where's the charger? Damn it!' she exclaimed, vaulting from her seat and hurrying into the kitchen.

She tried to bring the phone to life again, holding down the power button and willing it to be resuscitated.

She opened drawers in search of her charger, dropping things on the floor, cutlery and catering implements knocking her knuckles as she searched through the contents.

This was one of the craziest things he'd ever done. Taylor was there, everyone was there and he wasn't. He had escaped, paid off the people that needed to be paid off, because of her. Because what he felt for her wasn't diminishing now he hadn't seen her for twenty four hours, it was growing. He couldn't get her out of his mind. He couldn't settle, he felt uncomfortable with the amount of miles between them. He didn't want to give her up, he couldn't and he wouldn't.

Suddenly there was a loud thumping on the back door that jolted her, making her drop a pair of oven gloves and a cheese grater.

'Who is it?' she called, approaching the door with caution.

'Who d'you think?' Quinn's voice called back.

She couldn't believe it. This couldn't be happening. He couldn't be here! He wasn't supposed to be here, he was supposed to be at the other end of the country! She fumbled with the lock then hurriedly threw the door open.

'I don't believe you're here! How? Why?' George questioned all at once, her hands at her mouth in shock.

'How? Helicopter. Why? Because I couldn't stay away,' Quinn informed her.

He stepped onto the threshold of the door and looked at her, as if he was drinking her in with every glance. His breathing was already erratic, as he moved inside.

'I can't believe you're here,' George spoke, touching his face to check he was real.

'You'll have to thank the woman at number one in the morning. You didn't reply to my last message so I had to knock on a few doors to ask where you live. Remembered Raleigh Crescent, didn't know the number.'

'Oh God! You didn't!' George exclaimed.

'I had to see you. So, how pleased are you to see me?' Quinn enquired, pulling at her t-shirt and ripping it over her head in one quick motion, leaving her in just her bra.

'On a scale of one to ten?' George asked as he bent to deliver kisses to her neck.

'Uh huh.'

'About two hundred and forty five,' George responded, taking off his baseball cap and pushing him up against the table.

He turned her around, until she was backed up against it, and then he lifted her up and pushed her down on it, scattering the pans and containers on the floor.

He kissed her mouth and brushed her hair off her face as they lay in bed together.

'I still can't believe you're here, you only left this morning,' George said, running her hand over his shoulder.

'You knew I wanted you to come with me. If you wouldn't come to me I figured I'd just have to come to you,' Quinn answered.

'But where do people think you are?'

Quinn shrugged and moved off her, putting his arms around her and holding her close to him. She took hold of his hands and held them in hers.

'I don't care where they think I am,' he responded.

'But what about Taylor?'

'I don't want to talk about her. I want to talk about you,' Quinn answered.

'We talked about me last night. Why don't we talk about you?' George suggested.

'There's nothing to tell. I'm a thirty-something musician, you know that, that's it,' Quinn told her.

'Why don't you like talking about yourself?' George asked.

'Because there's nothing to talk about,' Quinn replied.

'Now that makes me think you're hiding lots of dark secrets,' George said with a smile.

'I wish,' Quinn responded with a sigh.

'What?'

'Nothing.'

'Quinn.'

'Look, I'm messed up George, that's all,' Quinn answered, sitting up and running his hand over his hair.

'I can't get it if you don't tell me,' George said.

'Sometimes it's best not to understand things, trust me,' Quinn spoke.

She didn't reply but rested her head on his chest.

She didn't want to push him. She enjoyed being with him, she knew their time together had a short shelf life and she didn't want to spend it fighting. Not when they could be doing so many other fantastic things.

'What's important is the here and now, the past's yesterday. It's gone,' Quinn told her.

'If only it were that easy,' George replied.

'It is that easy. Come here, let me show you,' Quinn said, pulling George on top of him.

George smiled down at him, letting him cup her breasts with his hands.

'Wanna hear something funny? Now this will get you. The other night I had this dream. You were dressed up in this school uniform, you had long pink hair and we were together at this God awful gig,' Quinn told her.

'That all sounds a bit kinky to me,' George replied, kissing his lips.

'Mmm, that's what I thought. In fact I didn't want to wake up.'

'I did dye my hair strange colours, a very long time ago now though,' George answered with a laugh.

'It was a good look; maybe you should try it again.'

'And the school uniform?'

'You still got it?'

The tap in the bathroom sink leaked and he wanted to get it repaired for her. What the Hell! He looked at himself in the mirror above the sink and let out a heavy sigh. What was he going to do? Tonight she'd whispered his name in his ear, kissed him so tenderly he thought he was going to lose it there and then. He wanted to share stuff with her. He wanted to open up to her but he was scared. He was scared, if he did, there was no going back.

Eighteen

He left just before 6.00am to meet his helicopter back to Manchester at the local recreation ground. The pilot had been paid well over the going rate to ensure his privacy, so there was minimal danger of their liaison being discovered. How long that situation would last depended on the intelligence and perceptiveness of the paparazzi. During the course of the short flight he also had to concoct a reasonable explanation for his night's absence. Something that would pass muster with Taylor and Roger.

He had kissed George goodbye in the kitchen and held onto her for so long she thought he might not manage to let her go at all. What concerned her most of all, was that she hadn't wanted to let go either.

Now it was almost 9.00am, she had showered and dressed and was busy rewashing all the pots and pans they had knocked onto the kitchen floor in their desperation to relieve each other of their clothes.

'Morning! Mother's having a bad hair day. Curling tongs blew up,' Marisa greeted as she and Helen entered through the back door.

'Thank you Marisa. Can't keep anything quiet around here can I? I mean as if George is interested in my hair anyway! Most of the time it's covered in a catering cap,' Helen reminded as she took off her coat.

'Your hair looks fine,' George insisted.

'No it doesn't. It's like all frizzy and flyaway, more so than usual...' Marisa began, pointing out sections of her mother's hair she disapproved of.

'Marisa, why don't you make some coffee,' George suggested.

'Can I put the radio on? Don't want any more of that hard rock nonsense on today,' Marisa spoke.

'Put on whatever you want,' George said.

She smiled at Helen and handed her an envelope.

'Here you go. There's that bonus for you and Marisa for all the work you did on the Hexagon after-show parties,' George said.

'Oh George, are you sure? You paid us overtime and we weren't expecting...'

'Take the money, treat yourselves, buy some more driving lessons. I'm going to look at vans tomorrow. It's about time Finger Food had something a little less cramped,' George said, remembering her night not sleeping in the back of the van.

'Er, am I being like totally thick here? Where's the bread?' Marisa asked, looking around the kitchen.

'Oh shit! Shit! The bread! Damn it!' George exclaimed in horror.

'What's happened?' Helen asked as George dashed to the telephone.

'I was supposed to find a new supplier, but what with Taylor Ferraro ringing up, I completely forgot about it,' George said, picking up a telephone directory.

'A new supplier? What happened to Simon? He's quite hot he is,' Marisa spoke.

'He doesn't want the job any more,' George replied.

'Why not?' Marisa questioned.

'Have you made that coffee yet Marisa?' Helen asked, trying to distract her attention.

'Just doing it. Think you need to get some dye on your hair too Mother, there's a few grey ones at the back,' Marisa informed.

'D'you think they'll notice?' George asked as she scrutinised the members of the Twitchers Association who had sat down to eat.

It was the afternoon and because she had forgotten Simon's resignation as bread supplier, she had been forced to buy supermarket bread to make the event's sandwiches.

'They've just sat through an hour and a half of slides on wetland species, I could eat mouldy bread right now. Supermarket's finest would seem positively luxurious,' Helen responded.

'I hate this. I hate serving up stuff I'm not a hundred percent confident with,' George replied, looking at a large man who had filled his plate with sandwiches, but was yet to eat any of them.

'It can't be helped. The important thing is we got all the bread and you got a reasonable deal with the other bakery to start supplying us from tomorrow,' Helen reminded.

'Yeah, I know. I feel bad about Simon though.'

'What happened?'

'He wouldn't take no for an answer,' George explained.

'Oh,' Helen responded.

'It's probably for the best,' George said as the large man bit into his first sandwich.

Her phone beeped. She got it out of her pocket and looked at the text.

Had a great time playing poker last night Taylor thinks i have gambling addiction Q x

161

George smiled to herself. He was so bad.

'Everything OK?' Helen asked.

'Yeah, fine,' George said, hiding her phone back in her pocket.

'You know George, if there is ever anything you need to talk about, you know you can talk to me don't you? I mean about anything that might be bothering you, you know, no matter what it is,' Helen told her.

'Yeah, I know, thanks. But everything's fine at the moment, apart from the dodgy bread,' George replied.

'Nice sandwiches love, particularly the prawn,' the Twitchers Association president informed as he appeared behind George and Helen.

'Oh, thank you,' George replied.

'Tea anyone?' Marisa enquired as she appeared from the kitchen with cups and saucers.

'Hey Adam,' George greeted that evening when she had sat down in front of *Masterchef* with a bowl of nachos.

'Hey, you OK?'

'Fine, how are you? All recovered from the accident?'

'Yeah, I was fine really, only in hospital as a precaution and I've got a nice new Volkswagen Golf now. Not brand new, you know, but new to me. Mum and Dad paid.'

'That's good.'

'So how are things with you and Mum?' he asked randomly.

She almost choked on the nacho that was in her mouth. Where had that come from?

'What d'you mean? We're fine. You know what she's like. She loves to boss me about and you know, I think I'm getting too old for that now.'

'Dad says you don't phone them much any more,' Adam continued.

'I'm busy aren't I? I barely have a minute to breathe most days and you know, she's busy too and Dad - he's - well, he's busy watching his golf and I don't know - growing tomato plants,' George spoke.

'You know about Mum and the hospital though yeah?'

His question jolted her and she had to put the bowl of nachos on the coffee table. Her mother was notorious for never being ill. She couldn't even remember her ever having more than a cold and even then it was done and dusted in no more than a few days.

'George? Are you still there?'

'Yeah I'm still here. No, I don't know about that. What is it? Arthritis of the jaw or something?' George asked, using humour to quell her concern.

'George, she's got cancer. She's having her breast removed next week.'

She couldn't hide the sharp intake of breath that filled her lungs now and she knew it would make Adam realise she had no idea about any of it.

'I can't believe she hasn't told you! What's happening to this family? Does no one even talk to each other these days? Man!' Adam exclaimed.

George couldn't speak, there was a huge boulder sat in her throat that was threatening to force tears into her eyes and she couldn't let it. She wouldn't let it.

'I knew she hadn't told you, because I figured you would've called me to talk, or you would have said something when I came down. But I just thought we were doing the whole Fraser 'putting on a brave face' thing we all do,' Adam continued.

'How long has she known?' George asked, forcing herself to speak.

'She told me a week or so ago. They were looking at options, she had a biopsy and decided to have a mastectomy,' Adam continued.

'So it's serious,' George said stupidly.

She couldn't think straight. She couldn't take all this in, in five minutes. Adam had been given time to digest things and now she had two seconds to react properly.

'It's cancer, it's always serious,' Adam said.

'Yeah, of course it is. Well, listen, I don't want you to worry, I mean she's as tough as undercooked braising steak isn't she? She's never ill. She'll have the op and she'll be back to normal as soon as she's recovered. Chairing the Bingo Society, or whatever it is she does these days,' George spoke, trying to be positive.

That's what people did didn't they? Bucked each other up, told each other it was a minor blip on life's path and everything would be back to normal as soon as. They said all this regardless of whether they really believed it.

'I don't think it's that clear cut but...'

'Of course it is! They deal with these sorts of things all the time nowadays don't they? I've seen it on the TV, it's straightforward, nothing out of the ordinary,' George carried on.

'Will you go round there and see her?' Adam asked.

The tone of his request tugged at her. This was someone asking from the bottom of their heart. Despite her and her mother's differences, Adam loved her and she had to remember that.

'Of course I will,' George replied.

'I mean properly go round there. For more than five minutes. Stay for Sunday dinner or something,' Adam carried on.

'Well...'

'Please George, for me. I hate it when you two are fighting,' Adam spoke.

'I know, but...'
'Please George.'
How could she refuse?

Nineteen

'We're low on tomatoes and olives and that funny Italian ham stuff and feta cheese and...' Marisa began as she looked through the fridge.

It was a few days after the Twitchers Association sandwiches and the new bread supplier was proving reliable and reasonably priced. The guy who delivered the bread was called Robert and he was at least sixty. George was confident he wouldn't try to hit on her.

'Basically everything then. I'll check the bookings, see what we need for those and get down the cash and carry,' George told Marisa.

George's phone beeped and Marisa raised her eyebrows.

'Your phone's never gone off this much ever. It's like going off every ten minutes,' Marisa exclaimed.

George picked it up and looked at it.

Need 2 c u recreation ground ten minutes Q x

George deleted the message and looked up at the clock.

'Why did you look at the clock?' Marisa enquired.

'To see what time it is,' George replied, putting her coat on.

'Are you going to the cash and carry now?' Marisa asked as George put her phone in her coat pocket.

'No, I er, think we're out of milk for coffee. I'll just pop out and get some,' George said, going to the door and letting herself out.

'Milk? Well there was like loads of milk this morning - George, there's almost six pints here,' Marisa called, taking a large carton out of the fridge.

Helen was out on a driving lesson in the brand new van, as her car was in the garage. George had no choice but to walk. It was almost ten minutes to the recreation ground and it was raining again.

Quinn had text her intermittently since his late night visit from Manchester, but her mind had been occupied with concern for her mother. Adam had text her too, most days, inquiring when she was going home for a roast dinner. She hadn't even picked up the phone to her parents. She didn't know how to. What did you say to someone who had disliked you intensely for so many years? And what did you say to that person now you knew they had a life-threatening condition? What did you say if that person was also your mother? She had made a promise to Adam, but she didn't really know if she was going to be able to keep it.

She pulled the hood of her coat up over her head and hurried down the street, periodically looking at her watch.

She got to the recreation ground and stood next to the pavilion. There were a gang of teenagers on mountain bikes, trying to bunny hop over the small metal fence, there were toddlers and their mothers on the swings and there was a group of children playing football on the pitch despite the drizzle. Ordinary people going about their ordinary lives, while she waited for goodness knows what to happen in hers.

She heard the helicopter before she saw it. It appeared out of the clouds and began to slowly descend onto the football pitch. All the children were looking up in amazement at the machine coming down onto the grass. In the end, they fled further down the field to avoid getting blown over by the wind it was creating.

It landed and George hurried over to it, ducking her head to try and avoid the draft from the rotor blades. The door opened and Quinn appeared.

'Hop in,' he urged, holding out his hand to her.

'Where are we going?' George yelled over the noise.

'Up there,' Quinn said, pointing to the sky.

He pulled her up into the aircraft and, as rapidly as it set down, the helicopter began to rise again. The children pointed and shouted, trying to see who it was, and George desperately looked around for a seat belt.

'You'll have to put these on!' Quinn yelled, passing her a set of 1980s style headphones.

She put them over her ears and moved the mouthpiece to her lips.

'You're lucky I'm here on time, I had to walk,' she informed.

'Sorry. I had a window of opportunity, I had to take it,' Quinn replied.

'I haven't heard from you for a few days. Is my appeal wearing off?' George asked as light-heartedly as possible.

'No, of course not. Roger flew in. He's been with me twenty four seven, literally. I did try and message you from the bathroom last night but, no signal,' Quinn said with a smile.

'So...'

'So I'm flying back to the States today. I have to be at the airport in two hours actually,' Quinn explained.

'Oh,' George answered.

'And that's where I'll be until the wedding.'

'Sure.'

'And not even I can conjure up a helicopter that can cross the Atlantic in double-quick time every time I need to see you,' Quinn told her.

'Are you sure?' George asked with a laugh.

'Hey, don't think I haven't looked into it,' Quinn said.

George looked at him and he took hold of her hands.

'God what am I doing?' he asked, squeezing her hands tightly.

'Travelling down from the other end of the UK in a helicopter? Yep, I have to admit I thought it was pretty over the top the first time,' George joked.

'No, leaving you,' Quinn responded, looking at George, a weight of emotion in his expression.

'Quinn, you have to go. You and me, we're a fantasy. A really good fantasy but a fantasy all the same,' George told him.

'Is that what you really feel?'

'That's how it is,' George said hurriedly.

'Is it?'

'It can't be anything else.'

'What if it could?'

'What d'you mean?'

'I don't know,' Quinn said, letting out a frustrated sigh.

'I can't help you unless you tell me,' George reminded him.

'I can't tell you unless you help me,' Quinn told her, fixing her with his blue eyes.

'What d'you want me to do?' George asked.

'Stop me getting married,' Quinn replied.

George looked at him, gathering in everything his face was telling her with its expression. She wanted to say the right thing, but she didn't even know what that was.

'I can't do that. Only you can do that, if it really isn't what you want,' she finally spoke.

'Of course it isn't what I want! Would you want to be married to her? Would you want to hear about handbags and haute couture and who's wearing what at the latest celebrity hangout?' Quinn snapped angrily.

'She must love you,' George replied.

'She loves the brand we are. Did you know, just after the wedding we're releasing his and hers fragrances called 'Ever After'?' Quinn asked.

'That sounds terrible. What does it smell like?'

'I've no idea,' Quinn answered, letting go of her hand and putting one hand to his forehead.

'Why don't you tell her the truth? Tell her you aren't ready for marriage. She might surprise you and understand,' George suggested hopefully.

'You've met her. She wouldn't understand and Roger, well he certainly wouldn't understand,' Quinn told her.

'Then...'

'I guess all I can do is pray for a plague of locusts or a tsunami to wipe out the whole of La Manga,' Quinn said, putting a hopeful smile on his face.

'That's a bit drastic.'

'Drastic times call for drastic measures.'

George let out a sigh.

'Are you OK? There's something on your mind other than table settings isn't there?' Quinn queried.

'No, not really. I've just got some stuff going on right now, that's all,' George began.

'What stuff?' Quinn asked, looking at her with concern.

'It's just family stuff, I'm probably going to be tied up for the next few weeks. So maybe space between us is a good thing,' George suggested.

'You think?'

'Yes.'

'I don't.'

Quinn smothered her mouth with his, kissing her passionately and holding onto her as the helicopter carried on circling the playing field.

'I want to help, with this family stuff. What is it?' Quinn spoke, searching for the answer in her eyes.

George shook her head, unable to find the words.

'George, come on, tell me,' Quinn urged.

'It's fine - it's just - my mother's ill and she needs an operation and...' George began.

She stopped talking to gulp in a breath and it was then she realised she was crying. Her shoulders were shaking with sobs and tears were spilling from her eyes like someone had turned on a fire hydrant.

'Hey, George, tell me what's going on here. Let me in,' Quinn begged as he wrapped her in his embrace and tried to soften her anguish.

George shook her head. She couldn't tell him, there wasn't enough time to even get started on everything she needed to say and she wasn't certain he was the first person who should hear it.

'I don't want to leave you like this,' Quinn said, stroking her hair away from her face and wiping her tears from her cheeks with his thumbs.

'Go. You have to get your flight. I'm fine,' George insisted, sniffing the tears away as best she could.

'I know you're not.'

'Go on. Get out of here,' George ordered, restoring some of her composure.

'I'll call you,' Quinn said as he indicated to the pilot to take the helicopter back down.

'It doesn't matter, if you can't. I mean you'll be having suit fittings and choosing flowers and stuff and believe me I've catered enough weddings to know exactly how long all that takes,' George said using the sleeve of her top to wipe her face.

'Don't,' Quinn said.

'It's going to happen unless you do something about it. I'm submitting the ingredients list at the end of the week,' George told him.

'At least the food will be awesome,' he answered solemnly.

The helicopter landed and Quinn took hold of her hand and placed it on his chest.

'I am yours George, no matter what you think. I'm yours in here,' he said, looking at her sincerely.

George swallowed, took his hand and placed it over her heart.

'I wish you were,' she replied sadly, taking off the headphones.

She kissed his mouth, touching his cheek with her hand and then she pulled the door of the chopper open and jumped down.

She put her hood over her head and hurried back towards the road, trying to avoid the uneven clumps in the turf. With every step, she tried to forget that every rotation of the helicopter's blades was taking him further away from her. Right now, she hated herself. She had broken down, she had sobbed over him, about her mother, over everything that had happened in her past. She hadn't shed a tear since Paul left, until today. She was usually stronger than that and she had to be. It was the only way she survived.

He watched her from the helicopter for as long as he could. She'd been so vulnerable. It had felt like he was holding her heart in his hands and throwing it back at her. He was an idiot. What was he doing? He was making things worse for everyone. He was defying Roger, cheating on Taylor and screwing George up at the same time. But what else could he do? He was f**ked no matter what he did.

Twenty

When she arrived at the front door, Lesley was chewing a marigold and swishing her tail suspiciously. She hated the damn cat. She had always hated it. It moulted, it permanently had fleas and there was the farting, that a specialised diet and liquid indigestion sachets couldn't cure. It looked up at George as she rang the bell and burped. Now it reminded her of Belch.

The 'William Tell Overture' chimed and it was a minute before her dad answered the door.

'Hello Georgina, come along in. Your mother's in the kitchen. I've just got to cast a quick eye over the golf. Justin Rose is progressing famously,' Brian said, disappearing back into the lounge and passing George the lavender room spray.

Right on cue, Lesley lifted her tail and the hallway filled up with putrid smog that threatened to engulf anything in its path. She sprayed the air freshener and made her way into the kitchen.

Heather was stood at the cooker, apron tied around a floral creation from Country Casuals and hair perfectly in place. Somehow though, she looked different. She appeared smaller, thinner, slightly weaker, less of the ogre she had been.

'Hello Mum,' George greeted, bracing herself for the usual lacklustre response.

Heather turned around and faced her daughter. At the sight of her expression, George almost crumbled.

Her mother's eyes were full of tears and she was wringing her hands together, like she didn't know what to do with them. This was completely out of character. Her mother was always so composed, so in charge and organised. She didn't do public displays of anything, apart from flower arranging.

'George, I'm so sorry,' she blurted out, bursting into tears.

George couldn't move. She knew she should. She knew she should put her arms around her mother, now in her hour of need. But the emotion wouldn't come. She was stuck fast to the spot, like someone had super-glued her boots to the floor.

'Do you need any help with dinner?' George asked.

She knew it was the most inappropriate thing to say, but she didn't know what else would cut it. What was appropriate at a time like this? Perhaps 'There, there, that's OK, I forgive you for making my life a misery' should have been the words spilling forth, but that was surely hypocritical. She didn't forgive her, not now when she was sick, not ever.

'I've been too hard on you, I know that now. I should have protected you more. I should have listened to you more. I should have helped you, not abandoned you,' Heather spoke through her sobs.

She was looking her age now. Was that the cancer? Sucking the cells of youth out of her and replacing them with older, weaker, disease-ridden ones? She didn't resemble a tyrant now, but that's what she was and always had been. Nothing she could say now could change that.

'I'm here because Adam asked me to come,' George said, picking up a sachet of bread sauce from the table.

174

'Did he tell you? About the lump?' Heather wanted to know as she dabbed at her eyes with a piece of kitchen roll.

'Yes he did. The operation's soon isn't it?'

'Tuesday.'

'I'm sure everything will be fine. I mean they deal with this sort of thing all the time now don't they?' George said, repeating the mantra she had said to Adam over and over since she discovered the diagnosis.

'Oh yes, they do. Mavis at the Choral Society had a breast removed last year and she kept her hair and everything,' Heather remarked.

'I don't know what you want me to say,' George said awkwardly.

'I don't want you to say anything George; I want you to sit down. I'll drag your father away from that television and the three of us are going to enjoy a lovely roast dinner, just like we used to,' Heather told her.

'With bread sauce?' George queried, looking at the packet in her hands.

'I know it's your favourite,' Heather said.

'Then let's make it from scratch, not use this packet stuff Dad always burns,' George suggested stiffly.

'Oh that would be lovely,' Heather agreed.

'That was superb love; I love a bit of turkey. I mean, most people say it should just be for Christmas, but I'm in the all year round club,' Brian spoke after the three of them had eaten dinner.

'It was chicken Brian,' Heather stated, sucking in her irritation as best she could.

'It wasn't was it? Well, I've always loved chicken. Used to buy one of those ready cooked ones for my lunch sometimes. It stunk the office out though, Miriam didn't like it,' Brian remarked.

'Miriam didn't like much if I remember rightly. Dogs – cats - pork pies – buskers – lifts - stepping on paving slabs...' Heather began.

'She had lots of insecurities,' Brian admitted.

'I'll make a start on the washing up,' George offered, standing up.

'No, don't do that. I'll do it later,' Heather said abruptly.

'Right then - I'd better catch up with the tournament. Let this chicken feast go down before pudding,' Brian said, getting up from the table and scurrying towards the door to the lounge.

'Sit down George, please,' Heather told her.

Now she really wanted to go home. Her mother seemed to be in the mood for some sort of reconciliation and she didn't want to have to react to that.

'Mum, I'm going to Spain in a few weeks. Perhaps it might be a good idea if you asked Aunty Linda to come and stay with you for a bit,' George suggested.

'I know all about it. Adam told me. You're catering the wedding of his favourite musician. It's apparently going to be the event of the decade,' Heather said.

'Well, I wouldn't go quite that far but...'

'It's a fantastic opportunity for your business. You should be very proud. I am,' Heather admitted her eyes meeting with George's.

'You're proud?' George said, checking she had heard right.

'Of course I am George. You're my daughter.'

'But I let you down, I disobeyed you and I got pregnant.'

'I know.'

'I got drunk and I started fights and I brought the police to your door,' George continued.

176

'I know and Mrs Jessop from number eighteen always finds some way to bring all that back up when we get chatting over her carnations.'

'You hated me,' George said.

'No I didn't. I hated myself for making you like that.'

'What?'

'Because that's exactly what I was like when I was your age Georgina. It was history repeating itself and I didn't want that to happen,' Heather blurted out.

Her confession made George retake her seat with a bump.

'We're not so dissimilar you and I. Of course it was Elvis in my day, not Billy Idol, but I was young once and keen to experiment with boys,' Heather began.

'Mum I don't know why you're telling me this now,' George said, toying with her fork.

'I'm telling you now, because I don't want to see out my days and leave you thinking I don't care. I do care, but I'm stubborn and proud, just like you. And as the years went by and we drifted further and further apart it was harder to get any sort of relationship back, whilst still saving face. I'm not so concerned with my face these days. Getting diagnosed with cancer makes you put things into perspective,' Heather continued.

'I don't understand,' George said.

'I had a boyfriend my parents didn't like. He was called Teddy. He had a quiff like Bobby Darin and he rode a moped. We used to go to all the dances, stay out past midnight, drink too much and because he was older than me, my parents put their foot down, forbid me from seeing him, just like I did with what's his name...'

'Paul,' George filled in.

'Yes, Paul. Well, to cut a long story short, I ended up in the family way.'

George's hand went to her mouth at this revelation. All the grief her mother had given her when

177

she had been in the same situation came back to her now. She'd called her a 'harlot' back then, 'cheap' and 'easy'. Her expression had been hard as rocks, her voice venomous, a tirade of poisonous words coming thick and fast.

And then George's eyes widened further still. What exactly was she telling her?

'Not me?! You're not telling me this baby was me! That Dad isn't...' George exclaimed her heart palpitating.

'No. No, it wasn't you. You know you have your father's eyes. Those soft, brown, caramel coloured eyes, with eyelashes to die for. Don't tell him I said that,' Heather said, smiling at her.

'Then if you knew what I was going through, why did you react the way you did? Why have you been pushing me away all this time?'

'Because I wanted the best for you and I knew you would never do what I did. I aborted my baby, I wasn't given a choice and I didn't have the relationship with Teddy that you had with Paul. When I told Teddy about the pregnancy he shrugged his shoulders. Shrugged his shoulders George! Well, I fell out of love with him pretty quickly after that, but it wasn't like that with you was it? You really loved Paul didn't you?'

George nodded her head, memories of him seeping into her mind.

'But despite what you felt for him, he'd left and I couldn't let a teenage pregnancy ruin your future like it almost ruined mine. I wanted more for you than that, so much more, and look at you now,' Heather spoke proudly.

'You should have tried to understand, when Paul left I had no one,' George told her.

'I did understand. In my own controlling and overbearing way. That's why I did what I did with the baby,' Heather said.

'I don't want to talk about the baby,' George said immediately her hand reaching for the chain around her neck and the ring that hung there.

'I know I didn't handle things as well as I should have, but I still think we did the right thing,' Heather continued.

'I've got to go, I've got some prep to do for tomorrow's events,' George said hurriedly standing up and pushing back her chair.

'George, sometimes we have to talk about difficult things no matter how uncomfortable they are. Like the fact that I might die from this disease,' Heather said bluntly.

'Mother you won't die. You're never ill. Our medicine cupboard only ever comprised Andrews Liver Salts and Vicks Vaporub,' George reminded her.

'I want to put things right just in case - with the baby,' Heather told her seriously.

'No,' George said.

'I think we need to.'

'I said no. I can't do this now. I've got to go. I'll phone you, at the hospital. It will all be fine, you'll see,' George said, hurriedly picking up her bag and heading for the door.

'George...' Heather called after her.

'Bye Dad,' George offered into the lounge as she hurried past.

'Oh bye love. Woods was just under par on that last hole.'

'I read about it. It was all over the papers. See you.'

Twenty One

He wanted to call her. He wanted to hear her voice, even if it was just for a second. Since he'd got back to LA he'd barely been alone for a minute. It seemed like he was even being accompanied to the bathroom. He could hardly breathe, let alone get time to speak to someone he shouldn't be speaking to. He ached for her, actually ached inside. He didn't even have a photograph of her. He had never wanted someone so badly and here he was, stood in a flower shop while Taylor asked his advice on which shade of pink he wanted for the bouquets. F**k this situation!

'So what do you think? For the wedding? The lilac maxi dress or the floral mini dress?' Marisa asked, holding both items of clothing up against herself.

George, Marisa and Helen were in George's living room, about to have an Indian takeaway. It was to celebrate an excellent afternoon's work at Bowater Manor where they'd been catering for a charity fashion show. It was also the night before their flight to Spain for the wedding preparations. It was an early morning departure and the women, along with Adam, were staying over.

Heather's operation had gone well. Her left breast had been removed and she was at home recovering and

180

waiting for the next tranche of treatment. George had visited a couple of times, brought her chocolates, told her about the intricacies of the wedding menu and refused to talk about the baby. She was saying anything about everything, just to stop her from having a long enough pause to even mention the baby.

She hadn't heard from Quinn at all since she'd left him in the helicopter. She wasn't surprised, but she was a little disappointed. She could have done with a distraction, something to take her mind off things for a while. She knew it needed to end, especially now the wedding was imminent, but she wished they'd had longer, been able to share some real time together, instead of rushed moments in a window of opportunity.

But in reality it had been a hot, urgent, tantalising affair that would never have lasted. Men like Quinn lived fast, hectic lives, travelling across the globe from event to event; she wouldn't have been enough for him. Before too long he would have got bored with her and moved on. Perhaps that was what he had done already.

'Marisa, you'll be wearing your white shirt and black skirt for serving as soon as the reception starts,' Helen reminded her.

'Yeah, like I know that, but come on! Half the world's press are going to be there, I can't be seen in the wedding pictures wearing a white shirt and a black skirt. I will be a lot of things, but I will not be monotone,' Marisa said horrified by the thought.

'You mean monochrome,' George told her.

'I mean like boring and ancient.'

'Marisa, waitresses are expected to wear black and white outfits, not maxi dresses or floral minis,' George said.

'Yeah but, just say I wasn't waitressing or catering or anything, just a guest. Which one?' Marisa wanted to know.

'The maxi dress,' George and Helen said at the same time.

'God you are both like *sooo* predictable,' Marisa complained sulkily.

There was a tap on the back door and George hurried to answer it.

'That'll be Adam with the food. Can you get some plates out guys?' she called, striding down the hall.

She opened the door and greeted Adam with four bags of takeaway food.

'Hey that van you've got now is awesome. I got it doing eighty, without breaking a sweat, down the high street,' Adam said with a smile, taking off his beanie hat as he entered the house.

'You better not have!' George exclaimed as she took the bags from him.

'He better not have what?' Marisa wanted to know as she came into the room.

'He's trying to break the sound barrier with my new van,' George complained.

'Isn't it cool? Sometimes when we're at the traffic lights I think she's stalled it the engine's that quiet. Hey, I hope you remembered to tell them no tomatoes in mine, because I'll be sick if I like even have them anywhere near my tongue,' Marisa told Adam.

'I remembered everything, I think. You did want a vindaloo didn't you Marisa?' Adam teased.

'You have got to be joking? You are joking aren't you? If you've got me a vindaloo I will like kill you. I am well starving,' Marisa exclaimed.

Adam laughed and Marisa hurriedly whipped him in the chest with a tea towel.

'So gullible,' he joked, taking a carton from George and helping to dish up the food.

'And you're full of it,' Marisa retorted.

'Come on you two. I'm not having a week of you sniping at each other. This is a big occasion we're catering for,' Helen reminded them.

'Yeah it's like the most awesome event of the entire year and we're going to be there, centre stage,' Marisa said.

'Not centre stage, in the background working hard,' George told her.

'Well, you two can be wallflowers if you like, but a wallflower I am not,' Marisa replied, licking the fork she was holding.

'Is Geraint OK about you going away for a week?' George asked Helen, referring to her husband.

'Yes fine. I stocked up the cupboards with meals for one and takeaway menus and he has the car to himself. He'll be more than happy. I totally expect him to have RSI in his remote control hand by the time we get back,' Helen told her with a chuckle.

'Well I'm really grateful to have you all coming over with me,' George spoke to the group.

'Where else would we be if we weren't with you at the event of the decade?' Adam asked, grinning at Marisa.

'It *sooo* is,' Marisa insisted.

'I know. But I appreciate your help and I know with the twenty or so staff we have to boss about and the state of the art catering wagon, the thought of which is really freaking me out, we're going to make the sort of culinary impression the world has been waiting for,' George told them.

'Here here,' Helen said, raising a poppadom in the air.

'God, let's go and eat before she makes any more speeches,' Adam said, picking up some plates.

'I am so going to get a tan. I can't wait,' Marisa spoke.

'You will not be getting a tan. You have dark hair and fair skin, it's factor thirty for you and I'll apply it myself if I have to,' Helen warned her.

'Jesus! You see what I have to put up with? Factor thirty; I'll come home whiter than I went!' Marisa wailed as they walked back into the living room.

'How's your mum?' Helen asked George quietly.

'She's doing OK thanks,' George replied, spooning rice onto her plate.

'My offer's still there you know, if you ever need to talk,' Helen said sincerely.

'Thanks.'

'I actually don't think they even make factor thirty any more. I'm sure I read about it in *Star Life*,' Marisa moaned.

'So what is a catering wagon exactly?' Helen enquired the next morning.

They had finally boarded the plane to Spain, after a short delay due to a 'technical issue'. Marisa had suggested rather too loudly that perhaps they had found a suspicious looking rucksack hidden under a seat and Helen had to rapidly convince the other passengers that she didn't travel often and she watched too many episodes of *Spooks*.

'I have no idea but, according to Pixie, it has about ten ovens and hobs and everything a mobile catering unit requires. Apparently it's going to be parked behind Channel Nine's television studio,' George informed, checking her boarding card and moving into a seat by the window.

'Now how glamorous does that sound? Television studio!' Marisa said still wearing the enormous sunglasses she had bought in Duty Free.

She squeezed in next to George and hit her nose on the back of the seat in front of her. Helen sat down next to her and Adam took a seat across the aisle.

George fastened her seat belt and leaned forward to smile at Adam. He smiled back and picked up the in-flight magazine. He looked at the cover and held it up for George to see. Before she had a chance to look, Marisa let out a squeal of delight and thrust the magazine into George's face.

'Look! It's Quinn! On the front cover! How like ironic is that?!' Marisa exclaimed.

George looked at the front cover. It was Quinn, dressed in a half done up white dress shirt, bow tie undone and dangling from his collar, chest exposed, violin in his hand, eyes dazzlingly blue.

She swallowed, a pang of longing clogging her chest. She needed to get him out of her system. Perhaps seeing Taylor in her wedding dress would finally do that.

'I'm starving. When do they start coming round with the food?' Marisa wanted to know.

'We usually have to be in the air first,' George told her, looking out of the window at the tarmac and the familiar green of the English countryside.

The captain introduced himself. Andrew Weeks with a clipped Home Counties accent that made him sound like he had studied aviation at Eton. George was reassured by the calm manner and air of authority in his tone and the fact he sounded educated. If the plane went into a nosedive because an engineer had left his mug of tea on the wing, Andrew Weeks sounded like the man to handle the situation.

The stewards and stewardesses performed their life saving/emergency exits demonstration, and before too long, they were at the end of the runway preparing to be given clearance to take off.

'Oh. My. God, I like hate it when the engines rev like that. Arrrrrrrrgh!' Marisa screamed out loud as the plane began to race down the runway to get up to speed.

'Sshh, you're freaking the little kids out,' George said as she gripped hold of the seat arm and braced herself for the take off.

'Argh! Argh! We're going to crash!' Marisa shouted.

Helen put a hand over her daughter's mouth and pushed her head down into her lap. Her cries were now muffled by a leg.

'Is she always like this on flights?' George enquired as the jet left the ground and began its ascent into the clouds.

'We used to go every year to Geraint's cousin's villa in France when Marisa was small. Two trips on a plane with her screaming and being sick and we took the ferry after that,' Helen replied.

'Give her something to suck,' Adam suggested.

'God! Rephrase that please,' George said.

'A sweet,' Adam added.

'Mint Marisa?' George offered, getting the packet of sweets out of her bag.

'Mint,' Marisa growled.

She shook herself free from her mother's hand-hold and sat up, grabbing the sweet and popping it into her mouth in one quick movement.

'It's not natural,' Marisa said, taking a deep breath as she sucked on the sweet.

'What's not natural?' Helen enquired.

'Flying - arrgh!' Marisa screeched as the plane bumped slightly.

'Lucky it's only two hours,' George remarked as Helen held her daughter's hand.

He was going to see her today and he was buzzing. He'd even managed a smile when Taylor talked about seating plans over breakfast. He couldn't give a toss who sat where, he was thinking about George and how much time he could manage to spend with her. God he'd missed her. He hoped she felt the same. He hadn't been able to call but she'd understand. She knew the position he was in. He'd spelt it out enough times. The fact he was stuck somewhere he didn't want to be. She would understand and when they saw each other again, the time apart would be history.

The plane touched down on time, catching up the delay in England, and George was glad to arrive in the airport terminal. Marisa had drunk can after can of Coke on the journey, kept getting up and down for the toilet and gripping her arm whenever they hit the slightest bit of turbulence.

'Oh. My. God, it's like boiling! Did you feel the sun out there?' Marisa questioned as they lined up to go past border control.

'Yeah, it's great. I know what I'm doing as soon as I get to the villa. Trunks on and into the pool,' Adam said happily.

'Well, let's not get carried away. Pixie might have plans for us,' George answered.

Pixie the wedding planner was an organisation obsessive. She had spoken to George almost every day since she was hired. She had checked and rechecked the ingredients and equipment they would require. She had finalised flight times and collection arrangements at least three times and only yesterday she had rung to inform them the flowers for their lapels had changed colour. Now it was coffee coloured roses instead of cream.

'Pixie sounds like a right pain in the arse and she talks like she should have a part in *Dallas*,' Marisa remarked.

'And what would you know about *Dallas*?' Helen wanted to know.

'God Mother, I watch it on Gold! And haven't you heard? It's coming back!' Marisa informed, flicking her hair back and adjusting her sunglasses as she got to the counter.

'Please take sunglasses off,' the passport inspector ordered her.

'Think they're going to be permanently attached to her face for the next week,' Adam commented.

'She's excited. We shouldn't be too hard on her,' George said, getting her passport out of her hand luggage.

'I wasn't – actually I quite like her,' Adam admitted his cheeks blushing slightly.

'Yeah, me too. She's a good kid - oh I see - you mean, you *like* her,' George said, lowering her voice as Helen was called forward.

'Yeah, I think so,' Adam answered.

'Well, aren't there any girls you like at uni? I mean you're in Wales a lot of the time and...' George began.

She wasn't sure she was keen on the idea of them together, as in exchanging saliva and holding hands. She had seen the other people Marisa had linked tongues with and it wasn't pretty.

'Next please,' the passport checker called.

George cursed under her breath, for not dealing with Adam's admission better and stepped forward to show her passport.

'Georgina Mary Fraser,' the Spaniard spoke, his dark eyes looking straight at her.

'Yes,' she replied, wondering why he was looking at her in a really unsettling way.

'You need to come with me,' he spoke, standing up from his chair and opening the door to his booth.

'Er, why exactly? Is there a problem?' George enquired.

'Please, come this way,' he ordered, keeping hold of her passport.

'But, my friends - I need to really stay with them and...' George began, looking behind her at Adam.

'It won't take a moment. This way,' the man spoke, holding his arm out and directing her towards a doorway.

'George? What's going on?' Adam called.

'I won't be a minute, some security procedure I expect. You carry on to arrivals,' George called back.

She saw the look of confusion on Adam's face, but he shuffled forward as a new passport checker entered the booth to continue dealing with the line of arrivals.

'I don't understand what the problem is. Do you need to check my bag? Or is there something wrong with my passport? It was all fine in England and...' George babbled as the customs official opened the door.

The heat hit her as soon as the door swung open and there, stood in front of an open-topped Jeep, was Quinn. He was wearing khaki linen trousers, a white shirt and Havaianas. On his face were Aviator sunglasses.

'*Senor* Blake, *Senora* Fraser,' the Spaniard called to him.

Quinn removed his sunglasses to look at her and he smiled. The smile that made her weak, the smile she hadn't seen for almost a month, the smile she hadn't been able to forget.

'Carlos, *gracias a mi amigo*,' Quinn spoke, saluting the customs official, as he handed back George's passport and retreated inside the terminal building.

George just stared at him. She had a suitcase on the floor next to her and she was standing outside some back exit to the airport that seemed to overlook the hire car sheds.

'Let me take your case,' Quinn said, hurrying forwards and picking it up.

'What are you doing here? Pixie's arranged transport for us to the villa complex,' George spoke.

She had to try and concentrate on the fact she should be angry with him, rather than the fact that he looked really hot in what he was wearing. He shouldn't be here; he should be with his wife-to-be, fanning her with ostrich feathers and feeding her local olives.

'Change of plan, for you anyway,' Quinn said, putting the case in the back of the Jeep and opening the passenger door for her.

'But Adam and the others will be worried. They just saw me escorted from the airport by a scary looking official,' George exclaimed.

'Give Adam a call. Come on, get in,' Quinn urged her.

'And what if I don't?' George asked.

'You'll totally ruin my surprise,' Quinn told her.

She let out a sigh, bothered by the fact she had little choice and by how much she wanted to be with him. As the sun started to scorch the hairs on the back of her neck she hopped up into the passenger seat.

Twenty Two

'So, how was your flight?' Quinn asked as he drove out of the airport.

'What's this? Conversation? You're speaking before you try and kiss me?' George remarked, looking out of the window as orange groves and olive trees flashed by.

Suddenly they were braking, the pads locking together and squealing in despair, as they veered to the edge of the road. He undid his seat belt and grabbed her forcefully, kissing her hungrily on the mouth. He tasted hot and salty and his face was rough with a thin coat of stubble. This was what she had been missing. It was even better than she remembered it.

She looked at him and he smiled at her.

'Feel better about talking now?' he asked.

'Well, I guess,' George replied, trying to get her breath back.

'Look, I know I haven't called, or messaged you, but it wasn't because I didn't want to. You must know that,' he told her.

'It doesn't matter. I didn't expect you to.'

'Why not?'

'Because I'm not going to be the bride to your groom. But, it's fine, it doesn't matter. Let's just get to the villas. I'd quite like to change.'

'We're not going straight to the villas. I've organised lunch,' Quinn told her.

'Oh,' George replied.

'And we're going to have conversation, instead of sex,' Quinn informed her.

'Novel,' George answered.

'Look, I'm serious about you George and I want you to believe that,' Quinn told her, taking hold of her hand and squeezing it gently.

'I'm starving. The meal on the plane wasn't up to much,' George told him, wanting to change the subject.

'Well, I only hope the little place I've booked can live up to your exacting standards,' Quinn said, pulling the car back onto the road.

Within thirty minutes they were driving along the coast and George was enjoying every second of the ride in the Jeep. Her hair was being buffeted by the breeze, the sun was warm on her face and she was enjoying the sights and smells of Spain. The earth was clay brown and rugged, the scenery mountainous with far-reaching views from every angle and her arms were starting to prickle under the intense heat.

Quinn turned off down a narrow road that opened up to reveal a small wooden restaurant. It was set beside the taupe coloured beach and the gentle tumbling waves of the sea.

He parked the car and took his sunglasses off to look at her.

'I've never taken anyone here before. I found this place when I was driving aimlessly around one day, trying to escape from Taylor and a hissy fit about the latest designer dress someone else wore before her. They do the most incredible paella and even better, they have no idea who I am,' Quinn told her with a smile.

'It looks like it's just been washed up by the sea,' George said, looking at the ramshackle building and appreciating all its authenticity.

'Come on, let's go in,' Quinn said, opening the door and getting out.

George opened her door and joined him on the sand. He took hold of her hand and they walked towards the entrance, as if they were a normal couple stopping by for lunch.

'*Buena tarde. Tenemos una tabla reservada para dos, en nombre de* Blake,' Quinn spoke to the grey haired Spanish woman who greeted them at the door.

'*Sí, por supuesto,*' the lady replied.

She smiled at George and led them over to a table by the window with the most amazing view of the ocean.

You couldn't fail to be impressed by the scenery; it was as perfect a beach scene depicted in any holiday brochure. And it was deserted. There wasn't a soul on the sand, just the waves lapping at the shore and the cloudless blue sky above.

Quinn ordered two lagers and reached across the table to hold George's hands.

'I can't believe we're sat here – together. Without having to worry,' he spoke, exhaling as if he had been holding his breath in forever.

'I can't believe how well you speak Spanish. How long have you been able to do that?' George asked, enjoying the feel of his hands in hers.

'I have no idea,' Quinn answered with a laugh.

'But when did you start learning?'

'I really don't know,' Quinn insisted. 'I speak French too, like a native.'

'That's really impressive. I mean I can't speak any languages. I never really studied hard enough and - well I just concentrated on catering really,' George said.

'You could always learn if you wanted. I could teach you,' Quinn offered.

'I wouldn't know where to start,' George insisted, taking a swig of her drink.

'Try "*Soy* George",' Quinn said.

'*Soy* George,' she repeated, flushing with embarrassment.

'There you go, *estupendo*,' Quinn said.

'I'm not very educated,' George admitted.

'Education's overrated. It's all about life experience,' Quinn told her.

'I've had plenty of that,' George said.

'How's your mom?' Quinn wanted to know.

'She's doing OK.'

'She going to be OK?'

'No one knows yet. We're waiting to see how the three 'T's go. Treatment, tests and time,' George told him.

'That must be hard.'

'Yeah, but you know, she's in the best place. So, tell me about this villa complex. It sounds huge,' George spoke, changing the subject.

'Yeah, it is. It's basically like a town in itself. Your villa has a view of the sea. I made sure of it personally,' Quinn informed.

'Marisa's jaw's going to be dropping so far from her face she's going to need help picking it up.'

'So, shall we try the paella?' Quinn suggested.

Neither of them had even glanced at the menu. It was enough just to be able to share some time together, to feel unrushed and not under pressure to squeeze a whole relationship into a half hour time slot.

'Yes, good idea,' George agreed.

'*Paella para dos por favor*,' Quinn called to the grey haired lady.

She nodded her approval and disappeared into the kitchen.

'God, does she work here on her own?' George asked.

'No, I think her husband and son are in the kitchen for her to boss about,' Quinn replied with a smile.

'And that's exactly as it should be,' George told him.

Quinn smiled at her.

'So what have you been doing?' George enquired.

She had been throwing herself into tea dances and committee meeting refreshments, trying to avoid visiting her mother, desperate to stop thinking about an unavailable pop star. She wanted to know what it had been like for him and whether he had thought of her.

'Since I left?'

George nodded.

'Well I've been working on my new album, attending film premieres and club openings. To be honest I was glad to get over here. I really like it here, I feel at home, you know?' Quinn remarked.

'Why don't you move out here?' George asked.

'I can't. I need to be in the States. That's where music central is,' Quinn told her.

'But these days people can work anywhere in the world. Music can be sent down the internet can't it?' George reminded him.

'It isn't as simple as that,' Quinn told her.

'It seems nothing's simple in your crazy world.'

'You're catching on.'

'But you must love what you do to keep on doing it.'

'Music's all I know. I'm good at it. I love walking out onto a stage and making people feel something. Sometimes I see people laughing and singing along. Other times they're crying and holding hands with the person next to them. No two nights are the same and I feel honoured to be in that position. I'm so lucky in so many ways but...' Quinn spoke, sitting forward in his seat and looking at George.

'But what?'

'I don't know - sometimes I just feel so trapped,' Quinn admitted with a heavy sigh.

The conversation was broken by the restaurant owner bringing a huge black iron pan to the table. The smell escaping from the steaming dish of paella was exquisite and George's stomach rumbled in anticipation of tasting it.

'¡muchas gracias!' Quinn said as the lady put down plates and cutlery.

'This looks amazing, but it's so big!' George exclaimed as she looked at the size of the pan.

'Don't worry about that. You've only seen me eat canapés and fries. I could probably eat this entire pan on my own,' Quinn informed her.

'Well I'm not having that. Ladies first,' George said, picking up a fork.

The paella was the best George had tasted. Everything had obviously originated locally because you could taste the absolute freshness of it all. The prawns were huge, the rice was cooked to perfection and now she felt completely stuffed. Quinn, however, was still eating and the pan was almost empty.

'Where do you put it all? If I eat anything else, I think I'm going to explode,' George said, watching him finish the meal.

'Running,' Quinn informed.

'You run?'

'Yeah, only about five miles a day. Outdoors if I can, on the treadmill if I have to. Running's great here, there's so much to see, so many hidden tracks,' Quinn said.

George let out a contented sigh and took a swig of her beer. She hadn't felt so relaxed in a long time. It was like he had appeared in her life again and taken away all her anxiety. That was pretty unbelievable, given the complexity of their situation.

'I want to show you some of it, while you're here. We can go up into the mountains and...' Quinn began.

Before he could finish the sentence, his mobile phone began to ring and he got it out of the pocket of his trousers and answered.

'Yeah? Yeah, I'm kind of busy right now - yeah I'm in town. Look, I'll see you a bit later - yes, I know what time the tailor's coming, I'll be there.'

George tried to concentrate on the scene outside and not on the phone call that was obviously from Taylor. She gazed out at the ocean, remembering one time the Frasers had gone to the beach as a family. Adam had been a toddler then and had got sand in every orifice and tried to eat the seaweed. Her mother had almost had a heart attack about that. She took him to the doctors when they'd got home, in case he had come in contact with any excrement.

'Sorry about that,' Quinn said.

'Taylor?' George guessed.

'Yeah, about the tailor,' Quinn replied.

'That's almost funny,' George answered.

'Yeah, almost,' Quinn said, finishing his beer and looking sadly out of the window.

George took hold of his hands.

'Thank you for lunch,' she said sincerely.

'*De nada.* You're welcome,' he replied, squeezing her hands tightly in his.

'I guess we'd better get back,' she said, looking at her watch.

'Is that what you want to do?'

'It's what we should do,' George spoke with a sigh.

'That wasn't what I asked.'

'The sensible half of me says we ought to show our faces before anyone puts two and two together...'

197

'And the other half?'

'Says, make the most of every moment before it's too late,' George responded her eyes meeting his.

'*Ese es el medio que usted debería escuchar, eres tan hermosa que me hace débil*,' Quinn spoke softly, taking her hand.

'What does that mean?' George questioned.

'He say, that is the half you should listen to. He say, you are so beautiful, you make him feel weak,' the grey haired Spanish lady spoke as she arrived with the bill.

George looked at Quinn, her cheeks flushing at the old lady's words.

'How do you say "I wish I could stay here forever"?' George asked her.

'*Me gustaría poder quedarme aquí para siempre*,' the lady spoke as slowly as she was able.

'What she said,' George said not attempting the Spanish.

'*Yo también*,' Quinn replied.

'He say "me too",' the lady told her with a smile.

Twenty Three

'So, here we are,' Quinn spoke as he pulled over a few hundred yards from the entrance to La Manga Resort.

The complex had giant golf balls sat on a tee at either side of the huge gates. There were beautiful looking villas, stretching as far as the eye could see, but the exterior was surrounded by a ten foot high fence. It looked more like a huge gated community, rather than a relaxing holiday complex. There were also four minibuses and at least twenty photographers stationed at the entrance.

'It's big,' George remarked.

'Hideous is the word you're looking for,' Quinn told her.

'Don't you like it? But I thought...'

'Oh, don't get me wrong, the villas are incredible but it's like a town in itself. I'm talking every shop you can imagine, from souvenirs to sound systems. There are bars and restaurants and of course the golf. You could actually come here and not set foot out of the complex,' Quinn explained.

'Not authentic Spain then,' George replied.

'No. Authentic Spain is what we just left behind at the restaurant,' Quinn told her.

'So why buy a villa here?' George wanted to know.

'Not my idea,' Quinn said.

'Roger?' George guessed.

'You're getting it,' Quinn replied. 'OK, this is where I get out. See those paps over there? They see me and they'll be over here before you can say "*buenos dias*".'

'What? Well what do I do? Where do I go? This place is massive, I...' George exclaimed.

'Take the Jeep; it's yours for the stay. Give your name in at the gate, follow the signs to *Calle Bosques* and your villa is number one hundred and eighteen. Just so you know, I'm up on the hill over there, *Calle Ballesteros*, number one,' Quinn informed.

'With a view of all your subjects,' George replied.

'There's only one subject I want a view of,' Quinn told her.

'That is so lame,' George said with a laugh.

'But true,' Quinn answered.

He leant over to kiss her and George pulled back.

'We can't. Not here. We're outside the venue of the wedding of the century. One false move, I'll hit the horn or something and we'll be front page news. Like you said, they'll be over here before you can say...' George said.

'Cold shower,' Quinn finished.

'Yeah.'

Quinn let out a sigh and just looked at her.

'You're right, I'd better go,' he said, opening the door of the Jeep and getting out.

'Quinn, I'm just being sensible, for you. I don't want to make trouble and...' George began, feeling a bit disappointed their wonderful afternoon had come to an end on a slightly sour note.

'*Calle Bosques*, one hundred and eighteen,' Quinn told her, ending the conversation.

He pulled his baseball cap down over his head and set off down the road on foot.

George climbed over into the driver's seat and started the engine of the Jeep. She looked at Quinn disappearing in the rear view mirror and then drove the car towards the entrance.

'Quinn! Over here! Quinn! Just a couple of shots!' the group of paparazzi shouted as they moved away from the gates and began following him down the street.

'Man! Can you give me a break? I'm getting married in a few days. How about a little privacy?' Quinn called back to them.

He watched George drive the Jeep up to security and made sure she was waved on through. Absence hadn't lessened his feelings for her; he'd been close to kissing her in front of the world's press and not giving a shit. She was pushing her way inside him and he didn't know how much longer he could hold back from telling her everything.

It was a five minute drive around the complex to reach *Calle Bosques* and it gave George a chance to take in the sights and sounds of La Manga Resort.

There was a huge lake in the middle of the complex, directions to two golf courses and villa after luxurious villa. There was a roman style hotel building, what looked like a mall full of shops and a three storey restaurant overlooking the lake. Everyone George passed, seemed to be pulling golf bags or driving around in golf buggies.

The villa had cream walls, a red roof and palm trees guarding the entrance. As George parked the Jeep, she could hear the familiar sound of Marisa's high pitched laughter and the splash of water. She got her case out of the back of the car and wheeled it towards the entrance.

The door was open and she went in. She walked through the marble entrance hall and into a large, state of the art kitchen. It was well equipped. If the catering wagon wasn't up to scratch, she was sure they could manage in here if they had to.

Marisa's laughter grew louder and George moved through to the sitting room. She took in large terracotta sofas, bowls of fruit and urns of flowers. Everything was perfect, not a thing was out of place. Looking through the patio doors she could see her team.

Adam and Marisa were in the pool and Helen was in a swimsuit, sat on a sun lounger reading *Star Life* magazine.

'Hey!' Adam greeted, noticing George walking out onto the terrace.

'Hi. I see you're all getting accustomed to your new surroundings,' George remarked, smiling at Helen as she removed her sunglasses and sat up.

'What happened at the airport?' Adam questioned, hauling himself up from the pool and joining her by the six seat teak table on the veranda.

'Oh it was nothing, just a random check. I had to answer a few questions and open my case,' George told them.

'But you've been gone like hours. You totally missed the fantastic lunch we were sent over. It arrived in like a golf buggy on silver platters. It was fish and salad and these gorgeous potatoes done with herbs and...' Marisa began.

'I hope it wasn't too good or they'll be taking our catering contract back,' George said.

'Oh they can't! That's why Taylor has to get in outside caterers. Would you believe it, there's another wedding here on the same day?! Some Spanish soap opera star is getting married in the clubhouse. Have you seen the clubhouse?'

'Yes, it looked like the Colosseum,' George replied.

'Well the famous Spanish chick – can't remember her name, it will come to me - she's getting married there and Quinn and Taylor are getting married in - wait for it - the castle,' Marisa announced.

'What castle?' George enquired.

'It's like huge, but it's not real. They had it built. It's right on the other side of the complex from here, on the cliff top. There's this like canvas tunnel thing they're building that leads from the hotel to the castle, like two hundred yards of it or more. And that's where our catering wagon is and all the television trailers. Dennis, our driver, took us for a tour and we have maps and instructions,' Marisa gabbled as she ducked up and down filling the cleavage of her swimsuit with water.

'Right,' George replied not wanting to think about the wedding at all.

'Shall I make you a drink? We've got a jug of sangria or there's fresh juice,' Adam offered.

'Sangria would be nice,' George accepted.

'Well, why don't you go and get your bikini on and get in the water. It's really warm,' Adam told her.

'Yeah and we still have a couple of hours before the briefing,' Marisa stated.

'Briefing?' George remarked.

'Yes, we're all meeting in a conference room of the hotel at five, to be briefed about the week's activities,' Helen informed her.

'That sounds ominous,' George said.

'I can't wait! A whole week of being in the thick of the wedding of the millennium,' Marisa exclaimed, splashing about in the pool.

'The wedding of the millennium now,' George said to Adam with a smile.

'You didn't see her when she saw her bedroom. She practically passed out,' Adam answered.

'So, you've all picked rooms. What am I left with?' George asked.

'Yours had your name on the door; Marisa sneaked a peek and got jealous. Said something about there being a box on the bed,' Adam informed her.

'Right, well, I'd better go and check it out. See you in a minute,' George said, taking her suitcase back inside and looking for the staircase.

She hurried up the marble stairs and her room was the first door she came to. She opened it up and let out a gasp.

It was filled with stargazer lilies, bouquets of them stood in vases in every space, the fragrance filling the air. The bed itself was at least a king size and it had crisp white linen covering it and sumptuous, plum coloured, silk cushions.

On the bed, was an expensive looking box. It was cream, with a plum coloured ribbon wrapped around it and seemed to coordinate perfectly with everything else in the room. She pulled at the ribbon and carefully opened the lid. Parting the tissue paper inside, she took out the contents.

It was a bikini, in midnight blue, with inch wide straps and a silver toned and diamante cross, joining the two cups in the middle. The bottoms were just her style, not too skimpy and made to complement her boyish shape. It was undeniably her.

She picked a card out of the box and smiled as she read it:-

> *Spain's too hot for jeans – I want to see you in this Q x*

'Oh. My. God. Where did you like get that bikini from?' Marisa exclaimed loudly when George joined them by the pool.

'Why? Is there something wrong with it?' George asked suddenly feeling self-conscious.

'It looks lovely. Is it new?' Helen asked.

'It's like designer! That must have set you back about five hundred quid or more,' Marisa informed.

'No way! For a bikini!' Adam remarked, staring at George.

'It wasn't anything like that much! I got it from Peacocks, it was about twenty quid,' George insisted hurriedly.

'Peacocks don't do stuff like that, not even copies. I shop in Peacocks and I've never seen anything like that in there,' Marisa continued.

'Well obviously they were popular and sold out,' George responded quickly.

'Leave George alone Marisa. Come on, I'll come in and swim with you,' Helen said, putting her magazine down and walking to the edge of the pool.

'What? You don't swim properly, you just kind of float and wave your arms around a bit,' Marisa said.

'Well we'll race each other then shall we?' Helen suggested, slipping herself into the shallow end.

'For money?' Marisa suggested eagerly.

George laughed as Helen splashed her daughter in the face and they set off swimming to the deep end.

Adam came and sat down on the lounger next to George and handed her a glass of sangria.

'Thanks. It's so hot isn't it? Have you got plenty of sun cream on?' George asked.

'Yes yes, factor fifteen. How about you?' Adam enquired.

'Yes, here it is, just about to do it,' George said, taking the lid off the bottle and squirting some into her palms.

Adam took a sip from his glass of sangria and picked up some paper he was writing on.

'So, you like Marisa,' George spoke quietly.

Adam looked up at her and his cheeks reddened straight away.

'Come on, I'm your sister. You can tell me anything. You told me you liked her at the airport - ah, I see. This song you're writing is for her isn't it?' George guessed, looking at the paper.

'Sshh, don't let her hear! I'm not going to play it for her or anything I just, you know, wanted to write something,' Adam said, trying not to appear flustered.

'She can't hear. She's too busy trying to beat her mother at swimming, or water bombing, or something,' George said as she watched Marisa pushing Helen under the water and laughing hysterically.

'You think it's stupid, to like her,' Adam spoke.

'I didn't say that,' George replied.

'You don't think she's right for me,' Adam spoke.

'I didn't say that either.'

'You don't need to, it's written all over your face,' Adam answered grumpily.

'Well, I like Marisa, you know I do, but I'm not sure she's really...' George began.

'Really what?'

'I don't know. She's just not - I don't know - not ambitious like you,' George said.

'Ambitious?! What does ambition have to do with anything? Anyway, how can you say that? She's a caterer, just like you,' Adam said, raising his voice.

'OK, well maybe ambition was the wrong word. She's sweet and she's funny but...' George began again.

'You don't think she's good enough for me,' Adam said bluntly.

'I think she might hold you back, take your focus away from your music, that's all,' George stated, taking her sunglasses off to look at him.

'I'm not talking about marrying her,' Adam said huffily.

'I know, but apart from the distraction, you've known her a long time and I work with her. When things go wrong it would be difficult,' George spoke.

'*When* things go wrong? Thanks! Maybe you shouldn't judge everyone by your own standards,' Adam snapped.

'Hey, that's uncalled for,' George retorted angrily.

'Yeah well, I wish I hadn't told you anything. I thought you would get it but you don't,' Adam said, standing up and preparing to dive into the pool.

'Adam, I do get it. Come on, sit down,' George encouraged.

'Pretty stupid of me to ask relationship advice from someone who's never had a relationship,' Adam snapped.

He dived into the pool and swam up to Helen and Marisa who were now playing with an inflatable ball.

George let out a sigh. She had handled that particularly badly. She was making Marisa into a female version of Paul and she was playing the role of her mother. Who was she to say who was right for Adam? That's what her mother had done and look what had happened there! She would apologise as soon as he had calmed down. The last thing she wanted to do was alienate him at the moment. There was enough fragility in their family right now.

'Oi George! Catch!' Marisa screamed, lobbing the inflatable in George's direction.

Twenty Four

At 5.00pm Team Finger Food were gathered in one of the conference rooms of the La Manga Resort hotel along with approximately one hundred other people. Everyone had name badges that also designated their role in the proceedings. George was stood next to 'Paco' who was apparently in charge of tablecloths.

'Ladies and Gentlemen, my name is Pixie Dean. I'm the wedding coordinator and I would like to welcome all of you to La Manga Resort and to the wedding of Quinn Blake and Taylor Ferraro,' Pixie spoke into the microphone.

She was wearing an emerald green trilby hat, a high-necked white blouse, green figure hugging shorts, white tights and black patent leather peep-toe shoes. She was completely how George had envisaged her, during their phone conversations. She looked like an over fashioned, ridiculously organised leprechaun.

'Now, before I run through the itinerary for the coming week, let me introduce the principal characters in this romantic fairytale. Firstly, the bride herself, please welcome Miss Taylor Ferraro,' Pixie squeaked excitedly.

George held her breath as Taylor came onto the stage, a picture of poise and elegance, dressed in a simple cream shift dress that showed off a newly acquired tan.

'Hello Taylor. Are you nervous?' Pixie questioned sticking the microphone in the actress' face and grinning like an overzealous game-show host.

'A little,' she replied, managing a coy smile.

'OK, let's introduce your Prince Charming. Please welcome, the adorable, the sexy, the multi-talented Quinn Blake,' Pixie continued.

Quinn walked onto the stage looking as handsome and devastatingly gorgeous as usual. He was wearing a white shirt that laced up at the front, jeans and Havaianas. George bit her lip as she looked at him. So many feelings ran through her, so many thoughts. The time they'd spent skin on skin, the drinks on the roof of the Hexagon, the beautiful Spanish restaurant. And here they were. Him on the stage, her just part of the group there to ensure the wedding ran like clockwork.

'Oh. My. God. Will you look at him?' Marisa whispered.

'Hello Quinn,' Pixie said, moving herself up to him and looking like a star-struck child.

'Hello,' Quinn answered.

'Looking forward to the big day?' Pixie enquired.

'Of course. Everyone here is in for a treat. The castle is amazing and the after party is going to go on for days,' Quinn told the crowd.

'And the getting married part?' Pixie asked.

The majority of the group let out a chuckle of amusement. George, on the other hand, was scrunching up a handful of her skirt, making her knuckles turn white.

'Can't wait,' Quinn replied, looking at Taylor.

George looked at the floor as her heart hit it. This was horrible. What was she doing here? It was nothing short of torture. He'd sounded so convincing. He had looked at Taylor like he looked at her. What was the truth? Could she really believe what he told her when they were together?

'Ah, so cute! OK, next we have the father of the bride; let's hear it for the head of Rock It Music, Roger Ferraro!' Pixie exclaimed.

A very tall, broad man with wavy jet black hair and an olive complexion bounded onto the stage and waved to the crowd. He was dressed in a dark suit, under which was a burgundy roll-neck jumper. It seemed a little inappropriate given the stifling heat.

George looked at Quinn and watched him move closer to Taylor and away from Roger as he joined Pixie.

'Well hello Daddy-O!' Pixie greeted as Roger kissed her on both cheeks.

'Hello Pixie. Hi everyone. I'm Roger, I'm Taylor's father and I can't tell you how excited I am about the wedding. Quinn's been like a son to me ever since we met and I just know he's going to make my little princess so happy,' Roger said, looking at Taylor, whose lip visibly quivered at her father's words.

Quinn looked exceedingly uncomfortable now Roger was on stage. He kept shifting about on the spot, wringing his hands together. George also noticed he was sweating. Although it was hot outside, the whole hotel seemed to be permanently air conditioned. It wasn't like he was wearing a roll neck jumper, like Roger. There was no physical reason for perspiration.

Next on stage were Carleen and Saffron, Taylor's Sindy doll bridesmaids, followed by best man Belch who sang his introduction with a guitar accompaniment. Finally Michael burst into the limelight. He was wearing a pale grey linen suit with a sequined silver shirt underneath.

'Saving the best 'til last Pixie weren't you? Well folks, I am Michael. I am Quinn's personal assistant, amongst other things and if you have any questions about anything at all then I am your man. No matter is too trivial. If you need your water cooling by a couple of degrees or if you prefer your bed sheets to be rubber rather than linen, then I will make the necessary arrangements,' Michael told the crowd.

The audience clapped for Michael and he bowed like an over excited seal who had just balanced a ball on his nose for a crowd of children.

George looked back to Quinn and saw he was looking very red in the face and was holding his head as if in pain. Taylor had a vice like grip on his arm and looked like she was telling him to perk up and fast.

Michael and Pixie formed a double act then and began to tell the teams of staff the itinerary for the week's events and what they would be expected to do.

Suddenly Taylor let out a blood-curdling scream and George looked on in horror as Quinn collapsed on the floor.

The crowd let out a collective gasp as Roger hurriedly bent down to assist.

'Oh God, oh God, is he like OK? He isn't dead is he?' Marisa questioned her mouth hanging open in shock.

'Maybe we should help,' Adam suggested as everyone stood dumbstruck not knowing what to do.

'Do you know First Aid? I mean someone here must know First Aid. I did a course when I was a Brown Owl but that was years ago and...' Helen began.

'Shut up Mother! He needs more than a sling and a leg splint, he's like unconscious!' Marisa exclaimed.

'I don't know CPR or anything but we're all here looking and someone ought to do something,' Adam said.

George's heart was in her mouth. She wanted to run up to the front but her legs were like lumps of concrete. All she could do was watch.

'Michael, call Nigel at once,' Roger ordered, propping Quinn into the recovery position.

'Yes, of course. Don't worry everyone; I'm sure it's just the heat. Perhaps we should adjourn? Pixie? Shall we adjourn do you think?' Michael suggested, getting his mobile from his pocket.

'Oh. My. God. It's serious. He isn't moving, oh God,' Marisa said, trying to outmanoeuvre people in front of her for a better view.

'Well, he's been put in the recovery position, so I think that means he's breathing,' Helen informed the group.

'I'm sure he's just passed out or something, it's been so hot today,' Adam said and he put an arm around Marisa's shoulders.

George was shaking and she couldn't stop it. She was worried about him. He had gone from looking crimson and hot to pale and lifeless in a matter of minutes. Roger was lifting him up now, aided by the black man who had delivered the room key and the VIP passes to George back in England. She didn't even know his name, that's how involved she was in this scenario. They were exiting stage right and heading out of the room.

'Oh, where are they taking him? How will we know if he's alright?' Marisa questioned not noticing the weight of Adam's arm around her.

George watched Taylor. Having recovered from her scream of shock when Quinn fell to the floor, she was now taking the whole situation in her stride. She was calmly telling people at the front not to worry, 'the heat did affect Quinn sometimes' and her father's physician would make sure he was taken care of. George was still trembling, yet there was no flicker of emotion on Taylor's face. It was almost like she didn't care.

'Are you OK?' Helen asked, putting her hand on George's arm.

George looked at her blankly.

'You look very pale,' Helen remarked.

'Oh, no, I'm fine. We should go,' George said, noticing other people were beginning to leave as Pixie desperately tried to hand out sheets of information.

'I'll go and get an information sheet, make sure we don't miss out on anything,' Adam said, letting go of Marisa and heading towards Pixie.

'What d'you think's wrong with him?' Marisa enquired of Helen and George.

'It was probably just the heat; the heat does funny things to people. That's why I'm always nagging you to wear sunscreen and put a hat on. It's UVAs and SPFs all the way from now on,' Helen told her daughter.

Michael was about to bustle past them but George hurriedly caught hold of his arm and brought him to a halt.

'Michael, sorry to bother you. I - er - just wondered - is Quinn OK?' George said, trying to hide the concern in her voice.

'George, darling, how lovely to see you. Yes, yes, Quinn's just fine. Just a touch of heatstroke I think. You try and tell these youngsters to cover up and not stay out too long but will they listen? Living in LA you would think they would know by now,' Michael gabbled, smiling widely.

'See Marisa, I told you, heatstroke,' Helen reassured.

'OK, well, that's good,' George said.

She was saying what she was expected to say but the truth was she didn't believe a word of it.

'So nothing to worry about, everything is still on course for the big day. Everything OK with your accommodation? Anything you need?' Michael asked George.

'No, everything's fine,' she replied, looking at Taylor who was checking out the condition of her nails.

'Good, good. Right, much to do. I'll give you a call to catch up on progress tomorrow,' Michael said hurriedly.

George watched him head over to a security guard at the door and begin speaking. The smile had left his mouth now and there was deep concern in his eyes. This wasn't heatstroke or dehydration; this was something much more serious.

'Looks like we're meeting our catering team tomorrow morning,' Adam informed, waving the sheet of paper in the air.

'Great, I've already thought of all the crappy jobs I can get them to do for me,' Marisa said, grinning.

'Come on Marisa, you're going to love taking the skin and pith off the citrus fruits and you know it,' Adam joked.

'That is *sooo* your job,' Marisa replied.

'Hey, how about we go into town and get some food? Local food, like omelettes or paella or something,' Adam suggested.

'Yes please, I'm starving!' Marisa agreed.

'What do you think George? Shall we go into town?' Helen asked her.

'Yeah, sure, that sounds good,' George replied, averting her eyes from Michael and the security guard.

'Right, well let's go and get the Jeep. I can't believe you hired a Jeep George, it's so cool. Can I drive?' Adam asked.

'Sure, why not?' George answered.

Twenty Five

When he came to he was laid on a chaise longue with Dr Nigel Collins peering at him through his half-moon glasses. He tried to sit up but was rapidly pushed back down again and a glass of water was summoned.

'What happened?' Quinn asked the doctor.

'One of your attacks. I thought these new pills were keeping things under control! I mean, right in the middle of the introductions!' Roger boomed with a snort.

'You were out for almost ten minutes,' Dr Collins informed Quinn, handing him the glass of water.

Quinn propped himself up and took a drink. His head was aching and his vision was blurred. He'd seen George looking like she wanted to smash his face in when he'd given his upbeat announcement about the wedding festivities. He'd wanted it all to be over so he didn't have to stand in line with Pixie, Roger and Taylor, like some sort of weird barber shop quartet. The black cloud had descended over him, strangling his brain and tightening his chest and the last thing he remembered seeing was the mad Welsh girl flapping her hands about.

George hadn't eaten. She had ordered a Spanish omelette, but had just pushed it around her plate pretending that constituted eating.

The restaurant they had chosen was in the nearest town to the golf resort and was extremely lively. Shortly after their plates were cleared, loud flamenco music had begun and diners had started to dance with each other anywhere they could find a space.

George wasn't in the mood for people laughing and being happy. She was concerned about Quinn. The lunch they had shared together, now seemed like it had happened in another lifetime.

She had looked at her phone constantly during the meal and she was looking at it again now. She wished he would text her, just to let her know he was OK. She didn't want to text him. She was never the first to text. She was too afraid he might be with Taylor, or Roger, or anyone else who shouldn't know. Basically anyone and everyone.

'Come on Marisa, let's show them how it's done,' Adam suggested and he stood up from the table and held his hand out to her.

'What? Like dance?' Marisa exclaimed with a nervous giggle.

'Yes, dance. Come on, everyone else is doing it,' Adam said, indicating the throng of people who seemed to be performing a mixture of flamenco and ceroc.

'Yeah, I know, but like I'm not very good at this sort of dancing,' Marisa said her cheeks reddening.

'Well, we don't have to do what they're doing. We can make up our own moves,' Adam suggested, winking at her.

'Alright then, but the second you like step on my feet I'm sitting straight back down,' Marisa told him, taking his hand and letting him lead her to the nearest empty space.

George didn't even notice them get up. She was too preoccupied, hoping that at any minute her mobile was going to announce a text from Quinn.

'Are you expecting it to ring? Because they don't if you stare at them too long. It's a bit like a watched kettle never boiling,' Helen remarked.

George looked up at her. Only then did she realise she was gripping her phone so tightly it could crack at any second.

'No, no, not really. Sorry,' George said, putting down the phone and picking up her glass of wine.

'Is everything alright George? You've been a bit distant all evening. Is it your mum? Are you worried about her?' Helen asked.

'No. No, she's fine. She'll be bossing her sister around by now,' George answered quickly.

'Are you sure that's all? I mean, it's only since we arrived here that the scale of the event has hit me. Did you see the press outside and the roving reporters in the complex?' Helen asked.

'Yeah, I did. I suppose I'm just a bit worried about being introduced to the catering wagon tomorrow. Not to mention meeting the other staff,' George responded.

'Well if that's it you can stop worrying right this minute and have another glass of wine. With all those people helping us it should end up being the easiest function we've ever catered,' Helen reassured her.

'Yeah, I guess,' George remarked with a sigh.

'He didn't look comfortable on that stage tonight though did he?' Helen said.

'Who?' George asked.

'Quinn Blake. He didn't look much like a man happy to be getting married in my opinion,' Helen continued.

'Well, he obviously wasn't feeling very well,' George reminded.

'I suppose not,' Helen mused.

'Look, I'm just going to get some fresh air. This music and the heat's giving me a headache,' George said, standing up and heading for the door.

All the Spanish guitars and loud stamping weren't helping her state of mind either. She needed to speak to Quinn or she was going to be distracted for the rest of the evening. She didn't know whether she was doing the right thing, but it was the only thing she could do. She sat on the low wall outside the restaurant and typed out a text.

R u ok?

She pressed send and her mobile confirmed the message had gone.

The humidity was still intense even in the late evening and the streets of the town were alive with people, some browsing gift shops, others stopping at bars for a drink.

She waited. He could still be unwell, or he might not have his phone with him. Anything could have happened, he could even be at the hospital. That thought really worried her and her anxiety was heightened by the fact she had no right for all this concern.

She looked back into the restaurant and saw Marisa and Adam trying to copy the flamenco moves of a middle-aged couple next to them, who seemed to be experts at it. Marisa was laughing hysterically and Adam was smiling more broadly than she had ever seen him smile before. She hadn't meant to be so harsh with him earlier, especially when he was confiding in her. She would have to talk to him again. He needed her to be a sister, a confidante, not a control freak. Who did that remind her of?

Her phone beeped with a new message and she quickly opened it, relieved to see it was from Quinn.

I'm OK did u like bikini? Q x

George smiled as she read it, so glad he had answered.

Its great wore it 2day G x
Want 2 c u
Where?
Where r u?
Restaurante Miguel in town
Meet by supermarket in 10 Q x

George locked the screen on her phone and put it back in the pocket of her jeans. She took a deep breath and prepared to go and tell Helen she was leaving.

'I'm not feeling very well, I'm going to go,' George said, finishing her drink and replacing the glass on the table.

'Oh poor you. Have you got some painkillers? I've got some in my handbag somewhere, let me just have a look,' Helen began, delving into her bag and pulling out Marisa's supersized sunglasses.

'That's OK I have some. Look I'll leave the Jeep, Adam can drive it back,' George said, picking up her bag.

'Well what about you? You can't walk, it's far too far and this heat does real damage if you're not used to it,' Helen began.

'I've got a taxi. I stopped one outside so I'd better go, he's waiting,' George said quickly.

'Oh OK. Well, take care and we won't be too late. It's a big day tomorrow,' Helen remarked.

'Yeah, bye,' George replied.

Twelve minutes passed before Quinn pulled up alongside her in a red Jeep identical to the one he'd given her to drive.

'Hey,' he greeted as she opened the door and got in.

'This is twelve minutes, you said ten.'

'So you do care huh? You were worried about me,' Quinn said, smiling at her as he pulled away.

'Just wanted to make sure I wasn't going to be left with two hundred Seville oranges to make use of, if the wedding didn't go ahead,' George said.

'I'm glad you messaged me. I've been stuck with Nigel the doctor since my dramatic collapse. He's probably on the phone to Roger right now wondering where I am,' Quinn informed.

'You left the doctor?'

'Everyone has to pee sometime. If he took my blood pressure one more time I swear I was thinking about strangling him with the stethoscope,' Quinn told her.

'Quinn it isn't funny. What happened back there in the conference room? Was it heatstroke?' George enquired.

'Heatstroke? Ah, that's the official line is it?' Quinn said with a laugh.

'That's what Michael tried to tell me.'

'But you didn't believe him. That's my girl,' Quinn said, turning off onto the coast road.

'Well what happened?' George wanted to know.

'In a second. I think there's a car following us,' Quinn said, studying the rear-view mirror.

'What? Press?'

'I don't know.'

'Well what do we do?'

'Lose him. Let's see how fast this Jeep can go,' Quinn suggested.

'Are you crazy? Just pull over somewhere and I'll get out,' George said as Quinn put his foot to the floor.

'And have them snapping photos for tomorrow's front pages?'

'Quinn!' George shrieked as they began to speed along the coast road at breakneck pace.

'Just hold on,' he urged.

The orange groves and cultivated earth were flashing past her eyes now, like the ground had earlier, onboard the plane in the approach to take off. The car in pursuit was almost matching them for speed and Quinn took a sharp right off the main road in a bid to shake him off. The Jeep skidded onto a gravel track with nothing but farmland at either side.

'Quinn! For God's sake stop!'

He ignored her and they carried on haring across the shingle and dust covered terrain, debris flicking up at them as they sped along.

Another right and then a left and, happy the tail was lost, he finally pulled the car over, underneath the shade of a tree.

'What the Hell was that all about?! You could have killed us!' George screamed at the top of her voice, throwing open the door in her anger.

'That Merc was following us! Did you want to get photographed for a celebrity magazine?'

'No! Of course not! But I didn't want to get showered with stones either!' George yelled back.

'I apologise! I didn't realise you were so precious!'

'What did you say?' George questioned, narrowing her eyes at him.

'Well what did you want me to do? Smile for the camera and offer them an interview?'

'This situation is just getting ridiculous! I haven't got time for it any more,' George said.

She started to walk away from him, up the track. She didn't know where she was going, but she needed to put distance between them. The whole scenario was just too much.

'Where are you going? George, for Christ's sake. Come back here!' Quinn yelled after her.

'No! I don't take orders from you! Leave me alone!'

'This is crazy! Come back!'

'Piss off!'

'Piss off? That's what you really want me to do?' Quinn asked, catching her up and grabbing her roughly by the arm.

She was so angry she could happily have punched him in the face. She was sick of this charade, the stupid La Manga Resort complex, Taylor and her designer shift dresses. She may have the biggest catering contract of her life, but she was never going to have what she really wanted. And that was him. Despite the rage she felt now at his recklessness, she hadn't felt this deeply about anyone since Paul. And it was going to come to nothing. All of a sudden she didn't think she could handle that.

'Well?' Quinn asked again.

'I can't compete! With this mad lifestyle of yours, with your fiancée, with car chases and furtive meetings. I can't do it,' George exclaimed.

'I know it's rough but...'

'But what Quinn? There is no 'but' anything. *This*, is all *this* is. *This*, is all we are. Sex between appointments with your wedding planner and secret lunches in a Spanish hideaway,' George stated.

'I want it to be more,' Quinn told her, looking at her with sincerity in his expression.

'So you say, but then you stood on that stage this evening and told a room full of people how much you were looking forward to getting married,' George blasted.

'That was all for show. You should know that by now! There were press there and most of the people coordinating the event, what was I supposed to say?'

'How can I believe anything you tell me about what you want and how you feel, if you're so capable of spinning a line? How do I know you're not spinning one to me?' she carried on.

'Come on George, I've told you things I haven't told anybody.'

'Like what?'

'Like how I don't want to get married. Like how I feel like a prisoner in my own life. What d'you think would happen if people knew all that?'

'You'd be free?'

'You think?'

'Well I don't know! I don't know because you won't tell me! You don't let me in! You're too busy keeping up appearances, being the macho pop star and all that means f**k all to me!' George screamed.

'I know. And when I'm with you I'm who I want to be. You know me George, better than anyone.'

'Do I?'

'Yes,' Quinn insisted and he brushed her hair off her face.

'I wish I believed it,' she said with a sigh.

'What can I do to make you believe it?'

'Trust me enough to tell me what's going on with you,' she replied.

Quinn let out a heavy sigh and dropped his eyes from hers.

'You can't do it can you?' George said her voice full of frustration.

'It isn't that straightforward. If it was then I would and...' Quinn protested.

'Forget it,' George snapped, turning her back on him and walking back up the track.

'George! Wait! Listen!' Quinn hollered after her.

She turned back to face him, her hands planted on her hips, the sun burning the back of her neck.

'What happened in the conference room - it happens sometimes. Not usually in public, but about a couple of times a month - maybe more - I kind of just blackout,' Quinn told her.

'What?'

'You wanted the truth, that's the truth.'

'But that isn't right. Are they doing tests?' George asked him.

'Believe me, I've had every test there is,' Quinn said.

'And they can't find the cause?' George questioned.

'It isn't quite like that.'

'Well what is it like?'

Quinn took hold of her hand and held it in his, gently stroking her fingers.

'I had an accident. A really bad one, years ago. I was in a coma for months. The blackouts are to do with that,' Quinn told her matter of factly.

'My God, what did you do?' George exclaimed.

'Apparently I was riding a motorbike without a helmet and I hit a truck,' Quinn said, looking at her.

'Apparently?' George queried.

'I don't remember,' Quinn admitted with a shrug.

'Is this what you've been trying to tell me before?' George asked him.

'Yeah, kind of. Lately it's become more than the blackouts. I've started having these dreams, about the accident, about playing in a band, about not liking bananas. I don't know if I like bananas for Christ's sake! I'm too scared to eat one! And it's freaking me out, because I'm worried that the bits about the accident and the totally shit band aren't dreams. I think they might be memories,' Quinn told her.

'Would that be a bad thing? If it was memory coming back?' George asked.

'I don't know, that's half the issue. Will I be better off knowing or not knowing?' Quinn enquired.

'What are you afraid of?' George asked.

'The truth. Just like you said,' Quinn replied, looking at her intensely.

'Everyone needs the truth,' George told him.

'That's what I think every day when I wake up and then there's Roger with the latest big news about Brand Blake. Then there's Taylor with her wedding entourage and all I want to think about is you and me and how much I want there to be a you and me,' Quinn said.

'You're getting married in four days,' George reminded.

'Am I?' Quinn replied, looking at her.

'I think we should stop seeing each other.'

'You want to stop it?' Quinn asked.

'No,' George admitted.

'Then why even think it? I couldn't stop seeing you even if I wanted to. I can't keep away from you George. I can't stop thinking about you. I want to be with you, every minute of every day and it drives me insane because I can't control it,' Quinn told her, running a hand through her hair.

'But you're getting married,' George repeated.

'And you think that's going to make a difference? You think having a ring on my finger is going to stop me wanting you?' Quinn asked her.

'It should,' George replied as his fingers began to massage the nape of her neck.

'Well I'm telling you, it won't,' Quinn said seriously.

'And what if it changes things for me?' George asked him.

'Will it?'

'I know what we've been doing isn't right, but it becomes a whole different thing if you get married. I won't be a mistress Quinn, not like that,' George told him.

'So what are you saying? If I get married you won't see me again?' Quinn asked, looking at her.

'Yes,' George replied definitely.

'So if I want to keep seeing you, I have to call off the wedding,' Quinn said.

'I didn't say that, I...'

'You did say that.'

'Quinn, this isn't about me, it's about you. If you love Taylor then marry her, like you were planning to do before you met me. But, if you don't love her, don't marry her. Because if you do, you'd be lying to her, yourself and your public,' George tried to explain.

'You know I don't love her,' Quinn spoke.

'You say that like it doesn't matter.'

'It doesn't matter. I'm not getting married for her, I'm getting married for Roger,' Quinn yelled, kicking at the gravel track.

He sent a foot full of shingle into the air and the dust swirled between them like a murky barrier.

George just stared at him, not knowing what to say. You didn't get married for your record producer, unless he was a member of the Mafia and you had a price on your head. That couldn't be what it was. That didn't happen in real life.

'Listen, we'd better get going. If I'm out too long they'll be calling and...'

'I don't understand. What hold has Roger got over you?' George questioned as Quinn began to walk back to the Jeep.

'It's complicated. I've said way too much already.'

'Why won't you tell me?' George wanted to know.

'I can't George, alright? I just can't,' Quinn exclaimed.

'But I'm not a member of the Press Association. I'm not someone who's going to kiss and tell to the tabloids. I'm just a caterer from Basingstoke,' George pleaded.

'Listen, no matter what you did, no matter who you did it with, I wouldn't be able to let you go, marriage or no marriage,' Quinn told her sincerely.

'I won't be the other woman. Not when that ring is on her finger,' George began, swallowing a lump in her throat.

'You won't even give me some time? Give us a chance?' Quinn asked as he got into the Jeep.

She didn't reply.

'Fine. I get it. Why waste your time on someone who's so f**ked up he's going to marry someone he couldn't give a shit about,' Quinn snapped angrily and he started up the engine.

'Come on Quinn, that isn't how I feel,' George insisted.

'No? Well how would I know? You say *I'm* holding back - what about you?' Quinn accused.

George didn't answer. She got into the Jeep silently and, as it pulled away, she put her hand to the chain on her neck.

Twenty Six

F**k it and f**k her! He'd told her more than he'd told anyone and it still wasn't enough! Now suddenly she had a conscience! Now she didn't want to be with him because he was going to have a meaningless scrap of gold on his finger. Granted the gold was the best that money could buy, but the cost didn't matter when there was no feeling behind it. And there wasn't, why couldn't she see that? This wasn't how he wanted things to go. He wanted to be with her, every second they had here. He wanted to show her Spain, play her the songs he'd written for her. There were twenty five of those and counting. He wanted to make love to her in the sand, he wanted to tell her he loved her.

He stopped pacing the villa and looked at his reflection in the patio doors. He expected to see someone different and was disappointed. He loved her. This wasn't just about lust. It had gone way beyond that and he couldn't let it go.

'Hey George! You'll never guess! Adam and me only came last in the dancing contest! Show her what we won Adam!' Marisa exclaimed as she, Adam and Helen entered the villa.

George was on her fourth bottle of beer and second packet of paprika crisps. Quinn had dropped her a decent enough distance away from the gates of La Manga Resort and she had blown a decent amount of Euros on comfort food at the on-site supermarket.

'Isn't it great?' Marisa said, producing a huge, bright red sombrero.

'I thought sombreros were native to Mexico, but according to Juan behind the bar they all wear them in this area of Spain,' Helen spoke with a wine induced giggle.

'Oh Mother he was trying to chat you up! He would have said elephants were native to Spain if he thought it was going to get him a quick one out the back,' Marisa replied.

'He was married and so am I!' Helen said, offended.

'And your point is?'

'You OK?' Adam asked George.

'Yeah. You know what, I'm going to go and get changed and get in the pool,' she said, standing up and heading to the stairs.

'What? Like now? There's absolutely no sun out there and it's like dark,' Marisa commented.

George didn't reply, but hurried upstairs to her room. There was the gorgeous bikini, dry, and lying on the bed waiting for her. She couldn't wear it now, not after the row she had with Quinn. He'd been so angry, he'd driven at full speed all the way back to the golf resort and hadn't even said goodbye when she'd left him. That wasn't how she wanted things to end.

Dressed in her plain black swimming costume, she came back downstairs, went straight outside and jumped into the pool where she began to thrash out length after length.

'Is she like alright?' Marisa asked as the three of them looked out of the patio doors at George motoring up and down the pool.

229

'She's been acting weird since the briefing,' Adam added.

'I expect she's just getting nervous about tomorrow, seeing the so called catering wagon, meeting the staff. It's a big thing for Finger Food isn't it? Lots of anticipation and the chance to show her creations to the world,' Helen reminded them.

'Yeah I know, but she's totally nailed the menu and, with all those helpers, it's going to be a piece of piss. I mean cake, a piece of cake,' Marisa said quickly, noticing Helen's eyebrows rising.

'I'll go and speak to her,' Adam said, opening the door.

'Perhaps she just needs to be on her own for a bit,' Helen suggested.

'If we leave her alone she's going to swim the equivalent of the English Channel,' Adam replied and he ignored Helen's advice and stepped out onto the terrace.

'Now *that* swimsuit is definitely Peacocks,' Marisa remarked with a nod, looking out of the doors.

George put her head under the water and powered down the pool. She just wanted to carry on swimming until she felt better. She was in an impossible situation and she didn't know what to do about it. She wasn't sure she *could* do anything about it.

She came up for air at the end of the pool and noticed Adam standing at the edge, looking at her.

'You in training or something? Think you could almost get into the Olympics if you carry on doing lengths in that sort of time,' he remarked.

George stopped and stood up to face him. She was completely out of breath and feeling the effects of swimming under the influence of four bottles of San Miguel, plus the wine she'd had in the restaurant earlier.

He handed her a towel and she accepted it.

'What's up?' he asked, offering her a hand out of the water.

'Nothing. Just fancied a swim,' George replied, towelling off her hair as Adam sat down at the table.

'Yeah, OK. You've never been a great one for lying. Who's pissed you off?' Adam continued.

'No one,' George insisted.

'Pull the other one. I know your pissed off expression when I see it and it's right there, plastered all over your face.'

'Yeah well, perhaps I don't want to talk about it,' George snapped back at him.

'God! That's what you get like when Mum's been having a go at you. She hasn't phoned has she?'

'What, to check I haven't left you out in the sun to fry or poisoned your dinner? I think she's actually got too much on her own plate at the moment,' George retorted.

'Whoa! This is bad,' Adam responded.

George let out a sigh and wrapped the towel around her shoulders. It was a balmy evening but she was starting to feel the cold now she had stopped swimming. However, it wasn't just the temperature, she was cold on the inside too right now.

'Look, about earlier. I shouldn't have said what I said about Marisa,' George admitted.

'I said some pretty stupid things too,' Adam said, avoiding her gaze.

'Yeah well I was wrong to say what I said. She's a lovely girl. I like her a lot and if you like her, then you go for it,' George said seriously.

'Mum doesn't like her, she thinks she's common,' Adam remarked.

'Yeah? Well that's what she said about Paul,' George spoke.

'Paul?' Adam queried.

'Oh, a boyfriend I had when I was younger,' George replied.

'You loved him?' Adam asked.

'Yeah, I loved him.'

'What happened?'

'He moved away,' George spoke.

'Didn't you keep in touch? I mean if you loved each other then...'

'We were young and you know, it probably wouldn't have lasted anyway. Things like that don't do they?'

'Why didn't Mum like him?'

'Because he was fun. Because he kept me out late and took me to parties, because he had a motorbike. Because he made me smile - I don't know - that and a hundred other reasons,' George said with another sigh.

'I wish she wasn't so black and white all the time. I mean, I'm not sure I would want to introduce Marisa to her, you know, as my girlfriend, well if she wants to be my girlfriend,' Adam babbled.

'Want my advice? Don't bother. She won't hold back in telling you what she thinks. Believe me, you could bring home the Virgin Mary and she would still see Katie Price,' George spoke her mind.

'Maybe, being ill and everything might have mellowed her. Does that sound really harsh?' Adam asked.

'No, I know what you mean and yeah, maybe it will mellow her,' George agreed.

'So are we friends again?' Adam asked hopefully.

'There was never any doubt about that,' George answered.

'You worried about tomorrow? Getting to grips with that catering wagon?' Adam asked.

'No, it'll be fine and if it isn't then so what?' George said with a shrug.

'Want a coffee?' Adam offered.

'Yeah that would be nice. I won't be long, just want to stay out here a bit,' George said as Adam stood up and prepared to go indoors.

'OK.'

He went back inside and George swept her wet hair back and looked out over the ocean. She had only been in Spain a day and things had started out so well. How had it ended up like this? She had feelings for Quinn, strong feelings, but it was so long since she had felt anything real for anyone, she didn't know whether she was interpreting them properly. What if he was just a passing infatuation? What if there was no substance to it? But on the other hand, what if he was the best thing that had ever happened to her? What if they could make a proper relationship out of their intensity? It could be special. Did she want to turn her back on that? And could she really let him go, married or not?

'Hey George! Come in here! Mum's actually worked out how to turn on the expensive TV and there's Quinn Blake's latest video on. He's not wearing much!' Marisa called excitedly.

'Coming straight in,' George replied.

Great! There was absolutely no getting away from him, whether she wanted to or not. He was absolutely everywhere.

Marisa had started an impromptu karaoke party, belting out tunes from VH1, using the television remote control as a pretend microphone. Adam accompanied her on makeshift drums using two pens and the coffee table. There was only so much Lady Gaga you could take in one night and George had headed for bed just before 11.00pm.

Not that she could sleep. It was now almost 1.00am and she had tossed and turned from one side of the king sized bed to the other, at least half a dozen times. It was hot, she had yet to work out how the air conditioning operated and she could hear crickets and other bugs, rubbing bits of themselves outside.

She closed her eyes and concentrated on the softness of her pillow. Then she heard a tapping noise. Fantastic! She turned over in bed again and pulled the covers over her head.

There was more tapping and she threw the covers off and sat up, listening in the dark.

More tapping and George realised it was coming from the window. She got out of bed, threw her t-shirt over her head and cautiously approached. She opened the glass and peered out through the shutters.

'Can I come in?' Quinn whispered.

'What are you doing here?' George questioned.

'Apologising,' he replied.

George opened up the shutters and, in seconds, Quinn had hauled himself up onto the window sill and leapt into the room.

She didn't say anything; she just looked at him, her heart already beating hard in her chest. He always had this effect on her. It was like someone had pumped her full of adrenalin.

'I'm sorry,' he said simply, swallowing nervously.

'Me too,' George told him.

Quinn kissed her, holding her tight to him and George didn't even try to resist. She couldn't and more importantly she didn't want to.

'Can you stay?' she whispered as he put his hands under her t-shirt, his fingers tracing the line of her breasts.

'Try and stop me,' Quinn answered, kissing her again.

George pulled his shirt over his head and steered him towards her bed.

Maybe it was time she stopped thinking about other people and started to think about what she wanted. If she wanted Quinn she could have him. She just needed to tell him how she felt. Was that so hard?

Quinn kissed her slowly, so slowly she thought she would combust if he didn't touch her again. It was like the inside of her mouth was being caressed by silk. It was sensual, it was sexy and it was making her ache with longing.

Outside it was starting to get light and they hadn't been to sleep. It had been agony trying to stop herself from shouting out when he made her come. She had gritted her teeth, buried her head into his chest and clung to him, trying to hold in what wanted to explode.

He stroked her hair away from her face and lightly kissed her lips.

'I'm sorry, for being an arsehole last night,' he said, looking at her with his piercing blue eyes.

'It's just hard. I don't know what to do. I'm trying to do the right thing and wanting to do the wrong thing,' George told him.

'I know and I was being a selfish prick,' Quinn stated.

'I love being with you Quinn,' George blurted out.

The second the words were out of her mouth she immediately felt self-conscious for sharing her feelings with him. She could feel her cheeks blazing and she avoided his gaze.

Quinn smiled and lifted her chin with his finger, forcing her to look at him.

'Even though I'm a selfish prick?' Quinn asked.

'Yeah. I must be a masochist,' George answered.

'A sexy masochist though,' Quinn said, rolling over on top of her.

'It's almost six, you'd better go. Helen's an early riser,' George told him, enjoying how he felt on top of her.

'Me too,' he replied with a grin.

George laughed.

'Not going to make me breakfast? I'm a breakfast lover by the way. Totally the best meal of the day,' Quinn informed her.

'I thought you musicians survived on alcohol and composition alone.'

'Don't be crazy. Alcohol, composition and eggs over easy,' Quinn said his fingers tracing her breastbone.

George let out a laugh and then stifled it with her hand as she heard movement coming from another room of the villa. She looked at Quinn, wide-eyed with concern.

'Maybe I should stay for breakfast and invite some of the paparazzi up here. Call a halt to this whole mad thing,' Quinn spoke.

'Sshh, someone will hear you,' George hissed.

'Do you care?'

'Yes!'

'Why? If everyone finds out about us the wedding's off,' Quinn said.

'But that isn't what you want. Not really.'

'Isn't it?'

'If it was, you wouldn't have got yourself into this position in the first place.'

'Maybe I didn't have a choice.'

'Everyone has a choice.'

'We'll agree to disagree.'

'Look, I don't want to argue. I don't want to waste another second arguing and I'm not the sort of girl who issues ultimatums,' George told him.

'OK, no arguing. So what shall we do instead? Ah, let me think, yes, OK, got an idea,' Quinn said, kissing her again.

'You have to go,' George repeated, kissing him but holding back slightly.

'I want to see what Marisa looks like first thing in the morning, before she puts her eyeliner on,' Quinn joked.

'Believe me you don't,' George answered.

236

There was another sound of movement and George slipped out from underneath Quinn and found her t-shirt and pants. She began putting them on, while he watched her from the bed.

'Where will Taylor think you are?' George enquired.

'At the villa.'

'Well, isn't she there?'

'No, she's at another villa with Carleen and Saffron. Stupid bitches they are. I think they share the one brain and play paper, rock, scissors to decide who's getting it for the day. Taylor thinks it's bad luck to see each other while the wedding preparations are going on,' Quinn said.

'So you're there on your own?'

'As if Roger would let that happen. No, Michael's there.'

'So where does *he* think you are?'

'He's not an early riser and he was paying quite a lot of attention to Paco last night at dinner,' Quinn told her.

'He's in charge of tablecloths,' George remarked.

'What?'

'Nothing, it doesn't matter.'

Suddenly there was a knock on the bedroom door.

'George? You awake? Mum says to tell you it's almost seven. Got to get to the catering wagon just before nine,' Marisa called through the door.

'Er, yeah, I'm awake, just getting up, thanks,' George called back.

Quinn stifled a laugh, holding a pillow against his face.

'Oh and George - can I borrow some of your foundation? Mine seems to melt in this heat and I don't want Belch to see me looking like a total minger,' Marisa continued.

'Yes, sure. I'll bring it to you when I'm up. Not actually dressed at the moment, so don't come in,' George exclaimed hurriedly.

'Oh OK, see you in a minute then. Adam's trying to make omelettes and Mum's instructing him. Bless her, she sounds just like Delia,' Marisa spoke with a laugh.

'I'll be five minutes,' George called back.

She listened; straining her ears to make sure Marisa was no longer outside her door.

'She's hot for Belch,' Quinn remarked with a smile.

'She's young. She doesn't understand that musicians have a girl in every town,' George answered, coming back to the bed and sitting down.

'That's what you thought about me,' Quinn reminded her.

'And I was right. But that's not all, Adam likes her,' George told him.

'Really? He seemed quite switched on,' Quinn said.

'He is switched on, but you can't help who you fall for. Besides she's a nice girl - a little over the top maybe - but she's harmless. Anyway, why are we having this conversation? You need to leave. Now,' George reminded him.

'And here I was thinking I might get omelettes.'

'I can't believe it's almost seven. There must be something wrong with my watch,' George said, looking at it and tapping the dial.

'Meeting your staff today then,' Quinn remarked still unmoving.

'Yeah, I hope they're capable of more than washing up,' George told him.

'I'm sure Taylor will have hired the best,' Quinn commented.

'I have very high standards,' George said.

'I know,' Quinn replied, kissing her firmly.

'You'd better go,' George told him reluctantly.

'Yeah I'd better go. I'm supposed to be meeting Taylor this morning along with the florists and the organist, at that hideous castle,' Quinn said with a sigh.

'The castle you had built. The castle you're getting married in,' George reminded.

'I didn't build it! Nothing about this wedding is how I'd do things,' Quinn told her.

'You'd better go,' George said again.

'Yeah, I'd better. Meet me later?'

'When?'

'I'll message you,' Quinn said, kissing her.

'OK.'

With that Quinn bounded out of bed and pulled on his jeans. He threw his shirt over his head and headed towards the window.

'See you,' he said, smiling at her.

'Bye,' George answered.

He pulled back the glass, opened the metal shutters and hopped out.

'George! Omelettes are ready!' Marisa's voice yelled from downstairs.

Twenty Seven

There were twenty of them, male and female, of every nationality, judging by the muttered languages and questionable fashions. Some of them looked alert, the majority of them looked half asleep and one of them, a young man in his early twenties, smelt really bad. He was called Milo. Hairs protruded out of his nostrils and he couldn't seem to stop biting his nails.

'They look like really weird,' Marisa remarked.

Marisa, George, Adam and Helen stood outside the now infamous catering wagon. It was another furiously hot day, at least thirty degrees. The worry George now had, was that unless the catering wagon had air conditioning, they were going to be in serious trouble once all the ovens got going. It would be like cooking up a storm in a sauna.

'They're just people Marisa, just like you and me,' Helen commented.

'One of them smells and that one over there, the one with the funny teeth, he's been picking his nose since he got here,' Marisa informed with a grimace of disgust.

'We need to check we've got enough gloves in that case,' George remarked.

'And hand wash and antibacterial gel,' Marisa added.

'Should you speak do you think? They seem to be looking for some sort of direction,' Adam whispered.

'I hate it, but I suppose I ought to,' George agreed, straightening the neckline of her t-shirt.

She mounted the steps to the catering wagon and turned to face her workers. She felt rather like Pontius Pilate, given the heat and her gladiator sandals. They all grew quiet and looked to her like she was the Pope, ready to address his followers.

'Hello everyone. I'm George and this is Helen, Adam and Marisa from Finger Food. I'm not sure how much experience you guys have with a function of this size, but I think if we all work as hard as we can and pull together as a team, then this wedding feast is going to be amazing,' George spoke.

The group in front of her suddenly began to clap and George hurriedly got down from the steps. She hadn't meant to sound like a politician trying to gain votes, but she knew that's how it had come across.

'A motivational speech,' Quinn said.

George squinted her eyes against the sun and saw Michael and Quinn had appeared at the back of the group.

'Oh. My. God. Are you feeling better? Was it really sunstroke? You need to hydrate, like you know, water,' Marisa blurted out before she could stop herself.

'I'm 100%. A little tired but apart from that...' Quinn replied.

He was looking at no one else but George and she felt the back of her neck start to prickle.

'Good morning Team Take! Now, you make sure you do exactly what this wonderful lady tells you to. She is a culinary Queen and you could learn a lot from her. George, you be sure to let me know if there's anything you need, anything at all, no matter how trivial it may seem,' Michael spoke his glossy hair bobbing up and down.

'Team Take. That is like *sooo* lame,' Marisa remarked only loud enough for Adam to hear.

'It could have been worse; it could have been Team Baylor or Quaylor or Berraro. Or how about Team Tinn?' Adam suggested.

Marisa let out a snigger.

'I will Michael, thanks,' George replied, avoiding Quinn's gaze.

'Right well, don't let us keep you, we're off to be interviewed for Channel Nine and then it's off to the castle. Toodle pip!' Michael spoke, waving his hand in the air like an eighteenth century courtier.

'Hey Adam. Meet me about three at the castle. I might have a job for you,' Quinn called to him.

'A job?' Adam queried.

'Yeah, I'll explain later,' Quinn spoke.

'Sure, I'll be there.'

'Oh. My. God Adam! He spoke to you!' Marisa exclaimed eyes bulging.

There were no variations in the questions. He had been asked the same set of questions numerous times in the last month. 'Will you be writing the wedding music?' 'Do you know what Taylor's dress is like?' 'Is Charlie Sheen on the guest list?' And he rolled out the same answers, 'Yes and it will feature on my new album out in the Fall.' 'No, she's kept it a closely guarded secret.' and 'You'll have to ask the wedding planner, but it could be fun if he is.'

His head was aching, his mouth was dry and the last interviewer had gone on so much about the wonderful relationship he had with his future father-in-law, by the time his fifteen minutes was up Quinn wanted to wallpaper the room with his body parts. Thank God he had plans in place for the evening.

'Hey,' George greeted later.

'Hey. Where are you right now? Not still giving orders to that team of freaks Pixie's hired you are you?'

She laughed out loud at Quinn's description and took a swig from her bottle of lager. She was sat on a lounger on the terrace of the villa, soaking up the scorching sun. Food preparation had finished early, Helen had gone to the market and Adam and Marisa had taken the Jeep to see the celebrity boltholes she was so keen to visit.

'I'm at the villa. Where are you?'

'At the castle. We're just about to rehearse these God awful, long, drawn out vows. The last timing of them was four minutes each. Four minutes! Half my songs are shorter than four minutes. Are you on your own?'

'Yep, just me, the pool and my best friend San Miguel,' George said, putting the bottle to her lips again.

'Give me fifteen and I'll be there,' Quinn told her.

'Don't! You can't! The others could be back at any time and anyway, you should stay there, rehearse the vows,' George said.

'Believe me, what I should do and what I want to do are poles apart,' Quinn said.

'I know, but we have to be realistic.'

'I am, four minutes each, that's eight minutes. Golf buggy to your villa say, four minutes. I've three minutes to spare.'

She laughed.

'OK, well even if I don't make it, you and me, we're going out tonight,' Quinn told her.

'Quinn we can't. Where will Taylor think you are? Where will I tell Adam and the others I'm going?' George asked.

'Make something up! Use your imagination. We're going to the opera. It's all arranged,' Quinn informed her.

243

'What?!' George exclaimed.

'Listen, I know it probably isn't your musical taste and I don't really think it's mine, but I like doing different things and, well, I want to do those things with you,' Quinn spoke.

'But what if we're seen? I mean the paparazzi are everywhere at the moment.'

'I've thought of that. We go in separate cars, we meet inside. I've hired a box, we'll have complete privacy,' Quinn assured.

'I don't know, it's too risky. I need this job Quinn and...' George started.

She was getting butterflies in her stomach, but it wasn't fear, it was a thrill just thinking about the risk.

'What *I* need is you,' Quinn told her.

There was a heavy silence and neither of them spoke. George closed her eyes, not knowing what to say.

'I've got nothing to wear,' she finally blurted out, trying desperately to break the intensity.

'All in hand. Say you'll come. With the bachelor party tomorrow and more rehearsals the day after, I don't know how much time we're going to have,' Quinn spoke.

'What are you going to tell Taylor and Roger?' George wanted to know.

'That I'm feeling hot and a little dizzy. It won't be a lie, not once I've seen you in the dress.'

George smiled, her resolve weakening rapidly. She was supposed to be maintaining her professionalism, building a platform for the future of Finger Food. But when she thought about spending more time with Quinn the business slipped down to second place. That had never happened before.

'It's the theatre in Murcia; I'll send you over directions with the ticket. Gotta go, four minute vow time,' Quinn said, ending the call.

George put her mobile down, put her iPod earphones back in her ears and took a deep breath. A night at the opera. How was she going to explain that away to her team? Especially Marisa. In some areas that girl was as sharp as a tack.

As if sensing she was being thought about, Marisa arrived, slamming shut the patio door behind her. She strutted out onto the terrace and began taking items of clothing out of carrier bags and putting them down on the table next to George.

'OK, right. Where do I start? I have been to *sooo* many cool shops; you won't believe what I bought!'

'What have you done with Adam?' George asked, taking her headphones out of her ears and sitting up.

'He's taken the Jeep to the castle. Said he didn't want to be late for Quinn. He's been humming and tapping and singing all the way round the town. We even had to go into a music shop so he could play guitar. Why didn't he just bring one with him?'

'You had to pay a fortune to bring excess baggage and he was worried they'd break it,' George told her.

'Look at these beauties! Aren't they just like the most gorgeous things you've ever seen?' Marisa asked, taking out a pair of banana yellow sandals with skyscraper heels.

'Are you thinking you might actually be able to walk in them?' George queried.

'I walked up and down in the shop.'

'Hmm,' George replied unconvinced.

'Well, look at these. Half price, aren't they cute?' Marisa said, holding up two flimsy looking mini dresses.

'They're tops right?' George asked.

'Argh! Mother! You said she would say that!' Marisa exclaimed loudly.

George looked round sharply. Helen was sat on the veranda underneath the canopy, seemingly engrossed in a book.

'Oh, Helen! When did you get back?' George asked, trying to quell her panic.

How long had Helen been sitting there? How much had she heard? George couldn't remember if she had said Quinn's name out loud.

'Not long ago. You were on the phone when I got here and then a package arrived for you. Then I had to hear all about Marisa's shopping trip. Just sat down,' Helen informed.

'Another package? Where is it? Is it another expensive looking box? Let me see,' Marisa spoke, stepping back towards the villa in search of the sacred parcel.

'It's just something for a function I have to go to tonight,' George said hurriedly, getting up and chasing after her.

'A function? What sort of function? Where is it? Are we invited?' Marisa questioned.

'It's just a get together, for the team leaders of each entity involved in wedding preparations. Sorry, just me,' George said, grabbing the box from the dining room table and clutching it to her chest.

'Well it isn't on the itinerary,' Marisa said, a sulky expression on her face.

'No it was a last minute thing, because the briefing ended so suddenly the other day,' George said, clutching the box tighter.

'Well we were all at the briefing, why can't we all be at this?' Marisa asked, scrutinising her.

'I don't make the rules Marisa. Right, well, I'd better take this upstairs,' George said turning and heading as swiftly as she could towards the staircase.

'Is that a dress? I saw dress material, poking out; it's a dress isn't it? Let me see!' Marisa exclaimed as George began to ascend.

'It's just something they hired, we all have to dress up, God knows why! It's probably one of Pixie's ideas. It will be something completely zany and not me at all,' George told her.

'It looks designer to me. Is it designer? Let me see!' Marisa begged about to mount the stairs after George.

'Marisa, will you stop badgering George! Isn't she allowed any privacy? Not everyone wants to tell the world their business do they?' Helen reprimanded sternly as she entered the villa.

'Well, I...'

'Come and show me how you walk in those ridiculous shoes and I'll decide whether or not to let you out in public in them. How about that?' Helen spoke.

George closed the door of her bedroom and eagerly opened the box.

On top was a map and typed directions to the theatre, together with a ticket for the opera *El amor y la pérdida* and a note from Quinn.

> ***Jeans don't cut it at the opera – hope you like it***
> ***Q x***

Twenty Eight

The material was as soft as silk. It had a pearlescent sheen to it and reflected the light as George moved around in front of the mirror. The colour was blue when she swished one way and grey when she turned another. It was full length and classic, nothing too flash or showy, just well cut and understated. The shoes matched the colour of the dress fabric. They were lightweight but high and not something George would usually wear, but they did look the part. Whatever part that was. Caterer to the wedding of the solar system? Mistress to the groom? Black sheep of the Fraser family?

She had smoothed down her usually spiky hair and had added some plain silver hoop earrings. She gazed at her reflection and then automatically her hand rose to the chain around her neck and she began to toy with the ring on it.

There was a knock on the door.

'Who is it?' George called.

'It's only me. You decent?' Adam's voice called.

'Yes, come in,' George invited.

Adam opened the door and let out a loud whistle of approval, when he saw what she was wearing.

'Wow! You look amazing!' he told her.

'Thank you,' George answered, smiling back at him.

'Marisa says you're going to some function to do with the wedding.'

'Yeah.'

'Well, they picked a fantastic outfit for you.'

'How did things go at the castle, with the music?' she asked him.

'Really good. I'm playing violin for the entrance of the bride. It's a fantastic piece Quinn wrote. It's soft and it's sensual and then it's vibrant and alive. He's an amazing songwriter,' Adam told her, sitting down on her bed.

'God! You're playing music for the entrance of the bride at the wedding to end all weddings! That's a big honour Adam,' George spoke.

'I know. I asked Quinn why he wanted me to do it and he said he'd never heard anyone play the violin with quite as much passion.'

'That's a massive compliment.'

'I know and he thinks I have a big career ahead of me,' Adam added.

'You do,' George agreed, looking at him.

'Yeah. It doesn't seem to impress Marisa though,' he said with a sigh.

'Oh?' George said, sitting next to him on the bed.

'I tried to let her know I was interested you know, by the things I said, by putting my arm around her, by opening doors for her and carrying her bags and stuff but - she just didn't seem to notice.'

'Listen Ad, sometimes, especially when you've known someone a long time, you have to be a bit more obvious about your change of feelings. I mean you two have always been friends, friends open doors and carry bags, I think you need to be more direct,' George said.

'What d'you mean?'

'I mean maybe you should ask her out on a date. Take her to that celebrity restaurant she wants to go to or something. Make it clear it's a date not just two friends having dinner together,' George told him.

'What if she says no?'

'Come on, this is Marisa! Being invited out to *the* celebrity hangout in the area! There is no way on Earth she is going to say no,' George said with a smile.

'But I don't want her to say yes because she wants to go there. I want her to say yes because she wants to go there with me,' Adam explained, looking at her with his big, soulful, brown eyes.

'Who wouldn't want to go anywhere with you?' George said, taking hold of his hand.

'You're biased, because I'm your little brother,' Adam said with a laugh.

He took his hand from hers and stood up.

'So how are you getting to this function then? Car picking you up?' Adam enquired.

'No, I'm driving,' George informed.

'In that dress and those shoes?'

'I was going to put sandals on and change when I got there.'

'Don't be daft, I'll drive you. Where is it?' Adam asked.

'There's no need to do that,' George said, picking up her bag and going to the door.

'But if I drive, you can have a couple of beers or champagne. Free drinks all night I bet,' Adam said, following her out.

'Honestly, I'll be fine. I don't really feel like drinking,' George said, hurrying down the stairs in a bid to get away from all the questioning.

'Hang on, what did you say? You don't feel like drinking? Are you alright?' Adam questioned.

'Look, keep your voice down or Marisa is going to be in here asking questions and to be honest she scares me when she starts asking questions,' George hissed.

'So what's the deal? Why the secrecy?' Adam wanted to know.

'I, well, er...' George began, racking her brain for something sensible to say.

'You've got a date haven't you? The dress, the shoes, there's no function, you're going on a date!' Adam exclaimed.

'Will you keep your voice down! Yes, OK, I'm going on a date, but don't you tell anyone,' George ordered him seriously.

'Well who with? How long's it been going on?'

'Not long. It's nothing serious,' George said as she looked around the dining room for her jacket.

'Well who is it? Someone you met here in Spain? That's freaking quick work.'

She didn't respond to the question, her heart was hammering on her ribcage. She picked up the keys to the Jeep and headed towards the door.

'Hold it! Where are you going? Aren't you going to let us see what was in that box? Holy shit! Look at you!' Marisa exclaimed in awe as she came out of the living room and stood gawping at George, chewing gum sticking to her bottom lip.

'I'll take it I look sick,' George responded, opening the door.

'She's going on a date,' Adam blurted out.

'What?! I thought you said it was a function. A date with who? Have you got a secret man here in Spain? Oh. My. God it's someone from the band isn't it? I know, I know, it's Eddie the drummer. Oh God I should have guessed. He kept making a detour for your canapé tray at the after-show parties. How long has it been going on?' Marisa wanted to know.

'Not long. Look I'd better go or I'm going to be late,' George said, checking her watch again.

'Bit dressed up for Eddie the drummer; I've never seen him in anything that isn't ripped. Maybe it's someone from management. Is it Michael? He's always all over you telling everyone how great you are,' Marisa carried on.

'Marisa, Michael's gay,' Adam informed her.

'Is he?' Marisa asked her eyes widening in surprise.

'He's gayer than Colin and Justin and John Barrowman all in the same room singing ABBA,' Adam told her.

'I'm going,' George said, opening the door.

'Honestly, let me drive you. I don't mind and I promise I won't loiter around to see who you're meeting,' Adam said.

'Am I going to be able to say no and leave this villa alive?' George asked.

'No.'

'OK, well, let's go but you are not bringing me home again, I'll get a taxi,' George insisted.

'Quiz her all the way there and come back with a name,' Marisa ordered.

His hands were trembling as he did up his shirt buttons. He had to stop this shaking lark; he had a reputation to uphold. He couldn't appear vulnerable to anyone around here. The truth was, he was both scared and excited about tonight. It was a big deal taking George to the opera, for lots of reasons. Tonight was going to be special for both of them and he didn't want to f**k it up.

He splashed some cologne on his face and looked at himself in the mirror. He let out a sigh of discontent and picked up his watch.

Adam talked all the way into Murcia, about university, about Marisa, about Quinn, particularly about Quinn and how much he had enjoyed working on music with him. It was thirty minutes before they were pulling up just across the square from the theatre.

The temperature was still in the mid twenties and the city was alive with people, walking up the picturesque boulevards. The theatre itself was an impressive building. Its facade was pink and grey and the unusual colour made it stand out amongst the other structures. It was both grand and statuesque.

'Where are you meeting him? Just so I know, not because I want to report back to Marisa,' Adam asked.

'I'm not completely stupid; there is no way I'm telling you that.'

'Then I'll have to sit here and see where you go,' Adam said, folding his arms across his chest.

'I'm not going anywhere until you drive off,' George replied, copying his pose.

'How childish.'

'Isn't it.'

'Come on George, why all the cloak and dagger stuff about this guy? What's wrong with him?' Adam wanted to know.

'There's nothing wrong with him.'

'Then tell us who he is.'

'No.'

'Why not?'

'Because it's nobody's business but mine.'

'Is he married or something?' Adam enquired.

George visibly stiffened, although she tried to disguise it by putting a hand to her hair. Adam picked up on it straight away.

'Jesus George! He's married right?' he exclaimed in horror.

'He isn't married, look; I'm getting out of the car. Drive home! What is this sudden obsession with my love life?' George wanted to know.

'We just care about you that's all,' Adam told her.

'Well thanks, but I'm thirty four, it isn't necessary,' George said, getting out of the Jeep and brushing down her dress.

'Alright, just trying to be the protective brother. I get the message; I'll go but just take care OK?' Adam said, starting up the engine.

'OK,' George replied with a smile.

'And I'll make sure Marisa doesn't wait up,' Adam told her.

'Thanks,' George said.

'See you,' Adam ended.

He started the engine and pulled back into the traffic.

She waited until he was out of sight before entering the square and walking towards the grand building.

There were other people going in, all of them looked amazing in different gowns, some long, some short. All the men were dressed in suits, some in dinner jackets, others wearing flowers in their lapels. She looked the part in her beautiful dress, but she felt like a fish out of water.

The theatre itself was beautiful. It wasn't particularly old inside, but it had obviously been sympathetically restored. There were people milling around in the foyer, chatting quickly in Spanish, laughing and enjoying the occasion.

George took her ticket from her bag and looked at it. She had no idea where to go. All the signs were in Spanish and her only hope was a dark haired twenty-something in an official looking uniform. She took a deep breath and prayed he knew some English.

'Excuse me, could you tell me which way?' George asked, showing him her ticket and speaking probably too slowly.

'*Si*, yes. Up the stairs, to the right,' he instructed her with a smile.

'Thank you - sorry I mean *gracias,* ' George said, attempting the language.

She held up her dress and went up the stairs as gracefully as she could. If she was honest, the nice shoes were killing her feet and she was starting to wish she had worn her boots. Underneath the long frock she might have just about got away with it.

Everywhere she looked there was glamour. There were a group of Spanish women, dressed in garish, bright outfits, drinking, talking loudly and laughing. They looked at George, as she walked by them. It was a look of desire for her dress. She smiled to herself as she made her way along the corridor. There was no way they would covet anything about her if they had seen her in jeans and her 'Rock Chick' t-shirt, sweating from the heat, Quorn all over her hands.

She checked the ticket again and looked at the sign above a small door. This was it; this was the entrance to the box. George pushed on the handle and stepped through. The scene before her took her breath away. The theatre was as spectacular on the inside as it was on the outside. She could see everyone in the whole place. People were taking their seats, ushers were moving amongst them, guiding the lost, and she could see right into the orchestra pit. But, what was more breathtaking than any of that, was the painted ceiling. The beautiful, luminous artwork looked down on her like it had been finished only minutes before. It shone, it almost breathed and it was like nothing she had seen before.

'Hey,' Quinn greeted as he stepped into the box and closed the door behind him.

'Oh, hi,' George replied with a blush, turning to look at him.

He was dressed in an expensive fitted black suit, with a white shirt, slightly open at the neck. The outfit only enhanced his attractiveness.

'You look amazing,' Quinn said unable to keep his eyes from her.

'You're so good at choosing clothes for me, I have a suspicion you're keeping a tape measure with you and whipping it out when I'm asleep,' George replied.

'As if I would waste my time with a tape measure, when there are so many more things I could be doing,' Quinn answered smiling.

'We're at the theatre. This is not the place for smut,' George told him.

'I believe, all those centuries ago, this was exactly the place for it.'

'You're just remembering history to suit your wicked mind.'

'Do you care?' Quinn asked her.

'No,' George admitted.

'Beer?' Quinn offered and from behind his back he produced an ice bucket, filled with bottles of Spanish lager.

'And here I was thinking it was bound to be champagne.'

'You can have champagne if you want. I'll order some.'

'No! I'm just kidding. I'm not really keen on it,' George said.

'Me neither. Not since I had to try twelve different varieties before Taylor would make a decision on what to have with the speeches,' Quinn replied.

George smiled, but inside her stomach contracted. He was getting married, she couldn't forget that important fact. It was real, it was happening in a couple of days and there was no getting away from it. His comment spoiled her anticipation of the performance a little, took the shine off the dress and made the shoes pinch her toes that bit extra.

Sensing what she was thinking, Quinn put the cooler down, on the small table to the side of the box, and came over to her. He kissed her firmly, but with all the sensuality of someone who knew what she was thinking and knew what she needed.

She kissed him back, and tried to force any thoughts of Taylor to the very back of her mind. He was hers, for tonight at least. She was the one he ran to, she was the one he couldn't get enough of. Taylor was just for show.

'I won't mention her or it again. Not one word. No talk about vows or seating plans, no mention of dove crap all over the priest, nothing about Pixie keeling over when the florist thought the wedding was next week. Nothing else,' Quinn told her.

'Dove crap all over the priest!' George said with a laugh.

'Yes, but I mean it - we are not going to talk or think about Saturday. We're not going to think about what it means or what it doesn't mean. Tonight we're going to watch the performance and we're going to talk, like there's nothing in the world but us,' Quinn continued.

'Pretend you mean,' George said with a sigh.

'Temporarily forget there are strings attached,' Quinn said.

'Can you do that?'

'Can you?'

'I don't know. Pass me a beer and we'll find out,' George spoke.

Quinn handed her a bottle and they sat down in their seats.

The opera was all in Spanish, but George was surprised how much you could pick up, just by watching the expressions on the faces of the performers and by the tempo and definition of the music. And the costumes also told a tale all of their own. They were bold and elaborate for the well-off and paupers' rags for the destitute.

The tale was of Maria, a young Spanish girl, cast out from the family home when her teenage sweetheart got her pregnant.

Maria was forced to live on the streets, met wrong man after wrong man, until she met a Mr Right who loved her, but couldn't love her child. So she had to decide what to do. Did she live a life of luxury with the man who loved her but couldn't love her past mistake? Or carry on how she was, whoring herself out to keep a roof over her son's head. And in the end, she chose neither. She did what everyone seemed to do so dramatically in opera, she killed herself. She slit her throat, rather too realistically, in the middle of the stage. And that was the end. Poor Maria, dead, no happy ending, no Mr Right and no child. Just death. The curtain came down.

Quinn looked over to George, as the orchestra performed their final notes and found her face completely awash with tears. Not just a trickle of emotion in appreciation of the performance, but big, fat, tears filled with sorrow. Her shoulders shook and she sobbed out loud. She looked up at him and he took her in his arms and held her as she cried.

'Hey. Sshh, come on. The story's bleak I admit, but then sometimes life is bleak isn't it?' Quinn spoke as he stroked her hair.

'She turned her back on her child. She was selfish, right to the very bloody end,' George replied, wiping at her eyes with her fingers.

She knew she was rubbing at her make-up, but she didn't care. It felt like the floodgates of emotion had finally opened after all these years and there was nothing she could do to shut them up again.

'She didn't want to give him up, she had to. She didn't want to live on the streets, she couldn't live with Roberto, what choice did she have?' Quinn asked.

'She should have told Roberto if he couldn't love her son then he didn't really love her. She should have made her own way in life, with her son, not slit her throat open in the middle of the market square. She should have fought harder, but she was weak. She let other people tell her what she ought to do for the best,' George spoke passionately.

'Hey, it's just fiction, it's not real. Maria's fine, her name's Sophia, she's a fantastic actress. I'll introduce you if you like,' Quinn suggested.

'No, Maria isn't fine. She's damaged and she's sad and she wants her son more than anything else, but she doesn't know whether that's really the right thing for him. What if she isn't how a mother should be? What if knowing the truth isn't the best for him?' George questioned.

She was screwing her hands up into fists in her lap. She didn't know what to do. She needed another drink. She wanted to shout and scream and tear at her hair. She wanted to break something.

'Is there something you want to tell me?' Quinn asked her.

The lid was off. It had been pressurised shut for so long but now, because of the opera, because of Quinn and how he made her feel it couldn't be contained. Not any more.

'I'm Maria. I had a son and I gave him up and I've been letting him down ever since by not acknowledging him, by letting him believe a lie,' George blurted out, looking back at Quinn with her puffy, sore, mascara-smudged eyes.

'You have a son,' Quinn repeated.

She saw him swallow, saw the shock in his eyes at what she'd said. She didn't care; she needed to tell him, no matter what the news did to him.

'I was young like her. I had nothing to offer him, but I wanted him. I wanted to be his mother but she told me not to. She told me it would ruin my life and I believed her,' George carried on.

'You believed who?'

'My mother looked after him, brought him up as her own and kept me away from him. I was just close enough to be able to see him grow up, but far enough away not to be involved,' George told him.

'Adam,' Quinn said, letting out a long, slow breath.

'And now she wants me to tell him, because she's really sick and we don't know how that's going to go.'

'So tell him,' Quinn told her.

'Oh yeah, because it's so easy. He's going to just say "oh great George, I thought you were my sister but now I know you're my mum and everyone's been lying to me for eighteen years I feel so much better".'

'Why don't you want him to know? What are you scared of?' Quinn enquired.

'He looks up to me now. His big sister, owning a catering company and working for you on the wedding of the millennium. He respects me. All that will fall apart if I tell him the truth.'

'You don't know that.'

'I'm scared,' George admitted.

'Come here,' Quinn said, squeezing her tighter and drawing her into his body protectively. She felt like a child being wrapped up and looked after.

He held her, stroked her hair and kissed her forehead until her crying subsided. After a while she started to breathe almost normally again.

'I'm sorry,' she said, raising her head and meeting his eyes.

'What for?'

'For laying all this on you. It was the opera. It was poor tragic Maria and her suicidal tendencies,' George told him.

'I'm having all the knives removed from your kitchen, first thing,' Quinn said with half a smile.

'That might make it difficult to prepare a wedding feast.'

Quinn smiled and smoothed away her remaining tears with his thumb.

'And how do you feel? Now you know,' George asked him.

'What d'you mean?' Quinn enquired.

'Well, I have an eighteen year old son. I had him when I was sixteen. You know, bad, dirty, schoolgirl pregnancy. I'm stupid and irresponsible and not the person you thought I was,' George spoke.

'Why would any of that change how I feel about you?' Quinn wanted to know.

'Well, I'm not just the owner of a moderately successful catering business. I'm not like you thought I was. I'm someone who got herself pregnant at sixteen and gave her son to her control freak of a mother. I've got issues and baggage and...'

'And your success in business is all I'm interested in is it? Because you have a past, I'm supposed to wash my hands of you. Maybe be shocked and disgusted and cast you out? Probably arrange to have you stoned or something?' Quinn suggested.

'Well, maybe not stoned.'

'George, there's nothing you could do, past, present or future that would change the way I feel about you. Nothing,' Quinn said sincerely.

He looked into her eyes and touched her damp cheek with his fingers.

'You don't mean that,' George told him.

'I do. Here, look - I got you something,' Quinn said, letting her go and reaching into the pocket of his jacket.

He took out a black leather box and handed it to her.

'You have to stop buying me things. Marisa thinks Peacocks have started doing a line in designer swimwear -

oh Quinn,' George exclaimed when she saw what was inside.

It was an exquisite watch. It was beautiful and classic with a slim gold band. It had an oval face outlined in silver and it was heavily encrusted with diamonds.

'I don't know what to say. It's gorgeous,' George said, swallowing a knot of emotion in her throat.

'I had it engraved.'

He took it out of the box and turned it over in his hand to show her the reverse.

G, I'm yours, Q x

She looked at the words and slowly traced them with her fingers.

'I mean it George,' he insisted.

'I know you do,' she answered, looking up at him.

'If I could give you more, you know I would.'

'I don't want to give you up,' George told him.

'You don't have to,' Quinn said sincerely.

'But I have to share you. We have to sneak about. We can't kiss in the street or spend a whole day together. We can't lie on the beach or go grocery shopping, or go out to dinner at the celebrity restaurant Marisa says does truffles...' George began.

'Is that where you want to go?'

'Well no, but if I did, we just couldn't do it.'

'It won't be like that forever,' Quinn told her.

'Won't it?'

'No.'

'Then for how long?'

'I don't know. Until I've done enough to pay back what I owe Roger,' Quinn stated with a sigh.

'Pay him back? Pay him back for what?' George asked.

'Just for helping me. When I really, desperately needed it,' Quinn replied.

'What did he do that's worth giving up your whole life for?'

'He saved it once,' Quinn answered.

'After the accident?' George guessed.

'Yeah - look, let me put this on. At least we can synchronise watches, make sure we don't miss a second,' Quinn said, changing the subject.

George unfastened her old watch and offered him her wrist. He paused.

'I didn't know you had a tattoo,' he said, swallowing as he looked at the black initial inked on the inside of her wrist.

'Yeah. Another stupid thing I did when I was sixteen,' George said.

'What does the 'P' stand for?' Quinn asked.

'Paul,' George told him.

'Is he Adam's father?'

'Yes.'

'So where is he now? I guess he left you right, when the going got tough.'

'Not like you think.'

'There. It looks beautiful on you,' Quinn said, admiring the watch.

'It's so elegant. Are you sure it's going to go with jeans?' George asked, admiring it.

'It goes with you,' Quinn replied, swallowing poignantly.

'What's wrong?'

'What's wrong? God, where do I start? I wish I could give you more. I wish I could just leave this stupid, dumb wedding fiasco and go somewhere where no one would find me,' Quinn said, sighing.

'That's going to be a bit difficult when you're one of the world's most famous stars,' George told him.

'Maybe anonymity is what I need back. Maybe I need to go back to being John Doe,' Quinn said, running his hands over his hair.

'John Doe?' George queried.

'It doesn't matter. I'm dwelling on what I've got to do on Saturday, when we said we weren't going to talk about it.'

'Everyone else has gone. We don't have to go yet do we?' George asked him, looking at the deserted theatre.

'No, we don't have to go yet,' Quinn told her.

'I've gone and told you everything there is to know about me tonight. It's all Maria's fault. Her and her tragic life. Why did you bring me here?' George asked with a half-hearted smile.

'I wanted you to see it. I wanted you to be moved by the music. This opera - well the score for the opera, I wrote it,' Quinn informed her.

'What!' George exclaimed amazed.

'I wrote it under another name. I didn't think it went with the image Roger's made for me. But it was just something I wanted to do,' Quinn told her.

'Why didn't you tell me before?' George asked him.

'Because I didn't know whether you would like it. I had no idea it was going to move you to tears and make you tell me all your secrets,' Quinn said with a smile.

'I wish you would tell me yours,' George spoke.

'I wish that too,' Quinn answered, holding her hand.

It was late when he got back to the villa, the early hours. Michael was asleep on the sofa, his mouth hanging open, snoring like a walrus, an empty bottle of Fanta hanging out of his hand. This guy did fizzy drinks like a junkie did crystal meth. Quinn closed the door and went back into the kitchen.

George had a son. How did that make him feel? He'd told her it didn't change things, but did it? He hated the sound of this Paul. The necklace she always wore and played with was obviously something to do with him. All these years and she was still wearing it like a constant reminder. He was jealous! Shit! He was jealous of a sixteen year old! What right did he have for jealousy? He was the one getting married. He needed to man up! He needed to get control back. He'd almost told her everything about him and Roger tonight. He couldn't do that. Not ever. If he did, he was finished.

Twenty Nine

'What time did she get in?'

'I don't know exactly. Probably around three.'

'Three! She *sooo* slept with him then.'

'We don't know that. I mean she was dressed up. They probably went to an exclusive club or something.'

'No. She slept with him for sure. Have you seen the bling on her wrist?'

'No. What bling?'

'Oh. My. God! Like the handmade gold and platinum watch encrusted with diamonds. Posh Spice had one on in *Star Life* magazine the other week.'

'So he must be rich.'

'He must be bloody loaded. I'm still not convinced it isn't Eddie the drummer.'

'I don't think it's him. He isn't George's type at all.'

'Has she got a type? Apart from having the absolute agony of hearing her flirt with Simon from the bakery, I've never seen her with anyone, or heard her talk about anyone.'

'She's a private person that's all.'

'Either that or she doesn't have a life outside of Finger Food. I can't believe you didn't get a name out of her.'

'Come on. I couldn't have interrogated her all the way to Murcia.'

'Why not? I would of.'

'You're one scary lady when you want to know something.'

'Hello?! Is anyone listening to me?' George yelled at the top of her voice.

They had been in the catering wagon since just after 9.00am and she couldn't cope with the amount of people in the small space. The extra numbers to 'help' were doing the exact opposite and no one could hear anything, because the radio one of them had brought along was at full volume, screeching out an irritating pop song, in Spanish.

Everyone heard George now, and someone realised it might be appropriate if the radio was turned down.

'Right, good. Finally, some attention! OK, now listen up. Ever heard of the expression 'too many cooks spoil the broth?' Well, my broth is in danger of being spoiled. Go! Come back to the castle tonight to help serve,' George ordered.

No one said anything, no one moved; everyone just stayed still and looked at their leader, waiting to hang on her next words.

'Didn't you understand what I said? I can't work like this. I can't move, I can't hear. There are too many people and you need to leave,' George ordered for a second time.

'That means go!' Marisa screeched out at the very top of her voice.

'Look, I don't mean to be ungrateful. But this many people to help prepare canapés for a hundred people isn't necessary. I do this all the time, with a team of two. Have the rest of the day off, I'll make sure you still get paid,' George told them.

At the mention of still getting paid, the enthusiasm for leaving increased substantially and people began to head for the door as fast as they could. Within a couple of minutes, everyone had departed and only the Finger Food team remained.

'God, I thought my head was going to explode. We cannot have all of them in the kitchen like that ever again. Not even on Saturday. We're going to have to load the trolleys, bump them down the ramp, and have them outside ready for them to wheel up to the castle,' George spoke.

'I have to admit it was getting a bit whiffy in here,' Helen said, cutting up avocados.

'God, yeah, it was. Especially when you were stood near the one with the crusty face. Although it definitely wasn't his face that reeked. His top had at least three day old sweat stains on it,' Marisa added.

'Oh Marisa! That's enough! And since when have you been the leading authority on sweat stains?' Helen enquired.

'Since they did a deodorant versus mint and tea tree oil lotion test in *Right Now* magazine,' Marisa answered, folding her arms across her chest and looking authoritative.

There were three theatrical raps on the door and then it burst open. Michael hopped into the wagon, beaming from ear to ear, a clipboard in his hands, his forehead glistening with sweat.

'Think he needs some tea tree lotion on that forehead,' Adam whispered to Marisa.

She giggled and popped another tablet of gum into her mouth.

'Good morning Team Finger Food! And how are we all today?' Michael greeted buoyantly.

'Fine. Now George has got rid of the hired help. They all smell and most of them can't even shell an egg,' Marisa told him.

'Oh George, is this true? Are they not up to standard? Shall I hire more?' Michael asked her.

'No! No more please. We're fine. Everything's fine, now we've sorted out the overcrowding,' George insisted.

'Good, good. So everything on course? Canapés being prepared for both parties?' Michael asked, looking around the room.

'*Both* parties?' George asked.

'Yes, the bachelor and the bachelorette. Did you not get my revised instructions? They should have been delivered to your villa yesterday,' Michael said, checking notes on his clipboard.

'No, I didn't. You want me to cater for the bachelor party too?'

'Yes, desperately! They were supposed to be going to a casino in town, but Taylor thought it would be nice to have both parties together, at the castle. So we will need food,' Michael explained.

'Vegetarian?' George queried.

'No! Good Lord no! Not for the men. I can't imagine Quinn being happy with that.'

'Then we have a problem. Taylor's having vegetarian, that's all the ingredients I have.'

'Oh. Oh dear. That isn't good. That isn't good at all. I'll give the suppliers a call,' Michael said his usual happy demeanour slipping as he got out his phone.

'Who has their hen and stag parties together? I mean where do you all look when the strippers arrive?' Marisa wanted to know.

'Don't ask me. I'm hoping there won't be any. Naked body parts near the avocado and walnut dip doesn't bear thinking about,' Helen replied.

'I don't know,' Adam answered with a grin.

'Mother! Like how old are you? Everyone likes a good stripper. I remember Cheryl's eighteenth. She got her top off, covered herself in squirty cream and got Big Brian to lick it off her,' Marisa informed.

'What a girl,' George answered, turning back to the filling she was perfecting.

'It was the working men's club,' Marisa replied.

'They're used to worse on a Saturday night,' Helen added.

'There's loads of chicken and stuff in the fridge,' Adam remarked, sticking his head out from behind the door.

'Yes I know that. But it's all for Saturday. We can't use any of it, some of it was allegedly flown in from Sweden,' George replied.

'OK, not so good news. It seems I can't get any supplies delivered until tomorrow which is obviously...' Michael began as he came off the telephone.

'Like a day too late,' Marisa interrupted.

'Yes, so I suppose...'

'Well, I guess I'll have to go to the local supermarket and see what they have,' George spoke, wiping her hands on a tea towel.

'Oh would you? That would get me out of a sticky situation. Just do the best you can with what they have,' Michael suggested.

'I hope they like chorizo,' George said, taking off her apron and approaching the sink to wash her hands.

'I'll get someone to drive you and to carry your bags. Put everything on your invoice, plus your inconvenience fee,' Michael said.

'Don't worry, I will,' George replied.

Just over half an hour later a Jeep pulled up alongside George. Quinn was in the driving seat, grinning over at her.

'Dennis tells me he's been detailed to take you to the supermarket and carry your bags,' he called, removing his sunglasses.

'That's right. No one told me I was catering for the bachelor party and apparently you can't go a night without meat,' George replied, looking over her shoulder to see who might be watching.

'Hop in then,' Quinn said, leaning over and opening the passenger door.

'What?'

'I gave Dennis something else to do. And you said last night you wanted us to go shopping together. Problem solved,' Quinn told her.

'Quinn, I didn't mean...' George began.

'Yes you did. Come on, get in before we get a crew from Channel Nine following us,' he ordered.

'I'm not sure this is such a good idea. There are paparazzi in town and there's another group by the entrance, I've seen them myself today. They're photographing anything that moves and most things that don't,' George told him as she got in and they pulled away.

'Yeah, I know. So what? I'm taking the caterer to the supermarket; it's my wedding, if I want to be more hands on what's wrong with that?' Quinn asked her.

'Let's just not get caught with our hands anywhere they shouldn't be,' George answered.

'Where's that sense of adventure gone?' Quinn enquired with a grin.

George smiled, slipping on her sunglasses.

They headed away from La Manga and drove out towards Pilar de la Horadada. Within forty minutes Quinn was pulling into the car park of the big Mercadona supermarket.

'Right, note this down. This is Quinn Blake and George Fraser shopping for groceries,' Quinn said, getting out of the Jeep.

'You think this is funny?' George asked him.

'Hell yeah! I've never been grocery shopping with anyone before,' Quinn replied laughing.

'Don't be ridiculous. Where do you get your food? You can't eat out all the time.'

'I have someone that takes care of it for me. Then someone who comes and cooks it for me,' Quinn told her.

'That's really bad,' George remarked.

'OK, so you show me what I'm missing out on,' Quinn said and he took hold of her hand.

George flinched and snatched her hand away.

'We can't hold hands here. It's too public, what if people see?' she asked him, looking around at the other customers, heading towards the entrance.

'We're forty kilometres away from the carnival. Can you see any of my team visiting a supermarket?' Quinn said.

'Er, well, no. I expect they have people to do it for them.'

'Yeah, you and me today. Come on,' Quinn urged and he took her hand again, holding it firmly in his own.

They entered the busy shop and Quinn picked up a basket.

'What are you doing with that?' George asked him.

'Well, don't we need something to put the stuff in?'

'Yeah and we're going to need something bigger than that, preferably something with wheels,' George spoke, pointing to a trolley.

'Jesus! How much stuff goes into making a few little canapés?' Quinn said, shaking his head.

'You don't have to have canapés,' George reminded him.

'Don't I?'

'No. I mean we can buy whatever you like. After all, it's your party and you're paying for it,' George told him.

'I've never had a choice before.'

'I don't know! Never been shopping, never choosing what you want to eat. Today's full of firsts for you isn't it?' George said.

'Are you laughing at me?'

'No, of course not,' George said unable to stop herself from letting out a laugh.

'You want a trolley?' Quinn asked.

'Yes please.'

'And I suppose you want me to push.'

'Well you can if you want to give it a try. But it might need experience, particularly if it has a dodgy wheel,' George replied.

'Experience huh?' Quinn said, collecting a trolley and bringing it over.

'Yeah. There's a knack to it,' George continued.

'OK, well how about I drive and you navigate,' Quinn said.

As quick as a flash, he picked George up and hurled her into the trolley.

'Quinn! Don't be stupid! Quinn! Get me out!' George screeched as Quinn set off, pushing the trolley down the aisle at top speed.

'I like shopping. I'm going to do it more often,' Quinn replied, laughing as he turned a corner and the trolley reeled to one side.

'Get me out of here or I swear I'll...' George began.

'Or you'll what?' Quinn asked, stopping the trolley and looking at her.

'I'll make you something really disgusting to eat tonight. Something vile. The most vomit inducing meal I can think of,' George told him.

'Is that the best you've got?'

'I'll tell the press you have a really, really, small penis,' George threatened.

'Ouch! But you know they would never believe it. OK you got me. Come on, out you come,' Quinn said, helping George jump from the trolley.

She brushed her t-shirt down and let out a sigh.

'Hey, come on. It was funny. These carts are great! Everyone was looking at us, like they've never seen anyone do that before,' Quinn asked.

'You say that like it's a good thing,' George replied.

'Come on. I'm a condemned man. Let me have a little fun,' Quinn told her.

George didn't reply.

'Don't be mad. Are you mad with me?' Quinn wanted to know.

'No, I'm not mad with you,' she began.

She paused, took a breath and held his eyes with hers.

'I'm falling in love with you,' she finished.

Quinn looked at her, seeing the expression of sincerity and sadness in her eyes. She looked to the floor, now feeling embarrassed and vulnerable. She had told him how she felt. It had crept up on her. She had held the emotion back as hard as she could, but there was no stopping it now. He made her feel like no other man ever had, in every way imaginable.

'I'm not falling in love with you George,' Quinn spoke, raising her head with his thumb and making her look at him.

George swallowed.

'I'm already there. And I've been there a long time,' Quinn told her.

He pushed her back against the shelves of long life juice and kissed her, firmly and passionately, in front of every shopper in the vicinity. His hands were at the waistband of her combats, her fingers were under his t-shirt, running along the ridge of his spine. For a second, neither of them cared who could see.

'*Disculpe. El jugo de manzana,*' a male voice spoke.

George hurriedly let go of Quinn and looked at a little old Spaniard in front of her.

'He wants to get to the apple juice,' Quinn spoke gently pulling George towards him and giving the shopper access to the shelf.

'Oh! Sorry! I mean – shit. What's Spanish for "sorry"?' George questioned.

'*Perdón senor.* Listen, I'm glad you told me you know - how you feel,' Quinn said, holding her hands.

'It doesn't change anything though does it? We're going to be living separate lives in a few days.'

'That doesn't mean we're separated,' Quinn told her.

'Doesn't it? Me on one side of the world, you the other - with a wife,' George spoke.

'I can't change that right now, you know that.'

'No Quinn, I don't know that, because you won't tell me why you're doing it. Why you're really doing it. I can't believe you're getting married, pledging yourself to someone, because someone else wants you to,' George continued.

'You don't understand.'

'No, I know I don't. Because you won't tell me the full story.'

'It's hard George.'

'You say you love me.'

'I do love you.'

'Then you should tell me.'

'I haven't told anyone. Not one person, ever. If it got out then...' Quinn said, taking a deep breath.

He was starting to perspire and his face was reddening.

'Don't you trust me?' George asked.

'Of course I do.'

'Then...'

'Look, I need more time,' Quinn said, shifting from one foot to the other.

'We don't have more time, you're getting married the day after tomorrow.'

'I can't talk about it now,' Quinn said, rubbing his forehead.

'Do you owe Roger money?' George wanted to know.

'I wish it was that simple,' Quinn spoke, closing his eyes and taking a deep breath.

'Are you OK?' George asked him.

'No, I think I'm going to...' Quinn began.

His sentence was cut short as his knees buckled and he collapsed on the floor.

'Quinn - HELP! Please, someone, HELP! Shit! What's the Spanish for "help"?' George shouted frantically.

Thirty

He could see her so clearly, but she looked different somehow. She was holding his hand and they were running down the road. They were screaming with laughter and they were out of breath. Their faces were glowing, their eyes were bright.

He didn't want to wake up. He was happy here, he was where he wanted to be.

'Quinn? Please open your eyes. I don't know what to do! They want to call an ambulance, I think. They keep saying something like *'ambulancia'.* I'm guessing that's what it is,' George spoke, holding his head on her lap.

He was pale now, clammy and his pulse was weak. She only knew about burns and eye washes from a vague First Aid course she had done at college. She hadn't taken all that much notice of it. She had snuck out of that lesson most weeks, to sleep with one of the A-Level tutors.

'See?' Quinn said his eyes beginning to open.

'Quinn? Are you OK? Should I get an ambulance?' George asked him.

A crowd of shoppers were circled around them, including the manager, on his mobile phone talking excessively quickly and gesticulating frantically.

'No, no ambulance. Let's just get out of here,' Quinn said, sitting up and attempting to stand.

He wobbled and had to hold George for support.

'Just sit for a bit. I'll get some water. Shit, what's the Spanish for "water"? Why didn't I bring a damn phrasebook with me?' George asked.

'Agua,' Quinn replied.

'Agua por favor,' George said to the group of people watching.

All of them hurried off, shuffling towards the bottled water section, where they started to take down two litre bottles of the stuff.

'Are you sure you're OK? Maybe you should go to hospital, to get checked over,' George suggested.

'I'm fine, this happens. You know it happens. I just had the weirdest dream though. I think we were going to get married and you had flowers in your hair,' Quinn told her, taking hold of her hand and smiling.

'Are you sure you didn't knock your head?' George replied.

'I'm sure,' he answered.

One of the shoppers passed over a bottle of water and George took it gratefully, passing it to Quinn. He drank some quickly, spilling it down his chin and wiping it away with the back of his arm.

'Let's get out of here. To Hell with the canapés, I'll order Chinese or something,' he said, getting to his feet and taking a breath.

'OK but I'm driving,' George insisted.

'Pull up over there,' Quinn directed.

'Where?'

'Just there, on the right.'

George brought the Jeep to a halt and turned off the engine.

'We ought to get back. I've left the team on their own doing the veggie canapés and...' George started, checking her new watch.

'Come on, there's steps. I run this way sometimes,' Quinn said, ignoring her and getting out of the car.

'Wait! Where are you going? You ought to stay out of the sun, Quinn!' George called as he disappeared over the edge of the rock face.

'You're sounding your age George! Start taking off your clothes!' he yelled.

George hurried out of the car and followed his lead, down stone steps carved into the hillside. The cliff was high and the path uneven, but she could see a small deserted bay at the foot of it. There was a short strip of golden sand and turquoise water lapping the perimeter.

Out of breath, in her haste not to get left behind, she stepped down onto the sand and saw Quinn was stood at the edge of the water. His bare feet were in the sea, his naked body was embracing the sun and his clothes were in a pile a few metres away.

'Are you mad?' George asked him.

'No, I'm naked,' he answered with a grin, turning to face her.

'I think you were lying. I think you definitely knocked your head on the floor of the supermarket back there,' George said, trying to keep focussed on his face.

'George Fraser, are you a prude? Do you have a problem with public nudity?' Quinn asked.

'I'm not a prude, you know that,' she replied, standing her ground and trying not to let embarrassment filter into her expression.

'Then take your clothes off,' Quinn told her.

He put his hand up under her top and dragged it over her head, leaving her stood in a bra that had seen better days and her work combats.

'Anyone could come down those steps and see us,' George whispered as he deftly undid the back of her bra.

'I know,' he responded his mouth meeting hers.

'We shouldn't be doing this. Any of this,' George breathed as he pushed her bra straps down her arms and removed it.

'I want to know what you feel like in the ocean, covered in sand and hot from the sun,' Quinn told her.

'Then I need to get out of these things,' George said, starting to unbutton her trousers.

'Yes you do,' Quinn agreed, pulling her down onto the beach.

She could feel the sun on her back, as she lay on her side on the sand. She felt hot and contented, alive and exhausted. Sharp grains were underneath her fingernails, and her hands were clasped together with his.

'I never thought I would ever find this,' Quinn said, looking at her.

'Find what?' George asked.

'This feeling I get when I'm with you. It's just so right.'

'I know. I feel the same,' she answered softly.

'So, what happened with Adam's father?' Quinn enquired, unlinking one of his hands to brush a strand of hair away from her forehead.

'It was a long time ago now. We were young,' George replied evasively.

Her feelings for Quinn had pushed Paul to the back of her mind, for the most part. Talking about him when they were together, felt almost treacherous, to both of them.

'I know that. I want to know why he left you. Does he know he has a son?' Quinn clarified.

George shook her head.

'His mother was ill. She had a rare form of cancer. The family moved to Canada so she could get treatment. The number he gave me - well I couldn't contact him,' George explained.

'Have you tried since? I mean have you looked him up on MySpace or Facebook?'

'Of course I have. He isn't on any social networking sites. To be honest, he wasn't a great one for technology. He gave up having a mobile phone, he was always losing it.'

'You loved him though? It wasn't just kids stuff,' Quinn said.

'Yes, I loved him. We loved each other,' George replied.

Quinn nodded and brought her hand to his mouth and kissed it.

'It was like you and me. We had this instant connection, we couldn't be separated,' George spoke.

'Until you were,' Quinn reminded.

'Yeah, like we will be,' George said with an air of finality.

'Not in here though. Never in here,' Quinn said, bringing her hand down onto his chest.

'What if that isn't enough? What if this 'debt' you owe Roger takes ten years to pay off? What am I supposed to do? Live on text sex, emails and the occasional visit? I mean transatlantic flights aren't a Ryanair hop across the water are they? And there's no Concorde any more. We're talking what? Eight? Nine hours?' George told him.

'It won't take ten years. I'm not waiting ten years for us to be together. I just need to get this wedding out of the way and let the dust settle,' Quinn spoke.

'And how long will that take? Six months? A year? All the time sleeping with her, while I what? Live like a nun surviving on the vibration of my Samsung?' George asked.

'What d'you want me to say George? I'm trying to be honest with you. You know I'm marrying Taylor, you've always known that. I just need to do it and then move on, as quickly as I can,' Quinn said.

'You're making it sound like a transaction. It's a wedding Quinn! You've just clung to me and cried out my name and torn at my back and you're going to stand up in front of the world and lie to them all. You're going to sell everyone a false fairytale.'

'I'm already lying to them OK! I'm lying to them everyday anyway! One more big, fat, costly, fiesta sized lie isn't going to make a bit of f**king difference!' Quinn blasted.

'What d'you mean?'

'We'd better go,' Quinn said, taking a breath and getting to his feet.

'No Quinn, not like this. We've just had the most perfect time here. We're going to talk this out. You're going to tell me what's going on with you,' George said, grabbing hold of his t-shirt as he bent to pick it off the sand.

'I can't talk it out and I don't want to,' he answered stubbornly.

'You don't want to! Oh, OK then. You don't want to so we won't! Listen, I'm not one of your minions who shops and cooks for you. I'm your - I'm - you know what? I don't know what I am,' George said.

She threw his t-shirt up to him and began hurriedly pulling on her clothes, scattering sand.

'George! Don't you dare walk away from me!' Quinn yelled as she began to stagger through the sand, fastening her trousers as she went.

'Why? Because you want to be the one doing the walking? No! I'm done. I'm out. Enjoy your marriage. Find another lover. I'm sure they'll be queuing up - well - before they read the article about your really tiny dick,' George screamed at him.

Tears were burning her eyes as she looked at him. There he was, topless and perfect, the sun glancing off his torso, the wind blowing his hair. Suddenly her heart was filled with memories of Paul. The despair when he left, her hand against the glass, Paul's expression of loss. She could still see the car disappearing around the corner at the end of her road. Her throat had been sore, her insides had ached. It was happening all over again.

She sank to her knees on the beach and hugged herself into a ball. What did she have if she didn't have him? Finger Food. Work was all she had and that had been all she needed, until now. Until she'd had a taste of something else.

'Now you listen to me! All this exhibitionist behaviour will get you nowhere with me. You hear?' Quinn said, pulling her head up from her knees and enveloping her against his chest.

'Leave me alone! I'm fine! It's you! You're making me remember things that hurt. You've opened up old wounds and poured rock salt in them! You've made me feel all over again and I don't want the pain! I can't go back there!' George blasted, thumping his chest with her fist.

'Hey, what do you think you've done to me? I've written thirty two songs since we met. Thirty two. That's going to be one Hell of an album! But they're all so personal I can't use any of them and I've got a big f**king deadline looming.'

'Well I apologise!'

'So you should because at least ten of those songs are the best I've ever written. Because I wrote them the night we first met,' Quinn told her, holding her tightly by the wrists.

'Let me go!'

'No.'

'Let me go,' she repeated.

'Never.'

'I can't be with you. Not when I know you're with her. Touching her the way you've touched me,' George said, biting her lip and raising her eyes to meet his.

'George, I've never touched anyone the way I touch you.'

She shook her head trying to shake romanticism out of it and let reason in. She wanted to believe him, but there was too much at stake.

'I know I'm asking so much of you, but can you trust me? Just let me handle this and then I promise you I'm yours. For good,' Quinn said, linking his hand with hers.

'Don't say that unless you really mean it.'

'Hand on my really small penis, cross my heart, hope to die.'

George shook her head and stifled a laugh.

'Come on, we can do this. What we've got, it's worth waiting for isn't it?' he asked, raising her head with his hand.

'Kiss me and I'll let you know.'

Quinn moved his head towards hers and slowly their lips met. She clung to his bare torso and pushed him back down to the sand.

Thirty One

He didn't see the punch coming. He faltered backwards, putting a hand to his lip.

'You f**king moron! What the f**k do you think you're doing? Have you lost your mind?!' Roger screamed at the top of his voice.

'What the Hell?! I don't know what you're talking about?' Quinn responded tentatively.

'Don't you patronise me you little bastard! Sit down!' Roger ordered.

'Hi guys. Sorry I was gone a while. I got all the way to the supermarket and then there was a change of plan. Apparently the bachelors are having takeaway tonight instead - what's the matter?' George asked.

It was three hours since she had left the catering wagon. Now she was hot and flushed from the sun and the sex and covered in sand. Marisa, Adam and Helen were all looking at her, anxious expressions on their faces.

'Nothing, everything's fine. We've almost finished the vegetarian canapés and we were going to make a start on the prep for the wedding,' Helen spoke quickly.

'Mother, you have to tell her!' Marisa exclaimed.

George removed her sunglasses and put them on the counter. Her stomach was already contracting in anticipation of what was going to be said.

'Tell me what?'

'Roger Ferraro wants to see you. He came here in person, looking for you. He looked really, seriously pissed off,' Adam filled in.

She felt sick. It could only be one thing. He wouldn't have visited in person to discuss culinary matters. That was Michael or Pixie's job; this was about her and Quinn. He knew. She swallowed the feeling down, and stuck her finger in a bowl of mixture in front of Marisa.

'This is good. Did you make this?' George asked her, eating it.

'George? Did you not hear what I said? What's going on?' Adam asked.

'Nothing. Nothing's going on. Why are you all looking so serious? It will be some stupid detail about serving green beans as well as mixed leaves with the main course or something. You know how they all faff about over things here. I mean Michael was practically having a heart attack over the napkins being a shade too cream the other day,' George gabbled.

'That's what I said! I expect Taylor's stamped her feet and got Daddy running around for her, chivvying everyone up and...' Helen started.

'Marisa's got a theory about your mystery man. She thinks it's Quinn Blake,' Adam stated his eyes fixed on George.

'I thought you were convinced it was Eddie the drummer,' George responded, dipping her finger into another bowl of mixture and tasting it.

'Well, it all adds up now. All the secrecy, the designer clothes, the three grand watch, Roger Ferraro looking pissed,' Marisa said energetically.

'Have you seen Quinn Blake's fiancée? Isn't she something like number five in America's hottest actress poll in *Star Life* magazine? Aren't we catering their wedding?' George asked them.

The scratches on her back were smarting against the thin material of her t-shirt as she avoided the accusations. This was not a good situation.

'She's mental though and spends days on end at beauty parlours, I mean you, you...' Marisa began.

'Spend all day making sandwiches and treating OAPs for binge drinking,' George offered.

'So your mystery man isn't Quinn Blake?' Adam asked directly.

'Look, I've been seeing Paco OK? You know, Paco, the one...'

'In charge of tablecloths! No George! Not him! He's so, Spanish looking, with facial hair and there is like no way he could afford a watch like that,' Marisa said, pointing to George's wrist.

'His family actually run a linen empire. They've got factories all over Europe. Not that his finances are any of your business. And while we're on the subject, neither is my love life,' George exclaimed.

With that comment made, her mobile phone began to vibrate in the pocket of her combats.

'That'll be him. That'll be Quinn saying the game's up. Is it him? Let me see!' Marisa squealed as George got her mobile out of her pocket and checked the display.

'Marisa! Will you leave George alone before she decides to sack you!' Helen reprimanded.

It was an unknown number, but she knew who it was.

'Hello,' she greeted quietly.

'Is that Miss Fraser?' Roger Ferraro's voice enquired.

'Yes.'

'Miss Fraser, its Roger Ferraro. I'd like to meet. Shall we say conference room three in ten?'

'About the catering?' George asked her team's eyes on her.

'I think you know this call has nothing to do with the catering. Ten minutes,' the now enraged voice said. The call was rapidly ended.

George quickly smiled at Helen, Adam and Marisa, replacing the phone in her pocket.

'Who was it?' Adam wanted to know.

'Roger Ferraro. Something about salad dressing. There's a meeting in ten minutes,' George said, picking up her bag and sunglasses.

'Ten minutes. Well I need to redo my lipstick. Mother can I borrow your mirror?' Marisa asked, dropping the fork in her mixing bowl and turning to Helen.

'It's not for everyone, just me,' George said, swallowing.

All this pretence was killing her. Roger must know about her and Quinn. The shit was going to hit the fan, she was going to lose the man she loved and the lucrative catering contract. She had lied to her closest friends and Adam for months. What would they think of her? Whatever was going to happen in conference room three was going to change everything.

'Of course it is! I mean why would he need the whole team to talk about salad dressing? I said about dressing the other day didn't I? I said, I expect they will want some sort of vinaigrette. That's what they're like these Americans. Can't have anything plain can they? Everything always has to be slathered in something,' Helen babbled, distracting Marisa as George prepared to go.

'He didn't look like he wanted to discuss salad dressing earlier. He actually looked like he wanted to kill someone - slowly,' Marisa said, looking straight at George.

'Right well, on that note, I'd better go,' George said her hand on the door.

'Just a second. Here, take a bottle of water, it must be over a hundred degrees out there,' Helen said, grabbing a bottle and going up to her.

George took it and it was then Helen whispered in her ear:-

'I know about Quinn and you have seaweed stuck on the back of your trousers.'

Conference room three had a brass name plaque with black writing stating what it was. The door knob was scratched in two places, and the kick plate had half a dozen small rubber lines on it, where people had thumped it with marking soles. She could see ugly troll faces in the grains of the wood and there was an indistinguishable orange stain about three quarters of the way up. It reminded her of the insides of a York Fruits sweet.

Should she knock? Who was in there? Just Roger? Roger and Quinn? Taylor? She balled her hands into fists and took her hundredth deep breath. Not only did she have to face whatever was going to be thrown at her from behind the door, now Helen knew the truth, she was going to have more explaining to do later. At least she would have something to do on the plane ride home, once she was unceremoniously booted out of La Manga.

She lifted her hand, knocked hard on the door and opened it, biting down on the inside of her cheek. She bravely stepped into the lion's lair.

The ice cold air-conditioned atmosphere hit her as soon as she set foot into the room, giving her immediate goose bumps on her arms. It made her instantly ill at ease and even more uncomfortable. If that were possible.

Roger and Quinn were sat behind a table facing her. There was a cream coloured tablecloth covering it and a large urn of orange lilies to Roger's left. All that was missing from this press conference arrangement, were the journalists, the row of microphones and the name cards. Quinn's head was hung. His eyes were focussed on the floor. Only Roger met her gaze and his expression wasn't pretty. His brow was furrowed deeper than a ploughed field, his olive complexion was glistening with sweat and he was drumming his fingers on the table.

'Sit down,' he barked, pointing at the chair in front of them.

She wished Quinn would just look up. She knew what was about to happen. She knew she was about to lose the best job Finger Food had ever had. But that faded into insignificance because she also knew, unless he made his stand now, she was going to lose him too.

She sat down in the chair and maintained eye contact with the music mogul. The man was a bully. He had some hold over Quinn, but she wasn't going to let him intimidate her.

'You know why you're here,' Roger said his drumming fingers increasing in intensity.

'Actually I don't. Should I?' George asked bravely, still wanting Quinn to do something.

At her reply, Quinn's shoulders seemed to arch even more, and his head sunk lower. His left shoulder turned in and he shifted uneasily on his seat.

Roger scoffed. Air seemed to shoot out of his nostrils as he threw an A4 manila envelope onto the table in front of her.

'Open it,' he ordered.

George reached for the envelope and slipped her fingers underneath the self-seal top. She pulled out the contents and held them in her hands. There were a pile of photographs. On each one were her and Quinn. They were all stills from that very afternoon, when they'd been together on the secluded beach. The heat crept up her neck as she looked at them. Apart from the fact they were both naked and engaged in more than picnicking, the thing that stood out more than anything else, was the intensity on both of their faces. It was passion and desire worthy of a Hollywood film.

George finished looking at the photos, put them back in the envelope and placed it back on the table.

'I was couriered these. You have no idea what I had to promise to keep them out of the public domain,' Roger informed her.

George didn't speak. She just held his gaze and waited for what was coming.

'This stops now. You get me? I am well aware of Quinn's inability to fend off overzealous fans, but this public display is an outrage!' Roger continued.

'Overzealous fan,' George spoke, looking at Quinn who was still engaged in studying his Havaianas.

'I am not prepared to let someone like you ruin this wedding. So let's strike a deal. You stay away from Quinn and make no mention of this dalliance to anybody, and you get to keep the catering contract, plus a little bonus of say – ten thousand dollars?' Roger negotiated.

'You're going to pay me to keep quiet,' George said, shaking her head.

'OK, twenty thousand. But that is my final offer and it's far more than you're going to get from any magazine deal,' Roger continued.

'I find that insulting,' George told him.

'Take the money,' Quinn said finally raising his head and looking at her.

'Take the money? I don't want the money! And I can't believe he is going to let his daughter marry you when he can see from these photos that you don't love her,' George said anger rising in her.

'George, please. Just take it,' Quinn begged.

'Tell him the truth. Tell him you don't love her,' George said her eyes pleading with him.

'This discussion isn't about love. It's about the wedding. A wedding we've been planning for a long time, a wedding that will be going ahead as long as there's breath in my body,' Roger informed her sternly.

'You know he doesn't love her? Oh my God! Is this for real? You know he doesn't love her and you're making them get married!' George exclaimed.

'This conversation is over; I'll have a cheque sent over to your accommodation. You may leave,' Roger said, holding his hand out and indicating the door.

'I don't want the money. But I'll take these,' George said, snatching up the envelope.

'I can't let you do that! Put them down!' Roger exclaimed, getting to his feet and flapping his arms about.

'Look at them Quinn. Look at your face, look at mine. Are you really going to let him make you say goodbye to that?' George asked, fanning the pictures out in front of him.

Quinn looked up at her, tears on the brink of falling from his eyes. He shook his head.

'We're done here. The next time I see you I'd like it to be fully clothed, carrying a plate of chicken and rice,' Roger told her.

She took a last look at Quinn and turned on her heel. She marched from the room, full of anger, despondency and desperation. It was over.

He was in freefall now, internally tumbling through the darkest, deepest ravine. He had lost her, the one person who got him, whoever that was. The one person who made him feel real. Why was he so weak?

Thirty Two

'So, what salad dressing did he want?' Marisa barked when George entered the villa an hour and a half later.

She'd drunk three bottles of San Miguel in the bar of the golf club, walked a mile around the complex and kicked a chunk out of the exterior wall of the wedding castle. She'd been angry and sad and mad, all at the same time. She didn't know what to do. She was angry with Roger Ferraro for being some sort of evil puppeteer, but she was more furious with Quinn for not having the balls to stand up for himself. What sort of man was he if he let himself be dictated to by someone who was prepared to sacrifice his own daughter's happiness for the sake of the perfect brand?

'What?' George asked, opening the fridge and taking out another bottle of beer.

'The big meeting with the Daddy of Pop. What dressing for the mixed leaves? Or should I say, what did he think about you and Quinn getting down and dirty on the sly?'

'Marisa! George is your boss! You don't speak to her like that, have some manners. You were brought up not dragged up. I know we come from Merthyr Tydfil, but we still have standards,' Helen told her.

'Have you been drinking?' Adam asked, scrutinising her.

'Yeah. So what?' George retorted, gulping down the lager.

'Oh. My. God. She's gone on a bender because Roger went all mental and...' Marisa started.

'Marisa! How many times do I have to repeat myself? Go and get in the pool. That's where you and Adam were heading to wasn't it?' Helen queried.

'Yeah but...' Marisa started.

'There's bugger all point talking to her when she's been drinking anyway,' Adam said harshly and he led the way towards the patio doors.

'Wait for me! Remember I've got first dibs on the lilo!' Marisa exclaimed, chasing after him.

George finished the bottle of lager and opened the fridge to retrieve another.

'Are you going to lecture me?' she asked Helen.

'Of course not.'

'Because I'm your boss?'

'No, because I can see you're not in the mood for a lecture. You've probably had to endure all sorts of terrible shouting from that brash American man, who looks like an overinflated Lenny Henry,' Helen said.

'How long have you known?'

'I overheard you on the phone the other day. I tried not to listen, stuck my fingers in my ears and hummed 'What's New Pussycat', but I'd already heard his name and...'

'He had all these photos - intimate photos. We weren't very discreet and he tried to pay for my silence,' George explained hurriedly, hugging the bottle to her chest like a comfort blanket.

'Quinn?!'

'No, not Quinn. Quinn just sat there and said nothing. Then he told me to take the money.'

'No! What a sod! I mean who do these celebrities think they are? They live on another planet they really do. Thinking they can use and abuse people, treat them badly and get away with it! I hope you told him exactly what you think of him,' Helen said, folding her arms across her chest.

'I'm in love with him Helen and he's in love with me,' George stated.

She took a long swig of her drink, savouring the burn on the back of her throat.

'But I thought he told you to...'

'Roger's controlling him. He's got some hold on him. I don't know what, he won't tell me, but the whole wedding's a sham,' George explained.

'Jesus Wept!' Helen exclaimed.

'We've still got the catering contract, but to be honest - he didn't stand up to him. He should have told him to go to Hell, that was his chance. Our relationship was exposed, that was his opportunity to man up and he just sat there,' George said, putting the bottle to her mouth and running her lip over the rim.

'I don't know what to say, you poor girl. To find someone and for it to be him, with all his celebrity hang-ups and a domineering manager and...'

'A fiancée,' George added.

'Yes, well, Geraint was engaged to someone when we got together, but for Christ's sake don't let Marisa find out. Bronwen she was called, liked cardigans and would have had Geraint tending her smallholding of sheep if she had had her way. Well, that wasn't my Geraint so I offered him a way out. Fried breakfasts every morning, no re-runs of *Countryfile*, more home-made wine than he could shake a stick at and absolutely no Fair Isle tank tops.'

'You can't tell anyone.'

'As if I would! What are you going to do?' Helen asked her.

'There's only one thing I can do. Serve them their wedding breakfast and act like I don't care. What other choice do I have?' George answered.

The upstairs of the castle had been decked out in candy pink by the evening. There were balloons, streamers, drapes at the windows and horrible fluffy love hearts dotted about the place. It was making George feel sick. The bachelorettes were downing champagne like it was going out of fashion and so far they were in a gaggle at a table at one end of the room, being played flamenco tunes by a three piece Spanish guitar band.

'Er, when d'you think it's going to like liven up? And where are like all the people? Wasn't she supposed to have ninety nine friends here? Not like about thirty,' Marisa continued.

'Apparently the plane carrying her family and friends got delayed. They're not going to get here until tomorrow now,' Helen chipped in.

'Where did you hear that?' George asked.

'I heard Michael on the phone,' Helen spoke, putting a platter down on the table.

'Great, canapés for a hundred, and twenty five people to eat them. Some bachelorette party this is going to be,' George answered.

'Stags might be extra hungry,' Adam suggested.

'For spinach and carrot tartlets and tuna and chive wraps?' George asked.

'Maybe,' Adam said.

'And where are the happy bachelors anyway? Shouldn't they be here by now?' George questioned.

'It's still early,' Helen assured her.

'Yeah well, I'm going back to the kitchen to fire the staff. We don't need them,' George said in a matter of fact manner.

'George! Don't do that! We might need them tomorrow! Oh Christ!' Helen exclaimed as George disappeared from the room.

"Is she OK Helen? Should she really be here? I mean how much has she had to drink?" Adam asked concerned.

"I'm sure she's fine, just anxious you know, about the wedding. She wants to make sure everything goes to plan, you know, for Finger Food,' Helen said, thinking on her feet.

The staff were picking up their bags and personal possessions, just as Helen and Marisa came out from under the tunnel.

'What's going on? Where's everyone going?' Marisa enquired.

'Away from here, out of my sight, anywhere, I don't care,' George informed, pushing past some of the staff and entering the catering wagon.

'What? But some of them are my team. They make good coffee and Sally's lending me some earrings that like totally match my outfit for the wedding,' Marisa exclaimed in horror.

'We don't need them. They're useless and they just get in the way,' George told her.

'But we can't do all the serving on our own at the wedding. I mean, if we do, we'll be moving up and down the tunnel like a Eurostar on speed,' Marisa continued.

'Best start practicing then,' George answered as the bell on the oven went off, indicating the readiness of the canapés.

'Marisa, why don't you take the food up to the castle, see if any stags have arrived. The Chinese food will be here any minute and you never know, Belch might be there,' Helen suggested to her daughter.

'You mean bachelors Mother, not stags,' Marisa said with a shake of her head.

'Here, put them on this platter and take them up,' Helen instructed as George began to rifle through the fridge for anything remotely alcoholic.

'You won't be long will you? I mean it's only me and Adam and...' Marisa began.

'Marisa, I'm putting you in charge,' Helen told her seriously.

'In charge?!' Marisa responded predictably.

'Yes. Now go and make sure everyone has enough to eat and check what needs restocking,' Helen ordered.

'OK. Will do,' Marisa replied.

She took the tray and hurried out of the wagon, the air of managerial status flying out with her.

'Why the f**k isn't there anything in here? Where's the white wine?' George questioned, turfing out ingredients and not caring.

'George, you have to calm down,' Helen told her kindly.

'Why? Why do I have to calm down?' she asked, glaring at Helen.

'Because if you don't, you're in danger of ruining the reputation of Finger Food. A reputation you've worked so hard to build up,' Helen continued.

'Who cares?'

'You do.'

'Yeah well, maybe not as much as I used to,' George replied, pulling out a bottle of white wine from the back of the fridge. It was supposed to be used in the sauce on wedding day, but what the Hell!

She unscrewed the lid and took a long swig from it.

'George, he's engaged to someone else. He's getting married in two days. Whether it's a sham or not, that's what's happening,' Helen reminded.

'Don't you think I know that? I can't get away from it. The whole wedding thing is going on twenty four hours a sodding day and I'm catering it!' George said, drinking more of the wine.

'It's going on twenty four hours a day because we're in the middle of it aren't we? Was it going on when you took the job? You and Quinn?' Helen questioned.

'I didn't want the job, not really. You and Marisa persuaded me it was the best thing to happen to the company. We were all going to get rich and well-known and win lots more lucrative contracts,' George spoke.

'That's unfair. We didn't know you were sleeping with the groom,' Helen retorted.

George chose not to reply and took another drink of the wine.

'Getting drunk and showing yourself up, isn't going to make any of this easier. I mean it might have worked at the pub back in the day but now...' Helen started.

'What will make it easier then Helen? Because I could really do with knowing that right now.'

'Nothing will make it easier I'm afraid, not if you love him,' Helen told her.

'Then what's the point?'

'The point is Finger Food. It's your business. The business you built up from nothing. You're a successful businesswoman George, with everything going for you. Don't lose sight of what's important. Think of all the hours you put in studying, getting that catering qualification, begging the bank for a loan. You made them all believe in you,' Helen told her.

'Oh Helen it isn't just this mess, it's everything else on top of it! It's Adam and it's my mother. I mean - get this - my mother has cancer and I don't feel a thing!'

'What do you mean?'

'My mother, she's ruined me! She's made me like this, the way I am! Did you know she spent every waking second since I let her down hating me? And now she has cancer she wants to let bygones be bygones and for me to tell her it's OK. Well it isn't f**king OK. She did this when she pushed me away. I'm cold and barricaded by some force-field for the emotionally inept. That's what you do you see, when you've given and been rejected. Up go the shutters, no admittance, sorry no second date. A nice kiss on the doorstep and a fumble in the car, but that's your lot,' George continued.

'Quinn got through the shutters didn't he,' Helen remarked.

'He burst through them Helen. He shattered them, tore them down, until there was nothing left,' George admitted, trying hard to stop the tears filling up in her eyes.

She couldn't give in to the tears. They made her feel weak and pathetic and she didn't want to feel like that. She wanted to feel angry and she wanted that rage to fill her up, right to the top.

'Oh George, I'm sorry if I sounded harsh,' Helen sympathised.

'Don't be nice to me. I don't deserve it. It's just no one's ever done that to me, not since Paul. And that was such a long time ago, I'd almost forgotten what it felt like,' George said.

She was shaking now and the bottle in her hands felt heavy.

'Why didn't you tell me when it started?' Helen asked her.

'Because I was finding it hard enough to admit what was happening to myself, let alone anyone else.'

Marisa burst into the wagon, hair flying across her face and beads of sweat glistening on her forehead.

'Can I like have some help now? Bachelors have arrived and they're already drunk. Belch has pulled down some of the drapes, Taylor's doing her nut and they're stripping Michael!' she said breathlessly.

Thirty Three

'This is like Archie Reeves' birthday party all over again, except we've got pink drapes instead of blackout curtains,' George remarked as she, Marisa and Helen re-entered the room where the parties were in progress.

'What should we do?' Marisa enquired.

Michael was in the middle of the room, stripped down to his lilac silk boxer shorts. He was being given the bumps by Belch, Eddie the drummer and Manny the keyboard player. A group of thirty other men were egging them on, chanting loudly and waving their beer bottles in the air. It was like a cross between the aftermath of football celebrations and an 18-30 pub crawl.

Pixie was the only other person who ought to be taking control and she looked wasted. She was trying to encourage the bored looking bachelorettes to get into the mood of the evening. She was stood on a table, a rose between her teeth, battering out a rhythm to the flamenco music the guitarists were playing.

There were upended chairs and tables, platters of food sprayed around the floor and some of the men were trying to pull the bachelorettes onto the dance floor.

Taylor was stood. Her shift dress was immaculate, her hair in an elegant chignon and her mobile phone pressed to her ear.

'What is she doing about it?' George asked Marisa.

'She started freaking out when the décor was being pulled down, but nothing's happening. That's why I came to get you,' Marisa explained.

'Great, just what I need,' George said and she walked towards Taylor.

'Oh I'm not sure this is a good idea. Adam, perhaps you should do something, not George,' Helen suggested.

'Why me? She's the boss.'

'...no Daddy, I need you to come now. They're messing everything up, we need security - no I cannot handle it. Quinn's not here and they're out of control...' Taylor squeaked into the phone.

'Sorry to interrupt, but I really think we need to sort this mess out,' George said firmly, breaking into Taylor's phone conversation.

'Hang on Daddy - I realise that Ms Fraser, I'm on the phone trying to organise something,' Taylor informed, taking the phone away from her ear and glaring at George.

'Well, if you don't get something arranged pretty quickly, it's going to turn into a free for all,' George continued.

'I am well aware of that too,' Taylor retorted.

Michael was beginning to yelp like an abandoned puppy and his face had turned the same colour as his underwear. Vomit was ensuing.

'Can you start by tidying up the food and arranging some replacements? Security will deal with the guys when they get here,' Taylor told George, looking over at the group of men, who were swinging Michael around by his ankles.

'Are you serious? We don't have replacements. We were lucky to get the food we did,' George reminded her.

'Yes Daddy, I'm still here - yes I know but...'

George let out an angry sigh of disapproval and she grabbed hold of Adam.

'She isn't going to do anything so we'll have to. The next time Michael bounces up, we'll put a stop to it. We can't wait for security to arrive, it's already turned into chaos and he looks like he's about ready to throw up. I can't cope with mopping up canapés mixed with Lilt,' George told him.

'I tried to stop them trashing everything, but there were too many of them,' Adam spoke.

'Don't worry - OK guys, I think that's enough bouncing about for poor Michael here don't you? He looks a bit puce. How about I organise some cocktails, before the strippers arrive?' George suggested to the men, clapping her hands together and trying to divert their attention.

'Strippers huh? Oh man, you mean Uptight Panties over there has dropped her 'no strippers' clause?' Belch replied.

'Yes, they'll be here any minute. So shall I make cocktails?' George asked as Michael scrabbled out of their clutches and began picking up his clothes.

'No, I've got a better idea. How about you strip for us? That waitress outfit really does it for me,' Eddie the drummer told her, a lecherous look on his face.

'I don't think so boys. I'm more cooking than stripping to be honest,' George said, trying her best to remain calm.

'Why don't you let us be the judge of that?' Belch asked, letting out a disgusting burp and grabbing George roughly by the shoulders.

'Hey, let go of her!' Adam ordered, taking hold of Belch's arm.

'Hot for her yourself are you?' Belch enquired, swaggering around and enveloping George away from Adam.

'I said get off her!' Adam ordered, pulling at Belch's t-shirt.

'Adam!' Marisa yelled, joining the mêlée.

'Marisa! Come back!' Helen called frantically as Marisa disappeared into the throng.

The Spanish guitarists seemed oblivious to what was going on and were still strumming at a frantic pace. Some of the bachelorettes were now stood up practising flamenco moves. They all looked the worse for wear and there were half-filled bottles of Cristal everywhere.

'You lay one finger on her and I'll kill you!' Adam yelled at Belch his eyes flashing angrily.

'Adam, it's alright. Everyone's just had a bit too much to drink and they're getting a little overenthusiastic, that's all,' George said, struggling away from the guitarist's clutches and trying to regain control.

Perhaps this hadn't been such a good idea. Maybe she should have waited for security. She hadn't bargained on being the entertainment.

'See, she likes it. Don't you George? Let's take your shirt off and see just how much you're really enjoying it,' Belch said, fingering the buttons on George's top.

As the guitarists launched into one of the Gipsy Kings' best known numbers and the bachelorettes started stamping out a beat, Quinn entered the room.

'Quinn, thank God you're here. Everyone's got out of control and Daddy's busy in a meeting about Saturday. Michael's left and I need you to sack the caterer. She's been rude to me and...' Taylor began to bleat, taking hold of Quinn's arm and gripping onto it.

'They all got pissed in town. Belch almost got arrested,' Quinn informed her.

'Well get them to stop. I've got the flamenco demonstrators arriving soon and they're ruining everything,' Taylor told him.

Quinn's eyes were drawn to the centre of the room and anger swelled over him when he saw what was going on. Belch was mauling George and she was desperately trying to get out of his reach, whilst trying to stop Adam getting into a fight over it. Marisa was being pushed from one bachelor to another, squealing and yelping like a human skittle.

'Quinn, the flamenco...' Taylor began.

He wasn't listening. He shrugged her off and marched up to the group of bachelors.

'What the f**k do you think you're doing?!' he yelled at the top of his voice.

He pulled Eddie and pushed past Adam to get to the centre of the commotion.

'Come on Quinn. It's just a bit of fun man, until the strippers get here,' Belch replied with a laugh.

'How dare you touch her,' Quinn spat, taking George's arm and pulling her away from his band mate.

'You need to chill out man. It's supposed to be your last night of freedom,' Belch replied, swigging from his bottle of beer.

'Look at this place! What the f**k is going on with you guys?' Quinn wanted to know.

'It's called having a good time. Marisa knows how to have a good time don't you honey?' Belch spoke, taking hold of Marisa and kissing her on the lips.

'Right, that's enough!' Adam shouted at Belch. He grabbed hold of Marisa's arm and wrenched her towards him.

'Adam, come away. They're drunk, they don't know what they're doing,' George told him.

'You touch her again and I'll have you,' Adam threatened Belch.

He was trying to create a barrier between him and Marisa by widening himself.

'So you're a tough guy now huh? Get a little credit on a song and you think you're in the band,' Belch taunted.

'Belch, you're way out of line,' Quinn warned still holding onto George.

'Speaks the almost married man. What's up with you man? She putting the pressure on already? Changing you? You'll be carrying her handbag next and getting one of those Shih Tzu's to go in it,' Belch said, reaching out and stroking Marisa's hair.

'What's your problem? Are you spoiling for a fight or something? Because if you want a fight, fight with me, not Adam,' Quinn ordered him.

'I told you to get away from her. Keep your hands off her,' Adam screamed, shielding Marisa protectively.

'I'm alright. Why don't I just go and make some coffee for everyone. I can make it really nice and strong, Sally taught me this really neat trick,' Marisa suggested trying to diffuse the situation.

'Yeah, sure. Coffee making's about your limit though isn't it babe? Best to stick to what you know darlin',' Belch said.

'What's that supposed to mean?' Marisa enquired.

'Well don't go hanging out for a modelling contract or anything. Because man, I think Hell might be freezing over first,' Belch said with a hearty laugh.

Before the group could join in with the cruel banter, Adam planted a punch on Belch's face that sent him reeling into the pack, knocking over Eddie and two others. Drinks hit the floor and Belch flailed about, stunned and momentarily unable to get up.

'Adam for God's sake! There was no need for that. He's pissed, he has no idea what he's doing or saying. Look at the state of him,' George said, moving Adam away from the crowd as Quinn helped to pick Belch back up.

'So that makes it OK does it? For him to unbutton your shirt and touch Marisa?' Adam asked still seething with anger.

'No of course not. But we're supposed to be professional, we're the caterers, not security,' George reminded him.

'Professional! Oh is that what we are? So it's professional to spend the afternoon getting pissed out of your mind and then sack all the staff is it?'

'Adam...'

'He deserved it! I wish I'd punched him harder!' Adam yelled, looking over at Belch.

'Get back to the villa, right now,' George ordered.

'What?'

'Get back to the villa. You're finished here for the night,' George told him.

'Come on! You heard what he said! You saw what he was like. You saw him touching Marisa,' Adam said angrily.

'And you let your feelings cloud your judgement. Go back to the villa,' George ordered again.

'Don't talk to me like that. I'm not a kid,' Adam told her.

'Then stop acting like one and do what I've asked!' George spat back.

'You're a hypocrite and you're blaming me for something that isn't my fault. I was trying to diffuse the situation!'

'By punching the best man?! Just go Adam!'

'Jesus Christ George, have you heard yourself?! You may be my boss but you're not my f**king mother!' Adam yelled.

The comment hit her hard. It was like a knife to the heart, the blade long and sharp, piercing and debilitating. Adam was looking at her angrily, the Spanish guitars were being strummed within an inch of their lives and Taylor was heading in their direction, Carleen hot on her kitten heels.

'Yes I am!' George yelled with every fibre of her being.

Thirty Four

'Security's on its way. I need replacement platters. I have more guests arriving and the flamenco demonstrators will be here soon,' Taylor told George, arriving at her side.

Carleen was like a mirror image beside her.

George and Adam didn't hear her. They were oblivious to everything, just staring at each other. Tears were welling up in George's eyes.

'What did you say?' Adam asked his voice barely more than a whisper.

'I said, yes I am,' George responded, swallowing a lump in her throat.

'I don't understand. I said "you're not my mother",' Adam repeated.

'And I said, yes I am,' George said again.

'Look, I have a party here. You're in charge of catering. I need more food, I need the tables to be fixed up, I need...' Taylor began.

'Just shut up!' George ordered, turning to face Taylor and truly despising her for the first time.

'How dare you speak to me like that!' Taylor exclaimed, putting her hand to her chest, like an arrow had just been speared through it.

'Oh my! You cannot speak to the bride like that!' Carleen added, patting her friend on the arm.

'You're saying you're my mother? Why would you say that?' Adam questioned, backing away from George.

'I want this mess cleared up. I want more canapés, I want...' Taylor began again, stamping her shoes up and down like she was auditioning for Riverdance.

George span around, drew back her fist and punched Taylor in the face. The bride-to-be fell to the floor and Carleen let out a deafening scream as if she had just been doused with Devil's spit.

The scream drew the attention of Quinn, Helen, Marisa and the less inebriated bachelors and bachelorettes.

'Christ George! You've just knocked out the bride!' Adam exclaimed, looking at the unconscious Taylor lying on the ground.

Carleen bent over her, a look of concern on her Maybellined face.

George grabbed hold of Adam and pulled him away into one of the corners of the room.

'Get off me! You're mental!' Adam said, shrugging off her arm.

'Adam, I know how this sounds but - I'm your mother,' George repeated in case there was any doubt.

'What's got in to you? You're still drunk aren't you!' Adam said, eyeing her suspiciously.

'I'm not drunk,' George exclaimed.

'Then why are you saying mad things?' Adam wanted to know.

'Mad things like what?'

'Mad things like you're my mother!' Adam exclaimed.

'Because I *am* your mother! How loud do I have to yell it before you believe it? Do you need me to write it down?!' George shrieked hysterically.

Adam just stared at her, trying to gather from her expression what was going on.

'Stop saying that! Just stop it.'

310

'It's the truth. I should have told you before. It never seemed like the right time. She wouldn't let me and then she got sick and she wanted to tell you and I didn't and...' George began the tears starting to spill from her eyes.

'No, this is all wrong! Why are you doing this? Because I answered back? Because I hit Belch? Why would you make something like that up? It's sick!' Adam yelled.

'It's not made up. Listen, let's just go back to the villa and I'll explain. I'll explain everything,' George begged as Adam backed towards the door.

'No, stay away from me. You've gone mental. Nothing you're saying is making sense,' Adam stuttered as he rushed towards the door.

'Adam, just come back!' George ordered, hurrying after him.

'No! You wanted me to go, now I'm going. I'm going before we really fall out. I'm not listening to anything else you have to say. I'm done,' Adam shouted. He turned his back on her and began hurrying up the canvas walkway.

'Adam, please! Don't go. Let me explain, please, just let me explain,' George called, hurrying after him.

Her words didn't reach him. He was already at the bottom of the walkway, making for the outside.

'George, what's going on? What's wrong with Adam? He just dissed me big time,' Marisa enquired as she and Helen arrived at her side.

'Nothing, he's just upset about Belch and everything. He just needs some space,' George spoke hurriedly, blinking away her tears and trying to ignore her hammering, terrified heart.

'Did you have a go at him for hitting Belch? Was it my fault?' Marisa questioned.

'No, it wasn't your fault.'

'Shall I go after him?'

311

'No Marisa!' George yelled.

Marisa looked like she was about to cry. Her bottom lip trembled and she defensively folded her arms across her chest.

'Look, I'm sorry. Just leave Adam alone for a while. It's been a bit of an evening and we're all stressed,' George said, regaining a little composure.

'Is everything OK?' Quinn questioned meeting them in the walkway.

'Marisa, why don't you and I go and see if we can put right some of the mess up there. We could knock up some more food,' Helen suggested, putting an arm around her daughter and trying to shepherd her away.

'This is the weirdest party I've ever catered for,' Marisa remarked, looking back at George.

George put her fist to her mouth and tried not to let her anguish get the better of her. The very last thing she wanted to do was look vulnerable in front of him.

'What's happened? I'm so sorry about Belch and the others. They've been drinking all day and...' Quinn began.

'Stay the f**k away from me. I have nothing left to say to you. Do you understand that?' George blasted her eyes meeting his.

'George, you and me, we're not done. I had to look like I was toeing the line today, but that was all it was,' Quinn told her.

'You know what? I don't care. None of that matters, not now. I've got more important things to worry about. Adam knows. He got mad and I got mad and I told him. I told him I'm his mother,' George informed him.

'George,' Quinn said, putting an arm around her.

'Get your hands off me!'

'Don't do this George, let me help you,' Quinn begged.

'If you want to help me, you'll tell me where the nearest piano is in this damn place,' George ordered.

He wanted to help her but she'd pushed him away and, shit, he didn't blame her. It had taken all the strength he had to make an appearance at his own bachelor party. But he'd put on the mask, buttoned up his persona and smiled at everyone. She couldn't do that now, he'd laid her bare. He'd got her to tell him all her secrets and there was no going back. *He'd* done that to her. *He* was responsible for making her world fall apart.

She could hear the piano outside the door. It was the piano that would be playing 'The Wedding March' located in the mock Tudor hall, on the lower level of the fabricated castle. She paused at the door and just listened. The player was hammering the life out of the keys in a tuneful, yet ferocious way. She didn't know what she was going to say to him. She couldn't imagine how he was feeling. She still didn't know whether he really believed her. But she had to talk to him. She couldn't leave things how they were.

She opened the door and saw him, right at the far end of the room, sat at the grand piano. His hair was damp with sweat, he had taken off his bow tie and his shirt was half undone. He didn't look up as she moved towards him. He just continued bashing at the keys, oblivious to anything else.

'Adam,' George started.

He ignored her, bowed his head and carried on playing. He was hitting each key harder and harder with every note.

'Adam, please. Can we just talk about this?' George asked him.

'Talk about what?'

'About what I said, about who I am. About who you are.'

'I phoned Mum. You know, my real mum, the one who brought me up. When I told her what you said she couldn't say anything. She didn't say *anything*. There was like this long pause, like she was holding her breath. I couldn't hear that breath just go on and on like that, without her speaking,' Adam informed her.

. 'Adam...'

'Why couldn't she say anything? Why didn't she tell me you were a liar?' Adam enquired, raising his eyes to meet hers.

'Because I'm not a liar. Because, for the first time in eighteen years, I'm telling you the truth.'

Adam just looked at her. His eyes were brimming with tears. He looked pale and scared and lost. He looked like someone had just pulled a dozen crucial pieces out of the jigsaw of his make up.

'Adam, I haven't told you this to hurt you. I told you, because Mum's sick and I want you to know that no matter what happens, I'm going to be there for you. And I wanted that to be on the proper terms, as your mum, not as your big sister playing some sort of guardian. Mum thought it was time you were told the truth and she was right,' George tried to explain.

'I can't believe it. I can't understand it. How? Why? And all the lies you must have told over the years!' Adam exclaimed slamming shut the lid of the piano and standing up.

'I was stupid Adam, I got pregnant very young. I was careless, *we* were careless, and I was alone and pregnant at sixteen years old.'

'You didn't want me?'

'No, it wasn't like that. I was scared, of being so young, of not being able to manage. But there wasn't even a second when I didn't want you,' George spoke quickly.

'Go on.'

'Well, you know what Mum's like. She felt let down by me, because I got pregnant, and she took over.

314

She came with me everywhere, to all the appointments. Most of the time it felt like she was the one having the baby, not me, and that's what happened. As soon as you were born she looked after you,' George said, trying to hold back her emotion as much as she could.

'And what did you do? Squeeze yourself back into your school uniform and go back to screwing boys behind the bike sheds?' Adam snapped.

'Adam, it wasn't like that. I tried to look after you; I longed to look after you. I used to steal you out of the house just to have some time alone with you. But she never let me get close. One bath, a couple of nappy changes and then weeks would go by before she would even let me hold you again.'

'And when I was older? Wasn't there any opportunity, before tonight, to tell me the truth?'

'I was scared. You were happy and Mum wanted things to stay stable,' George said, knowing her answer wasn't good enough.

'Who's my father?' Adam questioned.

'The boyfriend I told you about. Paul,' George said.

Her hand instinctively rose up to finger the ring on the chain around her neck.

'And he got you pregnant at sixteen and ran off and left you,' Adam scoffed.

'It wasn't that simple, he had to move away. He didn't know about you. He still doesn't know about you.'

'So you don't know where he is now?'

'No. But I'm sure we could trace him, if that's what you want,' George suggested.

'No, it isn't what I want. I have a father! Yeah, maybe he spends all his time drinking Earl Grey and watching golf, but he's still my dad. And he's the only dad I want to know!' Adam blasted.

'That's fine. Of course he's still your dad. Nothing has to change if you don't want it to,' George spoke.

'Then if nothing has to change, why did you bother telling me?' Adam asked, staring at her.

George let out a heavy sigh. It didn't matter what she said. She could speak for hours and it wouldn't make the situation any better. Adam was hurting. He didn't understand why he had been lied to. His whole past was being broken up and analysed in his mind. She could almost see all the thoughts riding through his brain, as he stood in front of her looking angry, confused and vulnerable.

'Like I said before, because Mum's sick and we don't know how that's going to pan out. I wanted you to know I'm here for you. No more pretence, no more lies, everything out in the open. I know I didn't choose the ideal time to announce it but...'

'What if I don't want you to be my mother?' Adam snapped viciously.

'That's your choice. I guess I would have to live with it.'

'And could you live with the fact that perhaps, after all this, I might not even want you as a sister?' Adam continued.

'You don't mean that. You're angry, I get that. I can't imagine what you must be thinking, but give it time, to think about things properly,' George suggested her heart up in her throat.

'You think angry and upset covers it do you? How about betrayed and let down?'

'We shouldn't have kept it from you for so long. But the longer it went on, the harder it was to change things. But, there's no reason to feel isolated, I'm here for you. I've always been here for you and that isn't going to change.'

'Isn't it? I think that's for me to decide,' Adam said, moving away from her and heading towards the door.

'Adam, don't shut me out. Talk to me, shout at me, but don't turn your back on me,' George begged, following him.

'Why not? You turned your back on me, gave me up,' Adam told her.

'I didn't want to. Adam, please,' George began tears finally escaping.

'You still did it,' Adam hissed.

'Adam, please. We can work through this,' George assured him.

'I'm not sure I want to,' Adam responded, opening the door.

'Adam, don't go. Please, not like this.'

'You'll have to call back some of the staff you fired tonight. I can't be in a catering wagon with you, I can't be anywhere near you right now, possibly not ever!' Adam informed her.

He slammed the door shut in her face with such force, it banged open again and hit the retaining wall. A piece of plaster fell off onto the floor and George crumpled with it. She slumped to her knees, putting her face in her hands. Torrents of tears fell down her cheeks and her body wracked with sobs. Her heart was breaking.

And then a pair of strong arms were around her, pulling her into an embrace she so sorely needed.

'Why did I tell him? Why did I go and tell him? I've lost him Quinn, I've lost him.'

He wasn't going to listen to anything she said right now. Even if she told him to f**k off he wasn't going anywhere. She needed him, whether she wanted to need him or not. They needed each other.

Thirty Five

When George woke, sunlight was streaming through the shutters of her bedroom. Her eyes felt grainy and sore, like she had been rubbing them with sandpaper.

She rolled over onto her side and was greeted by Quinn.

'What the Hell are you doing here?!' George exclaimed, sitting up and pulling the duvet around her.

'You asked me to stay,' he replied.

'Did I?'

'You were upset. You didn't want to be on your own,' Quinn spoke.

'You shouldn't be here. We're over, you're getting married tomorrow. I hate you,' George reminded.

'So you said last night when you hit me with a bottle of Jack Daniels.'

'Did I?'

'Yeah, right before you broke two strings on my favourite guitar,' Quinn added.

'I don't remember.'

'Listen, don't worry about Adam, he'll come round,' Quinn assured her.

Adam. Suddenly her chest tightened and she remembered all the anguish of the previous night. She had told Adam she was his mother and now he loathed her.

'You reckon? It didn't sound that way to me. I'm sure he said he couldn't stand to be anywhere near me,' George spoke.

'It's just the shock and the anger talking. He's young, he doesn't fully understand how the world works yet. He'll calm down,' Quinn told her.

'I'm not so sure. Sometimes he reminds me so much of his father. Paul was so stubborn, just like him. When he made a decision he stuck to it. He was headstrong and single minded. I thought they were good traits, but seeing Adam like that...' George told him.

'You two must have been some couple,' Quinn remarked.

'We were.'

'And we are,' Quinn said, taking her hand.

'Don't.'

'Don't what?'

'Don't say things like that.'

'Listen, I have a rehearsal with the orchestra at eleven, but the rest of the day I'm free. Let's do something,' Quinn spoke.

'We can't spend the day together. I'm not in this relationship any more Quinn, I told you that. You had a chance when Roger confronted us, you didn't take it. I don't know why you're in my bed now, but you need to get out of it,' George told him.

'You don't really want this to be the end,' Quinn told her.

'I can't deal with anything in my life right now apart from Adam. He's my priority. I need him to understand why the truth's been kept from him all these years and I need him to forgive me,' George told him.

'Forgiveness is going to take time.'

'I know.'

'*I* don't have time, *we* don't have time,' Quinn reminded her.

'Stop it.'

'We love each other.'

'I thought we did.'

'Nothing's changed except the paps took some fantastic x-rated shots of us and Roger had to kick in the damage limitation exercise,' Quinn continued.

'You're not taking this seriously.'

'Believe me, I am.'

Suddenly the door of George's room burst open and Marisa entered without warning, eating cornflakes from a bowl.

'George, we have to go soon. It's almost nine and where's Adam - Oh. My. God!' Marisa exclaimed, seeing Quinn in George's bed.

She dropped her spoon into the bowl and just stared at the scene, milk and soggy cornflakes drizzling out of the corner of her mouth.

'Get out Marisa!' George shrieked, pulling the bedclothes further up around her.

'Oh. My. God! I knew it! I said it didn't I! You! You and Quinn! Quinn and you! But, it's the wedding tomorrow. He's like getting married in twenty eight hours,' Marisa continued.

'Sshh, will you stop shouting!' George ordered her.

'I'd love a coffee Marisa, if you're making some,' Quinn broke in with a smile.

'This is like seriously f**ked up! Mother! Mother!' Marisa screamed.

'Can you give us some privacy to get dressed?' George ordered.

'Mother! Mother! Quinn Blake's in George's bed! I told you! Didn't I tell you?! It's so gross, they're like naked!' Marisa shouted as she left, swinging the door closed behind her.

George got out of bed and hurriedly began dressing.

'Now Marisa knows, you may as well put an announcement in *Star Life* magazine. Roger's going to go ballistic and Finger Food will have made its last canapé for this gig,' George said, putting a t-shirt over her head.

'Come on, I'm sure she can be discreet,' Quinn said, enjoying watching her dress.

'Are you mad?! Marisa doesn't know how to spell discreet, let alone know what it means. Don't you care any more? Aren't you in the least bit worried about this getting out? Your wedding's a day away. Roger's worried, yesterday he looked like he was ready to have a heart attack. I mean, if you don't care about this image you and Taylor are creating, why didn't you stand up to him when he was offering me a handout?' George asked him.

'Do you think Roger having a heart attack would call the wedding off? Or do you think he would sweat his way right on through to the speeches?' Quinn enquired.

'It isn't funny Quinn. I don't even know if I still have a catering contract. I mean it's one thing to sleep with the groom, it's quite another to knock the bride unconscious,' George fretted.

'Of course you've still got a contract. I'm not going through all that ceremony shit to get dished up some shit someone else has knocked together.'

'Is this all a joke to you?'

'Yes, of course it is. Tomorrow I marry someone I can barely stand being in the same room as. Ha f**king ha!'

'I need to tell Marisa and Helen about Adam. And I need to stop Marisa broadcasting anything she shouldn't to the entire universe,' George said, doing up her jeans.

'Fine. We'll do it together. But let's at least have a coffee first,' Quinn begged.

Marisa's eyes were still out on stalks when Quinn and George came down from the bedroom. Helen had made a pot of coffee and Quinn helped himself to a cup and poured some for George.

He drank a bit and gave Marisa the benefit of one of his well-practised smiles.

'Morning, again.'

'Hello,' she answered subdued.

'Look, I know this is really awkward and I'm really sorry for putting you both in this position,' George began, sighing and taking another drink of her coffee.

'I've explained things to Marisa, I hope you don't mind. I've told her the wedding is going ahead as planned and she's not to mention anything to anyone,' Helen informed them.

'Mum said it was one last fling before you got hitched. Is that what it was? One last fling? Because George has been acting weird for months. I put two and two together about the designer bikini and the bling, but no one would have it,' Marisa piped up.

'No, it isn't one last fling,' Quinn told her.

'Quinn...' George said, wishing he didn't feel the need to elaborate.

'It's complicated,' Quinn replied, taking hold of George's hand.

'Friggin' Hell! You're in love aren't you?!' Marisa exclaimed, putting her hands to her mouth.

'Sshh Marisa, we agreed. You have to be discreet,' Helen ordered.

'That's D-I-S-C-R-E-E-T,' Quinn told her.

'What?' Marisa questioned.

'Take no notice of him, he's an idiot.'

'But a hot idiot.'

'Listen, there's something else you should know - about Adam,' George began with a swallow.

'Like where he is? Because he didn't come home last night. Does he know about this fling that isn't a fling,

322

you know, the one I'm not supposed to mention?' Marisa asked them.

'No, he doesn't know and I don't want him to know. He's got too much other stuff going on right now,' George informed them.

'Then where is he? Why isn't he here?' Marisa questioned.

'Well, you know we had an argument and...'

'It's my fault isn't it? Because I didn't want Belch putting his hands all over me. I know I did before, but I don't now and Adam was only trying to help and I upset him and...'

'Adam's my son. I told him last night and he's obviously shocked and upset and he doesn't want to see me,' George blurted out as quickly as she could.

'You're shittin' me!'

'Marisa!' Helen exclaimed shocked by her daughter's language.

'OK, are we done here? I'm going to go and check on Adam. He's meant to be at a rehearsal this morning. I'll call you, let you know,' Quinn said, kissing George on the lips and heading for the door.

'Tell him I asked after him won't you,' George said, following Quinn to the door.

'I will. I'll see you later,' Quinn promised, smiling at her.

'For Christ's sake, what is going on here?! Have I slipped into an episode of *Lost* or something? I have no idea what's going on. Someone sane speak to me!' Marisa begged her mouth open so wide it was almost on the floor.

'George is Adam's mum. George and Quinn are in love with each other and he's marrying Taylor Ferraro tomorrow. Are you up to speed yet?' Helen asked her.

'You're really Adam's mum, not his sister,' Marisa said, staring at George wide-eyed.

George managed a nod.

'F**king hell. No wonder he's gone AWOL. Did he have like no idea?' Marisa questioned.

'Marisa, why don't you finish getting ready and let George have her coffee,' Helen suggested.

'Why can't I hear what you're going to say to her? I'm always the last to know everything around here,' Marisa moaned as she reluctantly mounted the stairs.

'Helen, I'm so sorry about all of this,' George said, sitting down at the table and offering her friend an apologetic look.

'So you finally told Adam,' Helen remarked, sitting opposite her.

'You knew?!' George exclaimed.

'Not for definite, but I had a feeling. You were always so concerned about him, always talking about him and always looking after him, much more than an elder sister would. I don't know it was just a feeling I had. That and the fact that having a baby so young might explain why you wanted to take on the world on the pool table and eat every man you could for breakfast back then,' Helen told her.

'God Helen, he hates me. He doesn't want to see me and he barely let me explain,' George told her, putting her head in her hands.

'He's just angry and confused, he'll come round,' Helen reassured.

'That's what Quinn said but I'm not so sure. I think I might have made the biggest mistake of my life by telling him. My mother said this was the right thing to do. Why did I go against my gut instinct and listen to her? I never listened to her before,' George said.

'Come on, we need you on top form today. We've got a lot of preparation to do for tomorrow,' Helen reminded her.

'We haven't been sacked yet then?' George remarked, sipping at her coffee.

'At this short notice? Where are they going to get another catering firm from?' Helen asked her.

'I'm sorry to leave you in the lurch last night. Was everything OK?' George enquired.

'Marisa worked really hard. The Chinese food never arrived so we had ravenous bachelors on our hands. She prepared hot dogs with a spicy salsa for the bachelors and courgette, asparagus and brie parcels for the bachelorettes. I don't know where she found the sausages from and I didn't really like to ask,' Helen informed.

'She made it all from scratch?'

'Yes, I was absolutely astounded. I never knew she had it in her but she took control. I handled things at the party and she beavered away in the kitchen. Once the security guys arrived and Belch and the others calmed down, things settled,' Helen explained.

'And what about Taylor?' George asked, feeling a knot of embarrassment rising in her throat.

'She came to and insisted she was taken back to her villa.'

'Oh.'

'She was back within the hour wearing a different outfit,' Helen replied.

'Good. I lost control. Adam wasn't listening to me and she was carrying on and on about the food and...' George began.

'You're only human George, not Superwoman. Anyway I don't like the silly girl. She swans around like the world owes her and she turned her nose up at Marisa's canapés - the bitch,' Helen said, biting into a bread roll.

Thirty Six

'So, what's he like in bed?' Marisa blurted out as she mixed up ingredients for the wedding day sauce.

It was another sweltering day and the complex was rife with golfers, media, holiday-makers and celebrity spotters. They were all making the most of the Spanish sun and the opportunity to get a real tan, rather than one sponsored by Piz Buin.

'Marisa! What are you like? We agreed not to talk about it!' Helen exclaimed.

'I didn't agree. You told me we wouldn't talk about it I said I wouldn't shout it from the rooftops. It's only us girls and that's the sort of thing girls talk about. Besides, if my employer has been having it off with *the* hottest rock star on the planet, I think I deserve details!' Marisa told them.

'He's not that good,' George replied roughly chopping herbs.

Marisa stared at her, a look of total disbelief and disappointment on her face.

'OK, I'm lying,' George answered with a smile.

'I knew it! So does he do that thing, you know when the guy...' Marisa started.

'Er, I don't want to worry you, but Taylor Ferraro just got out of a golf buggy and she's heading up here,'

Helen interrupted, looking out of the window of the catering wagon.

'Shittin' Hell! What are we going to do? Do you think she knows about you and Quinn?' Marisa questioned.

'We're going to act normal, because everything is normal right?' Helen ordered her daughter.

George hurried to the door and opened it before Taylor had a chance to knock. She was wearing a figure-hugging, lemon coloured dress with high, peep-toe shoes. A pair of large sunglasses were sat on her face and she had a lemon and white handbag on her arm.

'Ms Ferraro,' George greeted formally.

'Ms Fraser,' Taylor replied stiffly.

She gingerly removed her sunglasses and George got a look at her badly swollen eye. It was heavily covered in foundation.

'I am so sorry about last night. Your eye...' George remarked as Taylor brushed past her and entered the catering wagon.

'Yes, it's a mess. I'm having hourly ice compression. Luckily the make-up artist thinks the swelling will have decreased considerably by tomorrow. Even so, he will definitely be earning his fee trying to work miracles,' Taylor told her, putting her glasses back on.

'Look, I'm really sorry about last night. I apologise unreservedly and...' George began.

'She was under a lot of pressure and the bachelors weren't making it easy for anyone. I mean they were so drunk and completely out of control and...' Helen piped up.

'Believe me, if it wasn't for the fact I'm getting married tomorrow and over two hundred people are expecting food, I would fire you right now, without hesitation,' Taylor spoke firmly.

'I realise that and of course that would be no more than I deserve,' George replied.

'But Michael insists you stay. He keeps saying you're brilliant and I haven't got the time or energy to look for an alternative,' Taylor continued.

'She is brilliant. We're all pretty brilliant actually. And we're just preparing everything so it's all perfect tomorrow,' Marisa chipped in.

'All on schedule? You have everything you need?' Taylor enquired.

'Yes, everything's fine,' George answered.

'And where are your staff? I thought Pixie had arranged a team of helpers,' Taylor spoke, looking around for signs of other people.

'They were...' George began.

'Surplus to requirements,' Marisa added quickly.

'So how are you going to serve everything tomorrow if there are only three of you?' Taylor wanted to know.

'That's for us to worry about Ms Ferraro, not you. Now, why don't you go and have a rest? Get some more ice on that eye and leave the catering to Finger Food,' Marisa spoke, putting an arm around Taylor's shoulders and ushering her to the door.

'I'll call Pixie. I'll have her look into it,' Taylor said, walking down the steps of the wagon.

'Everything's under control. It's going to be the perfect wedding, better than - well - better than any wedding there's ever been and any wedding to come. The best! The wedding of all weddings,' Marisa told her, smiling broadly.

Taylor smiled at her unconvincingly and got back into the golf buggy where her driver was waiting for her.

'Bye!' Marisa called, waving a hand in the air.

When she was sure she was out of sight, she ran back into the catering wagon and picked up her mobile phone.

'I've still got Sally's number. I'll call her, get half a dozen of them back. Not the smelly one, or the one with the grim beard, or that girl with the plaits who thought she was like *sooo* cool, but the best ones, well the best of a bad bunch,' Marisa said, looking through her contacts.

'Marisa, you don't have to do that. Let me do it, I'm the one who sacked them all,' George reminded her.

'Exactly. Do you think they're going to come back for you? No, I'll do it. I'll put on my best grovelling voice and we'll have six people in here to help sort out the food today and serve tomorrow,' Marisa spoke, taking charge and putting the phone to her ear.

'What about Adam?' Helen suggested.

'I don't want to rush him into anything. He made it clear last night...' George started.

'Oh don't you worry about him. So his sister's really his mother. So what? Happens all the time on Jezza Kyle. Doesn't mean he can bail out on us, leave him to me,' Marisa insisted.

George exchanged a look with Helen, taken aback by Marisa's positive attitude.

'Hello Sally, it's Marisa from Finger Food. Now, I know you're probably down the beach, but I need you here...' Marisa began as she strutted up and down the wagon.

Within half an hour, Marisa's persuasive skills had managed to entice a small group of catering assistants to return to work for Finger Food and by lunchtime all the preparation that could be done was completed.

'I don't know how to thank you enough guys. You've all worked so hard this morning,' George told them all as the last bits of clearing up were done and foodstuffs were put back in the fridge.

'Bonus would be nice,' Marisa called out loudly.

'How about lunch?' George suggested.

'Yeah I'm like starving. But nothing accompanied by a sauce, because I've been looking at sauce like all day,' Marisa said.

'OK then, let's hit the clubhouse. Lunch and drinks on me,' George announced.

'Are you serious? You're going to pay?' Marisa quizzed, looking at George with suspicion.

'That's what I said. So come on, how about it? Before I change my mind,' George said, taking off her apron.

'Come on Team Marisa, let's go!' Marisa said, leading the charge for the door.

He wasn't listening to a word that was being said. They could have been talking in Hebrew and he wouldn't have noticed. He was circling his glass of wine with the thumb on his left hand. He had another headache, but he was damned if he was going to tell Roger that. There was no use thinking up excuses to stop the wedding now, it was too late. The snowball was of avalanche proportions and there was no halting it. He closed his eyes and immediately she came to mind. If he tried really hard, he could almost block out the incessant American drawl of Roger, running through the projects Brand Blake would be involved in straight after the nuptials.

'Quinn! Are you listening to me?' Roger barked.

He snapped his eyes open and swallowed, steadying the glass of wine as it rocked on the table.

When they arrived at the clubhouse they were stopped at the front door by a moustached Spaniard in the La Manga Resort's green and yellow uniform.

'I am afraid there is a dress code,' he said, looking at the jeans, cargo trousers and shorts worn by the majority of the group.

'Since when? I had ice cream sundaes in here the other day and I was wearing jeans then. You're making it up,' Marisa announced.

'I am afraid we have a private function in the *Ballesteros* suite...' the man began again.

'Well which is it? Either you have a dress code or you have a function we're not invited to! Make your mind up!' Marisa exclaimed angrily.

'We're here for lunch,' George informed him.

'A la carte, table d'hôte, we're not fussy. Table for ten,' Marisa continued her new found confidence bubbling over.

'I'm afraid...' the employee began again.

'No, 'I'm afraid' doesn't cut it. We're guests of Quinn Blake. Don't make me call him,' Marisa said warningly.

'I apologise Madam. This way please,' the employee said and he proceeded to lead them into the restaurant.

'Marisa! You name-dropper!' Sally shrieked excitedly.

'Oh dear, I don't think this was exactly what you meant to happen,' Helen said, reddening as she saw what was about to occur.

Quinn was sitting at a table with Michael and Roger. The La Manga Resort employee was directing their group to join them.

All three men stood up as the Finger Food party of ten arrived and the employee started to pull out chairs for them to sit on.

'What's going on here?' Roger demanded to know.

'Er, it's a mistake. We aren't appropriately dressed and Marisa said we were your guests so we could get in and eat and...' George began, trying not to notice how hot Quinn looked in the thin white shirt he was wearing.

'Is mistake?' the waiter asked almost upending a chair as he pushed it back in and left Helen without a seat.

'*Pablo, está bien. Ellos son mis invitados. Más vino para la mesa por favor*,' Quinn spoke hurriedly.

'What did you say to him?' Roger wanted to know, sitting down again.

'I said it was fine and I ordered some more wine. Hello everybody,' Quinn greeted, smiling and retaking his seat.

'Hello,' everyone muttered nervously.

The catering assistants were overawed by being in the presence of someone as famous as Quinn. The girls started to giggle and nudge each other.

'George darling, a bad night last night. All your lovely food going to waste and those naughty chaps thinking it was fun to make an idiot out of me. Thank you so much for coming to my rescue. She's a hero I tell you, stepped right into the breach,' Michael remarked as George sat down opposite him.

'I'm not sure about that,' she answered, feeling Quinn's gaze falling on her.

'This is insane. How can we discuss anything now?' Roger wanted to know, throwing down his napkin.

'I thought we'd made all the decisions we had to,' Quinn replied not taking his eyes from George.

'There are some matters that haven't been finalised. The honeymoon photo shoot, the press release for the perfume, the film premiere in Cannes, the...' Roger rattled off.

'Christ Roger! Can we not have lunch without discussing a freaking strategy?' Quinn blasted.

He picked up his wine and downed the contents.

'Perfume? Ooo, what sort of perfume?' Marisa queried, biting into a bread roll.

'It has lavender in it. It smells like a mortuary, don't buy it,' Quinn told her.

'QUINN! You can't say that! You're endorsing the product!' Roger yelled.

'If you don't want to stay and eat with us, then feel free to leave,' Quinn said, staring at him.

'Are you trying to tell me what to do?' Roger wanted to know.

Quinn ignored him and poured himself another glass of wine.

The table silenced as everyone waited to see what was going to happen next.

'I'm done here. It's a circus,' Roger said, rising to his feet and pushing in his chair.

'No, that's tomorrow,' Quinn muttered under his breath.

'Roger, come my man. You ordered the liver and onions didn't you? Don't let it go to waste, I've heard it's divine. Think of the succulent, velvety meat washing over your taste buds. Bliss,' Michael said as Roger brushed past Helen on his way out from behind the table.

'You eat it Michael. You savour every last morsel. I haven't the stomach for it,' Roger growled.

He turned his back on the party and strode out of the room.

'Ooo get him. I like liver and onions. What can we have George? Just one course? Because if it's just one course, I might just have to have ice cream,' Marisa announced.

'Have whatever you want, I'm paying. *Pablo, un poco de champán*,' Quinn ordered.

'You don't have to do this. It's my treat because they worked hard,' George told him.

'And you're all working for me, so I insist I pay,' Quinn spoke.

'Is there room for one more?'

George looked up at the sound of Adam's voice. He looked pale and exhausted, but he smiled at Marisa who stood up and threw her arms around him.

'Sit down you idiot. Who cares who your mum is? You do not leave me in charge of peeling oranges, we agreed at the start remember! We're both going to get citrus fingers on this job,' Marisa said, pulling out the chair next to her and virtually forcing him down into the seat.

'Good, everyone's here. Let's get your orders taken,' Quinn said, beckoning another waiter.

Adam hadn't spoken to her, but he had joined in with conversation at the table. Quinn had sung his praises and professed him to be his successor in the music business. George had seen Adam bristle with pleasure at that. He was enjoying knowing someone so highly regarded held him in high regard too. It was a start, sitting at the same table, but it still felt awkward. She didn't want to catch his eye. She didn't want to make him feel embarrassed, or talk to him and have him ignore her. But at least he wasn't shouting at her. It was a definite improvement on the night before.

After they had eaten George went out onto the terrace. She had a headache and she needed some fresh air. She took a swig of her lager and looked out over the golf course. The middle-aged men playing in the Spanish sun made her think of her dad. She had never really understood how someone as placid as her dad had ended up marrying someone as ferocious as her mother. Perhaps he'd been forced into it. Maybe forced marriages weren't uncommon. Perhaps there were thousands of forced marriages no one knew about. Or it could simply be that opposites did attract.

'Hey,' Quinn greeted, pulling up a chair next to her.

'Hi.'

'You OK?'

'Headache. Think it's the garlic fumes from the wedding breakfast I've been preparing.'

'Sounds terrific,' Quinn answered with a smile.

'Good. We've worked our fingers to the bone this morning.'

'Taylor came to see you.'

'Yeah.'

'And how was that for you?'

'Embarrassing, totally as it should have been. I'm lucky she didn't thump me back.'

'That isn't her style. I guess she might have swung her handbag at you, but that would have been as far as she would have gone.'

'I've seen how big her bag is. It could do some serious damage,' George replied with a smile.

Quinn smiled back at her and moved his chair until their knees were touching. It was both agony and ecstasy all at once. As usual, he was so close but still so far away.

'I want to kiss you but everyone's in there and...' Quinn whispered to her.

'I know.'

'George, you do know I don't want to marry her don't you?'

'Yeah, I get that. I think.'

'And you know how I feel about you.'

'I think so.'

'Believe it.'

'I do. It's just now the wedding's tomorrow, it all seems a bit final.'

'It isn't final.'

'Marriage should be though.'

'So, George Fraser is a believer in the sanctity of marriage is she?' Quinn said with a laugh.

'Why is that so hard to believe?'

'Because I had you down as someone who would burn her bra for equal rights, not someone who would want to dress up in a white meringue and waltz down the aisle.'

'Just because I wear a lot of jeans and drink beer, doesn't mean I'm not a traditional girl at heart.'

'So you'd do the whole white wedding, chicken and garlic sauce, chocolate flan thing if you were asked?' Quinn enquired, taking off his sunglasses and surveying her.

'Well, I'd have to check out a whole range of white jeans for the occasion obviously,' George answered, playing with the ring around her neck.

Quinn smiled and then he took a long, drawn out breath.

'Look, I'm going to tell you something and I don't want you to interrupt me or say anything, OK?' Quinn told her seriously.

'What?'

'Promise me. Don't stop me. Let me get it all out there. Yeah?'

'OK,' George agreed.

'OK,' Quinn said, taking another deep breath.

He looked nervous and George wanted to reach for his hand, but Michael and the table of catering assistants were just inside, parted from them only by the glass doors. Michael was onto another bottle of fizzy apple and Marisa was tucking into her third ice cream. Adam looked happy too, sat close to Marisa, filling up her glass with water every now and then.

She looked back to Quinn and saw the tension in his face.

'The accident I had really messed me up. I mean, really messed me up. Apart from almost dying and being in a coma for all that time, my body was wrecked. When I hit that truck, I wasn't wearing a helmet and when they removed the bandages I looked something like Freddy Krueger. I was hideous. I looked like something out of a freaking horror movie,' Quinn informed her.

George swallowed. She reached for him but loud laughter suddenly filtered out from inside and she quickly retracted her arm.

'Reconstructive surgery isn't cheap and I didn't have insurance. Back then, I thought I was destined to look like The Elephant Man for the rest of my life. There was stuff they could do, but it wasn't very sophisticated and I wasn't likely to see any real improvement for years. But one day, I don't know why, I just decided to stop hiding in my room and I went to the communal area where they had a piano. I played, all day that day and every day after that. My sight still wasn't great, but I played from memory. I have no idea where the music came from, or even how I knew how to play, I just did. It was like it came naturally. Then, one day, one of the plastics doctors hears me play, and a few weeks later Roger comes into the hospital. He sits and listens to me. I have no idea who he is, but he tells me he likes my music and he's willing to pay for state of the art, breakthrough surgery that's never been tried before, as long as I agree to sign for his record label. It was like a miracle. I had nothing to lose and everything to gain. Here was someone who was going to fund my treatment, radical, life changing, treatment and all he wanted was for me to sign a record deal with him. I mean can you imagine that? I had this f**ked up face, this broken body and here was a guy offering me the world,' Quinn explained.

'Is this what you've been trying to tell me? Is this the hold he's got over you?'

'Please George, let me finish,' Quinn begged.

George watched him take a deep breath, seemingly collecting his thoughts and marrying them up together.

'I had the treatment. God knows what it involved, I think I'm some sort of mishmash of latex and pigskin. I didn't ask. But whatever it was, it was pioneering and it was miraculous. I haven't one scar on my body and they made me into every woman's fantasy. You'd think what's not to like right? But with every procedure it bound me more to Roger. He paid for it all. He got rid of my hideous face and I owed him. At first it was OK you know, I love music and I found out I could play lots of instruments, not just the piano. My first album went platinum within a month. It was critically acclaimed, it won awards and I'm thinking, life doesn't get any better than this. But it isn't enough for Roger. He wants an album a year, he wants constant touring, he wants me to meet film producers and then he introduces me to Taylor. Before I know it, we're living in a mansion in LA with a butler, two housekeepers and a cook.'

'But if you hate it so much you have to leave.'

'I can't leave. I wouldn't know where to start. That's the problem, I don't have a beginning.'

'What d'you mean?'

'George, Quinn Blake doesn't exist. Roger created him, created me. I didn't just lose my memory in the accident, I lost my identity. When I woke up from the coma I had no idea who I was. I was John Doe, the guy with no name and half a face. I still have no idea who I am or where I came from and before, when all I could think about was not having the face of a monster, I could deal with that. But now, now I've met you, it isn't enough. I want to know who I am, I want to know how I can play music, how come I can speak three different languages, why I can't face eating a freaking banana anymore. I want to know who my parents are and I don't. No one does,' Quinn told her tears brimming up in his eyes.

Forgetting about the others sat inside, George took hold of his hand and held it in hers.

'Why didn't you tell me this before? What were you so afraid of?'

'Roger doesn't want anyone to know about the accident and how we came to meet each other. He's created a back story about me. I come from Arkansas, my parents are dead, and before their death we travelled a lot, so no real roots. It seems to be enough for the public, but it isn't enough for me. I mean I could be a wanted felon for all I know and I don't know! I go and make him millions every year, but that still isn't enough. He wants me to marry Taylor and give him grandchildren, musical protégés, Rock It Music's future security,' Quinn explained.

'Do you think he knows who you really are?'

'No. No one knows. I had no ID on me after the accident, no distinguishing marks. They checked the missing persons register, it was like I never existed. It was like I wasn't important to anyone. The only thing I had on me was a kind of friendship bracelet they had to cut off my arm. I kept it and I still have it. It's all I've got of whoever I was before I was Quinn.'

'Why do you sound ashamed?'

'Do I?'

'Yes.'

'I don't know, Roger says people won't feel the same way about me if they find out Quinn Blake's a fabrication. He doesn't want them to find out I was designed to look this good. He thinks they'll feel cheated and lied to.'

'You don't really believe that do you? People aren't like that.'

'They are in this business.'

'Well so what? Who cares? It doesn't matter who you were then. You're the same person with the same amazing talent, you've just got a different name.'

'But the thing is, without Roger, I wouldn't have a name. I wouldn't have a face I could look in the mirror at and I wouldn't have the career I have now. He's given me everything,' Quinn continued.

'And that gives him the right to make you marry his daughter?'

'I wouldn't have cared so much about that, if I hadn't met you.'

George looked at him, her heart aching for him.

'I'll marry her. But I can't give you up George. I just can't,' Quinn said determinedly.

'It's never going to work. I live in England, you live in LA. You're going to have a wife and children. I don't fit anywhere in that picture.'

'Move, move to LA. I'll get you a place.'

'Are you crazy? I have a business I've worked my arse off building up and I've got Adam. He needs me now more than ever. I can't just move, to be what? Your mistress when you can get away? It would never work. People would find out and I couldn't live that way,' George exclaimed, standing up.

'Then I'll move to England. To Basingstoke even.'

'Don't be stupid Quinn. There's nothing for you there.'

'There's you. I don't want to lose you. When we're together, everything seems to make sense. It's like I can be me, it's like you're what's missing from my life. We connect in every way and I don't know what to do,' Quinn admitted, looking at her with his wide, perfect eyes.

'You have to do what *you* want. Forget everyone else. If you want us, then you're going to have to choose us. And that means turning your back on Roger and Taylor and stopping this wedding,' George spoke, standing up from her seat.

'Don't go,' Quinn said.

'Shall I tell you how I really feel Quinn? About this whole thing? I'm in Spain catering the most publicised wedding of the century and I hate every minute of it. This was supposed to be what I dreamed of, big catering contracts, travelling, getting well-known for my food. But it's turned into a nightmare, because of you.

You came into my life and you turned it upside down. Most of the time, I can't think about anything else but you and it's driving me crazy. I've never felt this way about anyone. You get under my skin, you mess with my head and most of the time I can't decide whether I love it or hate it. You confuse me, you get inside me, you make me feel like I've never felt. And tomorrow I'm going to have to watch you promise eternal love to someone else,' George spoke, staring at him.

'But...' Quinn began.

'Don't you dare say I should know it isn't real. It doesn't matter if it's real or not, you're still going to do it. You're still going to say those words,' George snapped back.

Quinn just looked at her, his eyes filling up.

'We've had the most amazing time together Quinn and I will never forget you. But I won't play second fiddle to a make-up obsessed shopaholic. I'm worth more than that, and if you really care about me, if you really love me like you say you do, then you should know that,' George insisted her voice breaking.

Quinn got up from his chair and took hold of her hand, putting it to his chest.

'I'm yours George, you should know that.'

'You were never mine, not really. You were only ever on loan,' George replied, taking her hand away and heading for the door.

'George, wait, please - look - marry me – when all this is over, marry me,' Quinn called after her.

George looked back at him and shook her head.

'I can't.'

He could just step off the roof. He could just jump. He'd almost fallen climbing up after three bottles of wine, and now he was finishing the night off with a bottle of Jack Daniels. What was the point? What was the

341

f**king point of any of it? He had fame, he had money, he had status. He was doing a job he loved but he couldn't be any more f**king depressed. He didn't care about any of it. He just wanted her and if he couldn't have her, nothing else mattered. He took his phone out of his pocket and looked at it. No messages, no missed calls, nothing.

Thirty Seven

It was the day of the wedding and it felt like it was both a beginning and an end. George couldn't face getting out of bed. Quinn had text her all night, begging for her to reply, begging to see her. Then, he had started calling her. In the end she switched her phone off. She was too scared to turn it on this morning, knowing her resolve might not last. Half of her wanted to see him again, the more sensible half of her, told her to stay away. She had been having this fight with her conscience ever since they'd met. Besides, this morning he'd be dressing in his wedding suit, getting ready to get married. It didn't get any more final than that.

There was a knock on the door and then it opened. Marisa came in carrying a tray of food.

'Morning. I've made you ham, cheese and red onion omelettes with a tomato coulis. Mum made the coffee,' Marisa informed, bringing the tray over to the bed.

'God, I've been teaching you too much. Before long you're going to be taking over the business,' George remarked, pulling herself into a sitting position.

'I think I need to like, maybe, do a college course, in catering. Like, maybe in the evenings or something,' Marisa said, watching as George prepared to take a mouthful of the food.

'You want to go to college. That's great,' George told her.

'Yeah, I know, but the fees are like...' Marisa began nervously.

'You want me to pay?'

'Well Adam said I should ask, but if you can't then...' Marisa said.

'You get me the information from the college, I'll look into the finances. Is Adam OK?' George asked.

'I think so. I told him he should talk to you, properly like he used to and get over himself,' Marisa replied.

'Thank you,' George answered, eating some food.

'We - er - kind of - like got together last night. Not like, you know, in bed or anything, just, you know, a bit of...' Marisa began.

'OK, got the general idea,' George said hurriedly interrupting.

'I just thought you should know. You know, what with being his mum and everything,' Marisa said.

'Thanks and I'm pleased. He likes you a lot,' George spoke.

'He said he's liked me for ages but didn't think I liked him. Like how could I not? He's hot, I mean, he's really nice, and clever and everything and obviously like great on the piano,' Marisa said, blushing.

'So, is he helping us out today?' George asked.

'Yeah, he's downstairs messing about with the violin Quinn gave him for his solo thing today. He's really nervous, though he wouldn't admit that. So, don't say I told you.'

'OK, I won't mention it,' George agreed.

'He says Quinn's a mess. Apparently he got drunk last night, climbed up onto the roof of the villa and sat there for hours, just drinking on his own,' Marisa informed her.

'You haven't told Adam about me and Quinn have you?'

'No, Girl Guide's honour. I'll take it to the grave.'

'Were you a Girl Guide?'

'Well, no. But I was in Brownies for a while, you know, made cups of tea and tied knots and stuff like that,' Marisa answered with a grin.

George smiled at her. Despite her previous reservations about Marisa and Adam, she couldn't help but admire her youthful enthusiasm and joie de vivre. Perhaps that was exactly what he needed in his life, something light and uncomplicated - something fun.

'Are you going to be OK today? I mean, seeing him, getting married, you know, in front of the entire world,' Marisa asked.

'Yeah, I'll be fine,' George replied with more confidence than she really felt.

Marisa stayed standing by the bed, just looking at George. The scrutiny of her stare got too much and George looked up at her.

'You've nothing to worry about. You're going to romp the catering course, these omelettes are really good,' she told her.

'Really?!' Marisa exclaimed excitedly, jumping up and clapping her hands together.

'Really,' George assured her.

'OK, time check. How long have we got?' George questioned later, flicking her hair back as she bent over a mixing bowl.

George, Marisa and her team, Helen and Adam had been working in the catering van all morning, preparing the wedding banquet. Outside it was over thirty degrees and inside, with all the ovens going, it was almost melting point. It was a perfect, blue sky day and the wedding photos would look fantastic. It almost seemed

345

like the weather had been choreographed, as well as everything else.

'It's forty one minutes until the ceremony starts,' Marisa informed, looking at her stopwatch.

'OK, then we're doing fine,' George said, wiping the sweat from her brow with her sleeve.

'I'd better get changed and get up there. I'm sure they won't want the lead violinist dressed in an apron,' Adam spoke with a smile.

'You look sexy in that apron actually,' Marisa piped up.

'Enough already. Is that what they say these days when they want it to stop?' Helen said.

Although he was there, Adam had been quiet all morning, diligently working, sharing the odd joke with Marisa, but he still hadn't really communicated with her. Before he left the van George needed to try and make things better. She caught his arm as he passed her.

'Look, Adam. Thanks for helping us out today.'

It sounded pathetic. It didn't sound nearly enough, when she had shaken the foundations of his world.

'That's OK,' Adam answered, shrugging.

'Adam, listen. I don't want things to change, you know, between us. I don't want you to think I'm suddenly going to develop a passion for bingo or that I'm going to start controlling your life,' George told him.

'I've already got someone who tries to do that,' Adam reminded her.

'I know and I wouldn't want to step on anyone's toes. Honestly, I can still be annoying and boss you about like I always have and you can still tell me how much you drink at the Student Union.'

'I never really told you the truth about that,' Adam answered with half a smile.

'I know it must be weird for you, but we can just take things slowly, one step at a time - or we can never talk about it again. All I ever wanted was for you to know the truth and for you to know how much I love you,' George assured him tears pricking her eyes.

Adam nodded soberly.

'So, are we friends again?' George wanted to know, swallowing back the emotion.

'Will you tell me about my dad? Properly I mean. What he was like, what he looked like, you know - stuff I should know,' Adam asked.

'Of course I will, if that's what you want. I've got photos,' George spoke, nodding.

'OK, well I'd better go,' Adam said, checking his watch again.

'Yes, well, break a leg or whatever they say in the music business,' George said awkwardly.

'I will,' he replied and he hurried down the steps, nearly bowling over a Channel Nine film crew.

George closed the door and looked at her employees, hurriedly preparing things to go in the oven or the fridge. All this work for a sham wedding seemed criminal, but she knew there were guests from American magazines, people would notice the food and it was important to get it right. It was the only thing in her life she had a chance to get right now.

'You OK?' Helen asked, looking up and noticing the expression on George's face.

'Yeah, fine. You know, I don't think I'll come up for the wedding,' George said, wiping her hands on the front of her apron.

'What?! But you have to! Adam's playing for a whole castle full of celebrities. Taylor's dress is like encrusted in at least ten million diamonds or something and Quinn's apparently wearing a dove grey linen suit with turquoise trimmings. I can only imagine how well that's going to go with his eyes,' Marisa exclaimed, looking up.

'Marisa!' Helen exclaimed.

'Oh God, I completely forgot you'd...' Marisa began.

Helen coughed loudly and hissed at her daughter.

'Do not inform the entire room of it!'

'Shit, sorry!' Marisa said to George.

'It's OK. You can tell me all about it afterwards and I'm sure there'll be plenty of pictures in *Star Life* magazine,' George spoke.

'They've got a special souvenir issue going on,' Marisa informed.

Helen went over to George and patted her affectionately on the shoulder.

'Is it definitely over?' she asked her quietly.

'Yep. He's marrying Taylor, there's no going back after that,' George said with a determined nod.

'There is someone out there for you George,' Helen assured.

'Yeah, maybe. Not that it matters, I mean who needs a man anyway right? They're nothing but trouble, the ones I fall for anyway,' George said.

Her defences were back up and her tough exterior, although not completely restored, was definitely going to withstand the crater-sized cracks that had opened up. It would take time, but she had lots of that and maybe more business off the back of the wedding would help her through it.

There was a knock on the door and Marisa leapt to open it, getting cream and garlic sauce on the handle.

'Hello,' she said, greeting Dennis, the larger than life security guy.

'I've got a packet for George Fraser,' Dennis informed in his usual gruff manner.

'Oh she's here. I'll give it to her,' Marisa offered.

She shut the door and looked at the packet.

'Dennis brought this for you,' she said, holding it out to George.

George took it from her and put it to one side.

348

'Well aren't you going to open it?' Marisa questioned.

'No, I need to check the chicken and I need to do another batch of sauce and...' George began, walking across the room to distract herself.

'I'll open it then,' Marisa said, picking up the parcel and turning it over in her hands.

'You will not Marisa,' Helen spoke warningly.

'Just leave it, please. In fact there isn't long to go now. Why don't you guys go up to the function room and check it's all been laid up correctly. Marisa, Helen why don't you go up to the wedding,' George suggested.

'I'm not really fussed about going to be honest. All that expense, releasing pink doves, elaborate harpists and water fountains. It isn't really my thing,' Helen remarked with a sniff.

'Mother! You have to come! Quinn invited us! And we have to support Adam! After today, he's going to be hot property. Well he already is, but like, not on the music scene, yet,' Marisa spoke excitedly.

'Yes, go Helen. You can tell me all about it afterwards. The toned down, proper version, instead of the over the top, exaggerated version I might get from Marisa,' George said.

'I take offence at that!' Marisa called.

'Are you sure you don't want any help here?' Helen checked.

'I'm sure. Everything's under control,' George insisted.

'Right! Let me get out of this apron and slip into something more chic,' Marisa said, untying the pinny and throwing it down.

It was like a fairground. All that was missing was the Ferris wheel and the candyfloss sellers. People were smiling at him. They were all dressed in their finest, the

349

whole colour wheel represented in silk, linen and chiffon. He felt sick to the stomach. Getting married shouldn't be like this. It shouldn't be about putting on a show, it should be about the main players, the bride and the groom and how they feel about each other. He was damn sure creating an eau de parfum wasn't the right basis for a life together. But what he'd shared with George was. He had no doubt about that. And she'd said no.

The castle was full to capacity with beautiful people in flamboyant outfits. The orchestra was situated to the left of the front doors, and to the right were the water fountain and the elaborate harpist. She was playing music by Handel, as the guests took their seats.

'He's here then,' Marisa remarked as she adjusted her dress.

She and Helen took a seat each at the back of the room.

'Who? Adam? Yes, doesn't he look gorgeous in that suit? I'm very pleased about you two Marisa. He's a lovely boy,' Helen told her.

'I wasn't talking about Adam, I meant Quinn. He's at the front there, with Belch looking as scruffy as ever. I mean, like he's wearing a suit, but he still manages to look like he's spent all night in a ditch. The state Adam said Quinn was in last night, I'm surprised he's not got a bucket by the side of him,' Marisa commented.

'Poor George, it must be hard for her, knowing he's marrying someone else. I think she really fell for him,' Helen whispered to her daughter.

'And now she knows she's second best. That's gotta hurt,' Marisa added.

'He doesn't look too well though does he? He looks very pale and he keeps glancing back at the door,' Helen remarked.

'Well, that's what they do don't they? All grooms do that. They get all sweaty and clammy and start adjusting the collar of their shirt and whispering nervously to the best man. And when they're not doing that, they're like smiling at their mad old aunts with the freaky hats,' Marisa informed.

'You haven't been to that many weddings.'

'No but I've seen them on *EastEnders*. I'm hoping for some face slapping and a paternity reveal at the reception.'

'I think we've had enough revelations this week, don't you?' Helen remarked.

The harpist stopped playing and silence fell over the guests as Adam got to his feet and tucked the violin under his chin.

'Oh. My. God! Have you seen her dress? It's like *sooo* over the top. I totally love it!' Marisa remarked loudly as the congregation rose to their feet.

Taylor stood at the entrance to the room, wearing a white, full-length gown in satin, encrusted with diamonds and pearls. She was wearing a veil over her face and her silk gloved hand was holding tightly onto Roger's arm. She smiled at people who greeted her with happy, hopeful expressions and then walked confidently forward, as Adam began to play.

George swigged from a bottle of lager and looked at her watch. The wedding would be starting and she couldn't pretend it didn't hurt. She couldn't see him marry Taylor. It would be like having her face rubbed in it. It didn't matter whether he loved Taylor or not, he didn't love *her* enough to stop it.

She looked at the packet on the worktop and picked it up. She took a deep breath and ripped open the top, shaking out what was inside. It landed on the worktop in front of her, a leather bracelet, old, worn and broken in half.

George picked it up with a trembling hand and just stared at it. It couldn't be. She couldn't breathe, she felt sick. She looked again at one of the pieces and her heart felt like it was going to burst open. This couldn't be real, it was someone's cruel trick. Roger's revenge maybe? But there it was, in her hands, and her conversation with Quinn the previous day played through her mind.

She looked at her watch, her whole body trembling. She knew what she had to do. She had to stop the wedding.

Thirty Eight

Adam played the violin solo and Taylor and Roger, followed by Carleen and Saffron, made their way up the aisle to the front of the room, where the priest was waiting.

Quinn looked behind, but not at Taylor. He was looking at the doors of the castle, hopefully and almost expectantly. He was starting to sweat.

Taylor reached him and Roger smiled at Quinn, giving him his daughter's hand.

'Good afternoon everyone and a very warm welcome to this beautiful castle, where the sun is shining upon us and upon the marriage of Taylor and Quinn,' the priest began.

Taylor looked at Quinn and smiled, but Quinn stared straight ahead, unable to connect with the event. His mouth was dry and he felt light-headed.

'Marriage is a symbol of unity, unity between husband and wife, but also unity between family and friends. Everyone who has been invited here today will become part of this special union, whereby I hope you will love, cherish and support Taylor and Quinn throughout their married life together,' the priest continued.

'Bit OTT,' Marisa whispered to Helen.

'If they can't support themselves, they shouldn't be getting married at all,' Helen agreed.

'As you all know, it is a legal requirement for me to ask if anyone here knows of any lawful reason why Taylor and Quinn cannot be joined in holy matrimony. And if anyone knows of any reason, they must declare it now,' the priest announced.

'Marisa, am I too late?' George hissed, bending down at the side of Marisa's chair.

'What? Too late for what?' Marisa asked, looking at George.

'To stop the wedding,' George said her voice faltering.

'Oh. My. God. You *are* like joking! This is the wedding of the millennium,' Marisa said.

'I can't do this,' Quinn said in barely more than a whisper.

'Sorry?' the priest said, moving closer to Quinn and leaning towards him.

'I can't do this,' Quinn repeated a little more firmly.

'Marisa, I need to stop the wedding. I need to stop it now, it can't go ahead,' George babbled, looking up the aisle and shaking with fear.

'OK, I get it,' Marisa replied.

In her six inch heels, Marisa clambered up onto her seat and waved her hands in the air like a fan at a pop concert.

'EVERYBODY STOP! STOP THE WEDDING!'

A hush descended over the guests and there were murmurs of shock and surprise. Everyone was staring at Marisa, including a horrified and bemused Adam.

'Do you want some water Quinn? I'll have whoever that is removed and we'll carry on. It's just nerves isn't it? It's a big day for everyone,' Roger said, taking hold of Quinn's arm.

Quinn didn't reply.

'I'm afraid I have to speak to that young lady. If she thinks she has a reason to halt proceedings, then I need to hear it,' the priest told Roger.

'She's insane, a publicity seeker. It was always going to be inevitable with a wedding of this scale,' Roger insisted.

'Now what are you going to do? I've stopped the wedding and the priest is like looking at me funny. You need to do something if you're going to do something,' Marisa shouted at George.

'I know, I will,' George said, standing up and taking a deep breath.

The leather bracelet was still tight in her hand.

'Well, what are you waiting for? Get up there!' Marisa ordered and she pushed George out into the aisle, bringing her to the attention of all the guests.

'Go with her Marisa,' Helen told her daughter.

'Go with her? Are you like crazy? She's about to wreck the wedding of all weddings,' Marisa exclaimed, looking over at Adam who was now on his feet with the rest of the orchestra, wondering what was going on.

With every step George took up the aisle, her legs felt heavier. She squeezed the bracelet in her hand and prayed this was the right thing to do.

'I don't want any f**king water!' Quinn exclaimed, shaking Roger's arm off.

'Quinn, what's wrong? It's natural to feel a little nervous. Maybe we should take a break,' Taylor suggested, lifting up her veil and looking at him.

'Yeah come on man. Let's chill for ten minutes, have a beer or something,' Belch spoke.

'Is that what you would like to do?' the priest asked Quinn.

'Yes, that's a good idea. We'll adjourn for fifteen minutes. You can have some water and some of your pills maybe and then we'll reconvene,' Roger suggested.

'I stopped the wedding,' George spoke her voice shaking as she finally reached them.

The wedding party all turned around to look at her.

'For Christ's sake! I thought I'd made things clear for you. What is it you want if you don't want money?' Roger asked her.

'Why would you stop my wedding? You're catering the reception. It's in your interests the wedding goes ahead,' Taylor wailed.

Quinn looked at her and she held out the leather bracelet to him.

'Is this yours? Is this what you were wearing when you had your accident?' George asked him.

'What the Hell is going on here Quinn? We have a castle full of guests and Channel Nine recording every second in high definition!' Roger blasted.

'Yes. It's the most important thing I own and I wanted you to have it,' Quinn answered, looking only at George.

Tears spilled from her eyes and she hurriedly wiped them away with the back of her hand. She had to carry on. She had to be strong because there was no going back now.

'For Christ's sake! What's with the dramatics? What the f**k has that stupid thing got to do with this wedding?' Roger demanded to know.

'You said - you told me - you didn't have any identifying marks on you. No birthmarks, no scars, no tattoos. Is that really true?' George continued.

'I don't understand. Daddy, what's going on? What's all this about? This is meant to be my wedding and she's ruining it. It's going to be all over the news,' Taylor spoke her eyes welling up with tears.

'That's what I was told. I don't know, I was in a coma for months, I don't remember much. Roger?' Quinn asked, turning to his mentor.

'I don't know anything. I don't know what you're talking about and you've made a big mistake crossing me like this. I am going to have you removed and then perhaps we can get on with this wedding,' Roger ordered, beckoning security.

'I asked you a question Roger, answer it,' Quinn ordered him.

'Security, please remove Ms Fraser,' Roger spoke as two burly men stepped forward to join them.

'Don't you lay one finger on her,' Quinn hissed, pointing threateningly at Roger.

'What are you all talking about? What accident? When? Quinn, what's going on?' Taylor asked, looking completely bemused.

'I asked you, if I had a birthmark or a tattoo or something? Answer me!' Quinn screamed.

'Oh, what does it matter?' Roger asked.

'It matters to me,' George told him her whole body quaking.

'You had multiple injuries, you were covered in lacerations. Everything was restored, you were made perfect. Everything, every blemish was wiped out,' Roger spoke quietly his shoulders hunching over.

His desperation not to let people hear was paramount.

'Did he have a tattoo on his wrist, like where a watch might go?' George demanded to know.

Roger raised his eyes to Heaven and shook his head at Quinn.

'You f**king tell me now!' Quinn bellowed.

'Jeez! It was about two centimetres big. It was like a crescent moon or something!' Roger replied.

'Like the letter 'C'?' George spoke her voice wobbling with emotion.

'Yeah I guess. Whatever. Right, good, now that's cleared up. Please take Ms Fraser back to her catering unit and we can get on with the ceremony,' Roger ordered.

'No,' George said the tears rolling down her face as she tried to stop herself from sobbing aloud.

'George whatever it is, tell me,' Quinn begged, taking hold of her hands and gripping them in his.

'You can't marry Taylor, Quinn. You're already married - to me,' George informed.

The emotion rode over her like a tidal wave and now she let out an audible sob.

'What d'you think she's saying? She's crying now. God, this is terrible and it's going to be all over the souvenir edition of *Star Life* next week,' Marisa remarked, squinting her eyes to try and get a better look at the scene.

'Taylor looks devastated and Roger looks like he's been given a puncture. He's liable to go whizzing round the room deflating and squealing any second,' Helen said.

Neither of them noticed Adam had come over to join them.

'What's going on Marisa? You stopped the wedding. What's happened?' Adam wanted to know.

'Er, well, it's a bit complicated, but George wanted the wedding stopped so I, er, like stopped it,' Marisa spoke, blushing.

'Helen? Am I going to get anything like the truth from you?'

'We don't know what's going on,' Helen responded not meeting his eye.

'I don't understand,' Quinn said, looking at George his expression beyond shocked.

'No, I know you don't. I don't even believe it myself but somehow it's true,' George said, through her tears.

'I have no idea what's going on here. Quinn isn't married. I think I would know if Quinn was married. He is my fiancé!' Taylor screamed.

'And you have no place at this wedding, no place at all. How many times do I have to say it? Get her out of here!' Roger demanded, looking to the security team.

'No! Leave her alone. Tell me George, all of it! I want to know,' Quinn demanded.

'Come on man, I thought we were having a beer break and getting this wedding back on track,' Belch spoke.

'Change of plan. Ignore them, ignore all of them. Look at me and tell me,' Quinn urged her.

'Here?' George queried, looking around at the full castle room where people were all staring at her and the wedding party.

They were all nudging each other and commenting amongst themselves about what was going on.

'Yes, here. Right now!' Quinn ordered.

'I know who you are,' George began, swallowing a lump in her throat.

'Yeah and so does half the world. He's Quinn Blake, rock star. Now if you haven't got anything else to say you can get on your way,' Roger interrupted, grabbing hold of George's arm himself.

'You're Paul,' George told him hardly able to believe she was saying the words.

'Paul?' Quinn queried.

'Paul who?' Belch asked.

'Paul Simon? Paul Rodgers? Paul Mcf**kingCartney? What planet does this woman live on?' Roger blasted as Taylor just stared at George, hanging on her every word.

'Paul Robbins. My Paul. *This* Paul,' George said.

She took off the watch Quinn had given her, reminding him of the tattoo on her arm.

Quinn put his hands to his face, immediately whitening as tears brimmed in his eyes.

'I don't understand? What are you saying here? That he's someone else? That he isn't Quinn Blake? Why would you say that?' Taylor wanted to know, glaring at George.

'Because it's the truth and I should have seen it before. I should have known, somehow I should have known, but I just didn't,' George spoke, watching as Quinn dissolved in front of her.

'Well why would he pretend to be someone else? Daddy, I don't understand. Tell me what's going on!' Taylor begged.

'I think we just need to go into the green room and take five minutes. Get away from all the people and the cameras,' Roger suggested, taking hold of Taylor's hands.

'Quinn, talk to me, please. Say something. You've got to believe me, I didn't know. I had no idea. I mean, you don't look like him. You don't talk like him, or laugh like him or even move like him and I swear to you, I didn't know,' George begged as she watched him crumbling.

She wanted to help him. She wanted to take away the shock, the confusion and the realisation, but she didn't have room to do it. She was still reeling from it herself. All these months, falling for him, finally thinking she was moving on from Paul, when all the time she was stepping back to him. There really was only one person out there for her and she had fallen in love with him all over again, without even knowing it.

Quinn raised his eyes to meet hers, his expression bereft.

'Are you sure?' he asked her.

She nodded her head and looked again at the worn bracelet in her hand.

'I made Paul this. This was what I gave him when we got married. He gave me the ring I wear round my neck. No one knew, but us,' George told him.

'This makes no sense. I've known Quinn for the last ten years. I think I would have known if he'd gone out and married someone,' Taylor spoke.

'It was a long time ago, we were sixteen,' George informed.

'Shit man, what did you do? Go to Vegas or something?' Belch questioned, laughing.

'Right, well, this is a great story and all, but where's your proof? I mean, you say you're married to him, well show me the certificate. Show me the certificate that says you're married to Quinn Blake,' Roger said, puffing up his chest and smiling smugly at George.

'I have a certificate, not here obviously, at home,' George informed him.

'Well I don't believe a word she's saying. It's absurd and preposterous. Are you trying to tell everyone here that he isn't Quinn Blake, he's someone called Paul. And, that this Paul married you when you were sixteen?' Roger questioned.

'Yes. And I can prove it,' George said, staring at Quinn.

He was now a shade whiter than Taylor's dress, looking like the ground had been taken from under him.

'Oh yeah? How? Now this will be good,' Roger stated.

'We have a son,' George stated, daring to look across at Taylor.

'Man! This just gets weirder!' Belch exclaimed.

Taylor burst into tears and, picking up the skirts of her wedding dress, she fled past the priest and into the curtained off area.

Roger looked like he was about to spontaneously combust and Quinn just stared at George, not knowing what to do or say.

'We're leaving Quinn, come on. The sooner we sort this mess out the better,' Roger said, taking a vice like hold of Quinn's arm.

'No,' Quinn stated.

'Don't be stupid Quinn. We'll go and see the doctor. We'll get you a sedative or something,' Roger said, trying to steer him the way Taylor had gone.

'I said no. Get off me! I don't want a sedative, I want the truth and she's the only one who can give me that. Come on George,' Quinn said, taking hold of her hand.

'Where are you going? Quinn, we're in the middle of a wedding here for f**k's sake!' Roger yelled.

'Not any more. The wedding's off,' Quinn replied, pulling George down the aisle towards the exit doors.

'George! What's going on? What's this got to do with you?' Adam asked, catching her arm on her way past him.

'I can't explain now Adam, but I will. Just give us a bit of time,' George said as Quinn pulled her away.

'Us?' Adam queried, looking at Marisa.

'Yep, was sworn to secrecy about that, but I guess the whole world's going to know soon enough. Quinn and George, been at it like the cast of *Watership Down* since she got the catering job at the Hexagon. I only just found out, well the other day, when I walked in on them in bed together. Looks like it might be love if she's like stopping the wedding. Wonder what Taylor's going to do with her dress? Maybe she'll put it on Ebay,' Marisa said thoughtfully.

Thirty Nine

'Quinn, stop! Where are we going?' George questioned as Quinn pulled her along at a quick pace, up the castle steps towards the next level.

'Somewhere no one will bother us. In here,' Quinn said, pushing open a door.

George followed him up a second set of stairs to the roof of the castle. He climbed up onto the battlements and held his hands out to her. She hauled herself up and then followed him, scrambling up the tiled roof to the very peak, next to the bell tower. The slates were hot from the sun and her hands were sore, but she still clung to the bracelet.

'Can't see any paparazzi climbing up here,' Quinn remarked.

'Did you not see the helicopter earlier?' George replied.

Quinn let out a breath. It was so long and low, it sounded like he'd been holding it for a lifetime. George didn't know what to say. She didn't know where to begin.

'You know I knew there was something more about you, the first time I saw you at the party. I didn't know what it was then, but there was this immediate connection. I don't make a habit of kissing caterers you know, but that night, I just couldn't help myself,' Quinn spoke.

'And there I was thinking it was my tomboyish charm.'

'Well, there was that too,' Quinn said, looking at her.

'Look, Quinn, I didn't stop the wedding to stake my claim on you.'

'No?'

'No. I mean it wasn't right, legally I mean.'

'And that was why you stopped it?'

'Yes.'

'Well, do you think anyone would ever have known?'

'I don't know. Maybe, maybe not.'

'Do you love me George?'

'What d'you mean? Why are you saying it like that?'

'Do you love *me*, Quinn. Or do you still love Paul?' Quinn asked her, looking at her intently.

'I never loved anyone the way I loved Paul, *until* I met you. You taught me how to love again. Finding out you're Paul, doesn't change the way I feel about you,' George told him.

'But the way you feel about me wasn't enough for you to stop the wedding.'

'I could say the same about you.'

'No. I stopped the wedding, before the whole Marisa screaming her lungs out bit. I told them I couldn't do it. I wasn't going to do it, because of you,' Quinn informed her.

'I don't understand why it's important,' George told him.

'It's important, because even if I am who you say I am, I can't connect with him, me – whatever - not yet,' Quinn exclaimed.

'I realise that. I can't imagine how it must feel, to know, after all this time. I'm as shocked as you are. When

I saw that bracelet - well I haven't seen that bracelet, since Paul left,' George spoke.

'Yeah, since he left you.'

'It wasn't as simple as that.'

'He left you and worse than that, you were married! Why didn't you tell your parents? Why didn't he tell his? Why didn't he tell everyone where to get off and tell them you were married and you were going to make things work together?' Quinn asked her.

'That's exactly what he would have done, in normal circumstances. His mum was so ill Quinn. His dad got the new job in Canada and they were going there to get specialist treatment for her, treatment that could save her life. I couldn't expect him to stay behind with me when his mum was like that. She needed him and his dad needed him. As much as he liked to do what he wanted, he was also fiercely loyal and he loved his parents. I've told you all this,' George tried to explain.

'But he didn't keep in contact. He didn't call you.'

'No.'

'Why not?'

'Quinn I don't know. He was sixteen, maybe he moved on, maybe he lost my number. I don't know.'

'He can't have moved on that much, he was still wearing the bracelet in his twenties,' Quinn blasted.

'Quinn, this isn't my fault. I didn't make this happen. I don't know what happened after Paul left. You're as much in the dark as I am,' George told him.

'I can't believe I would have left you and not contacted you. If you and him, if *we* were so much in love that we got married! I mean, Christ! You paint the two of you like Romeo and f**king Juliet,' Quinn spoke.

'I don't know what you want me to say, but there's someone else we should be considering here. What am I going to say to Adam?' George wanted to know.

'Adam,' Quinn said, taking a deep breath and running his hands over his hair.

'He's Paul's son - your son,' George said barely able to say the words.

'I don't know how to deal with that. I mean he's how old?' Quinn asked.

'Eighteen.'

'So how old does that make me? Because Roger tells me I'm thirty every single f**king year.'

'Thirty four.'

'Thirty four, with an eighteen year old son,' Quinn said with a shake of his head.

'Yeah well, at least now he's toilet trained,' George blasted.

'George, I didn't mean it like that.'

'If you don't want to be part of his life, then that's fine. I guess he doesn't have to know. I suppose I could hold the truth from him - it's not like I don't know how to do that,' she snapped.

'Come on, that wasn't what I meant. It's just a shock, I mean Christ! A few minutes ago I was just me and now I've got a wife and a child I knew nothing about and I'm someone else. I'm just slightly freaked OK?' Quinn told her.

'I know. So am I,' George said, taking hold of his hand.

'OK, maybe slightly freaked was a bit of an understatement. Totally freaked doesn't even begin to cover it. Should we have some sort of test? DNA?' Quinn asked.

'Yes, you should. Then you'll know for certain who you are and Adam will have something concrete to tell him who his father is,' George agreed.

'What do you think he'll say?'

'Shit, I don't know. He's only just found out I'm his mother.'

'Yeah, it's going to be a shock,' Quinn said, rubbing his mouth with his fingers.

The Channel Nine helicopter took off again and began to buzz about, getting closer to the castle. The news of the wedding being brought to a halt was filtering out of Spain and hitting the media in America.

'Do you remember anything about us? I mean, about me and Paul?' George asked him.

'The pink hair? The bad punk band? I'm guessing the dreams were memories,' Quinn started.

'Yeah, I had pink streaks in my hair when we were together and you were in a punk band. But they weren't that terrible. They were quite good actually,' George informed him.

'Jesus! Really! Are you sure? They're always awful when I hear them.'

'They were good. They could have been really good but then you left - well Paul left - you know.'

'And the tattoo?' Quinn asked.

'We both decided to get tattoos. We lied to the guy that we were both eighteen and I had mine done first. It hurt like Hell but I wasn't going to admit that. Then, when it was Paul's turn, he practically fainted the second the needle touched his skin. The guy managed to start the top of the 'G' and that was it, he couldn't take any more. I laughed for days about that. For someone who was supposed to be fearless, he couldn't even manage a tattoo!'

'So it was supposed to be a 'G'.'

'Yeah, but it ended up like half a 'C' – that's why he started calling me 'C', to make up for being such a total wimp,' George replied with a smile.

'Don't you feel any resentment towards him? I mean he left you and he didn't contact you. Why aren't you angry?' Quinn wanted to know.

'I was never angry with him because I knew he loved me. There was a reason why he didn't contact me. I don't know what it was and I guess I'll never know, but there would have been a reason. Like you said, he was still wearing the bracelet when he had the accident - and he gave me Adam. He's the best thing that's ever happened to me. I can't be mad at someone who gave me something so precious,' George told him.

Quinn shook his head and took another long, slow deep breath.

'I wish I could remember. I just can't,' he said, putting his head in his hands.

'It doesn't matter.'

'It *does* matter. I need an answer, even if you don't. I want to know what happened to my parents, I want to know why I didn't call you, I want to know where I was going on that motorbike without a helmet and I want to remember marrying you,' Quinn told her.

'I've got pictures of the wedding. It was in Scotland. We hitchhiked there and back and used all our money for one night in a hotel.'

'It sounds terrible,' Quinn said.

'It was perfect, apart from you being sick. We drank too much and you ate the whole – oh my God.'

'What?'

'You ate the whole cake I made - a chocolate and banana cake.'

'Bananas huh?'

'Yeah,'

'Well that explains that then.'

'I guess so.'

'All these years though and you never got a divorce or an annulment? Why?'

'Because I still loved him. There was never any reason to.'

'What are we going to do?' Quinn asked her.

'We're going to get down off this roof and then I'm going back to the villa to pack. You need some time Quinn, to take this in, to get your head around things - to talk to Taylor,' George reminded him.

'I don't want you to go.'

'Look, you're confused, you've got a lot to think about and all this to come to terms with. You don't need me getting in the way. This whole new situation wasn't how it was supposed to be,' George spoke, pulling herself to her feet.

'You're my wife,' Quinn reminded her, swallowing as he said the words.

'Yeah, I know, but in the weirdest of ways. Anyway, we can talk about that. I mean, you've been thrown into it, if you want an annulment or whatever I'll do it. Like you said, it's probably about time,' George said matter of factly.

'You want out? You find the guy you've been in love with all these years and now you want to let him go, let *me* go?!' Quinn exclaimed.

'I don't want to force you into a situation you aren't ready for. I mean a wife and a grown-up son...' George began.

'Why don't you let me decide what I'm ready for? OK, I'm terrified about being Adam's father. I mean, I know nothing about being a father. I have no idea what I'm meant to do. But, I'm not concerned about being married to you. I asked you, remember? I asked you to marry me and you said no,' Quinn spoke, looking up at her.

'You would have said anything to stop me ending things. You didn't mean it,' George replied, trying to avoid looking at him.

'Yes I did,' Quinn insisted.

'Don't say that Quinn. You don't mean it, you're emotional, we both are. Look at everything we've just found out,' George said her voice breaking.

'Forget all the Paul stuff for a minute. Forget about Adam. *I'm* asking you, *Quinn* is asking you. Just imagine for a second it was just you and me, nothing else, no strings attached. Would you marry me?' Quinn asked her, taking hold of her hand.

George looked at him, looking at her. The handsome guy who broke down her defences and made her feel alive again for the first time in almost twenty years. There was only one answer she could give.

'Yes.'

Quinn stood up and pulled her towards him, kissing her mouth, holding her tightly, his hands cupping her face softly. Then he broke off, untied the chain around her neck and took off the ring. He slipped it on her ring finger and held her hand in his.

'Then that's what we're going to do. We're going to get married, again. Although this time, I want more than one night in a hotel and definitely no hitchhiking,' Quinn insisted.

'Not even for old time's sake?' George asked with a smile.

'I don't want to do anything for old time's sake. Everything starts from now,' Quinn told her, squeezing her hands.

Forty

'Are we doing the right thing do you think?'

'Marisa, people have travelled a long way and they've been waiting around all morning. They're starving, the food's here, the least we can do is serve it to them,' Helen said as they pushed another trolley of food up the walkway.

'Where d'you think George and Quinn are?' Marisa asked, bumping the trolley over a rut in the carpeting.

'I don't know.'

'I mean d'you think the wedding's really like off, like completely? I mean sometimes these things sort themselves out don't they?' Marisa continued.

'I would say it's definitely off,' Helen replied.

'Did you see Adam's face when I told him about George and Quinn? I mean, talk about freaked! Well, I guess it is his mum. Urgh, how gross is that?' Marisa exclaimed.

'Yes and we shouldn't forget that. Perhaps a bit more sensitivity is called for,' Helen suggested.

'Yeah, you're right. I mean, you wouldn't want everyone talking about your mum, the one who broke up the wedding of all time would you?' Marisa spoke.

'Hey,' George greeted, meeting the trolley just before the castle entrance.

'Oh, George is everything OK? What's happened?' Helen enquired.

'It's too complicated to explain right now,' George replied, running her hand through her hair.

'Is the wedding definitely off? Does Taylor know about you and Quinn? Is she going to auction her dress?' Marisa wanted to know.

'The wedding's definitely off, no idea about the dress.'

'Not that I would necessarily want a dress that's so like obviously unlucky, but if it was a bargain then I might be persuaded. I could always insist people bring horseshoes and invite a few chimney sweeps or nodding dogs. Nodding dogs are lucky aren't they?' Marisa said.

'Where's Adam?' George wanted to know.

'He's serving the guests with Team Marisa. We didn't know what to do, but people were directed to the reception room and we thought we ought to stick to the schedule and serve the food,' Helen explained.

'I'll come and help,' George said, taking hold of the trolley.

'Er, not being funny or anything but like are you sure that's a good idea? I mean, you're the woman who stopped the wedding. Well OK, I'm the one that climbed on the chair and hollered out, but you're the one that did the talking and there seemed to be a lot of talking. What was all the talking about?' Marisa wanted to know.

'Maybe you're right. Maybe I shouldn't go anywhere near it,' George mused.

'Where's Quinn?' Helen wanted to know.

'He's gone to see Roger and Taylor,' George spoke.

'Into the lion's den then. Hope he makes it out alive. Roger's really scary, *Star Life* magazine reckons if someone gives Quinn bad press he makes sure they never work again,' Marisa informed.

'Marisa, that's enough,' Helen ordered.

'OK, well, do you want me to organise some stuff in the kitchen?' George suggested.

'Oh. My. God! Wait one second! What the Hell is that on your hand? Is that a ring? Mother! She's wearing a ring on her wedding finger!' Marisa exclaimed her eyes bulging.

'Sshh, keep your voice down! It's nothing,' George said as wine waiters passed by them.

'Where did it come from? Who gave it to you? What's it doing on your wedding finger?' Marisa continued to question.

'It's just the one I usually wear around my neck.'

'So why's it on your finger now?' Marisa demanded to know.

'Marisa, it's none of our business. Now, let's get this food up to the reception,' Helen ordered.

'But...' Marisa began.

'George, we had to tell Adam about you and Quinn. He was asking questions when you stopped the wedding. We didn't know what else to tell him,' Helen explained.

'It's OK,' George said with a nod.

'I think he thinks it's a bit gross, you know, what with you being his mum and everything. But I didn't mention the word 'cougar' honestly,' Marisa began.

'Marisa, that's enough. We need to get this trolley to the party before the sorbet melts,' Helen said.

'Look, there is a lot I need to tell you but I can't right now,' George informed them.

'We understand,' Helen said.

'No we don't and we need to know now!' Marisa shouted from behind the trolley.

'I'll find something to gag her with,' Helen assured, pushing the trolley up the incline.

George watched her colleagues go and then she stopped and took a breath. She was shaking. Everything was coming home to her now. Quinn was Paul, he was

Adam's father. It was both a dream and a nightmare rolled into one. How were they going to deal with it? And more importantly, how was Adam going to deal with it?

He was a father. He had a son. And he finally knew his name and where he came from. Despite the shock, despite knowing he was the heartless bastard who left the woman he loved high and dry with a baby on the way, at long last he felt grounded. He had a past. He had a start and a middle and now he had a future.

George buried herself in her work, like she always had done and began plating up chicken breasts and sauce. The food looked wonderful. The green beans were blanched to perfection and Marisa had done a fantastic job on the potatoes.

'Hey, you're here. You OK?' Adam asked, entering the catering wagon and pulling a trolley with him.

'Yeah, just trying to get these meals served up. Is everyone there?' George enquired.

'Well, apart from the bride, the groom and the father of the bride, yeah, pretty much,' Adam responded.

'Good, I'd hate for this to go to waste, I mean...' George started.

'There would've been no chance of it going to waste if you hadn't stopped the wedding,' Adam remarked.

'Yeah, I know,' George said, sighing.

'Marisa told me about you and Quinn.'

'Yeah, I know that too.'

'Bit rich of you making comments about me and Marisa when you were having an affair with an almost married man. And Quinn, of all people! You denied it, you said it was Paco,' Adam said harshly.

'Oh Adam, just don't,' George said, putting the bowl of sauce to one side.

'Don't what?' Adam asked.

'Don't lecture me, not today,' George begged him.

The door of the catering wagon opened and Quinn stepped in. He had taken off his jacket and cravat and had undone the top three buttons of his shirt. He looked stressed and overwhelmed, like he was melting from the heat of the day, as well as all the revelations.

'Hey Adam,' he greeted his face lighting up at the sight of him.

George swallowed as she looked at them both. There were no similarities between them. Not even their height or their stance. How could she have been expected to know?

'Hey. I guess I ought to leave you two to it. Whatever *it* is,' Adam said, making for the exit.

'Don't do that,' Quinn said, stopping him.

George's stomach tightened. Quinn couldn't tell Adam any of this yet. It would overwhelm him more than it had overwhelmed her. He was sensitive, he'd just found out his mother wasn't who he thought. He thought he knew who his father was now. He couldn't deal with the truth, especially an almost unimaginable truth.

'Look, just because you're sleeping with my mother, it doesn't mean you get to order me about. Not even *she* gets to do that yet. It's all still a bit new for me,' Adam said stroppily.

'Quinn, don't, please,' George said, sensing what he was about to do.

'I've broken all ties with Roger. He can sue me over my contract if he likes, but I'm going to sign with someone else. There are more than a couple of labels that have wanted me for a long time now and I'm going to set up some meetings. Hang what anyone thinks about me not being the person they think I am, they'll have to get over it or just stop buying my songs. The perfume will definitely be shelved, so there is a silver lining,' Quinn informed them both.

'I need to go and help Marisa,' Adam said, opening the door.

Quinn took it from his hands and slammed it shut.

'Look, what's with you? I'm not interested in what you two have got going on. I like you Quinn, I think you're a cool guy, but this is all a bit weird and I'd rather not be part of it,' Adam told him.

'I'm glad you like me, that's a start,' Quinn answered.

'Quinn, stop, please. It isn't the right time,' George begged.

'What's this all about? What isn't the right time?' Adam questioned, looking at George.

She shook her head. She couldn't tell him, she didn't want to tell him, it felt too soon. She hadn't grasped the reality of it herself.

'Look, I'm not going to fancy it up with stuff. The fact is, I'm your father,' Quinn blurted out.

'Christ Quinn!' George yelled in horror.

Adam turned to face his idol. He just stared at him, not a hint of an expression on his face.

'Look, I know how that sounds. It sounds totally crazy but...' Quinn started.

'It doesn't sound totally crazy. It *is* totally crazy. What the Hell is going on here? Why would you say that? Is this some joke doing the rounds on Facebook or something? First George, now you! She says she's my mother, now you're saying you're my father? You've only known each other a couple of months and I'm eighteen, even I can do the maths on that one!' Adam exclaimed.

'It's kind of complicated,' Quinn told him.

'Yeah, I get that, because it's not true. I know who my father is, his name's Paul Robbins, George already told me. So, I don't know why you want to jump on the bandwagon, but the spot's already taken,' Adam blasted.

'I'm Paul Robbins - we think. We don't know one hundred percent yet, but you know, ninety nine point nine or something close,' Quinn continued.

'Adam, I know this is going to be difficult to understand but...' George began.

'Why are you doing this?'

'I had an accident. I don't look like I used to look, I didn't know who I was, but I do now and George knows. We were so in love back then we got married and she had you and I'm your father, that's it,' Quinn continued.

'I cannot listen to this. Do you know how this sounds? It sounds like someone has taken *The Jerry Springer Show* and turned it on its head. It's deranged! It's totally unbelievable!' Adam carried on.

'We can have a test. I think we should have a test so we know, so we both know for sure,' Quinn told him.

'George? What's going on? Is this true? What he's saying,' Adam asked, looking for guidance.

George couldn't manage words. Seeing his anguish all over again was too much. She nodded and then had to turn away.

'Right, so we'll fix a test and then me and George, we're getting married - again. So, you take as long as you want to get your head around it, but when you do, I'm going to want to know everything there is to know about you,' Quinn told him.

'Yeah?' Adam scoffed.

'Yeah,' Quinn replied, staring back at him.

Adam sucked in a breath and then punched Quinn so hard, he reeled back against the kitchen worktop.

'Adam!' George exclaimed.

Quinn put his finger to his split lip and nodded at Adam.

'I'll give you that, just this once. But you know what? Now I know I'm your father, I'm going to tell you things straight. You have real talent, but sometimes you play that piano like you're typing or something. You need

377

to put more passion into it, leave the sheet music behind,' Quinn informed him.

Adam glared at him and flew from the catering van, slamming the door with force.

'Well, that didn't go too badly. What's this? Is this my wedding breakfast?' Quinn asked, dipping his finger into the sauce on one of the plates.

'Didn't go too badly?! For Christ's sake Quinn!' George remarked, taking the plate out of his reach.

'He'll get used to the idea. Well, he'll have to won't he?' Quinn said biting into some green beans.

'You don't know him yet, he's sensitive,' George told him.

'Yeah well, he'll need to toughen up, especially if he wants a career in the music business,' Quinn replied.

'Quinn, this is a big thing, what's happened today,' George reminded him.

'I know. But this is the only way I can deal with things. No more pretence George. I'm his father, we're married, let's deal with it. Let's tell everyone, let's start living our lives, instead of letting other people live them for us,' Quinn said, taking hold of her hands.

'It's not going to be that simple for everyone. Other people are going to take longer to adjust to the situation, like Adam. All this has been sprung on him, as well as us,' George told him.

'I know, but my way of adjusting is getting on with it,' Quinn said, kissing her on the mouth.

George held onto him, enjoying the taste of him, loving being in his arms again.

'We're going to be OK, you, me and Adam,' Quinn said, holding her and brushing her hair with his hands.

'I hope so, because that's what I want more than anything,' George replied with a sigh.

'Me too. I'm yours remember. Always have been apparently, but more importantly, always will be,' Quinn said, holding her hand to his heart.

George smiled and entwined her hand with his. She had been waiting her whole life to feel like this again.

'By the way, there's way too much garlic in that sauce,' Quinn told her, dipping his finger into another plate.

'Hey! Enough! That's the sort of thing Adam does,' George announced, slapping his hand away.

'So we're alike huh?'

'Maybe I should have seen it before. The musical talent, the non-stop eating, the good looks, the charm...' George reeled off.

'Shit, he has all that *and* youth? I'm not sure I'm going to like that sort of competition,' Quinn replied.

'You will be a good father you know,' George spoke.

'I think I'm going to need a lot of help,' Quinn admitted.

'Look no further,' George replied, smiling at him.

Epilogue

12 months later – Los Angeles

'Oi Adam! You need to put more sun cream on!' Marisa screamed across the pool, sitting up on her sun lounger and dropping *Star Life* magazine on the floor.

'Marisa! How many times have I got to tell you? You don't shout like that, it sounds common,' Geraint, Marisa's father spoke, taking off his sunglasses and looking at his daughter disapprovingly.

'Mother, why did we have to bring him? Couldn't we have left him at home with a kitchen full of microwave meals and the Special Brew?' Marisa questioned, scowling.

'Marisa, don't be so rude to your father. He's going to take you shopping later,' Helen told her.

'Am I?' Geraint asked, looking at Helen, bemused.

'Are you?! Oh Dad, thank you. I've seen like this amazing outfit in a boutique in town and there's like shoes to match,' Marisa began, moving her lounger closer to her father's.

'Adam, Marisa's right you know. It is time you put more cream on,' George said, looking at her watch.

'Christ are you serious? You're timing it?!' Adam exclaimed, getting up from his lounger.

'Not down to the minute but...' George began.

'Just put it on Ad, keep the ladies happy,' Quinn replied, sitting up and reaching for his drink.

'Pass it here then,' Adam said, reaching out for the bottle.

'I say Quinn, do you really think Tiger Woods might be at the course tomorrow when we play?' Brian asked, looking over from his position under the parasol.

'It's a definite possibility. One of my drivers says he's there every Tuesday without fail,' Quinn answered.

'I don't know why you're getting so excited Brian. He isn't exactly going to ask you to caddy for him is he?' Heather spoke harshly.

'I should hope not Heather. Brian's going to have his own caddy tomorrow,' Quinn informed.

George smiled at her mother's po-faced expression and leant over on her side to look at Quinn.

'I can't believe my whole family are here and I'm Mrs Blake,' George whispered to him, toying with the ring on her finger.

'I can't believe you made me wait a year,' Quinn answered, taking off his sunglasses to look at her.

'It wasn't my fault Finger Food went global, that was your fault. Well, Michael's really I guess. His PR, and the fact I was labelled as the girl who stole Quinn Blake from the fifth sexiest actress in the *Star Life* poll,' George replied.

'Can you give me a warning if you're going to snog. I don't want to be anywhere in the vicinity,' Adam announced.

'Adam! I'd rather you didn't use that word,' Heather called.

'Kiss, pucker up, lock lips, neck, cop off...' Adam continued.

'Hey, have some respect,' Quinn ordered him.

Heather adjusted her sunhat and reached for her mineral water.

'Why not get Marisa in the pool. Quick, go - and close your eyes,' Quinn said as he leant forward and kissed George.

'God! I don't care how in love you are. Your parents snogging in front of you just isn't right,' Adam announced, throwing the sun cream back down and walking over to Marisa.

George watched Adam trying to entice Marisa into the water. He tickled her, made her scream and then took hold of her hand and gently kissed it.

'He called me dad the other day you know. It was a slip of the tongue and he corrected himself afterwards, but he still said it,' Quinn informed her.

'I don't want him to call me mum, especially with my mother here. Plus it makes me feel old and I do not want to feel old, not when I've only just got married. OK, well technically for the second time, but who's counting?' George asked.

'Not me. So how does it feel this time around? Was it better getting married on the beach or better in Scotland in the rain?' Quinn enquired.

'Do I have to be honest?'

'Yes.'

'On the beach. How about you?'

'I'm just glad I can remember this one,' Quinn told her, laughing.

'And I'm never going to let you forget it. The only way this ring is being removed is by surgical procedure,' George informed.

'Please! I've had enough of those!' Quinn exclaimed.

'I just meant I'm never letting you go. I'm yours,' George said, taking hold of his hand and putting it to her chest.

'Yes you are,' Quinn said and he leaned across his lounger and kissed her again.

'Oh. My. God! Like pass a bucket! They're at it again! Get a room already! It's sick,' Marisa yelled at the kissing couple.

'So how she used the word there - was that a good "sick" or a bad "sick"?' Helen wanted to know.

'BAD!'

'Good, most definitely good,' George replied, holding Quinn's gaze.

Acknowledgements

I would like to thank the following people for their help during the creation of Strings Attached:-

Sharon Goodwin and Louise Graham

Both of you have provided me with so much support, not just frantically tweeting and re-tweeting my book news, but reviewing the manuscript, giving me advice on writing competition entries, making me laugh and picking my chin off the floor on bad days! Thank you so much xxx!

Jane Dixon-Smith – for the fantastic cover design I immediately fell in love with!

Andrew Riley – for again doing the final proofread of the manuscript! You found the gremlins!

All the authors and Associate Readers at Loveahappending.com – particularly my lovely Team Baggot members Rea Sinfield, Lindsay Gentles and Sue Fortin - for supporting my work, and for promoting and befriending me. I love being part of our gang!

Jane Holland (formerly Embrace Books) - for giving me probably the best quote ever to use on the cover! Thank you!

Mr Big – for being my soundboard when I'm thinking out loud and firing questions at you! I know you believe in George and Quinn's story and I know you believe in me too! Love you xxx.

My girls – Amber and Ruby - for being the best daughters in the world! Love you lots xxx.

Lightning Source UK Ltd.
Milton Keynes UK
UKOW050842050112

184790UK00001B/2/P